Civil Blood

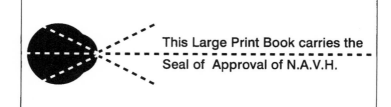

This Large Print Book carries the
Seal of Approval of N.A.V.H.

Civil Blood

A CIVIL WAR MYSTERY

Ann McMillan

Thorndike Press • Waterville, Maine

Map of the City of Richmond, Henrico County, Virginia. Prepared from actual Surveys and published expressly for Subscribers to the Richmond Directory. By Eugene Ferslew, 1859. Reprinted by *The Virginia Guardsman* in May 1935. Courtesy of the Map Collection, The Library of Virginia. Map altered to show details.

Published in 2001 by arrangement with Viking Penguin, a division of Penguin Putnam Inc.

Thorndike Press Large Print Americana Series.

The tree indicium is a trademark of Thorndike Press.

The text of this Large Print edition is unabridged. Other aspects of the book may vary from the original edition.

Set in 16 pt. Plantin.

Printed in the United States on permanent paper.

Library of Congress Cataloging-in-Publication Data

McMillan, Ann, 1952–
    Civil blood : a Civil War mystery / Ann McMillan.
        p. cm.
    Includes bibliographical references.
    ISBN 0-7862-3614-0 (lg. print : hc : alk. paper)
    1. Richmond (Va.) — History — Civil War, 1861–1865
— Fiction. 2. African American women healers — Fiction.
3. Female friendship — Fiction. 4. Race relations —
Fiction. 5. Large type books. I. Title.
PS3563.C38657 C5 2001b
813′.54—dc21   2001041569

To Hunter Loy Hallman, born 1992,
and Delilly Hunter, born 1792,
this book is dedicated.

1. NAVY HILL

2. SHOCKOE HILL

3. BUTCHERTOWN

4. TO SEVEN PINES

5. TO DREWRY'S BLUFF

6. CAPITOL BUILDING

7. ST. PAUL'S CHURCH

8. LANCASTERIAN SCHOOL (FREE SCHOOL)

9. CITY JAIL

10. MCV EGYPTIAN BUILDING (MEDICAL COLLEGE)

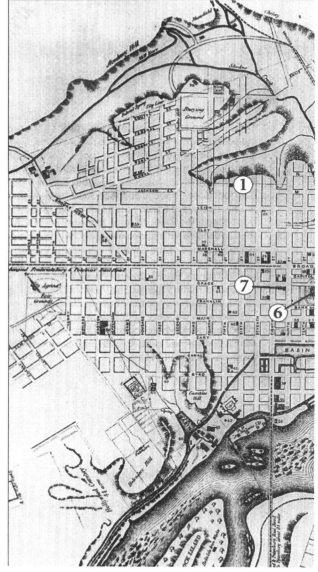

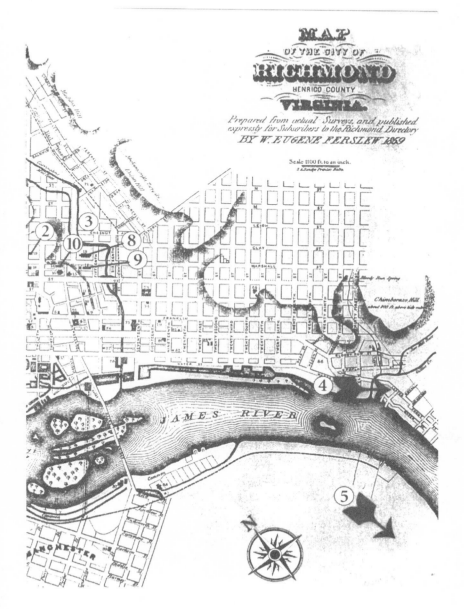

Acknowledgments

I wish to thank the following individuals (whose titles, degrees, and honors would run to several pages): Kathy Albers, Colleen Callahan, Carolyn Carlson, Glenna Jo Christen, Charles L. Cooke, John and Ruth Ann Coski, Elizabeth A. Fenn, Gertrude Jacinta Fraser, Robert Hancock, D. A. Henderson, Peter Houck, Audrey C. Johnson, Robert Peter Johnson, Gregg Kimball, Jodi Koste, Nancy Reed, Ann Reid, Terry Reimer, Todd L. Savitt, Terry Sharrer, Kent and Sarah Smith, John Vial, Nancy Yost; and the following institutions: the Black History Museum and Cultural Center of Virginia, the Conference on Women and the Civil War, the Medical College of Virginia/Virginia Commonwealth University, the National Museum of Civil War Medicine, the Pamunkey Regional Library, the Florence L. Page Memorial Library, the Richmond Public Library, the Valentine Museum/The Richmond History Center, the Virginia Historical Society. My apologies to all the above for any errors I have made despite their help.

I owe a special debt of gratitude to Alexander Hunter of the 17th Virginia Regiment, whose memoir *Johnny Reb and Billy Yank* gave me many of my best stories, including the one about the forged pass. And special thanks to Randy and Hunter.

CHAPTER ONE

Richmond, Virginia

WEDNESDAY, MAY 14, 1862

Josiah Harrald wondered if he might already be dead. The fever, and the pain it brought, had gone from him, but he had not the strength to move. Thought was left to him, enough to register these facts, but whatever emotion he might have supposed himself to feel at such a time was singularly absent. It was as if he had passed through a door that had shut behind him. Rage, bitterness, and ennui, the blue devils that had plagued him by turns throughout his life, he had left on the other side. Was this what it meant to *rest in peace?*

As he lay there in a milky darkness, Josiah felt his chest rise, then fall. Breath; he was alive, then. He could scarcely feel it, this breath, and it weighed nothing, but

Peabody Public Library
Columbia City, IN

it tied him down like the heaviest of chains; it bound him to life.

At last he tried to move his fingers. They felt as stiff and remote from sensation as if he were wearing gloves. He stroked one hand with the other, exploring. The skin was rough as a toad's, covered with wartlike bumps. He brought his fingers up to touch his face — the face that he would live or, more likely, be buried with. It was a swollen, shapeless thing on which the skin had bubbled up into pustules that covered even his eyelids, his lips, the inside of his mouth.

He could open his eyes just a little. He held his hands in front of his face and found he could see them, blots and bands of shadow between him and the merciless light that burned his eyes. Tired with the effort, he lowered his hands again and shut his eyes. Fluid drained from the roof of his mouth into his throat, and it hurt to swallow, but he lacked the strength to cough it up. He remembered a night — how long ago was it? — how he had struggled to get away. They had tied him down. Even if he had succeeded in escaping, what would have been the use? He could not run away from his own body.

He heard a sound, quickly interpreted it

as footsteps; then, men's voices, black men, two of them, laughing and talking. Then a rasping like the movement of rusty hinges: his own breath, he realized, drawn in with sudden fear. He had seen these men, or men like them, in the field hospital, and at the medical college hospital. He knew what they were here for. But he was not dead yet. He could not let them grab him around the ankles and under the arms, as he had seen them do to others; throw him onto a cart; wheel him and tip him into his grave. Or . . . this makeshift quarantine hospital was the basement room which the medical students used to perform dissections. Would the surgeons cut him open before burying him, to see how far the rottenness had spread beneath his skin?

He pushed the thought aside. He was alive. He was Josiah Harrald, a man of wealth and standing, an officer, accustomed to being obeyed. He had something important to tell. But he had to be very careful to whom he told it.

The men were very close now. Josiah felt his lips move, heard himself whisper, "Alive."

There was silence for a moment. Then one of the black men called out, "He ain't dead." Josiah could feel the man bending over him, and wondered how even a slave accustomed to such horrors could bear to look at the corrupted thing that had been Josiah Harrald. (The man was beyond doubt a slave, for who else would do this work?) Josiah opened his eyes and strained to see the man's face. Then he understood. The slave was himself pitted, his skin ravaged as if burrowing insects had been at it. The rough-edged scars were without pigment, white against the man's dark skin, giving the impression that his bones were showing through. Of course, a strong back and a strong stomach were all that was needed for this job. But Josiah had seen a flicker of concern in the brown eyes. The man was fighting it down, looking away.

Josiah Harrald seized on that small betrayal of compassion; he could make use of it. "Water," he whispered through lips that had swollen and cracked. The slave sighed, but what could he do? He went off, returning after a few minutes with a battered tin cup. The water was warm and tasted of iron. Most of the cupful ran down Josiah's face, but a little wet his lips and eased his throat.

"Not dead," Josiah said again. The slave looked at him, as if to say, *Not yet.*

"Mrs. Powers." Josiah was pleased at the strong sound of his voice. "Make her come . . . here. Must tell her . . ."

Doubt creased the slave's ruined face.

"What's your name?" Josiah asked.

The answer was made reluctantly. "Jim." And then, "Jim Furbish — sir."

"Jim . . . she must come. Now."

Josiah saw the slave, Jim Furbish, blink and move his head like a mule trying to dodge the halter. Then the slave was gone, and Josiah lay exhausted. He thought about Narcissa Powers, the young widow who had been his nurse at the medical college hospital following the amputation of his left leg. Strange, how the loss of his leg had seemed a tragedy at the time. Narcissa . . . he liked the name. Many things about her had pleasantly surprised him: her fine-grained skin, not plump and yielding as was the fashion but smooth, so smooth. . . . He could almost have lusted for her. But that particular bedevilment of the flesh was gone from him, as absent as his severed leg. He needed her now because she listened. She had a tender heart. He could trust her. Now, if only he could remember what it was he had to tell. It was hard to keep hold of a thought. The fear of death was pressing him again, a devil at his side, while at his other side beckoned the angel Sleep.

Josiah's breath slowed to a lulling susurration. The weight on his chest was lifting, and it seemed he was held to the earth by the lightest of tethers. It was very peaceful to be floating so.

Jim Furbish whispered to his cohort, Nahum McCall, "I know you thinking he going to get us in trouble."

Nahum pouted but said nothing.

The two slaves were attendants at the medical college hospital, now drafted to serve in this temporary pest-house whose current occupants, in addition to Josiah Harrald, were two soldiers from the western part of the state who looked as if they might recover. The attendants' jobs were to clean, remove soiled bedding, and take out the dead. Seldom did patients ask them for anything, other than perhaps a drink of water, that they were able to give. Never, to Jim Furbish's recollection, had a patient asked him his name.

Jim tried cajoling. "You stay here, keep an eye on things; I'll go across and get her."

Nahum still resisted. "Might be he seen what happened. He tell that nurse, next thing you know we got all them doctors asking us what about this and what about that. Just let it be."

He stared insistently at Jim, who shied away from his gaze. It was hard for Jim to look people in the eye, even those who, like Nahum, were so used to his face that their own registered no horror at the sight of it.

But Jim refused to back down. "I can't be pretending I ain't heard a man's dying wish. When he stand before the Lord, I don't want him complaining about Jim Furbish."

Narcissa Powers tied a clean bandage on the leg of a man named Tunstall, a volunteer from Alabama who had risen to the rank of sergeant. He had told her that and more about himself just the day before, falling silent when the surgeon began to reopen the wound. The surgeon's probe had brought out a jagged piece of metal that fortunately had missed the bone. Today, the wound was hot and oozing yellow liquid. The formation of laudable pus meant the wound was discharging its poison so that healing could begin. But the smell of it always seemed to carry a message of death.

Narcissa rose quietly and came away, carrying the fouled bandages to be boiled and used again. She dropped them into the basket at the end of the hall. At the washstand she poured water from the pitcher into the basin and grasped the rough cake of soap, cleansed her hands and forearms, then brought up her damp hands to push back the tendrils of black hair that clung to her forehead. She stood looking out the window onto the street below, glistening and filthy under a gray sky. Spring had fled, along with many of the city's occupants, from McClellan's glittering army, a hundred thousand strong, marching with its siege guns from Norfolk up to Richmond. But those who remained in the city saw passing through its streets the defenders, gathered from throughout the Southern states, ready to fight and die for the Confederate capital.

"Mrs. Powers!" The voice, pitched low, carried along the hall to her. She turned to see the hospital's surgeon in charge, MacKenzie Stedman, beckoning to her. Having caught her eye, he turned away. Narcissa hurried to follow.

In the bare room that served as his office, Stedman waved Narcissa into a straight-backed wooden chair, then dropped wearily into his seat behind the desk. Stedman folded his hands on top of the pile of papers that lay before him, inches deep, flanked by similar stacks on either side. Stedman looked beleaguered, his cotton-fluff hair standing out as if he had been running his fingers through it.

MacKenzie Stedman was the father of three daughters, and he seemed to think of Narcissa in that way. He had opposed her serving as a nurse at the medical college hospital, but that was a year ago, at the outbreak of war. When the wounded had come in from Manassas, all that had changed. And now the war had come to their very doors. The siege McClellan was preparing would fill Richmond with hundreds, perhaps thousands, of soldiers wounded in its defense. If McClellan took the city, the defending soldiers would be forced to make a stand somewhere else. Richmond would fall — as Norfolk, New Orleans, and other cities had already fallen — into the hands of the enemy. Perhaps it was concern for his wife and daughters that was affecting Stedman so. Narcissa wondered why he had not sent them away from the endangered capital, as President Jefferson Davis had sent his own family.

"I was looking for you, Mrs. Powers, in the hope you will help me with *this.*" Stedman picked up a piece of paper and flourished it in front of her. She took it from him, glancing at the thick, creamy paper on which a few lines were written, then looked up at Stedman, a question in her eyes.

"Roland Ragsdale," Stedman stated, as if the name itself were sufficient explanation. "How he thinks he can come here, today of all days, with enemy gunboats practically in firing range of the city. . . . But he is a wealthy man, and so used to being obeyed. And the gift he proposes is a generous one."

"Roland Ragsdale?" Narcissa repeated, mystified. "I can't recall ever having heard the name before."

Stedman shrugged. "Man of business. Owns a gambling house, engages in various enterprises, some of a dubious nature no doubt. Came here from Norfolk when the war broke out. Was in Baltimore before that, I believe. Now he proposes to make a substantial gift of his *earnings* to the military hospitals. Claims I did him a favor, though I would hardly call it that."

"A gift? That speaks well of him, don't you think?" Narcissa could not imagine

Stedman turning down a donation. Medicines and supplies smuggled through the lines or brought in by blockade-runners came dear.

Stedman smiled wryly. "Makes you wonder exactly how profitable his business is, does it not? Be that as it may, I have no time to spend being charming. And I'm sure he would appreciate your efforts in that direction far more than mine!" Stedman drew his gold watch from his pocket and frowned down at it. "He was supposed to arrive at four o'clock, and it's now five past. Maybe — Ah, here you are, Mr. Ragsdale."

Stedman stood to greet the new arrival. Narcissa rose and thrust the letter into her pocket, concealing her curiosity with a polite smile. She saw a man of middling height and age, brown-haired and bearded. A glance at his clothes told her he was indeed wealthy. With his fine wool suit and silk vest, he looked like a man dressed for his own wedding.

Stedman shook Ragsdale's hand, then turned to Narcissa. "Mrs. Powers, may I present Roland Ragsdale. He has announced his intention to —"

"Allow me to tell it, Doctor." Ragsdale's prominent, heavy-lidded eyes flashed a look at Stedman, then fixed with searching intensity on Narcissa's face. "I have been most fortunate in my business dealings here in our Confederate capital. I propose to make a gift — a sizable gift — to help care for our wounded heroes. And I hope to make the presentation to one of our heroines. Now that I have met you, I dare hope that it will be *you*, Mrs. Powers." With the words, he took her hand and held it for a moment, his bright eyes seeming to see more of her than was actually on display.

Dr. Stedman cleared his throat and said dryly, "Mr. Ragsdale has enjoyed a great deal of success in his . . . *investments* . . . in the city." Clearly Stedman meant the remark to take Ragsdale down a peg. Apparently there was nothing to be said about Ragsdale's family.

Ragsdale's smoothness remained unperturbed. "The gift I propose is of ten thousand dollars. And I will challenge the other gambling-house owners to make similar gifts."

"Ten thousand dollars! That is extremely generous of you, sir." Narcissa did not feign her surprise. How could anyone afford to give away such a sum, at a time when cotton and tobacco, cut off by the blockade from sale in Europe, sat unsold? And to think there were more like him in the city, men who could give away thousands! The thought troubled her. And yet his gift would benefit the wounded.

Ragsdale's smile plumped the smooth skin of his cheeks above his dark whiskers, and his full lips curved back to reveal strong teeth, the canines prominent. Narcissa felt the contrast between him and the poorly fed, chronically ill soldiers who had retreated up the Peninsula to Richmond's hospitals.

Ragsdale seemed to sense her disapproval. His eyebrows lowered, dimming the light in his eyes. "What I have heard of you is true, Mrs. Powers. You — as a nurse to our wounded heroes — represent the finest qualities of Confederate womanhood. I will make my gift into your hands, Mrs. Powers. Or not at all."

Ragsdale smiled again, but Narcissa felt the threat behind his words. She forced herself to smile back at him. "I would be happy to do whatever I can to help our soldiers."

"Excellent," Ragsdale replied, looking over at Stedman and nodding. "Then I shall make my plans."

"We are all very obliged to you, Mr.

Ragsdale." Narcissa smoothed her skirts — rubbing off, she realized, the feeling of his hands pressed on hers. "Now, if you gentlemen would please excuse me?"

"Certainly, my dear," Stedman replied. "Oh, I intended to mention, our friend Cameron Archer is back from Williamsburg. I asked him to stop in. I'm sure he hopes to see *you*."

Williamsburg. Stedman's tone held nothing of the horror that word now carried for those waiting anxiously in Richmond. All those men lost, as many as at Manassas, just to slow down the enemy's advance.

She shook off her depressed imaginings, conscious again of Ragsdale's scrutiny — made more intense, it seemed, by Stedman's jesting reference to Archer's admiration for her. She felt her face grow warm. Friends like Dr. Stedman saw what they wanted to see, she told herself. If Cameron Archer felt any interest in her, he had fought against it quite successfully for more than a year.

"Pray excuse me," she said again. Ragsdale made an exaggerated bow. She felt him watching as she hurried away. *A man of business,* Dr. Stedman had said. A speculator, buying up goods and reselling them to the quartermaster, or to city shops, at exorbitant prices. Not a gentleman, nor did he act like one, though perhaps his manner toward her reflected the notion that a nurse was not quite a lady. Still, she was both nurse and lady enough to accept ten thousand dollars for the Confederate hospitals, and to behave graciously toward the giver.

As Narcissa stood gathering her thoughts, she glimpsed a slight, fast-moving shape in the hall, darting between the bigger, slower forms, heading for her. Benjy. The slave boy was one of the first people she had met in her volunteer employment as a nurse. She had needed his help interpreting the doctors' demands — she'd learned quickly not to ask the doctors themselves to explain. That was a year ago, when the medical college's new hospital building, with its eighty beds, had seemed so spacious and well planned. Now there were hospitals all over town, including one on Chimborazo Heights with the capacity for thousands of ill and wounded soldiers. Somehow, despite the decades-long warnings of speech makers and editorial writers, the war had taken them all by surprise. Benjy had become a reassuring constant. He could almost always come up with whatever she asked him to find, from clean bandages to a chicken for soup.

Benjy stopped before her, gave a quick bob of his head, and said, "Mrs. Powers, Jim Furbish come over from the pest-house with a message for you."

Narcissa knew what the message must be. "Josiah Harrald is dead."

"No, ma'am, he ain't dead. He asked Jim to send for you, said he got something to tell you. Jim say he ain't got much time left."

Narcissa breathed out a long sigh. So that battle would be lost, despite all their efforts.

She had met Harrald about a month before. At an engagement in the Shenandoah Valley, a conical ball had passed through his left leg below the knee. The wound had grown infected, and he had been sent home to Richmond. There the leg had become gangrenous, so that Harrald had had to undergo amputation. A medical student had cut and sawed under MacKenzie Stedman's blandly smiling gaze, then tied a dozen ligatures, hurrying to finish the last one as Stedman moved on to the next patient. Narcissa had remained to dress the stump with cold water and maneuver Harrald into bed with the help of a male attendant.

She had thought it strange that a wealthy man whose family lived not a stone's throw away should choose to remain in the medical college hospital. But Josiah Harrald had an eccentric and irascible humor, which Narcissa had discovered when she brought a Bible to his bedside. *Holy trumpery* and *the greatest hoax ever perpetrated on mankind* had been among the mildest of his phrases on that occasion, but a gleam in his sharp hazel eyes had told her he did not aim to drive her away. So she had put away her Testament but held her ground, and soon discovered that, by serving as audience for his outrageous pronouncements, she could get him to swallow the bitter-tasting sulphate of morphine ordered by Stedman.

Of patients who underwent amputations like Josiah's, roughly half survived. But Josiah was young — not yet forty, the brown of his hair and beard unmixed with white — and his kind of agile, restless temperament usually made a good recovery from wounds that were only in the flesh. He had smiled sometimes, a smile attractive with respect to good, sound teeth but not warmed by any human feeling. She had doubted whether, once he returned to health and left her care, she would like him.

Then, a week after the amputation, fever set in, of the type associated with virulent infection, perhaps influenza or typhoid. Josiah had been isolated. A few days later, when the characteristic sunburnlike rash appeared, he had been banished to the makeshift pest-house. He suffered from the malignant confluent type of smallpox, and death could come from any number of causes, of which blood poisoning was the most likely. A white quarantine flag was nailed to the basement door of the Egyptian building — but most Richmonders already avoided the building where medical students practiced their craft on bodies brought by the sack-'em-up men.

Those who had come in contact with Harrald had been sought out and inoculated. Just as well that Harrald did not seem to have many friends. As far as anyone knew, this most contagious disease had not claimed any other victims through Josiah Harrald.

Narcissa passed under the buzzard-winged sun disk that adorned the entrance to the medical college's Egyptian building and descended the steps into the basement. The building's thick walls kept the air chilly, and she shivered as she changed out of her neat brown-and-red-print calico into a servant's discarded homespun already tainted with the miasma of infection. Though she changed all her clothing and scrubbed herself afterward, it took hours or days for her to lose the feeling that she carried the contamination. Perhaps that was because no one seemed to know how the disease infected its victims. Some said it spread through contact with the pus, others, through the breathed-in effluvia, while still others claimed it was none of these. She imagined smallpox drifting like spores from a poisonous toadstool, only waiting to find the right soil — in the case of smallpox, a human body — to take root again. Until they found that human soil in which to grow, the spores could wait a year or more, lying inert as dust, on cloth, paper, almost anything.

Soon she was kneeling by the pallet on which Josiah lay on his back. His face was a swollen mass of dark red bumps that oozed foul-smelling pus. His left hand, knobbed with pustules, lay atop the sheet that covered him to his chin. Fighting down the nausea that the smell of smallpox evoked in the most battle-hardened surgeons, Narcissa took his hand, her fingers resting briefly on the inside of the wrist before closing around his palm. His pulse was weak and irregular.

It struck her that a smallpox hospital was a strange, out-of-this-world place, untroubled by the woes affecting the rest of humanity. The threat of Federal invasion that had driven Richmond to the verge of panic did not touch the occupants of this room. If the Federals won, the inmates of the pest-house would be the last to know and, knowing, would not care.

Josiah Harrald's eyelids opened into slits. He turned toward Narcissa, away from the light — painful, she knew, to the eyes of smallpox sufferers — that seeped through the veiled window and diffused in the damp air. The effort it took him to see, and to think, showed in the grimace that bared his teeth. Narcissa, seeing he was trying to speak, remained silent. His hand tightened on hers, and hers responded, sharing his struggle.

"Money. Tainted . . . money."

Josiah fell silent, as if he had lost the thread of what he was saying. After a moment, he brought his free hand up to his chest. His fingers probed the thin cloth over his heart where his uniform pocket would have been, the place in which a man might keep those things most precious to him — a Bible, a photograph in its leather case — or money.

"In my pocket."

"It's all right, Major Harrald," Narcissa said in a light, firm voice. "Any money you had with you was destroyed. It will not spread the contagion."

Josiah moved his head with a suggestion of his old impatience. "No, no. Stolen. Cats. Came in the window."

Narcissa looked up at the little, diamond-paned windows, one on either side of the long, narrow room. They were curtained with black cloth to shield the eyes of the smallpox sufferers. From the outside of the building, they would be at ground level. They would open barely wide enough for a cat to come through. Surely Josiah had imagined it. She probed gently. "Have you seen cats here?"

Harrald's strength was fading. The hand she held felt cool, as if the blood had abandoned his extremities. His tongue worked in his mouth. Narcissa reached for the tin cup and found it empty.

"Let me bring you some water. And I

will ask the attendants if they have seen any cats. I will be back in a moment. Now, try to rest." The water would make him more comfortable, but she doubted whether he would be strong enough to speak again. What could she say to him to ease his mind, to turn his thoughts away from this fever-induced preoccupation? Perhaps it did not matter so much what words she chose. She would stay with him until the end came. It could not be much longer. Narcissa hurried away.

Josiah Harrald lay still, his hand over his heart. He was a solitary witness, as it were, of that organ's shuddering efforts to preserve his life — a beat, then a writhing spasm, then frantic, overhasty beats, then a frightening pause that made him wonder if the next beat would ever come. He remembered an exhausted horse he had seen once, flogged by a teamster. The horse had fallen to its knees in the spring mud and was struggling to rise, sinking back, struggling again, the tendons in its neck taut with effort. How much easier, he had thought at the time, to sink into the mud and die. But now he dreaded the silence, the nothingness that would quiet his heart forever. Was that to be the last emotion left to him — fear?

Many men had tried to frighten him. Only one had succeeded: his father, Thaddeus. At last Josiah had told him, *Enough*. And it had ended, the old man's attempt to run his eldest son's life. But it had ended too late, and the wrongs that had already been done because of it had never been put right. Because, Josiah now realized, his father had won the larger victory. Josiah had taken on his father's cold detachment, strapped it on piece by piece like a suit of armor until it enclosed him.

Narcissa crossed to the door, where the attendant Nahum had settled himself on the floor to watch and wait — like a buzzard, she thought, but she did not blame him. She dipped some water from the barrel into the dented cup, then addressed herself to Nahum.

"I suppose his uniform has been burned, and any — anything in his pockets." It was not even a question, so certain she felt of the answer.

"Yes'm, sure was."

One more question remained. "Have there been any animals in here?"

This time the answer came more slowly. "Well, they's rats sometimes. But we drives 'em off."

Narcissa fought down her revulsion. Rats, she knew, were impossible to keep out entirely from any hospital. Had cats come in to chase them? Or could Josiah have mistaken a large rat for a cat? Neither of these explanations would ease the distressed imaginings of the dying man.

Grasping the cup in both hands, Narcissa hurried back to where Josiah lay.

Josiah wondered. Should he forgive his father, or seek forgiveness from those he himself had hurt as a result of his father's training? No time for that now. Even fear was slipping away. Again Josiah felt himself floating free. His eyes strained against the tormenting light to see a woman standing over him, her face gentle. His mother? He breathed a prayer to the unknowable source of life: *Take me back to you.* He felt his remaining life gather itself, then let go.

Josiah Harrald was dead. Narcissa knelt beside him, setting the cup down on the floor beside her. It tipped over despite her care, unable to stand on its dented bottom. The water — which Josiah Harrald would never drink — spilled onto the stone floor. Narcissa blinked back stinging tears. She dared not cry, for fear she would not be able to stop. So many had died.

She looked again at Josiah. Had he survived, he would have been badly scarred. For a proud man it could be well-nigh unbearable to live trapped in such a hideous shell. But she knew he had not wanted to die. She had seen men with worse deformities than smallpox scars fight off death — men with no arms who would forever need help even to feed or relieve themselves; men with no legs, no eyes; a man whose lower jaw and tongue had been blown away. Somehow they lived, some of them. *Thy will be done,* she tried to pray. Josiah Harrald's last breath still hung in the air, but it could not be recalled. God's will *would* be done, in this if in nothing else. *The silver cord is loosed, the gold bowl is broken.*

She spent a moment checking the condition of the other two sufferers. Both were sleeping, apparently peacefully. By some diabolical quirk, the disease let its victims sleep during the day, only to lie awake through a night of pain, fear, and loneliness. Narcissa was relieved to see no sign of hemorrhage or sepsis in either of the men.

Narcissa crossed the hall to the little room where she had left her own clothes. Now that Josiah was dead, the urgency had drained out of her, and she felt bone-weary. Slowly she undid the hook-and-eye fastenings of the bodice and waistband, then stepped out of the dress. Standing in her camisole and drawers, she bundled up the dress together with the cloth that had covered her hair and wedged them into a shelf where the others who came and went, physicians and attendants, also left their tainted clothes. She washed her hands, arms, and face with water dipped from a barrel, then dressed again in the brown-and-red print. She had had the dress made when she decided to put away her widow's weeds. It had seemed to her not quite right to wear mourning for her brother, dead for more than a year, and her husband, dead more than three years ago now, when for so many the grief was immediate and raw. Better that she be a soothing presence at the soldiers' bedsides than a reminder of what their own loved ones might soon have to undergo.

Now Josiah Harrald's family would mourn. She would report Josiah's death to Dr. Stedman, who would dispatch a convalescent soldier to take the news to Josiah's family. Tomorrow, or the next day — if all should be well, if their city should be standing against its enemies — she would call on the Harralds herself.

Judah Daniel caught sight of Jim Furbish and set down the heavy iron she was using. With all the rain they'd had lately, the sheets would not dry. They hung in the hospital's washhouse for days until they began to sour, fouling the air and the tempers of the folks who worked here. She had to go over each sheet three or four times, changing for a hot iron every few strokes, just to get the sheets dry enough to be used on the patients' beds.

Judah Daniel felt glad of a rest, and glad to see Jim Furbish. She had nursed Jim through the smallpox, several years ago now. She had made a reputation as a healer in her own free black community, so that now white men, like Jim's owner, often called on her to care for their slaves. She had kept Jim clean and comfortable, given him styptic gargles to close the oozing pustules in his mouth, kept his bowels open with plant concoctions. But even she, who knew the healing secrets of the Indians and Africans, could not cure the smallpox. Neither could the white surgeons trained in their fine hospitals. Thanks to God, working His will through her hands, Jim Furbish had lived.

Feelings made little show on Jim's masklike face, but she could tell that something weighed on him. He walked over close to her and spoke in a low tone, though the laundresses at the far end of the room could not have heard him over the din of their own work and chatter.

"Judah Daniel, some boys done broke into the pest-house. They stole some things. Must have been more than one, because this one put the bundled-up things through the window, and I saw somebody out there, taking it off him."

"Jim . . . you telling me a boy came through the window and went out again?" In spite of his troubled face and honest eyes, she could not take what Jim had told her for the truth. "And took something out with him?"

Jim nodded. He looked near tears. "Nahum made me promise not to tell nobody. But I don't reckon he meant you."

Judah Daniel knew what Nahum meant well enough. *Don't tell the white folks, they'll blame it on us.* She put her hand on Jim's arm to steady him through his confession.

He began again. "When me and Nahum was first sent over there to work, we wasn't sure what we was supposed to do with the things, the money and clothes. We set them over against the wall. But then one night I was laying on the floor asleep, and I heard a noise and woke up. I thought I was dreaming it at first, this little boy going out through the window, handing something out."

Judah Daniel still wondered if maybe he had been dreaming. "Did you get a look at him?"

Jim nodded. "Seem like I seen this boy with the Cats. You know, them boys that fight in the streets, throw rocks and bricks at each other. One of the littlest ones, a white boy, real light hair, six year old maybe, real skinny."

Oh, yes — the Cats. Judah Daniel sighed inwardly. They were unruly, those boys, and some of them prowled and fought near the medical college, the poor Cats of Butchertown against the rich-boy Shockoe

Hill Cats, hurling rocks and brickbats. There were black boys and white boys in both: in Butchertown, poor whites and free blacks rubbed elbows in uneasy near-equality, while on Shockoe Hill, white boys sometimes brought their slaves along. The medical college — a block south of President Jefferson Davis's mansion and less than a block northwest of the city jail — sat on the edge of Shockoe Hill looking down into Butchertown.

Jim went on. "Anyway, I knowed I wasn't dreaming because Major Harrald's uniform jacket was laying over there under the window, and it was gone."

Judah Daniel thought this over. Any white man of the right age could use an officer's uniform just like a signed pass to enjoy the pleasures offered by the capital. A uniform jacket with a major's braid could bring a good price in Richmond. Not enough, maybe, to tempt the wealthy Hill Cats to steal. The Butcher Cats might be a different story. The shinplasters earned by the sale of a uniform jacket might mean they would eat that night. She thought of the boys she had seen brawling in the streets. Yes, it was possible. But a uniform jacket taken from the pest-house would carry disease and death through the streets with the wearer. Would anyone, even young boys, be heedless enough to steal from the pest-house, on the chance of being able to sell what they stole? These days it seemed like the city was feasting on run-mad mush.

Judah Daniel thought back over what Jim had said. "Was there money in the uniform jacket?"

Jim nodded miserably. "Yes'm, a lot of money. Maybe a thousand dollar."

Judah Daniel had to smile. "Jim, you know you ain't seen more than a few dollars in all your life. How you know it was that much?"

Jim's brow knotted. "I don't know for sure. It was a lot of notes. They had pictures of slaves putting cotton on a wagon."

Yes, well — that was enough to prove it was Confederate money. But, what with bank notes being issued by the new national government, the states, cities, even banks and railroads, she could not tell the worth of it from that description. Not a thousand, maybe, but enough to tempt anyone young and foolish enough to risk the fate of Jim Furbish or Josiah Harrald. But another question occurred to her. "How'd they know it was there?"

"I don't know, Judah Daniel, I swear.

41

Nahum and me, we didn't tell nobody. I reckon they seen the uniform jacket through the window and thought to sell it. But this . . . we scared we get the blame, Nahum and me."

She understood their fear all too well. The white doctors would likely blame him, and Nahum; no doubt both men feared the lash, or imprisonment, or being sold south. Still, the danger was too great to keep the secret. "Jim, how long ago was this?"

Jim looked miserable. "A week."

"A week! God have mercy." Judah Daniel drew a deep breath. If the disease had got out, people could be showing up sick any time now. "I got to let folks know about the danger. But I'll try and keep you and Nahum out of it. You keep your eyes and ears open. You hear of anybody getting sick, you let me know."

"All right," Jim murmured, and took his leave. He looked happier now, with the weight of his knowledge transferred to Judah Daniel. It was an awful fear: the boys could bring down a plague on themselves, and on the city.

Judah Daniel went back to ironing, her mind on the problem of Jim and the Cats. If she told the authorities, Jim and Nahum would be punished. Jim had already borne more than his share of suffering. But it was as she had told him: she couldn't just keep his secret.

It wore her out sometimes, having to go back and forth between the two worlds of black and white, relaying just enough information but not too much, hiding what could not be accepted. But with this . . . Smallpox endangered both the black and white communities. Since she had to tell someone, she would start with Narcissa Powers.

Lifting her skirts out of reach of the ubiquitous mud, Narcissa made her way toward the washhouse, where she had been told she could find Judah Daniel. The free black healer was as learned in her own way as the surgeons were in theirs, though her medicines were the humble plants of the field, swamp, and wasteland. Some of these medicines appeared as well in the medical man's armamentarium, given the glamour of Latin names. And Judah Daniel's craft had its own secrets, rites carried out to harmonize relations between the living and the dead. Did Josiah Harrald's spirit linger, after all? Could the conjure woman perform some rite to help him find the peace that had eluded him?

The hospital washhouse was Narcissa's second descent into hell that day: stinking with human filth, steaming hot from the boiling pots suspended over constantly burning fires, and on a rainy day festooned with clinging, sopping sheets. She felt the impact of the wet heat the moment she stepped through the door. Her soles slipped on the wet brick floor. She peered through the steam, blinking away drops of perspiration that formed on her forehead and streamed into her eyes. The washerwomen fell silent, glancing her way with looks that questioned her presence. At last she saw Judah Daniel, holding what looked like thirty or forty pounds of wet laundry in a basket on her hip, one strong arm half-encircling the basket and the other crossing her body, steadying the load. With a glance Judah Daniel let Narcissa know that she had seen her. After placing the basket with others at the far corner of the room, Judah Daniel crossed to where Narcissa waited, and the two women stepped outside into the cooler air, sheltered from the rain by the building's shallow porch.

"Josiah Harrald is dead," Narcissa told

her. "He called for me before he died, to tell me something he thought was important. But I don't understand what he said — he was delirious, I think."

"Well, what'd he say?" Judah Daniel folded her arms as if preparing to listen to a long story.

Narcissa found the gesture comforting. *Doctors . . . do they ever really listen?* She took her time, trying to recall Harrald's exact words. "He said something about money. *Tainted money,* he called it. Then he moved his hand around over his chest as if he were searching for his breast pocket, in his uniform. I told him that the money he had with him would have been destroyed, but he didn't seem to believe me. He told me it was stolen."

"Stolen?" Judah Daniel's thin, arching eyebrows rose a fraction. "That be some stupid thief."

Narcissa nodded. "I know. But he said — he said it was stolen by *cats*. That they got in through the window." Narcissa put her hand to her left temple and rubbed the place that sometimes throbbed with an old wound. "He must have been feverish and imagined he saw cats. It could have been rats he saw. I asked Nahum about it; he said they'd had a problem . . ." She shuddered and left the sentence unfinished.

Judah Daniel's reply was puzzling. "Nahum ain't the one to ask. You talk to Jim Furbish?"

Narcissa shook her head. "He wasn't there. Should I?"

Judah Daniel breathed out a sigh. "I reckon I can save you the trouble. It weren't the animal cats, but them boys that fight in the streets."

"Oh — the *Cats!* You mean, Major Harrald *did* see something?"

Judah Daniel nodded. "Jim seen one of them boys go out through the window. Major Harrald's uniform jacket was stolen, with some money in the pocket."

Narcissa recalled the pest-house windows, scarcely large enough to admit a real cat. She imagined a child, a boy, slipping in secret into that foul atmosphere, then going out again, carrying a bundle in his arms, and both of them poisoned, the boy and the bundle. . . . Then the image dispersed, and she saw Judah Daniel. What was she staring at with such intensity? Narcissa followed her gaze along the street to where Shockoe Hill sloped down to Butchertown — where the territories of the Hill Cats and Butcher Cats met. She looked back at Judah Daniel. The black woman's hair was pulled back, invisible under the white cloth wrapped turbanlike around her head. Her dark copper skin stretched taut over her prominent cheekbones. Judah Daniel's face kept its troubles to itself. But Narcissa could tell that she was worried. So it was true.

"When did it happen?"

Judah Daniel stiffened slightly. "A week ago."

"Who was the boy?"

Judah Daniel shook her head thoughtfully. "Jim say he was real small, looked six years old maybe. White boy, with light-colored hair. The other boy, the one outside, Jim didn't see nothing but the shape."

"And the money: how much was it?"

Judah Daniel's mouth twisted. "I ain't seen nothing much bigger than a fifty-cent shinplaster myself, so you tell me: what note got a picture of slaves loading cotton in a wagon?"

Narcissa tried to see it in her mind. "It could be a hundred-dollar note." The Confederacy backed its money not with gold, but with cotton. And with the labor of slaves.

Judah Daniel nodded slowly. "Well, Jim said he had a bunch of them bills."

Narcissa's eyes widened. "Goodness!

Are you sure that Jim and Nahum didn't —"

Judah Daniel shook her head. "If they took that money, why tell *me?* Why not light out for Canada? With that kind of money, reckon they could go in style."

Narcissa frowned. "Why wait so long to tell?"

Judah Daniel returned her gaze. "They was scared they'd be blamed. So they come to me . . . and me to you."

Narcissa mulled this over. Surely, Jim and Nahum should have told what happened. But what good would it do to punish them now? It would only prove their fear had been justified.

So: the Cats? Narcissa tried to recall what she had seen and heard of the boy gangs. "I've heard President Davis's own son, Jeff Junior, fights with the Hill Cats! Thank God the family's left town. They'll be safe." *Strange to think that while an enemy camps at our gates, another prowls in our streets.*

Judah Daniel's sideways glance seemed to say, *It won't be the rich boys bearing the danger.* "The Cats been accused of stealing before. The Butcher Cats, not the Hill Cats. Accused of breaking into shops. But the detectives can't catch them at it."

Judah Daniel did not trouble to hide her skepticism concerning the detectives' efforts. Narcissa could understand it: Judah Daniel was herself frequently harassed by the provost marshal's men, the Public Guard, or some other group supposedly out to maintain order. Now that Richmond was under martial law, the Military Guard's detectives were running the city to their liking, impounding gentlemen's horses and riding around in style. The Baltimore detectives known as "plug-uglies" were particularly hated. Meanwhile, the ranks of the day police force and night watch kept increasing, though always behind the pace of crime in the city.

It was too bad, Narcissa thought; if they had been trustworthy, the provost marshal's men could have been called on to help locate the Cats and prevent an epidemic.

Narcissa spoke her thoughts aloud. "We have to tell Dr. Stedman about this. We have to find out who the boys were, inoculate them and their families, friends, anyone they may have come in contact with. If the clothes were sold, we have to find out who bought them. . . ."

Narcissa fell silent, and the women exchanged a look. It might be impossible.

But they had to try. If an epidemic were to break out as a result of this, it would strike first among the children.

Out of nowhere, it seemed, Judah Daniel asked, "Why you think Major Harrald kept that money in his uniform jacket, instead of giving it to his family?"

Narcissa shrugged. "He chose not to go home after the amputation. I suppose he didn't want to be a burden."

"Still," Judah Daniel responded, "a pile of money ain't a burden they be like to complain about. But he kept it, and after it got the smallpox on it, it weren't no good to nobody."

Narcissa frowned. "He didn't expect to get smallpox. He didn't expect to die. I suppose he thought he would need it for something." She gathered her skirts in an automatic gesture before stepping into the street. "Let's go to Dr. Stedman."

The door to Stedman's office stood open. Narcissa's anxious haste carried her into the room before she took in the fact that it was Cameron Archer seated behind Stedman's desk. She stopped short.

"Mrs. Powers." Archer pushed the chair back and stood, sketching a bow.

"Major Archer." She held out her hand to him across Stedman's cluttered desk.

Archer clasped it for a moment. His hand felt rough and sinewy. His beard had grown in along his jaw, obscuring what had been a neatly trimmed Van Dyke. The strong Virginia sun had darkened his face, save for a band of white at the hairline that his hat had kept in shade. His eyes looked tired, bloodshot, creased at the corners and circled underneath.

"You are back, then . . . from Williamsburg." Again her mind filled with images of the horrors he must have endured. She wanted to reach out to him, but she could find no words. *How stupid I must seem.*

"As you see." Archer's dry tone repelled further comment. "Stedman was called away. I borrowed his office to write my report."

His gaze shifted to a spot behind her. Judah Daniel had come up to the door. Narcissa gestured for her to come in. Archer spoke a word of greeting, then looked back at Narcissa, a question in his eyes.

"Josiah Harrald has died," Narcissa began. Archer blinked but said nothing, though he must have known Harrald. They were of an age, and they shared the drawling speech of Richmond's elite. *Had* shared, she corrected her own thought. Josiah Harrald had met an enemy that his cavalier blood could not conquer. "He had smallpox." Again she watched for his reaction. It did not do to tell a doctor something he already knew. "It's not known where he got it, and no new cases have been reported."

Archer shrugged. "Harrald likely was infected by someone who brushed past him on the train coming here. By now that person is God-knows-where — Atlanta, maybe."

"We learned today" — Narcissa glanced at Judah Daniel — "before he died, Major Harrald told me he saw two boys, a week ago, there in the pest-house. Little boys, around six years old. They stole Major Harrald's uniform jacket, and the money that was in it."

Archer frowned. "Why were the things not destroyed?"

It was the question Narcissa had been dreading. Jim and Nahum had made a terrible mistake, but had anyone troubled to tell them what they should do, or why it was so important? Hot anger burned away cold dread. "What does it matter?" Her face matched the surgeon's, frown for frown. "There are *children* out there, and they're in danger."

She braced herself to take his response. But when he spoke, the surgeon's practicality had won out over the surgeon's pride. "Go find them, then, and make sure they haven't started an epidemic."

The surprise, and the relief, of his capitulation so struck Narcissa that she came near to laughing. A year ago he had not thought her fit to spoon-feed an injured soldier. Now he was trusting her to prevent a smallpox outbreak!

Archer frowned, seemingly aware of her thoughts. "The Confederate army can't spare any men — especially surgeons. Smallpox is not the scourge that it was, before we had inoculation. You can do what needs to be done." He managed to make this expression of confidence sound like an insult.

"I must have Judah Daniel's help," she pressed, bending over the desk in her urgency. "Write her a pass to that effect. Also, we must have a supply of the virus to use for inoculations. Please," she added, hoping her momentary assumption of equality would not so irritate him that he would refuse.

Archer hesitated. Then he spoke, as if to himself, not meeting her eyes. "General

Longstreet has not been the same since scarlet fever took three of his children back in the winter. Three, within a week." Archer picked up a sheet of paper and began to write. "I will get you what you ask for, Mrs. Powers. A plague among the children is the last thing we need."

So, thought Narcissa, he does have feelings other than anger.

It was near dark when Narcissa arrived back at the Powerses' home — her home, now. Her late husband's father, Professor Powers, and his daughter, Narcissa's good friend Mirrie, lived just west of town, close to the site of Richmond College. Narcissa walked slowly toward the house, breathing in the scent of honeysuckle. The overtaking vine was running wild in the front yard, climbing up through the boxwood. There it would flourish as long as more pressing tasks than rescuing the boxwood were occupying her attention — and Mirrie's, who was spending most of her time reading all the newspapers she could get hold of, not only the Richmond papers but those from New York, London, and Paris that made their way through the blockade and into her hands, sometimes weeks after they had been printed. Looking for the truth in these newspapers seemed to Narcissa a little like divining the future from the sodden flecks of tea left in the bottom of the cup. But Mirrie seemed determined to try.

Was it only this morning she had left Mirrie at the breakfast table and hurried down this walk, impelled by fear for the besieged city? But the long hours had seen that crisis pushed aside by another. Now it seemed to her that silent death had breached the city's defenses and walked among them, wearing the innocent face of a young boy.

Tomorrow — unless an enemy bombard-ment should intervene — she and Judah Daniel would begin looking for the Cats. And she would call on the Harralds. She had imagined their mourning for his death, but as she thought of it, she wondered how deep their grief would be. She wondered especially because it was unusual for a patient with family nearby to linger in the medical college hospital following an amputation, as Josiah had done. By the same token, once Josiah's smallpox was diagnosed, he could have remained in quarantine at his home; instead, he had exiled himself to the pest-house. Had he made these choices because the family was not a close and loving one? Or was his decision made to spare them the danger of infection and the inconvenience of quarantine?

She thought how profoundly she herself had felt, and still felt, the deaths of her own brother and her husband. Nothing could have kept her from Charley's bedside, or from Rives's.

And now she saw women — mothers, wives, sisters — arrive at the hospitals from as far away as Alabama, Florida, and Texas, determined to care for the men they loved. Sometimes she envied them their hardships, she who no longer had anyone of her own to love, to care for. . . . Still, she thought she could understand why some family members might stay away, overcome by their helplessness in the face of terrible suffering.

"Halloo! Mrs. Powers! In a brown study?"

Narcissa looked up into the bright blue eyes of Brit Wallace. Her own eyes widened as she took in the change that had come over the young reporter since last she had seen him several weeks before. His formerly smooth face was sunburned and

56

stubbled with a half-grown beard. His curling black hair looked as if it had been cropped by grazing sheep. The faultless white shirt and handsome blue cravat were gone, replaced by a checked shirt. A loose-fitting sack coat and trousers of brown jean cloth completed the young Englishman's suit.

Narcissa heard a familiar laugh ring out and looked up to see Mirrie standing in the doorway, her strawberry-blond hair haloed against the light.

" 'What have you done with our Mr. Wallace?' I said to him!" Mirrie called out to Narcissa. "It was not until he spoke in his John Bull voice that I would believe it!"

Brit drew Narcissa's hand through his arm, and together they walked up the steps to join Mirrie. In the light from the lantern that hung there, Narcissa could see lines of fatigue around Wallace's eyes, and the growth of beard covering his dimples, but his grin was merry as ever. He had been traveling with the army, she knew, gathering material for dispatches to his London newspaper. The difficulties of that life were turning him from a boy into a man. But he seemed to be bearing up well, and she could not look into his face without smiling in return.

"You would not believe how the boys chafe a fellow. I had just bought an overcoat, in the new longer style. Everywhere I caught the volleys: 'Mister, I see your feet!' and 'How long does it take for the water to dissolve you?' Finally I traded it to a sutler for this checked shirt." He gestured with both hands along his shirt front. "If I were to appear at home in these, well, my own mother would not recognize me, Miss Powers" — he nodded at Mirrie — "anymore than you did!"

"You will be wearing Confederate gray next," Mirrie said, her mouth twisted in a wry expression. "What will your mother say to that?"

Brit smiled and shrugged. "The pen is my weapon. It is said to be mightier than the sword, though I would like to show old Bulwer-Lytton the effects of well-placed artillery, and see what odds he would give the pen."

Mirrie turned and, with a sweep of her hand, beckoned them into the house.

In the warm and welcoming back parlor, Narcissa greeted frail old Professor Powers by a gentle pressure on his shoulder rather than her accustomed kiss on his cheek. Though she knew it was irrational, and though she knew the Powers and their servants had been inoculated, she could not quite shake the feeling that the smallpox miasma clung to her. And Professor Powers seemed so frail these days, with his fine white hair and translucent skin. Mirrie and the servant Beulah coaxed and badgered him to eat, but it seemed what little he took in found no purchase on his bones.

"Josiah Harrald died today — of smallpox." Narcissa spoke loud enough for the professor to hear. "I was with him when he died," she added, her voice trembling slightly.

"Oh! Josiah Harrald, Father!" Mirrie leaned toward the old man and put her hand on his arm, making sure he understood.

Professor Powers nodded. "I taught his father, Thaddeus. Rather an insolent young pup. Sorry to hear about the boy."

Mirrie and Narcissa exchanged a glance that mingled humor and concern. The professor tended to remember the young men he had taught over five decades as young men still. In his mind, a son of Thaddeus must be a mere child.

After they had all filled plates with cold chicken and biscuits, Brit told them of what he had seen and heard in Norfolk,

Yorktown, and Williamsburg. The Confederates under Johnston had conceded Norfolk, backed up to Yorktown, taken a stand, then slipped away before Union general McClellan was quite ready to deliver the crushing blow he had envisioned.

"McClellan is an engineer, you know. I can see him as a boy in the nursery, lining up all his little tin soldiers, all the miniature cannon, just so." Brit smiled as his fingers mimicked the careful placement of small objects. "If his sister knocked one down, he would sweep them all away and start over. McClellan prepared so well for the attack at Yorktown that, when at last he gave the order, there was no enemy left to fight."

"But Williamsburg . . ." Narcissa almost whispered the words.

Brit's face grew solemn. "There was terrible carnage there. Manassas was nothing to compare. Jubal Early — he was wounded, you know — and Harvey Hill led an attack on a Federal battery that . . . well, it was disastrous for the Confederates." Brit's averted eyes and tight jaw told more of the story than he would say to them, but Narcissa had heard it already, from wounded men brought into Richmond the week before, in the first wave of the retreat. It was this disaster that had kept Dr. Archer behind enemy lines, caring for the Confederate wounded, one of a handful of doctors working night and day among the groans of the dying and the terrible silence of the dead.

Thinking of the wounded men who had come into the city, and the others who likely would come soon, reminded Narcissa of Roland Ragsdale and his promised gift. "A man named Ragsdale came to the hospital today. He plans to donate ten thousand dollars for the care of the wounded!" To her consternation, Narcissa felt her face grow warm. What was it about Ragsdale that made her so uncomfortable?

Brit sat back and watched while Narcissa recounted her meeting with Ragsdale. The pink flush on Narcissa's pale face was becoming, but he found himself resenting this rich man. He knew a little about Ragsdale: a speculator, an owner of gambling houses that were now closed — at least, according to the law. But it would seem mean-spirited of him to speak ill of the man now. He would find out more about this Ragsdale, he promised himself, then changed the subject.

"I attended the Virginia General Assembly's meeting today. They have vowed to hold Richmond 'to the last extremity.' I believe the flight of the Confederate government only strengthened their resolve."

Mirrie's mouth twisted in an ironic smile. "Now the Confederacy has seceded from *us!* Narcissa, I do believe that if you and I stay right here — the two of us, for Father is not political, and you must be our chronicler, Mr. Wallace — we will be our own sovereign government before this is over!"

Brit laughed heartily. "You and Mrs. Powers? Highly as I regard you both, I know that one of you would be seceding from the other within a week."

Mirrie and Professor Powers laughed, and even Narcissa, preoccupied as she was, had to smile. It was true, the politics of each followed the bent of her temperament. Mirrie, idealistic, all-or-nothing, was committed to the abolition of slavery and ready to light the fire that would bring on the brave new world. Narcissa was more inclined to think of individual slaves, and to wonder what kind of a world it would be if the old ways were destroyed in a sudden blast of refiner's fire.

"Well," Brit added, "at least we could call back the diplomat Nat Cohen and employ him in running from one to the other of you with offers and counter-offers." ♦

Mirrie smiled and looked down, made shy for a moment by the mention of her fiancé, now employed as a representative of the Confederate government in France.

At last Professor Powers retired for the night, and Narcissa felt free to bring up the subject that was obsessing her mind. "Josiah Harrald's death is not the worst news. Some little boys — boys from one of the Cats gangs — got into the hospital a week ago and stole the major's jacket. There was quite a lot of money in it. They may have sold the jacket, and they must surely be spending the money. The infection may be all over town. There could be an epidemic."

Brit leaned forward. "How much money?"

"Maybe a thousand dollars," Narcissa answered unhappily.

"A thousand!" Brit's eyebrows rose. "Who knew it was there?"

"I don't know," Narcissa admitted, "except for the orderlies who work in the pest-house, and they swear they didn't tell anyone. I believe them," she added. "They know the horrors of the disease better than most."

"Well . . ." Brit said slowly, "someone knew. The person who gave Josiah the money in the first place."

Narcissa sat up straighter. "That's right!"

"It wasn't his army pay," Brit remarked dryly. "So, let's see. He could have won it in a poker game. Soldiers in the camps are much addicted to gambling. Was Harrald?"

"I've no idea."

Brit smiled reassuringly. "Never mind. That should be easy to find out. Or maybe someone owed him money, and paid it to him in the hospital?"

"Or maybe," inserted Mirrie, "he had the money with him in order to pay it to somebody."

"Well, I'll investigate along those lines," Brit stated, smiling as if pleased with himself. "What else?"

Narcissa thought for a moment, then outlined her plan. "Judah Daniel and I will find out more about the Cats whose territories are near the hospital — the Shockoe Hill Cats and the Butchertown Cats. It would help immensely to find the boys

64

who stole the things. But it's not likely they'll want to admit to it. They may be frightened. Maybe if we could find the person who bought the jacket? How awful, to think that someone may put it on and go out among our soldiers!"

Brit frowned. "How long does it take for the symptoms to appear?"

"A week, or a little longer." Narcissa looked down at her knotted fingers. "But it's been a week already —"

Brit shook his head at the difficulty of the task. "We won't know we've gone down the right path until we find someone with smallpox at the end of it! Why has the United — er, the Confederate — States not required vaccinations?"

"Well," Narcissa responded, smarting a little, though she knew the accusation was justified, "most families do inoculate their members whenever the scabs are available. We're not often well-organized enough to use cowpox —"

"*Vaccination*, as opposed to *inoculation*," Mirrie broke in, sounding a pedantic note, "*vacca* being the Latin for *cow*." Her tone abruptly shifted. "As to why we do not require it, we Americans — especially we Confederates — are morbidly sensitive to requirements, even to save our skins . . . or our souls. And this war proves it."

"If grown men want to risk their lives," Brit countered, "I suppose they have that right. But to leave children unprotected . . ."

They sat in silence for a moment.

Narcissa tried to soften the harshness of the indictment. "The Cats may not have understood the danger beforehand. But when we locate the boys, we may find they've lost their nerve — or regained their senses — and thrown their ill-gotten gains in the fire." Still, she had to admit to herself, it was as Brit had said. The path they had to follow would most likely lead to disease — and possibly to death.

Benjamin Givens, whom everyone called Benjy, had seen just about every kind of death, except sudden. He hadn't seen any much worse than death from smallpox. Major Harrald had swelled up and festered but had still clung to life. On his errands for the medical college, Benjy had gotten close enough to see the sick man, and hear him, moaning and raving. Jim Furbish had warned Benjy against coming too close. Jim's face was enough of a warning for anybody against the dangers of smallpox.

Even though he had been inoculated, Benjy dreaded smallpox more than just about anything. That was why, when Timmy and Samuel had told him what they had done, he had come near to panicking, to running away and letting the little boys fend for themselves. But he had calmed himself enough to make some plans for their protection. They could hide, the two of them, in the old shed behind the free school. The school, where the white boys went to learn to read and write and do sums, stood empty at present because of the threat to the city. The stout, two-story brick building was only a short way from the medical college hospital. Benjy could bring them food, check on them. In a week or so, he told them, they would know it was safe to come out — that they wouldn't get the disease. He didn't tell them that if they did get the disease, they would have to go across the street to the pest-house.

So Benjy found them a hiding place, made it comfortable as he could with straw and rags, brought them bits of food borrowed from the hospital (after all, *this* was a hospital of sorts, now). He made the promise of secrecy they demanded. The boys had done wrong. If it came out, their parents would beat them bloody, the police too maybe; they might even go to jail. If he didn't keep their secret, they said, they would go back home and act like nothing had happened. That frightened Benjy, to think of how the smallpox could spread while they argued, him a slave against a white boy and a free black.

Benjy didn't think to wonder *why* they had stolen into the pest-house and carried out Major Harrald's uniform jacket. Little boys did crazy things. But after a while it dawned on him that something was frightening them — something that, to the minds of the boys, was much worse than smallpox. He began to ask questions: Why had they gone into the pest-house anyway? What had they done with the jacket they had stolen? They wouldn't answer.

Then — on the seventh day after the boys' theft from the hospital — he slipped over to the shed and found Timmy feverish and nauseated. The meaning of what they had done, what *he* had done, hit him with a new force. He couldn't handle this on his own.

So he had told one person, not the wisest or the kindest, but — he supposed — the easiest and most natural. And he was sitting here in the dark of night, outside the closed door of the shed in which the boys were sleeping. His heart pounded against his ribs. He knew he would catch a beating at the very least. But he had to do this, he had to get help. Timmy needed medical care, Samuel too maybe. He was doing the right thing, he told himself. The thing to be afraid of was the disease, not the nameless, faceless terror that spooked the little boys.

And so, when he saw the figure approach, he stood up and stepped forward. The figure drew closer, just a darker shape in the darkness, silent and swift. He tried to call out, but his voice caught in his throat. Then something slammed him, much harder than any blow he had ever felt, in the middle of his chest. He fell, the shock of it fading into merciful blackness.

CHAPTER TWO

THURSDAY, MAY 15

The crack of a sharpshooter's rifle brought Cameron Archer wide awake. In a moment his vision and brain had cleared enough to tell him that he was in his own chair, before his own fire, at his home on Shockoe Hill in Richmond; and that the pop of a twig as the fire caught it had wakened him. His watch showed it was a quarter past five in the morning: near time to get up, though he had not yet gone to bed. He was sweating; it was too warm for the fire he had had lit to banish a chill deeper than its heat could reach.

Without thinking, he put his hand out for the brandy glass that Gideon filled, and refilled once, every night that Archer was at home. As his fingers closed around the stem, his sense of the moment shifted again. He had come home, but with him had come war, in earnest now. Most of the liquor and wine from his ancestral cellars had been given to the hospitals. He had saved for himself six bottles of an excellent brandy. He would drink only half a glass, now, on the nights he was home, until one was finished: the war or the brandy. He held the glass in front of his eyes, gazing into its golden heart as if it held the answer to the question. Then he tilted it, drained the last drop, and set the glass down.

Archer's thoughts drifted to a memory from nine days before. The Confederate army had suffered heavy losses at Williamsburg. Still, it had escaped the crushing blow McClellan had been so long — *too* long — in preparing. Archer himself and a dozen others, mostly medical officers, had returned to Williamsburg under a flag of truce. They had ridden through fields littered with dead men, many of whom, killed in a hot exchange of fire, lay staring up at a blue sky that mocked them with its beauty after so many days of rain. Others the cannon had blasted into travesties of the human form, like one whose head had been blown away, leaving only the face, an empty mask, still attached to the body. Horses had been swallowed up in mud, dragged down by the cannon they

71

had tried to pull.

From among the dead had come the wounded, hundreds of them, borne by ambulances loaded to groaning, wagons, stretchers, and their comrade's backs and supporting arms. Those strong enough to withstand this rough transport had left in the vanguard of the retreating army. Still, hundreds had remained, too badly wounded to be moved. Hospital flags — yellow for Confederate, red for Union — had flown from the old college, churches, and homes of Virginia's colonial capital. Bandaged men, with little left to distinguish between Yank and Rebel, sitting propped against the buildings, hard by the piles of amputated limbs awaiting burial.

Then his gaze had come to rest on a little party of soldiers, wearing blood-stained blue uniforms and bearing a flag of truce. At first he took them for wounded. A man whose insignia marked him as a surgeon stepped forward from the group. There was something familiar about him, Archer thought, and then recognized him — Stephen Goodell, his friend from Hampden-Sydney College, who had gone to Philadelphia to train as a surgeon.

Archer dismounted and stepped forward to meet him, but Goodell had not known him until Archer said his name. "Hello, Stephen."

Now, remembering, Archer wondered if the conflicting emotions he had seen in Goodell's face had also been visible in his own. The eyes had widened, the smile had begun; then a hesitation, a shutting down. The two men stood for a moment as if unsure what to do. Then Archer offered his hand, and Goodell clasped it briefly in his own.

At last Archer said, "General McClellan was most gracious in extending protection and care to our wounded. We" — he indicated the others with a sweep of his hand — "have been detailed by the surgeon-in-chief to help with their care, until they are able to be moved to Richmond."

Goodell looked tired, most of all, but his narrowed eyes and compressed lips revealed anger just under control. His gaze swept over Archer's comrades. "Not many, for several hundred wounded. General McClellan was gracious, indeed." He sounded as if he himself would not have been so gracious.

Archer had felt his own anger mount. The other medical officers had gone to prepare for the defense of the Confederate capital, to which the army was withdrawing, Union forces in pursuit. Richmond was his home, where Stephen Goodell had visited his family in former days and been treated like a son. In that moment Archer had resolved that neither Stephen Goodell nor any other enemy soldier should ride through the streets of his city and glory in its fall.

Stephen's tone when he spoke again had been chilly. "Tell the others they can go make themselves useful. And you, Archer, come with me. There is something I want to show you." Goodell set off across the street, making for a building that flew the Union red. Archer had spoken to the men with him. Then, curious, he followed Goodell. He entered to find a makeshift hospital no different from others in which he had labored. Men were lying on the floor. The lucky ones had pallets of straw. Those whose wounds were bandaged helped the others. A bloody rivulet running across the floor marked the way to the operating room, where a surgeon and orderly labored over a table constructed of a door mounted on trestles.

Stephen had gone to a dark corner where he stood looking down at something covered with a blood- and mud-stained sheet. As Archer came up beside him, Stephen pulled the sheet back. There was a smell of sulfur and charred flesh. Archer, who thought he had seen every horror, realized it was what was left of a man, the lower half of his body blown away, the upper half blasted gray with black powder that had burned into every visible inch of his skin.

"One of your torpedoes did this," Goodell said. "This man was not engaged in battle, not even on picket duty. He was merely walking along the road when he stepped on a torpedo fuse hidden by your retreating forces." He dropped the stiffened sheet back to cover the remains. "I did not think your army would stoop to such a dishonorable act."

Archer had heard of the torpedoes — artillery shells buried in the road, rigged with percussion fuses that the pressure of a foot would set off. They were an innovation of modern warfare, the brainchild of a general who had used them against the Seminoles in Florida twenty years before. Archer himself thought the use of such mechanisms cowardly and unworthy, but in the face of Goodell's outrage, he had found himself in a defensive position.

"I am sorry for the waste of any man's life," Archer responded. "I am grateful for the flag of truce that allows us, you and me, to save as many as we can regardless of their uniforms or their sympathies. But you should know that every advance in weaponry by one army is seen by the opposing army as dishonorable — at least until it has produced its own. And you are the invaders here."

He had seen Goodell's fists clench. In a moment the Federal surgeon lashed out, though not with a blow.

"You must know there is a difference — an absolute difference — between honor and dishonor. Years have passed since you trusted your reputation to my honor. Now that we are enemies, has that changed? Is *honor* a mutable quality?"

The reference had first puzzled Archer, then sparked an angry retort that he'd bitten back. At last he said, very quietly, "The honor of another was involved. *That* has not changed."

For a moment they had stared at each other, Archer and his old friend, until the familiar sounds of the hospital, the barked orders of the surgeons and the moans of the wounded, recalled them to the oath they shared as physicians. "Our duty calls us," Archer said, and Goodell led the way. For the next five days, the two men worked side by side without touching again on personal subjects. Then the Confederate medical officers and their patients had begun their removal to Richmond, a laborious journey that had taken another three days.

Then this afternoon — yesterday, it would be now — Archer had sat down in Stedman's office to write his report. He'd been drifting into sleep, his thoughts confused, when Narcissa Powers rushed into the room, startling him. A beautiful woman, clean and sweet-smelling, she seemed in that moment to represent everything they were fighting to keep sacred. But what she said, about Josiah Harrald's death and the possibility of a smallpox outbreak, had chilled him. Why did it have to be Harrald? To hear the name again, so soon after Goodell's words had recalled the whole shameful incident to his mind! And to think Narcissa would have to go out, with only Judah Daniel to help her, and try to prevent an epidemic. . . .

Now, as he sat before his too-warm fire, he felt the same chill. But what could he do? In the midst of a war to protect Southern womanhood, he could not protect one woman.

Today was Thursday. Today, in all likelihood, the defenses on the James below

Richmond would be tried. A shock of nervous agitation ran through Archer, bringing him to his feet. This was no time to be moping in front of the fire.

The Chapmans were always at work long before dawn, preparing the baked goods that would be delivered to the sutlers that supplied the troops, then to the hotels, and later sold in their little shop fronting Main Street. By six o'clock in the morning, the first flurry of baking was over. Judah Daniel helped them out when she could, though she was more skilled at mixing potions than pastry. Now she sat drinking a hot brew made from parched corn and trying to imagine it was coffee. John Chapman and his son Tyler loaded the goods onto the wagon. Tyler's wife Elda, awkward in her eighth month of pregnancy, rolled out pie crusts. Their son, Young John, slept with his head in Judah Daniel's lap. Old Honus Chapman, patriarch of the family, drowsed in the heat from the cooking fires. Two other men well up in years — Zed Truesdale, whom everybody called the Reverend, and the blacksmith Webb Clark — were at the shop earlier than usual.

"Well, now, Tyler," Webb called out to the younger man. "Reckon that bridge y'all built done stood the test so far."

Judah Daniel could see the tendons stand out in Tyler's neck. He was angry, but he was determined to respect the older man. It wasn't really Webb that had Tyler riled, anyway.

"Reckon it'll hold to let in Mr. Lincoln's troops," Tyler said levelly.

Webb shook his head slowly in response and smiled, unexcited. It was an old argument now, sharpened on this day by the possibility that Mr. Lincoln's troops really could come riding in, if the Union navy could only blast its way past the guns on the bluff seven miles below the city. Tyler had been impressed by the Confederate army to help build the pontoon bridge that provided quick access from the Richmond side of the James to the fortifications on the south side, overlooking a sharp bend in the river. For two days and a night Tyler had labored without resting. He had worked alongside other men, five hundred of them, white and black, laborers, servants, and thieves from the wharves. The bridge had been completed, a triumph for its designer. What it was to the men who built it, no one asked.

"All right, son," John Chapman said in a voice that soothed but carried a warning. "You can go on now. Keep your ears open, and your mouth shut, and don't believe half what you hear — them hotel folks love a new piece of gossip better than a new dime."

"And keep your eye out for them Cats!" Judah Daniel called to him. Then she turned to Elda. "You wasn't here when I told the menfolks. There was some things stolen from the pest-house. Jim Furbish seen a boy, a white boy, that he seen before fighting with the Cats over between Shockoe Hill and Butchertown."

"Smallpox!" Elda's furrowed brows showed how seriously she took this news.

John Chapman stood with his arms folded across his chest, still scowling at the door through which Tyler had passed. At last John crossed over to his daughter-in-law and put his arm around her. "Let's rest a little while, honey," he said, and drew her over to the plank table where Judah Daniel and the others were sitting. Elda settled on the bench next to Judah Daniel and gently touched the curly hair of her son.

Chapman sat across from the women. He sighed deeply and said, "I'll sure be glad when all this is over and things get back the way they was."

"Things won't never be the way they was," Elda said sadly, her voice a whisper.

John Chapman answered her with a false heartiness. "Well, they could be a heap better than they is now. Got the government printing more money than they's making things to buy with it. Got the white trash of the Baltimore slums laying down the law for folks born and bred here.

"You talking about them Cats," John went on, glancing at Judah Daniel. "Them boys getting blamed for breaking into shops, busting things up, stealing. Plug-uglies always gets there too late to catch them at it." Chapman's lip curled in distaste. "Course, some people ain't going to have no trouble. That Mal Evans, I reckon they knows what he's up to, and if they ain't caught him at it, they's looking the other way. I mean to say, when a bunch of growed men goes into a filthy little old confectionery all hours of the night and comes out with a wrapped-up package —" Chapman mimed taking a drink.

So John Chapman suspected Mal Evans of selling illegal alcohol along with candy. But John and Mal had never liked each other. On the couple of occasions she had seen them together, they had circled each other like dogs, each warning the other not to give him a reason to fight.

Something John had said brought Elda out of her sad daydream. "Didn't Sam, Mal Evans's son, used to fight with them Cats? You know, that little boy who like to follow Tyler around, ride on the wagon with him? But he ain't a bad boy, and he ain't no thief. Just love to brawl, like boys do. Not that this one ever going to fall in with such foolishness." She looked down tenderly at her own son. "I ain't seen Sam around much lately, though. I hope and pray he ain't got the smallpox."

Elda's little shudder of dread disturbed her son, who sighed and wriggled in his sleep. Judah Daniel settled him more comfortably, then raised her eyes to Chapman's once again. "So you don't think the Cats is doing the stealing?"

John Chapman shrugged. "They's just boys. Stand to reason any sort of a *man* could clap a hand on them and get them to stop." His tone left no doubt what sort of men he thought the plug-uglies were. "I mean for Tyler and me to take turns watching out. Maybe that trapdoor Tyler put in come in useful after all."

The trapdoor led to an earthen crawl

space that ran for about thirty feet between the bake shop to the little lean-to stable behind it. John Chapman had opposed his son's making the tunnel, which readied the bake shop to serve as a hiding place for runaway slaves. But, as Chapman had told Judah Daniel, his talk on how much they had to lose — not only their property, but their freedom — seemed to mean no more to Tyler than the buzzing of a fly. Tyler was the third generation of a prosperous family. The way John figured it, Tyler couldn't imagine how thin the line was between his own lot and that of the slaves escaping on the Underground Railroad. But Judah Daniel wondered if the opposite was true: if Tyler felt more keenly than John himself how flimsy the division was between freedman and slave.

Suddenly Main Street came alive with noise — pounding hoofbeats, men and boys calling out. Judah Daniel scooped up Young John and followed Chapman through the door into the bake shop, then out onto the plank sidewalk, with Elda and Webb close behind them.

"The Union fleet's been sighted, coming up toward the bluff!"

Elda held out her hands for her son, took him from Judah Daniel, and clutched him to her heart, settling one chubby leg on each side of her swollen belly. The boy smiled and put his arms around her neck.

"We best get inside," Chapman said quietly. "Don't matter what color uniforms they be wearing, the soldiers going to want biscuits."

From Hampton Roads to Richmond, seagoing vessels have found their way up the James since the land it flows through belonged to the king of that name. There they must stop: for at Richmond come the falls, where the river renounces its kingly depth, though not its name. Below Richmond, the James loops like a ribbon dropped by a careless hand. The last bend, just before the ribbon unfurls into Richmond, is overlooked from the south by a hundred-foot-high bluff.

Brit had composed these words the night before, looking at an officer's map. Now he stood at the top of the bluff, breathing hard from the climb, and looked out to where the river ran high and brown. It was barely light enough to see, cool and rainy still, but he hardly felt it in his excitement. At any moment the Federals might round the bend. . . .

Here, "Fort Drewry" — begun this winter with the construction of a redoubt and placement of three heavy cannon — has over the last few days received heroic, if much-delayed, reinforcement. The owner of the land, a Mr. Augustus Drewry, is today defending it as captain of the Southside Heavy Artillery. The Confederate Navy, unable to meet the invaders on the water, has retreated behind a line of obstructing debris sunk into the river — stone pilings and cribs, logs, and the scuttled vessels of unlucky merchants, together with one of their own warships.

But the navy has put its men, and its guns, to the defense. At the fort, Commander Ebenezer Farrand, a grizzled veteran, is ranking officer. He commands troops plucked from heavy artillery batteries and infantry regiments. The eight-inch smoothbore from the ironclad warship Patrick Henry *is mounted on the bluff, as well as other guns, both rifled and smoothbore, from the* Patrick Henry *and the scuttled warship. The guns are secured in part with sandbags sewn by the ladies of Richmond in their own heroic efforts to stand firm against the invaders.*

The recent arrival of the navy men on the bluff had been greeted with jibes. "Ain't you fellows supposed to have a ship with you?" The sailors retaliated, letting it be known that they viewed the Southsiders as nothing more than a bunch of farmers whose bacon the navy had come to pull out of the fire. The grumbling fell silent when the men had to save their breath — it was hard work hauling heavy guns up a nearly perpendicular hundred feet. And doubtless the men would pull together again when the enemy came in sight. But now, delay and dread were trying the men's patience, and the grumbling started up again. "Don't know why they had to destroy the *Virginia*," remarked a landsman to his mates, looking sideways over his shoulder to see the effect of his words on the navy men nearby. "They say Abe Lincoln danced a jig when he heard the news!" Brit, resting on his haunches with his hat pulled down to keep the rain out of his eyes, got up and walked to the easternmost edge of the emplacement.

Across the river, a little less than a mile downstream, rises Chaffin's Bluff. Here we must pause and remember the pride of the Confederate Navy, the hoped-for defense of the city, that was the Union's old warship Merrimac. *Rechristened the* C.S.S. Virginia, *it was rebuilt according to a revolutionary, though unimpressive-looking, new design that concealed the ship itself below the waterline, exposing only its stoutly casemated guns to view. Those guns, together with an iron ram on the bow, inspired hope in the breasts of Southerners and a corresponding fear in Union hearts. Just four days ago, off Craney Island in the lower James, the* Virginia's *crew blew up the* Virginia *rather than risk its falling into enemy hands. Today some of those same crew members are having their revenge, digging rifle pits and stationing themselves as sharpshooters on Chaffin's Bluff.*

Jesus God! There they were! Brit opened his mouth to call out, but the cry was already loud in the air. Suddenly he was all eyes and ears, picking up snatches of what the men were saying to him and to each other, massed together as they were now, distinctions of service forgotten.

At six-thirty in the morning, with a light rain falling, the Federal fleet is sighted. The Galena, *covered with iron plates overlapping like fish-scales along its sides, comes first. Its captain is John Rodgers, commander of the Federal fleet on the James. Next is the curious craft* Monitor, *which, like its ill-fated adversary* Virginia, *conceals its vulnerable parts below the water, and which like that vessel terrifies its enemies. Viewed from above, its shape is that of a weaver's shuttle, pointed at both ends. Its revolving turret, which has been com-*

pared to a cheesebox afloat on a raft, mounts two eleven-inch smoothbores that can fire shot or shell. These are followed by the ironclad Naugatuck *and wooden gunboats* Aroostook *and* Port Royal.

It was a slow and graceful dance of bulky partners, down there in the river. The navy men on the bluff watched the skillful maneuvers of their Yankee counterparts in admiring silence.

The Galena *anchors approximately six hundred yards from the fortifications on the bluff. She swings about broadside. At about 7:45 A.M., the* Galena *opens fire. An hour later, the* Galena *still has done little damage to the Confederate fortifications, yet the Confederate guns are taking their toll at close range. The* Monitor *comes up above the* Galena. *The* Monitor *proves impervious to Confederate shot and shell, but, unable to elevate her guns to reach their target, she swings back below the* Galena. *That ship is by now pock-marked by the shots that have pierced her armor. One can only imagine the condition of the men inside.*

Brit made a mental note to find out about the casualties.

The booming of the cannon, the whiz and ping of the rifles — ah, that was lively music. Brit put away his notebook and pulled out his telescope. The firing grew hotter, forcing Brit, who now felt himself to be serving in the role of target, to stand down. Before long he was glad he had done so, as a heavy ball from the Federal flagship hurtled over the edge of the emplacement and into the structure of earth, logs, and sandbags holding up one of their biggest guns. It was now that the men's courage and dedication would be tested. They had to go up, into the line of fire, and right the gun. As many had to go as could fit around it, for it was longer than a man's body and weighed six thousand pounds. Brit watched them go, their faces set in grim lines. He watched some of them fall and be dragged away, while others stepped into their places. For a moment it overwhelmed him. *My God . . . what makes men able to do this?*

A blow from the Galena, *or from the hand of fate, has dislodged the eight-inch gun from the* Patrick Henry *off its log casemate. The gunners swarm around to get it back into position, exposed all the while to enemy fire. The carnage is dreadful. One man has the top of his head shot off, the brain blown away with the skull. One man has half his body torn away down the side. Another loses a leg. But at last the gun is mounted and firing again.*

"Hip, hip, hooray!" As the *Galena* slipped its moorings, the cheer went up once, twice, three times. Ebenezer Farrand, sober and stern as he was, joined in the clamor. Brit grinned at the boys, their rivalry forgotten, slapping each other on the back, jumping and hollering.

Now, with the sun high in the sky, a shell fired from this very gun delivers the coup de grace to the Union flagship, blasting its way into the Galena *and lodging there, sending out a billow of smoke. The* Galena *moves downriver, exposed all the way to the depredations of the sharpshooters. Three and a half hours after it commenced, the attack is over.*

All Richmond celebrates its good fortune.

The hospital had been quiet all morning, its occupants straining to hear the firing from the river as if it carried some message of victory or defeat. Even after the firing ceased, around midday, it seemed as if they coughed, talked, even breathed as quietly as possible. When at last the message came that the attack had been repulsed, all but the sickest patients roused themselves to join in the cheering.

For Narcissa, the message held a different meaning. It was time for her and Judah Daniel to go out and look for signs of a smallpox outbreak. They found Dr. Stedman back in his office, just as before, with no sign that Archer had occupied his chair the previous evening.

As they stood hesitating, Stedman smiled and beckoned them in. "Well, Mrs. Powers, we've turned back the attack on the water. Now it remains to be seen whether we can do the same on land. And you're engaging another enemy, I hear. There's some prepared virus here for you and Judah Daniel." He handed Narcissa a leather pouch. "Go find Dr. Cumber and get him to show you how to use it. He does the procedure for the hospital personnel — probably did it for you, as a matter of fact."

As Stedman turned to address another questioner, Narcissa and Judah Daniel went to look for Dr. Cumber. They found him giving instructions to some convalescents detailed as nurses. They stopped a few paces away, not wanting to interrupt, but Cumber saw Narcissa and Judah Daniel and beckoned them to join the group.

"They can all hear this," Cumber said,

indicating the convalescents who were gathered around him. "May need to do it someday themselves." He took the leather pouch from Narcissa, drew out one of the little tin pillboxes, and opened it to show the gelatinous contents. "This is live vaccine, taken from the scabs of inoculated children. It can be kept in glycerin, as this is, or in wax. You introduce it through a wound in the arm — a good, bloody scratch or a small puncture will do. Apply the serum directly to the wound. In about a week you should see a well-formed pock at the site, followed by a fever and a mild case of the disease itself. It is rarely fatal — perhaps one death in a hundred, as opposed to one in four or five. Well, then." Cumber handed the leather pouch to Narcissa. "Any questions?"

One of the convalescents, Private Simms, whose pitted face showed his own past experience with the disease, looked shyly at Narcissa. "I heard you was with Major Harrald when he died. That was right Christian of you. I tended him some after his leg was took off. I reckon his family —"

Cumber frowned impatiently, but Narcissa stepped closer to the private and in a low voice urged him to continue.

"Well —" Simms looked torn between wanting to speak and fearing rebuke. "Well, him and his family wasn't on the best of terms, I reckon. I only ever seen his brother and sister here one time, and his fiancée one time, right after he come in. Just glad you showed an interest, that's all." Simms bowed his reddened face in a sort of awkward tribute. Cumber was striding away, the convalescents following in his wake. Simms turned to follow.

Narcissa paused a moment, wondering, then put a hand on Simms's arm. "Major Harrald had a fiancée?"

Simms blinked. "I reckon that's what she was."

Narcissa pressed for details and learned that the lady had dark hair and was "very handsome" — as evidence of which, the soldier's blush and downcast eyes were more forceful than his words. Under her cloak she had worn a wide-skirted dress, red in color, with bows on it. Josiah and the lady had talked quietly, she leaning close to him, for about ten minutes, after which she had left quickly, her face veiled. The visit had taken place late one evening soon after Harrald had arrived, he thought, the same day as the amputation or the day after.

As she and Judah Daniel slipped through the crowded halls, Narcissa wondered about Josiah's fiancée. Some wellborn young lady, no doubt, delicately reared and perhaps constrained by an overcareful *maman* from visiting a vulgar, offensive place like a hospital! So she had slipped in, this young lady, on her way to a ball or a reception. That would account for the elegant, wide-skirted dress. Red was an odd color, though perhaps Simms had mistaken a more ladylike shade, mauve perhaps. . . .

Why had Josiah Harrald not mentioned his fiancée? Most men took comfort in talking about their loved ones. Simms himself had shown her the little leather-bound daguerreotype of his wife, a pretty, shy-looking woman. But Josiah had had a prickly, standoffish manner; perhaps he hadn't wished to speak of something so personal. Or perhaps Josiah and his visitor had had a disagreement and severed their connection, so that Private Simms had witnessed not a tender reunion but a final leave-taking. Of course, neither Major Harrald nor the unknown woman could have known how final it would be. She wondered if the woman felt regret, now that Harrald was dead.

Narcissa stopped in the doorway and turned to Judah Daniel. "Here, take this handkerchief. I'm going to give you half of these." Narcissa began pulling tin pillboxes out of the leather pouch and placing them in the handkerchief. Then she tied the corners of the handkerchief together. "You start down in Butchertown, and I shall start up here. When we meet, we'll compare notes."

Out in the street, a fine rain was falling. Richmonders who had kept to their houses through the morning were now pouring into the streets, eager for news. Judah Daniel passed among them in silence, down the slope of Broad Street from Shockoe Hill into Shockoe Valley, to the area known as Butchertown. Over the years, the slaughterhouses and tanneries had vanished: there were no butchers in Butchertown. There was no town, either, just a hundred or so houses — some sustaining their owners as boardinghouses, groceries, bakeries, or confectioneries — and a few warehouses. In the depths of the Valley they seemed to hunker down as if to escape notice among their more imposing neighbors: the fine homes and public buildings of Shockoe Hill to the west, and to the east, the mansions and spires of Church Hill. The division between Shockoe Hill and Shockoe Valley was marked by nature with Shockoe Creek, which flowed between them on its way to the James; and marked by man with the railroad line that took a course through the Valley parallel to the creek.

As she passed a shabby little confectionery fronting Broad Street, Judah Daniel halted. It was the shop of Mal Evans. According to Elda Chapman, Mal's son Sam was a Cat. Mal had a second, younger son as well.

Judah Daniel hoped it wasn't true, what John Chapman had hinted at: that Mal was selling illegal liquor, with the plug-uglies turning a blind eye, if not taking a cut of the profits. Whatever the truth might be, one thing was certain: none of the Evans family would want to talk about any of this. They might know her and trust her as a doctoress, but they also knew she was John Chapman's friend. All Judah Daniel could do would be to warn Mal and his wife Juney about the danger of smallpox and offer inoculations.

Behind the counter stood Mal's wife,

tired circles like bruises darkening her brown skin under the eyes. *Might as well get started,* Judah Daniel thought. "Juney, don't know if you heard about the smallpox being around? No? Some things, clothes and such, gone missing from the pest-house up at the Egyptian building. Some people think it was the Butchertown boys. I ain't saying so," she added quickly. "And you know I don't have no truck with the police. But I'm telling you, best be careful if you see any clothes laying around in the street that you don't know where they come from. I'm going around to do inoculations. You got two boys, right?"

Juney nodded, not meeting Judah Daniel's eyes. "They ain't here right now."

"They been inoculated?"

"No, they ain't," Juney admitted.

"How about you and Mal?"

Juney picked up a napkin and flicked it at a fly spiraling down toward the countertop. "We both had it."

"Well, I'll come back, then, when the boys is here." Judah Daniel stated it so it couldn't be argued with. Then she pointed out the candies she wanted to buy. Juney grabbed up the ones she pointed to, avoiding Judah Daniel's eyes all the while. Then Judah Daniel left, with a paper full of sweets and a mind full of questions.

Among the fine houses of Shockoe Hill, Narcissa was surprised to find the boys willing to admit to gang membership — even boasting about it. Perhaps it was because Jefferson Davis's own son, as well as the free black boy called Jim Limber who lived in the Davis household, fought with the Hill gang. Or perhaps the Hill Cats, already endowed with the self-confidence of wealth and power, did not fear getting into trouble with the authorities.

At the McClennan house, she found eleven-year-old Natty. Mrs. McClennan, Natty's mother, sat nearby, knitting a very large and lumpy gray sock, but she jumped up and hurried from the room when a baby cried somewhere in the house. After his mother left, Natty undertook to explain to Narcissa about the importance of the Shockoe Hill gang. "We can't have the boys from Butchertown coming up here, pretending they're as good as we are."

"But your fathers are soldiers," Narcissa replied mildly, "fighting for the same side."

Nat's mouth turned down at the corners.

"*Their* fathers take orders from *my* father. That's how it should be. If those Butchertown boys would give it up, and take orders from us, that would be all right."

"What would you do, then," she asked him, "if your two gangs should combine?"

Narcissa saw the gleam of an idea in Nat's eyes.

"We'd have the biggest gang around! We could take on the boys from Church Hill, and beat them, too!"

Narcissa breathed an inward sigh and gave up her dreams of peace-making. "Nat, have you heard any rumors about boys breaking into the smallpox hospital in the Egyptian building?"

Nat stared at her in surprise. Clearly he had heard nothing. But he wrinkled his brow and bit his lip — signs that he was taking in what she had said.

"Must have been those Butcher Cats!" he exclaimed, punching his fist into his open palm. "How dare they come up here and do a thing like that? We'll get them!"

Narcissa thought she was going to have to hold him down. "Nat, smallpox is a very serious disease. Any boys who might have been exposed are in great danger. So are their families, their friends — even their enemies," she added, fixing him with a serious look. "Have you been inoculated?"

"Yes, ma'am," Nat answered, a little abashed.

"That's good. Now, you hadn't heard anything about the theft until just now, had you?"

Nat shook his head.

"Then you really can't say the Butcher Cats are to blame, can you?"

Nat did not reply, but the look on his face reminded her of men she had seen in the hospital — men who could hardly stay to have their wounds bandaged before going back to kill more Yankees.

Just then Natty's mother returned, carrying a baby bonneted and dressed in such a foam of white batiste that only its pink face and chubby arms were visible. Narcissa got up to admire the baby, and Natty went with her. "Her name is Alice," he said, chucking the baby under the chin. The baby gave a toothless smile and captured her brother's finger in her little fist.

Narcissa smiled, fighting down the wave of grief and loss that threatened to engulf her. Her own baby, hers and Rives's, would be four years old now if he had not died within a few hours of his birth. Old enough to enjoy being the big brother of a little baby like this one. Would it never leave her, this painful mixture of longing and despair that swept over her whenever she saw a baby?

Judah Daniel made her way toward a little wooden shack, backed up to the creek and close to the train tracks, in a part of the Valley known as the Flats. Cassie Terry's place was no more than a shanty. What yard there was, was mud, packed and slimy on the high ground and puddled in the low. Boards were loose, in the steps and in the walls, or missing entirely. The shutters hung loose from their hinges.

Judah Daniel knew the house all too well. She used to be called regularly each year to deliver Cassie Terry's latest baby. Who the fathers were, she hadn't known; likely Cassie hadn't known either. Going on a year ago now, Cassie, her eyes blacked and her belly covered with bruises that looked as if they'd come from a square-toed boot, had delivered a stillborn child. A few weeks after that, a man's body was found dead, clubbed in the head, in an alley near this house. No one had ever been arrested for the crime; probably the police had been glad to be rid of one more drunken bully.

After that, there had been no more babies. Instead of men, Cassie had gone to taking in boarders, one of whom was the hospital's errand boy, Benjy. For the past three years Benjy's owners, who lived somewhere east of town, had hired him out to the hospital. They must pay Cassie to house and feed him thinking that, being white, she could be trusted with their property. But sometimes Benjy slept on the hospital floor rather than go to Cassie's.

A glance into the filthy room showed her that Cassie's situation had not improved much. The smell of alcohol was strong, though the door was open at the other end of the little shotgun house, and children's voices could be heard out back. Cassie looked up from the low chair in which she slumped, and her face, white and soft as dough in a mixing bowl, broke into a smile. "Judah Daniel, you know I ain't got no need of you no more." With an arm as thick as a man's, Cassie lifted the bottle she was holding, tipped it toward Judah Daniel as if offering a toast, and drank from it. "My youngest brat's going on three years, and there ain't going to be no more, I'm making damn sure of that."

Judah Daniel repeated the story of the theft from the pest-house, again expressing disbelief that it was Butchertown boys who were to blame. "We going around looking for children need protecting against the smallpox. If you want, we can inoculate your children. It won't cost you nothing if you'll let us have the scabs when they come."

Cassie pulled her hair away from her face and turned so that the light from the door fell on her cheek. Judah Daniel saw the scattering of pits in Cassie's pale skin. "I done had it," she said. "But the kids . . . yeah, you might fix them up so they won't get it."

Judah Daniel smiled to herself. At least Cassie would let her children be protected from the disease as long as it didn't cost her anything.

Cassie's mouth wrinkled, and she took another swig from the bottle. "Damn. As if there wasn't enough to worry about, what with the Yankees beating on our doors. I ain't heard of nobody sick. You say it was them Cats?"

"Might be," responded Judah Daniel.

Cassie got up from her chair and lumbered toward the back door. Judah Daniel followed her. The yard back of the house was another bare patch of earth, about ten feet square, bounded by outbuildings that a strong wind would knock flat. The high brown water of Shockoe Creek could be seen through the gaps in the snaggle-toothed fence. Here a half-dozen children played in the mud, a few bedraggled chickens scratched, a slat-ribbed dog bolted down something. A girl of eight or nine, Cassie's oldest, looked on in resignation.

Cassie stopped at the door and yelled, "Rose!"

The oldest girl answered. "Yeah, Ma?"

"Get the young'uns."

Rose looked beyond her mother to Judah Daniel. Her eyes widened with surprise and, Judah Daniel thought, a little fear. She must be wondering what the doctoress was wanting with her brothers and sisters.

"Rose." Judah Daniel spoke to the girl in a gentle tone. "I'm going to treat you and your brothers and sisters to keep you from getting the smallpox. If you know anybody been exposed, you'd be doing them a favor if you told me." Judah Daniel's eyes searched the yard again. "Where's Timmy?"

Rose looked toward her mother. Cassie wheeled around to face Judah Daniel. "He ain't here." Then she turned back to the door. "All right, you brats. Come on, and don't make me use my fist on you."

"Will it hurt?" A girl who looked to be about four years old asked the question.

Judah Daniel returned her gaze. "Yes, honey, it'll hurt. But it'll hurt a lot less than the smallpox. And we got some peppermint sticks, and lemon drops —"

Rose's voice broke in. "It'll hurt a whole lot less than the beating I'll give you if you try to run off." Rose grabbed a dark-haired little girl and a pale-haired little boy and, face set in a scowl, dragged them toward the house. Being a mother to them, thought Judah Daniel, the only way she knows how.

For hours, until the sun was low in the sky, Judah Daniel passed through the streets of Butchertown, knocking on the doors of unpretentious but mostly comfortable homes and explaining her errands. She inoculated four women, two elderly men, and a dozen children, a few of whom might be members of the Butchertown Cats, though none of them admitted to it.

In the streets the party continued, livelier than ever, with bonfires and impromptu concerts. The city and its uniformed saviors — including thousands who'd not been anywhere near Drewry's Bluff that day — were dancing and dining in the streets.

Judah Daniel straightened her shoulders. Seemed like she always carried her burden there, even if the weight of it was in her mind. Sam Evans, Timmy Terry, both missing, and both mothers more anxious than they'd let on. Might be they were the thieves. But even to ask the question carried a danger. Fear of smallpox contagion could close down Mal Evans's confectionery. Cassie could lose the boarders whose little money kept her from having to sell her body. And both of them were likely to take out their misery on their children.

With that fear in her mind, Judah Daniel told herself to be careful.

All Richmond celebrates its good fortune.
With these words Brit ended his dispatch on the subject of Fort Drewry and the salvation of the Confederate capital. He had scribbled almost without pause until he had covered a half-dozen pages. It wasn't until he turned the stack over and read those words again that he thought how naive they were. The throngs in the streets,

their shouts mingling with the boom of the cannon that yet reverberated in his head, had deafened him to quieter voices. But those voices were Richmond too: the slaves condoling with each other that the men who had been their masters this morning were their masters still; the outspoken Unionists sitting in their cells at Castle Godwin, mourning their lost chance for vindication; the spies and traitors moving like rats in the shadows, conducting their activities just out of sight. The croakers who had prophesied doom, and hidden their stores of tobacco to trade with the conquerors, were no doubt celebrating the loudest, pretending they had held fast all along.

Still, what he had written was a good start: enough to earn him dinner at Zetelle's chop house. And there he could begin to follow up on an idea he had had in connection with the theft of the smallpox clothing. If he wanted to don Confederate gray, as Mirrie Powers had mockingly suggested, where would he go to get it?

A crowd of excited men, civilians most of them, jostled each other in the smoky, dark-paneled room. Brit elbowed his way in — no one seemed disposed to take offense on such a day — and soon found himself slipping into a little space from which a white-jacketed Negro was whisking the plate and glass. He glanced at the two across from him, then stared. Both had on overcoats buttoned to their chins, though the place was warm with the press of bodies, and wide-brimmed hats pulled down to hide their faces. Brit could not help leaning sideways just a little to peer under the hat of the one nearer to him, and he found himself looking into the smooth-cheeked, boyish face of Archer Langdon — *Private* Archer Langdon of the Alexandria Rifle Grays.

Langdon smiled, shrugged, and elbowed the similarly clad man sitting next to him. Brit heard Langdon's conspiratorial whisper, "It's only Brit Wallace." The other young man pursed his lips and blew out an exaggerated sigh of relief.

Archer Langdon, an eighteen-year-old Virginia gentleman, had, it seemed to Brit, a very particular code of honor. *Noblesse* obliged Langdon not only to do his duty when battle was engaged but to avoid doing his duty when the drums fell silent, no matter how great the difficulty or the risk involved in either exercise.

Langdon, apparently deciding to relax

his guard, pushed the hat away from his face and rolled up the too-long sleeves of the overcoat to show Brit the gray wool underneath. "We've got on our uniforms, ready to answer our country's call."

"Though not ready to answer roll call," Brit couldn't help pointing out.

Archer shrugged. "Our brigade's on the move, coming closer to the city. General Johnston wants the Chickahominy River at our front. *I* wish it were in — well, never mind! We were there this morning when the provisions were given out — one cracker and a slice of meat to each man, to march all day in the mud." Langdon paused to wipe a crust of bread through the gravy on his plate, pop it into his mouth, and swallow it almost without chewing. "So Watkins and I said" — Henry Watkins looked up at this as if to say, *Leave me out of it* — "why not triangulate? March into Richmond: it will be faster, seeing as there's just the two of us. Take on edible reinforcements." Langdon gestured at the dishes in front of them. "March back, primed and ready to fight. For it won't be long, I think," he added, his tone matter-of-fact.

Brit leaned back, smiling at the pluck of the youngsters. "It may have been easy for you to walk through the town this morning, when all eyes were focused on the river. But suppose the guards stop you on the way back?"

"Oh, we have a pass, signed by General Johnston himself."

"Oh?" Brit raised a quizzical eyebrow. "I thought they were rarer than phoenix eggs."

Henry Watkins leaned forward to tell the story. " 'My Dear Aunt: As requested, I hereby send you the autograph of our Commander-in-chief, General Johnston.' " Henry and Langdon exchanged glances, then both bent nearly double with suppressed mirth. Watkins was gasping too hard to continue, so Langdon took up the tale. "The message was in pencil, of course. We erased it and wrote 'Pass in and out of Richmond, at will, the bearer and friend for two weeks.' But," Langdon added, his smile fading, "I doubt whether we will get the good of it. In another week, it will be hot."

Brit knew he didn't mean only the weather. He took a bite of his chop and thought of a way to raise the question Narcissa had suggested to him. "Where could I get a uniform, at a good price?"

Langdon froze, his fork halfway to his

mouth. "You thinking of joining up?"

"Ha! No. But where could one get a uniform, shall we say, *used?*"

Langdon and Watkins exchanged a glance, then looked back at Brit, their faces serious now. "It's a crime that our own side — or those pretending to be on our side — strip the uniforms off the dead bodies and leave them with nothing but their shirts. But it does happen. And men buy them, I suppose, and wear them, bloodstains and all, though how they could be so cold-hearted —"

Watkins's eyebrows rose in anxious peaks. "Perhaps they don't know."

Langdon gave a short, cold laugh. "Perhaps they think lightning won't strike twice in the same place."

Brit persevered. "Where would one go to purchase . . . ?"

"Go to the passport office. Ninth and Broad. Winder's plug-uglies have just about everything for sale."

Brit laughed, even as he registered the information. "And another question — I am a reporter, after all! Does either of you know a man named Ragsdale?"

Langdon nodded. "Owns a gaming house or two, doesn't he? He must be seeing a lot of the plug-uglies. They're trying to get the gambling hells closed, except to themselves and their friends. And of course, they're making sure no one can buy alcohol."

Watkins blinked owlishly. "And the" — Watkins mouthed the words — "bawdy houses?"

"Course not!" Langdon looked at his friend with contempt. "Why should they be closed? They're against the law to begin with! But no doubt the plug-uglies are sticking close there, too." He added, with a wink at Brit, "I wouldn't mind taking on that duty myself."

Brit started to laugh, then covered it with a fit of coughing. He told himself sternly that the beardless, ninety-pound Langdon had proven himself a man on the battlefield and — moral and medical considerations aside — might very well seek to do so in the boudoir. He himself, on occasion . . . "Don't be taken in by women like that. True pleasure cannot be bought and sold."

Langdon laughed. "You are as prudish as my uncle Cameron Archer. I'm sure he would have some warning from a surgeon's point of view, though I hear he cut quite a caper himself in his younger days. Funny that you're both . . . I mean . . . sorry!"

Brit's face froze in a bland smile. Of course, Langdon had seen him with Narcissa Powers. Had seen Cameron Archer with her as well. Were they both, he and Archer, so transparent in their admiration?

Langdon shrugged apologetically. "She prefers you, I'm sure of it. If she doesn't, she should."

How little "should" weighs with women, Brit thought ruefully.

Brit came out of Zetelle's at last to find the gas lamps lit and the street still crowded with people. The whole town had turned out to fete the victors of Drewry's Bluff. Slender, blushing maidens and fat farmwives offered the contents of their larders to anyone wearing a Confederate uniform. Purposeful traffic had run aground in the milling throng of celebrants. Barefoot boys darted in and out, leaving him to wonder if they, or someone they knew, carried with them the smallpox infection. Soon the truth would begin to appear, in the form of pus-filled pocks and debilitating fever. But further questions would have to wait the dawn of a calmer day.

CHAPTER THREE

FRIDAY, MAY 16

In the late afternoon, a few glum civilians inconvenienced by the ban on alcohol sales gathered in the saloon of the Exchange Hotel. Brit took a seat among them and, after exhausting the more pressing subjects of war, expressed casual admiration of Roland Ragsdale's financial success in the city. A few fish rose to his bait — a be-whiskered, long-legged man; a youth whose collar stood a half-inch away from his neck; and some smaller fry.

"Well, Ragsdale's faro bank will have to close," Whiskers said with a wink. It was an open secret that anyone with enough money to bribe the plug-uglies could still find admittance about anywhere he chose. "But I heard he bought up a lot of shoes at seven dollars a pair. Reckon he'll get twenty-five when he lets 'em go." Brit could not help glancing down to see the nearly new brogans on Whiskers's long feet. Did he think the pair would last the duration of the war?

Chicken-Neck grinned sourly. "Must have been a bad moment for Ragsdale, when they was first talking about the tobacco being destroyed. He'd just bought all them warehouses full of the stuff."

There was scattered laughter.

Here was something of interest. Brit played him a little. "Was that not a wise investment?"

"Well!" Whiskers leaned forward, getting the jump on Chicken-Neck. "You see, the Confederate government passed a law saying any tobacco that was in danger of falling into enemy hands had to be burned."

"Burned! Couldn't they just hide it somewhere?"

Whiskers laughed. "Mister, a hogshead of tobacco ain't the size of your snuffbox. It's near as high as your head and take two men to reach around it. And you know how much tobacco is in Richmond? *Sixty million dollars' worth.*" Whiskers paused to enjoy the effect of his words on Brit, then went on. "Stand to reason every big building in the town, if it ain't full of sick soldiers or Yankee prisoners, it's full of tobacco."

Whiskers looked around, taking in the admiring glances of his audience, then resumed his lecture. "So, there was talk of firing the warehouses. But then the government skedaddled" — he smiled, baring teeth yellowed like his coat — "and folks started saying the tobacco warehouses couldn't be burned, because they was too close to buildings used as hospitals. Well, them hospitals was tobacco warehouses too, before the war."

Chicken-Neck broke in. "Them that was rich enough, and smart enough, sent their tobacco overseas before the war broke out. Their money's over there waiting for them, and it ain't Confederate." He frowned in disapproval — though if he were so patriotic, Brit wondered, why wasn't he in uniform?

Whiskers nodded impatiently, unwilling to yield the floor to Chicken-Neck. "Anyway, the City Council's been debating, if Richmond falls, what to do with the tobacco: burn it, or dump it in the James. And if they dump it, how many men will they hire and how much will they pay them?" He laughed and looked around at the half-dozen other men who lounged on the saloon's chairs and sofas as if over-zealous army surgeons had removed their spines. "So there they're stuck, and there they'll stay, and it don't look like no tobacco will drown or burn."

"Not unless the whole city burns," Chicken-Neck said with morbid zest. "I heard some of the important buildings has been loaded up with powder in the basement, just like them torpedoes. The last Southern man out going to set the tripwire, and the first Yankee in going to blow that building to kingdom come!"

The others laughed appreciatively. Whiskers took a swig of lemonade, then set down his glass and stood up. "I got to find me something fit for a man to drink. You with me, boys?" A half-dozen "boys" cheered and jumped to their feet.

As they streamed out the door, a newcomer pushed his way through them into the saloon. He was holding a round-brimmed felt hat bashed in on the side. "Damn and blast the imps!" he growled to no one in particular. "They came close to braining me! If only we could set them Cats on the Yankees, we'd see them turn tail!"

So the Cats are battling. Brit shot out of his seat and hurried over to the newcomer.

"Where are they — the Cats?"

"Up on Shockoe Hill, near the medical college. If you're so eager to test yourself under fire, my good fellow, why don't you enlist?"

Laughter followed Brit out the door, but he paid it no heed. With any luck, he would find out something to help Narcissa.

Judah Daniel was carrying yet another load of soiled linen from the hospital building to the washhouse when she heard two orderlies talking about the Cats. She called out a question, and one answered, "Looks like they's fixing to go at it now, down past the jailhouse. It's the Butcher Cats and them Hill Cats, fighting each other."

Judah Daniel called her thanks to the men's retreating backs and headed on to the washhouse to drop off her load and get her bearings. She would go down the hill and behind the free school, so as to come out behind the invading Butcher Cats. A look down Fifteenth should give her a view of the boys. If not, she would go on down to Sixteenth.

The Cats most often fought their battles after the churches let out on Sundays, when traffic was light. Today was a Friday.

But now that the Confederate government had hightailed it and Richmond was hunkered down behind its defenses, the traffic was often light enough for the Cats to chase each other through the streets any day of the week. And at last the weather was clearing after three days of rain. Yes, a perfect day for a fight.

And the reason — if they needed a reason — could be the rumors that were no doubt circulating, down in Butchertown and up on Shockoe Hill, about the thefts from the pest-house. Where there's bad feeling already, rumors turn to accusations quicker than cream turns to butter. All it needs is some willing hands to churn it.

Hearing reports, laughing or chagrined, that the Cats were fighting nearby, Narcissa hurried out of the medical college hospital. As she came out onto Marshall Street, Narcissa heard a cry go up, something between a human's wail and an animal's howl. It was joined by another, and another. The wildness of it made her skin prickle. She hurried up the steep, grass-covered slope to the portico of the Egyp-

tian building. Below her she saw the boys
— the Hill Cats, surely, since they occupied the higher ground — two, three, five
of them, maybe more, darting out from
behind the cover of buildings. She thought
she recognized the McClennan boy, Natty,
though the furious and flailing youth she
was watching looked very different from
the tidy-haired, self-possessed boy she had
met the day before. She had put that
war-light in his eyes, with her questions
about the theft from the pest-house. He
was reacting in the simple, inevitable way
those who have weapons react to any
threat, even an imagined one. Thank
goodness the weapons were only rocks and
bricks.

Downhill from the Egyptian building,
the Hill Cats paused and began flinging
their fist-sized missiles. Then, apparently
having pushed their enemies back, they
gave their war cry and charged again. Suddenly an answering cry came from the
boys' opponents, hidden from Narcissa's
sight by the buildings that lined the street.
Rocks and bricks flew. Then the boys who
had charged down the hill ran back up it,
arms crossed behind their heads. A few of
the missiles thwacked against backs and
thighs, raising howls from the wounded

but not slowing their retreat. One reddish, jagged-edged object bounced up the hill to land almost at Narcissa's feet. She looked down to see a broken half-brick, then looked up again, with more urgency this time, in the direction from which it had come. The Hill Cats were picking up rocks now, reloading for another attack. Down the hill, the Butcher Cats were undoubtedly doing the same. She decided to take cover behind one of the Egyptian building's stout columns. *Only* rocks and bricks? It must be true that Cats have nine lives.

Brit paid the hack driver and stepped out at Fourteenth Street on the south side of the railroad that ran down the middle of Broad Street. He was ready to discard his brogans, stiff and gritty from days of immersion in mud, and put on a good pair of English-made boots. With a hefty surcharge paid to the blockade-runner, he should have new boots in a month or so, providing the blockade-runner succeeded in running the gauntlet there and back. If not, he thought, he might be reduced to buying shoes from Roland Ragsdale's hoarded stock.

He could hear them — the Cats. *Sounds like a damned Rebel yell.* The mad yell was succeeded by more typical boyish sounds: laughter, shouted taunts, curses when a rock or piece of brick found its mark. He had covered half the block toward Marshall Street when he heard a too-familiar sound that echoed off the surrounding buildings, stopping him in his tracks — the percussive burst of a pistol shot.

There was silence for a moment, then shouts and screams as the boys ran for cover. In another moment a boy appeared rounding the corner, a medium-size dog at his heels, coming at breakneck speed. The boy saw Brit and pulled up. He seemed to make up his mind to take his chances with Brit rather than with whatever might have been behind him — it wasn't the dog he was running from, apparently, for it was running with its head down and its tail between its legs, clearly frightened itself. Suddenly the boy put his head down and ran straight for Brit. He was holding his right arm close to his chest, and Brit wondered if he were hurt. As he came closer, Brit could see that the boy was clutching a pistol. This fact made the whole matter rather more serious.

Still the boy came on straight at Brit as if meaning to bowl him over. At the last moment the boy dodged right; but Brit, who had done some running from pursuers himself in his time, anticipated him. He thrust out his walking stick level with the boy's shins and sent him sprawling. The dog skidded to a stop and crouched low to the ground, watching them, the picture of canine misery.

Brit grabbed the boy's shirt collar, hauled him up, and, using his walking stick, held the boy tight against his chest. Brit found himself looking down at a tangled thatch of dark hair and the top of a freckled nose. The boy was struggling like a madman, but Brit held on and said, "Here now! Did you shoot someone with that thing?"

The boy tilted his head to look up into Brit's eyes. "No!" he panted out. "One a them damn Hill Cats took a shot at Popcracker!" He nodded his head toward the dog. "I saw that damn Stone drop this, so I run to pick it up." The boy wriggled his right arm free and held out the mud-spattered pistol, its barrel pointing at Brit's face. The dog whined and writhed in misery, though it didn't appear to be hurt, only scared. Swearing, Brit moved his grip to the boy's arm, then grabbed the gun by the barrel. It was an old single-shot flint-lock, converted to percussion. He pulled back the hammer, took out the percussion cap, and rolled it between his fingers. The tiny copper cap was dented and stained with verdigris. So the pistol had been fired.

He looked again at the boy. At close range, Brit could see that what had appeared to be freckles were actually smallpox scars, little pits strewn more or less evenly across the boy's face and darkened with ground-in clay dirt. Here at least was a Cat who would not fall prey to the disease.

Judah Daniel stood squinting into the shadowed alley behind the free school. The shot had come from behind her, higher up the hill. Why, then, was this boy lying sprawled in the mud? Dread hung heavy in her heart as she made her way toward the familiar figure.

It was Benjy. His eyes were open, blurred with the rain that had fallen all day. She knelt beside him. *Why, God, does it have to be Benjy?* He was enslaved, he had nothing, not even his family except for a few days at

Christmas. She pushed the anger away long enough to pray, "Jesus, take his soul into your care." Then grief rushed in where the anger had been. She took his head in her lap, stroked his short-cropped hair. She saw on his upper lip a few fine dark hairs breaking through the smooth skin of the child. The sight brought a bitter-tasting lump to her throat. Then she saw it: a hole almost at the center of his collar-less white shirt, darkened, as with a little blood. The body was cool to the touch, and loose-limbed, the stiffness of death already passed over. Benjy had been dead long before the Cats had come out to fight.

The pistol's report seemed to explode among the boys, scattering them in all directions. Narcissa stood frozen, under cover of the column. Several boys hurtled past her, seeming not even to notice her presence. Then one stopped, turned back, and ran up to her. "Go, get away!"

The boy looked so frightened. Narcissa reached out to him. He stepped closer, and she asked him, "Are you all right?"

"Those crazy Butcher Cats fired on us!" the boy sobbed out, looking back over his shoulder. "Someone could have been killed." The boy sagged into Narcissa's arms and clung to her as sobs racked his body. Narcissa looked down the street in the direction he had come but saw nothing. She wanted to go down there, to make sure no one had been injured — but this boy had claimed her attention. She would not leave him.

Judah Daniel heard the thud of hooves in mud, the creak of leather, the sound of men's voices. The plug-uglies were here, too late as usual. They had to dismount to come into the narrow alley; she had time to calm herself, outwardly at least. It was a good thing it was too dark in the alley for the guardsmen to read her expression. They wouldn't know what had happened, they would suspect she was involved somehow, they would accuse her and abuse the dead with their laughter. *Vengeance is mine, I will repay,* she told herself. Her anger couldn't help Benjy, while it could hurt her, and those she loved. She ought to weep, she knew; the guardsmen would expect it of her, but that she would not do it. *I will repay, sayeth the Lord.* By the time she looked up into their faces, she was cold as iron.

"This here boy one of them Cats?"

Judah Daniel looked up at the man and said slowly, "This here is Benjy. Benjy Givens. He hired out to the medical college. I work there. I found him laying in the street like this. Look like he been dead a day at least."

The man snorted with laughter, mocking her. "It ain't been five minutes since that shot was fired. And you didn't see no fight? Didn't see no boys?"

Judah Daniel shook her head slowly.

"Ah, Christ, go on home, auntie." He turned to the two men behind him. "We ain't going to get nothing out of her. Go find them Cats, drag them out from under their mamas' skirts if you have to. Provost marshal have our hides if that damn *Examiner* gets onto this. By the time the damn editor's finished with it, this dead nigger be the most pitiful damn thing you ever heard of."

Judah Daniel slipped off her apron, laid it on the muddy street, and eased Benjy onto it so that it pillowed his head. Then she got to her feet and spoke to the man who had given the orders. "What you going to do with his body?"

The sneering man glanced down at Benjy. "Oh, this here's evidence. Get along now, auntie, before I get to wondering how you got here so quick."

Judah Daniel got up then, praying silently, and headed down the hill toward Butchertown. She thought about what the plug-ugly had said about the *Examiner*. A few weeks back, the *Examiner* had reported an old slave being beaten and robbed. Two soldiers who fled the scene were not pursued by the Military Guard, and the newspaper had called the guardsmen "humbugs." Word of the report had gone around Richmond's free black community. Today, the provost marshal's men were all taken up with the Cats, looking for a crime to catch them in, to quiet the rumblings of the newspapers. Strange, that the guardsmen's fear of ridicule had helped her to slip away. She could only hope that the same fear didn't lead to trouble for some innocent boy.

"You there! Halt!"

Brit looked up to see a red-faced, red-bearded guardsman riding toward him and the boy.

"God damn. Now we're in it."

The boy's *we* was not meant to include him, Brit realized, but wondered if he might not be "in it" just the same. After all, it was he who now held the gun. He moved his hand to an avuncular-looking, though tight-fingered, grip on the boy's shoulder and whispered, "You won't try and run for it, will you?"

The boy shook his head. Brit let him go then and said in a low voice, "What is your name?"

"It's Coffin," the boy hissed back. "What's yours?"

"Wallace, correspondent of the London *Weekly Argus*. That's in England."

"I ain't stupid, mister."

"Well, if you *ain't*," Brit responded, "then listen, and play your part." Brit hallooed to the approaching figure. "Well met, officer! You see my young friend, Coffin, here, found a pistol. It's not loaded." He proffered the gun, holding it by the barrel so that the guardsman would perceive no threat. "He brought it to me to take to the provost marshal."

The red-faced man had drawn up in front of Brit and Coffin. Now he leaned down from his stamping horse and jerked the pistol from Brit's hand. Popcracker whined. The guardsman stuck the pistol in his belt and frowned at them. "Got a report them Cats was fighting again. We come up here and find a nigger boy laying dead in the street, shot through the chest."

Brit felt Coffin wince as though he had been struck.

"And here we got the leader of the Butcher Cats with a pistol in his hand! Or in *your* hand, mister — what's your name, anyway?"

Red Man had finally noticed him. "William Wallace. Correspondent for the London *Weekly Argus*. I have resided in the Exchange Hotel for a year, more or less." Brit thought it prudent not to mention those days he had spent exiled to Washington City or those spent imprisoned in a Richmond tobacco warehouse after he'd been rounded up by the victorious Confederate troops after Manassas. It was fortunate the Baltimore detectives were less familiar with his history than were the Richmonders.

The guardsman's interrogative gaze traveled slowly from Brit's hat, now soaked and shapeless, to his filthy brogans and back again. Then he gave a little shrug as if to say, *It takes all sorts.* Since Richmond had become the Confederate capital, long-term residence in the Exchange Hotel was evidence of both wealth and importance. Brit was well-supplied only in the former, and that was thanks to his family, but to his relief the prestigious address had the desired effect.

"Well, sir," the man said at last, much to Brit's gratification, "suppose you tell me what you seen."

Brit smiled. "I saw nothing, really. I heard some yelling, then I heard a shot. I thought I had better investigate. Just then, young Coffin here came up to me and told me he had found this pistol. He asked me to go with him to turn it in to the authorities, and I told him I would. Then you came riding up, saving us the trouble. And what is *your* name, sir?"

Red Man turned and spat tobacco juice before answering. "Smith. All right, Coffin, why don't you tell me what *you* seen?"

Coffin looked up the hill past the mounted guardsman. He was biting his bottom lip, maybe to keep from crying. "We got word the Hill Cats was looking for us, saying we done something underhanded to some of their boys. They's always spreading tales like that, but they's the ones, not us. We didn't want them saying we was yellow, so we come out.

They sent some rocks, we sent back, and we was all staying on the move to keep from being hit. Then I heard the shot from up on the hill. I seen Popcracker running down the street to beat the devil. I seen them Hill Cats screaming and running away up the hill. Stone was with them, and it looked like he was holding a pistol. He seen me running after him and he dropped it, I picked it up, and Mr. Wallace done told you what happened then.

"You know," the boy went on, his eyes narrowing, "come to think of it, might somebody want to know how you all got here just in time to miss the whole thing and catch the wrong person."

Smith's grin told Brit that Coffin had gone too far. "Maybe you ain't heard this town is under martial law. Or maybe you don't know what that means. Just come along with us, and we'll explain it to you." He turned to the men with him. "Boys, we're taking this one in." Then he turned back to Brit. "Go along now, mister. We'll call for you at the Exchange Hotel if we need to hear your story again."

"Stop a minute!" Brit protested. "Can I not at least take word to the boy's mother?"

Smith grinned again. "Every man in

town want to meet Coffin's mother —
ain't that right, Coffin?"

"Well, then?" Brit pursued.

Smith turned to Coffin. "Want to tell
him where to find your mother?"

Coffin spat on the ground in front of
Smith, then looked up to glare at Brit. "In
hell!"

Smith grinned, obviously pleased to have
provoked the boy so easily. "He's wild, you
know," he said to Brit. "That's how he got
his name. Sneaked into the medical college
and spent the night in the dissecting room
on a dare. So you run along now, Mr.
Wallace. Coffin Avery ain't some little lad
you got to nursemaid."

Brit pressed, careful to be deferential.
"Sir, could you not release the boy to my
custody, then? I should think —"

One of the guardsmen leaned down and
hoisted Coffin up onto his horse. As the
riders turned, Brit started to follow on
foot, to see where Coffin would be taken.
Smith turned his chestnut horse sideways
in Brit's path. "Run along," he repeated.

Coffin twisted in the guardsman's grip.
"Go on, Popcracker! Go find the boys!"

The dog — a mutt whose hair might
have been fluffy had it not been stuck flat
to his sides, and a male, Brit noticed —

raised his ears in interrogation. As the horse on which Coffin was seated moved away, Popcracker stood looking after it for a moment, running his tongue around his mouth. Brit took a step toward him, and that made up Popcracker's mind — he was off again, tail between his legs, running down the hill toward Butchertown.

Seeing no better course, Brit obeyed the guardsman. But he repeated the name softly under his breath: *Coffin Avery.*

After a few moments, the boy pulled away from Narcissa's reassuring embrace, wiped his nose on his sleeve, and said, "I'm Stansbury Harrald. But Stansbury's an awful name. Call me Stone."

"Well, Stone, I'm Narcissa Powers, and —"

"Oh, Jupiter — they've seen me."

Three men on horseback were just coming over the rise of the hill. They seemed to be staring at Narcissa and Stone, and one seemed about to spur his horse in their direction. Something that the others said appeared to calm or distract the lead horseman, however, and after a moment the three turned their horses and began to ride away at an ambling pace, looking down the streets, talking and gesturing to each other, until they disappeared.

"Recognized me, I suppose," Stone commented with a self-assurance that contrasted with his panic of a few moments before.

"Are you a relative of Josiah Harrald?"

The boy nodded. "He just died, did you know?"

Narcissa nodded. "Yes, I know. He died of smallpox. I was with him when he died. He told me that some of the Cats stole his uniform jacket from the pest-house. I went around the houses up here yesterday, giving inoculations. Have you been inoculated?"

Stone nodded. "I hope you realize it wasn't any of *us*."

Us would be the Shockoe Hill Cats, the boys whose familial wealth and connections appeared to protect them from the authorities.

"Oh, Jupiter!" Stone swore again. "Here comes my Aunt Aurelia."

Josiah's sister. Narcissa looked up the street to see a woman dressed in full mourning, but with her head bare, coming toward them at a jolting half-run. Mud covered her shoes and splattered her skirts, but she seemed unaware of it. Aurelia rushed up the steps to where they stood, and Narcissa expected her to gather Stone in her arms, but she pulled up short a few feet away from him. Her face was pale and tear-streaked.

"Thank God you're all right!" Aurelia panted out the words. "Jensie should never have let you out of her sight! And now I find that you . . . !"

Stone's cheeks colored. "I . . . I didn't think there was any harm in it."

"No harm!" Aurelia's voice climbed to an almost hysterical note.

Stone straightened his shoulders, and said, "I came out to warn those Butcher Cats, to tell them they'd better not come around here anymore."

"Why did you think they would listen to you?" Aurelia almost sobbed out the words.

"I don't know." Stone, red-faced with embarrassment, glanced at Narcissa. This seemed to remind Aurelia that a stranger was witnessing the scene. She turned to Narcissa and said with a rather distracted air, "Oh! I . . . I'm much obliged to you for coming to Stansbury's aid."

"She didn't!" the boy responded indignantly. "I came to hers."

"We must be going." Aurelia's voice was firmer now. She turned away, and Stone fell into step beside her, looking back once to wave good-bye to Narcissa.

So, Narcissa mused — that was Aurelia Harrald. A fine lady, blessed with attractive features (as well as could be judged in such a moment) and the accoutrements of fortune. But the errant behavior of the boy had jolted her so that she had come out into the street bareheaded and wearing her dainty house slippers. A woman of feeling, then; Narcissa felt disposed to like her on account of it.

Brit headed down Marshall Street toward the city jail, his failure to rescue young Coffin dogging him like an invisible Popcracker. It was his duty, however randomly incurred, to see that the boy wasn't made a scapegoat.

They couldn't suspect Coffin of shooting anyone, the voice of evasion whispered. *They were taking him in for insulting the Military Guard. Surely, if the boy didn't have any more discretion . . .*

Discretion? The voice of duty was scornful. *Surely you remember when you were that age!*

Well, he would do what he could, Brit decided, ending the internal argument. Maybe the men at the city jail could tell him where Coffin was being taken. He would visit the boy, find his mother, talk to anyone he could think of who might have some influence with the provost marshal's office. The boy shouldn't have to suffer for being poor and friendless. Then, too, Brit thought, if he could earn Coffin's gratitude, he would perhaps be rewarded with information concerning the Cats' involvement in thefts from the smallpox hospital.

Brit entered the jail and looked around for someone at leisure to exchange a few words. He settled on a fellow wearing a grease-spotted striped vest over shirtsleeves who had taken a moment to smoke a pipe. "There was a brawl just now, out in the street. A boy was arrested." He paused to see what reaction he might get.

"I heard about that." Grease-Spot took the pipe out of his mouth and gestured toward the door. "Heard a black boy was killed, shot with a pistol." The pipe went back into Grease-Spot's mouth as if that were the end of it.

"Did anyone here see anything?"

Grease-Spot shook his head. "Nope. We learned to keep our heads indoors when them Cats is fighting."

"Did you know the Military Guard took someone up?"

"Yeah. That boy Coffin. They said he tried to palm a pistol off on some damn fool foreigner." If he suspected the aforesaid foreigner was standing in front of him, he made no sign of it, Brit's accent notwithstanding.

Brit persisted. "Do you know where they've taken him?"

"Castle Godwin, I reckon."

"Castle Godwin?" Brit was taken aback. "Is he accused of sedition?"

Grease-Spot frowned. "Why not? With the Yankees camped at our door, it ain't helping any to have them boys fighting in the streets, putting honest folks at risk. And Coffin, he's one of the worst — leads the younger boys into it."

Brit made a grimace, the meaning of which was open to any interpretation, then changed the subject.

"Do you know Coffin's mother?"

Grease-Spot shoved the pipe to the corner of his mouth and answered in a somewhat indistinct voice. "Pauline Avery. Her name come up from time to time." A smile appeared around the pipestem.

"Where would I find her?" Brit pursued.

The smile disappeared, and the pipe came out again. Was Grease-Spot disapproving, or envious? "If I was you I would look for her down on Cary Street."

So, thought Brit, Coffin's mother is one of the Cary Street women. A prostitute.

"But then again I wouldn't, if I was you," he went on. "Lest you want to explain your interest to Mr. Ragsdale."

Judah Daniel skirted the edge of Butchertown to Cassie Terry's shanty, where Benjy had boarded. Benjy's owner had taken a few dollars out of the boy's little earnings each month to pay for — what? What kind of cooking could the drunken Cassie have been doing? Most likely it was her eldest daughter Rose, a child younger than Benjy himself, doing the cooking. And his *room* couldn't have been more than a pallet on the floor, since the Terry house didn't have above two rooms. It struck Judah Daniel that, painful as it was to bring news of a death that would grieve the hearers, it hurt more to bring the news to those who would not

140

grieve. She hoped that whoever told the bad news to Benjy's mother would find some sorrow there, and would offer a comforting shoulder, maybe even a few words about the likely young man that Benjy had become — as she herself longed to do.

Cassie Terry met Judah Daniel at the door. "What's wrong?" She sounded as if she expected bad news. Cassie had dirty blond hair, while most of her children were white-blond. That fit Jim's description of a boy with light-colored hair.

"Benjy's dead," Judah Daniel said quietly.

Cassie took a minute for the news to settle. "Well, damn. Now I got to find me another paying boarder. What he do?"

"He was shot in the street, out where the Cats was fighting. He been dead for a while, though. How long it been since you seen him?"

Cassie frowned. "Three, four days, maybe. Reckon he had something to do with that theft from the smallpox hospital you come around asking about?"

"Reckon he might have knowed something about it," Judah Daniel said, her eyes searching Cassie's face. "Reckon I might talk to Timmy about that."

Cassie frowned. "Our boys, don't none

of them own a gun. If they was lucky enough to find one, reckon they'd sell it. Them Hill Cats, now, that's a different story. I wouldn't put it past one of them."

Judah Daniel nodded slowly. Clearly, Cassie wasn't going to come right out and say if Timmy were home or not. She couldn't force Cassie to tell her. She needed the goodwill of the folks of Butchertown, the poor whites and the blacks. They called on her when they needed doctoring, and the little money or goods they sometimes paid her helped keep her and Darcy fed and clothed.

Cassie made to shut the door in Judah Daniel's face. Before she could do so Judah Daniel brought out a fifty-cent note and held it out to her. Cassie stopped, eyes fixed on the money.

"I need something of Benjy's, a cup or a bowl."

Cassie shrugged, but her pale eyes lingered on the money. She turned and disappeared into the dark house. After a few moments she returned, carrying a small baked-clay cup. She thrust it toward Judah Daniel, grabbed the money, then shut the door.

Judah Daniel walked away, bearing the cup between her hands like an offering,

and bearing rage in her heart like a banked
fire.

Narcissa had gone back to the hospital
to look for Judah Daniel. Finally one of the
laundresses had told her that Judah Daniel
had gone out to watch the Cats battle. Yet
Narcissa had not seen Judah Daniel in the
street, nor could she find her in the hospital. Thinking she may have had some
reason to follow the Butcher Cats down
the hill, Narcissa set out in that direction.
She had gone only a few steps when she
recognized Brit Wallace coming up Marshall Street. He was headed away from her,
but he must have felt her eyes on him, for
he hesitated, turned, then hurried toward
her. In a moment he reached her side.

"You should not be here alone, Mrs.
Powers." Brit's eyes searched hers. "A boy
was shot dead. A Negro boy."

"Oh, no —" Narcissa put her hand on
his arm. "We've got to find Judah Daniel. I
think she went down to Butchertown."

Brit looked as if he might argue, but in a
moment he nodded, and they set off
together down the hill.

Narcissa felt sick at heart. "Do they

know who shot the boy?"

"They think they do," Brit answered bitterly. "They've taken up a boy who was no more guilty of the deed than I was. His only crime is being poor and without family connections."

One boy shot, killed. Another arrested. And a third, from whom the guardsmen had turned away: Stone. He could not have known — could he? Had the boy who wept in her arms been holding in this terrible knowledge? "Josiah Harrald's nephew Stansbury — he's called Stone — is one of the Shockoe Hill gang. He was there. After the shot was fired, the boys were running away, but he turned back to warn me. He was terrified. He may have been about to tell me something, something he saw. But just then Aurelia Harrald came rushing up, and —"

Narcissa broke off and turned to see what it was that Brit was staring at so intently. Judah Daniel was walking slowly toward them, coming up from Butchertown. One glance at her face told Narcissa that something was very wrong. Her dark skin looked ashen in the gray light, and deep lines dragged down the corners of her mouth. Narcissa had seen Judah Daniel tired, in trouble, fleeing for her life, but never so weary, so defeated. The dead boy — had Judah Daniel known him?

Impelled by the instinct to comfort, Narcissa went to her. "The boy who was killed —"

"It was Benjy."

The words took Narcissa's breath away. All she could say was, "Oh, no. Not Benjy." She turned tear-filled eyes to Brit.

Brit looked from her to Judah Daniel and back. "Benjy, the boy who took messages in the hospital?"

Narcissa looked at Judah Daniel as if hoping it weren't true, but the woman nodded. "Not so little. Almost a man," Judah Daniel said quietly as if to herself.

"Shot?" Brit looked to Judah Daniel for confirmation.

She nodded. "He was laying in the mud, in the alley off Fifteenth behind the free school. I seen bullet holes before, on soldiers in the hospital, but never one this big. Seem like somebody stood close to him and shot him. Soldiers shot like that, they don't make it to the hospital." Judah Daniel glanced down at her hands. Narcissa noticed the bit of cheap crockery Judah Daniel was holding as if it were a treasure. Something of Benjy's, she supposed. How little he must have left behind. . . .

"And you saw no one?" There was urgency in Brit's voice. Narcissa wondered if he feared to hear Judah Daniel's answer — feared his new friend Coffin might be guilty after all.

"No one . . ." Judah Daniel said slowly. Narcissa could see her expression sharpen as thought pushed grief aside. "But that ain't so surprising. He been dead a day or more, I'll be bound."

"So the shot we heard had nothing to do with Benjy's death!" Brit's voice lightened with relief.

"No." Judah Daniel shook her head. "Not that the plug-uglies going to believe it. They just make whatever use of it they can, or keep it quiet if that suits them."

Narcissa thought of something. "Mr. Wallace, give me a piece of paper, and your pencil." Brit handed her his pocket notebook and silver pencil, and she stood scribbling.

Brit looked back at the scene of the Cats' fight. "I hope someone saw the shot fired and will come forth to tell who fired it. But where did it come from? From what I've seen in the field, a rifle's report can bounce off any sort of wall, even a line of trees. All these buildings" — he waved his arms to take in the length of the street — "would pass the sound back and forth among them until there would be no way to tell where the shot was fired."

Brit turned to Narcissa. "Your friend Stone, where was *he* when the shot was fired?"

Narcissa went to the defense of the boy who had, for a moment, lowered his defenses in front of her. "Stone Harrald is a good boy. I'm sure if he'd fired the shot, he would have admitted it."

Brit raised an eyebrow. "That is as may be. Still, Coffin did no more than pick up a gun he had found, and he's been taken up by the Guard on account of it."

"But why?" Narcissa burst out. "Why would anybody want to kill Benjy?"

Judah Daniel crossed her arms over her chest. "I reckon he knowed something about that theft from the pest-house. Best I can tell, neither Timmy nor Sam's been around for a couple days. Timmy got light hair like Jim Furbish seen on the boy done the thieving. Might be both boys run away from somebody they's afraid of: the police, or their own folks . . . or Benjy. On the other hand, might be somebody put them boys up to the stealing, and now he's got them hid someplace. Or worse," she added under her breath.

Narcissa handed the piece of paper on which she had been writing to Judah Daniel. "Please, Judah Daniel, make sure Dr. Archer gets this note. I've asked him to examine Benjy's body. He will be able to tell whether the shot could have killed him." *And the plug-uglies will believe him,* she added to herself.

Judah Daniel took her leave. They watched her stride up the hill and out of sight. Then Brit turned to Narcissa, concern in his eyes. "Mrs. Powers, it will be dark soon. I will escort you home. Then I must go down to Castle Godwin and find out what they've done with Coffin Avery. He may have a murder charge against him at this point."

Narcissa shook her head impatiently. "How could I go home at such a time? I'm going with you."

Their destination was only a short walk away, across Broad and down Lumpkin Alley to what had been the old Negro Jail — a holding pen for slaves awaiting sale — but was now known as Castle Godwin. Some of the white population of Richmond were learning what it meant to be imprisoned there — a few dozen outspoken Unionists, suspected spies, and others whose activities were seen to endanger the government.

Brit quickly realized that Narcissa's presence aided his purpose. Nowadays his British accent was met with suspicion — a man claiming to be British had recently been exposed as a Union spy — and Brit's correspondent's role never seemed to make a favorable impression on city authorities. So as he stated their request to visit Coffin, Brit played the role of chivalrous supporter. "I'm sure you understand. Mrs. Powers has a womanly concern for so young a boy being incarcerated in such a place." Brit glanced around as if the terrors of Castle Godwin were making their impression upon him.

The jailer, a leather-skinned old man who, Brit judged, had spent most of his life as a farmer, curled his lip. "They's boys younger than this one fighting for our country, drummer boys and powder monkeys. Best she save her tears for them."

"Oh," Brit answered quickly, "Mrs. Powers has spent her tears and more for the soldiers. She's been a hospital nurse since the war broke out."

The old jailer looked back at Narcissa, this time with a new light in his eyes. "Oh, a nurse? Well, why didn't you say so? I got three boys in the army, and a grandson." His hard face softened for a moment.

Brit felt with a pang the old man's vulnerability, even as his journalist's instincts sought to turn it to his advantage. "I'm sure the boy is crowded into a cell with grown men. I would hate for Mrs. Powers to have to undergo such discomfort, such embarrassment. If you perhaps have a space more private —"

The farmer-turned-jailer stomped off, and Brit feared having asked for too much, but the man returned after a few minutes and went over to Mrs. Power. "Ma'am, please come this way," he said, his courtesy worthy of the cavaliers. Soon he had ushered Narcissa and Brit into a little room furnished with a deal table and three wooden chairs.

In one chair sat Coffin Avery, slumped and scowling. At the sight of Narcissa his eyes widened with surprise, but the frown returned as he caught sight of Brit. The old jailer looked as if he would like to haul Coffin out of the chair and knock some manners into him, but Brit grabbed the old man's hand and pumped it, thanking him profusely and backing him out the door.

"What do you want?" Coffin directed

the words to Brit.

"Mrs. Powers, allow me to present Master Coffin Avery." Brit bowed as Narcissa extended her hand to the boy, who stood and shook it, then threw himself back in the chair with a *whoof* expressive of disinterest in the proceedings.

"I don't need you." Coffin's deep-set eyes stared gimlets into Brit. "They know I didn't do nothing. They going to keep me here anyway, just for the" — he broke off, glancing at Narcissa — "just for the fun of it," he finished, apparently softening his customary language. "They going to drag us in one by one until the Butcher gang is finished." The thought brought Coffin upright in his chair. "You tell the boys to keep it up! They can't scare us! We got to defend our honor."

Brit sat on the edge of his rickety chair and leaned forward, legs wide apart and hands on his knees. "So you've heard then. About Benjy."

Coffin looked down, the bravado wiped away. He nodded. "The guards was talking. I knowed who it was."

"I knew Benjy," Narcissa said gently. "I'm a nurse at the medical college. He has been there since before I came a year ago. I can't imagine what it will be like, not having him around."

Coffin shot her a glance. "He liked it there. Sometimes he'd sleep there in the hospital, anywhere he could find. Me too. We hated it at Cassie Terry's."

Brit smiled. "I heard that's how you got your name — sleeping among the dead at the medical college."

Coffin's head jerked up. Gradually the defiance drained away, leaving only sadness. "Benjy stayed with me. Didn't nobody know it. It weren't something he'd brag about."

"He didn't fight with the gangs, did he?" Narcissa's calm voice held only interest.

"No."

"Then what was he doing there?"

"I don't know. I didn't even see him."

Brit thought about the terrain he had mapped in his mind. "Both gangs were swarming all over the place. The shot could have been fired by a member of either — or neither," he added, watching Coffin closely.

Coffin's mouth twisted. "They won't believe a Hill Cat shot him, because them boys got money. Don't you know what goes on? Stone Harrald's uncle Aaron bought his way out of the army, paid a poor man to do his fighting for him. If

Stone wanted to kill one of us, he'd get himself a substitute to do that too. I reckon he throwed down that gun on purpose so's I'd pick it up. Reckon he knowed the plug-uglies was coming!"

It was plausible, Brit had to admit. "But how would he know you would pick it up? You're clever, I think, and no doubt Stone knows it. How was he to know you would do something so foolish? Anyway, the fact is, Stone didn't shoot Benjy. Whoever shot Benjy was well away by the time you boys were fighting."

Coffin stared. "But I heard it!"

"You heard a shot," Brit corrected, "but it wasn't the one that killed Benjy. Whoever did that must have muffled the sound of it somehow. Then he, or someone else, fired the shot that scattered you all."

"How'd you reckon?"

"Someone we know — and trust," Brit added, with a glance at Narcissa, "came upon Benjy right after he was shot."

Coffin was silent for a long time. "Had to been one of them Hill Cats killed him," he said at last.

Narcissa leaned forward. "Do you know about the thefts from the smallpox hospital?"

"I never!"

Coffin's response was, Brit thought, the automatic one of a boy who is used to being accused.

"Oh. . . . I thought someone might have said something. . . ."

But Coffin didn't answer.

Narcissa was gently insistent. "Don't you have any family? Anyone?"

Coffin shook his head, glancing at Brit as if to say, *Keep quiet.* "I done told you I used to board with Cassie Terry. Would anybody live there, long as he had somewheres else to go?"

CHAPTER FOUR

SATURDAY, MAY 17

Major Josiah Harrald could have had a funeral procession with military honors. But some consideration — perhaps the fear of smallpox contagion clinging to the coffin — had led his family to choose a simple burial in Shockoe Cemetery. It was not, of course, the only burial taking place that morning. All around them, it seemed, the drums of the Dead March beat like a slow, sad heart.

Narcissa and Mirrie stood at the far left-hand side of the semicircle that was gathered around the grave. As all eyes were focused on the coffin, the raw hole in the ground, or the minister, Narcissa felt free to examine the little group of mourners.

There was Stone — Stansbury — Harrald, looking subdued in a handsome suit, taupe trimmed in dark brown, with perhaps his first long trousers. He wore a band of black crepe around his arm. Standing next to him was Aurelia, wearing what looked like the same dress Narcissa had seen yesterday — the servants must have worked hard to clean it — as well as a beautiful black silk mantle and a mourning bonnet with long ribbons and veil.

On the other side of Aurelia stood a man whose mourning crepe marked him as a close relative of Josiah. Narcissa remembered there was a brother, Aaron. His frown spoke more of ill temper than of grief, though some men did hide their feelings that way, Narcissa knew.

A few uniformed officers and a half-dozen men in civilian clothing made up the rest of the mourners. One of them looked familiar: Roland Ragsdale, she realized. It surprised her to see him here. She couldn't help but feel the Harralds, with their old Richmond blood and money, would despise him as a parvenu — Josiah most of all. She looked away, but not quickly enough. Roland Ragsdale's smile acknowledged her interest — an interest he seemed to find much more flattering than it was meant.

For the rest of the service, Narcissa kept her eyes down, trying to find comfort in the minister's words. *Delivered from the burden of the flesh.* Whether or not Josiah Harrald shared in the everlasting glory promised to the faithful, his was a merciful death. But Benjy — his death had not been merciful. Why had anyone thought they needed to kill him? It wasn't possible — was it? — that another child had shot Benjy dead? That a child had gotten hold of a gun, and decided to see what it could do? Did Benjy's death have no more meaning than that?

When the service ended, Mirrie and Narcissa picked their way through the wet grass to where the Harralds stood, together yet apart.

Mirrie spoke to Aurelia, who had lifted her veil to show a pale face and reddened eyes. Despite these signs of grief, she looked much more composed than she had on the previous day. Narcissa could tell that Aurelia was indeed a handsome woman, her brother's rather heavy jaw softened by a pretty mouth and well-molded chin.

"Oh! Mirrie. I appreciate your coming."

Aurelia sounded surprised, thought Narcissa; but in the year that Narcissa had lived with her sister-in-law, Mirrie had never mentioned the Harralds. Of course

Aurelia would not expect Mirrie to attend Josiah's funeral.

Mirrie murmured some words of condolence, then turned to Narcissa. "This is my brother Rives's widow, Narcissa Powers."

Aurelia eyed Narcissa warily. "You were . . . I saw you yesterday," she said at last.

Narcissa only nodded, but Mirrie spoke for her. "Mrs. Powers attended Josiah in the hospital. In fact, she was with him when he died."

Aurelia, eyebrows raised in surprise, turned back to Narcissa. "Really? Then you must come to the house. I — *we* — would like to hear —"

Narcissa nodded. "Of course, if you would like us to."

Again Aurelia looked away from them. Her eyes sought, then found, their object, and the sad lines of her face softened into tenderness. Narcissa nudged Mirrie, and the two of them moved away. Who had inspired this feeling in Aurelia, Narcissa wondered, and the confidence to display it so openly? She turned her head to see Roland Ragsdale. Aurelia stepped forward to meet him, and he bowed over her hand. As he did so, he glanced sideways at Narcissa with a look that said, *I would rather pay these attentions to you.*

Narcissa turned away, frowning to herself. How could it be that these people could put on false faces, express polite sentiments as far removed from their real emotions as wax flowers from living blooms? Did they not know that death walked among them, silent as smallpox or loud as a pistol shot?

Traveling through the mud-slicked streets in the Powerses' carriage, Narcissa asked Mirrie to tell her about the Harralds.

"They are an old family, I'm sure there was a Harrald among John Smith's men, but they've been townspeople, not planters — selling it, not growing it. They are certainly among the first circles, though I don't believe they move much in society now. It's odd that all three children have remained unmarried. Aurelia must feel it especially, since all her girlhood friends are long since wives and mothers.

"Around five years ago," Mirrie went on, "Thaddeus, who was a vigorous man in his sixties, injured his back in a fall and took to his bed. It's said he is in constant pain. At any rate, he never goes out."

They were coming up on the Italianate building that formerly housed the Female Institute and now was a hospital for officers. They had not far to go now. "What about Aurelia Harrald?"

"Aurelia —" Mirrie tipped her head back and looked down her nose as she did sometimes. The mannerism seemed to foretell criticism, though Narcissa could not be sure, as most of Mirrie's remarks were critical.

"Aurelia —" Mirrie said again. "Rather a sad waste of a good mind. She is between you and me in age, probably thirty or near it. Everyone expected her to make a brilliant marriage, but she went away to school — perhaps her mother thought she was becoming too fond of an unsuitable man. While she was away at school, her mother died. She returned home, and has been under her father's thumb ever since. Thaddeus was always a cold, unpleasant man, and from what I hear, his illness has embittered him."

Narcissa thought of Stone. "The boy, what do you know of him?"

"Stansbury was the family name of Thaddeus's late wife. A very distinguished family from South Carolina. I suppose he is a relation on her side."

"And Aaron?" Narcissa probed.

Mirrie shrugged. "A cypher. He fell in love with a woman whose family Thaddeus thought inferior. He forbade Aaron to marry her." Though they were alone in the carriage, Mirrie's voice dropped to a whisper. "I hear he keeps her as his mistress."

That reminded Narcissa. "What about Josiah's fiancée?"

Mirrie looked surprised. "I didn't know he had one. But, now that I am an abolitionist pariah, I'm sure I don't hear half the gossip I used to!"

At the Harralds', the maid admitted them into the front parlor. The shuttered windows and draped mirrors followed the conventions of mourning. A damp, smoking fire and a few low-burning gasoliers only deepened the gloom, serving to illuminate dark, heavy furniture and wallpaper with a flocked design in moss green.

Aurelia moved forward to meet them, crossing in front of Aaron, who was taking his time getting up from the low sofa. Narcissa caught sight of Stone at the far end of the room near the fireplace. He straightened and bowed to her and Mirrie. But after a moment, when Narcissa again glanced in his direction, Stone had disappeared. Perhaps he was afraid she would mention something about the incident of the day before. He was of the age to be embarrassed at having shown unmanly weakness.

Aurelia spoke some conventional words of welcome, then turned to the man who was slowly moving their way. "Aaron!"

"What is it, Aurelia?" Aaron Harrald's luxuriant whiskers disguised the full-jawed appearance he shared with his brother and sister.

"You know Miss Powers." Aurelia's tone accused her brother of neglecting his manners.

"Of course. Miss Powers." Aaron extended his hand to Mirrie, a rueful smile acknowledging his lapse in courtesy without apologizing for it.

"And this is Mrs. Powers," Aurelia went on, "Rives's widow. She nursed Josiah in the hospital. Now that I think of it," Aurelia added, looking into Narcissa's face as if seeing her for the first time, "I believe Josiah spoke of you. Did he not, Aaron?"

"Oh, I am sure he did," Aaron responded in a dry tone that conveyed his lack of interest in anything his brother would have had to say. "He spoke of so many things — army life, his experiences in battle. I believe he planned to write his memoirs." Aaron brought his hand up to his mouth to cover a yawn.

Aurelia looked away. "I'm afraid we did not visit him as often as we should have. Aaron is so occupied with business matters, and I — I only went once. I must confess I could not bear the place." Aurelia looked away.

Narcissa tried to reassure her. "It is very hard for those who are not used to it. I'm sure Josiah's fiancée —"

"Fiancée!" Aaron burst out. Narcissa turned to stare at him, unable to imagine what had made him so angry. "Josiah had no fiancée!"

"I'm sorry!" Narcissa said hastily. "It's only what the nurse called her. I suppose she was a woman friend."

Aaron glowered at her. "Josiah had no woman friends. The nurse made a mistake. Perhaps he mistook Aurelia for some *woman*." He snarled the word as if it were an insult.

Narcissa winced, but Aurelia made no sign she had heard her brother. "Father will want to see her."

Aaron turned to the servant who was standing near the door. "Jensie, find Stansbury and remind him of the behavior appropriate to a house of mourning — if it is not already too late." Then he turned

163

back to Narcissa and Mirrie. "Well, then," he said, with a mocking tone in his voice that Narcissa did not understand, "let's go to Father."

What could she say to Josiah's father concerning his son's last moments? However she couched them, Josiah's dying words would not bring consolation.

As she passed close by Narcissa, Aurelia whispered, "Please don't tell Father about Stansbury."

Thaddeus Harrald occupied a spacious bedroom on the second floor. Aurelia knocked at the half-open door, then swung it open and stepped into the room. Narcissa and Mirrie followed her, with Aaron trailing behind. Here the fire burned brighter than downstairs, illuminating large, costly-looking paintings of classical subjects, crystal-and-gilt candlesticks, inlaid and gilded furniture — all the trappings of luxury that Narcissa realized she had not seen in the rather dismal parlor downstairs. It was as if Thaddeus had drawn the most visible reminders of his wealth into this room with him.

Thaddeus watched their approach, frowning over his pince-nez. He was sitting propped up on pillows in a massive bed whose carved posts reached high above Narcissa's head. A wooden stand like a sawed-off pulpit, over which lay an open newspaper, boxed in his torso. Thaddeus was wearing a dark-red quilted jacket over a shirt and vest, and a little embroidered cap covered the top of his head. His gray beard was neatly trimmed.

Despite the obvious signs of invalidism — his pale, finely wrinkled face, the bedside table covered with little bottles — Thaddeus still had the power to dominate his children. Narcissa observed Aurelia's hesitation — perhaps an ingrained response to the old man's frown. But she approached her father and said something in a low voice. Narcissa saw Thaddeus look past his daughter to where she and Mirrie were standing, saw the corners of his mouth turn up in a mocking smile. It seemed to amuse the old man that his dying son had chosen her to confide in. But the look vanished in a moment, and Thaddeus beckoned to them. Aurelia moved away from the bedside as if to say, *I've done what was required of me; do not blame me for the consequences.*

Thaddeus greeted Mirrie first. "Miss

Powers. I knew your father. He was a bright man, a professor of ancient languages, was he not?"

"He still is!" replied Mirrie tartly, but Thaddeus did not seem to hear. He turned to Narcissa. "So Josiah made a pet out of you at the hospital? Did he make you any promises of what you could expect at his death?"

Narcissa felt an angry flush rise to her cheeks, but she fought it down, unwilling to respond to his needling. "No, sir, quite the contrary. *I* tried to assure *him* of the promise of the resurrection. He was not very interested."

Thaddeus stared at her for a moment, then put his head back and laughed a dry, wheezing laugh that ended in a choking cough. He motioned angrily toward Aurelia, who hurried up to hand him a glass of water. He snatched it from her and drank from it.

"Well." Thaddeus went on as if nothing had happened, but his tone was less insulting. "Did my son have any messages for his family? If he made you his confessor, he may have put you in a rather uncomfortable position."

Narcissa breathed in and out slowly, forcing herself to go slow, to be careful.

"Your son died of smallpox."

"We know that." Aaron's voice startled Narcissa, who had forgotten he was in the room.

"It is a lonely and terrible death," Narcissa went on, not acknowledging the interruption. "It seemed that, at the end, he had been dwelling on some details of the disease. He talked about money that had been tainted by smallpox. I have heard that he had some money on his person when he fell ill. Anyway, the danger from tainted money weighed on his mind. I tried to assure him it had been destroyed, but he insisted that it had been stolen . . . by some boys from the Cats."

"Stolen!" Aaron's exclamation was sharp. "He was delirious. Feverish, no doubt. And yet, the instinct to make himself the center, and the concern with money — both those things were typical of Josiah."

"Be quiet!" Thaddeus snapped at his son. "Was that all? What else did he say?"

"Nothing, really. Only . . . I am sorry to distress you: it seems that Josiah might have been right. One of the servants who works in the smallpox hospital saw a boy. He thought he recognized him as one of the Cats who fight in the streets around here. If smallpox-tainted things, money and clothes, were stolen, there is danger of an epidemic. Are you certain everyone in your household has been inoculated?" The sudden stillness in the room alerted Narcissa to the storm coming. It did not take long to break.

"By God, I'll not have it!" Thaddeus roared. "It's a vile practice, and I'll not have it. Don't you try to interfere with my family, any more than you have already."

The strength of Thaddeus's anger had brought him bolt upright. Narcissa stared as the red flush ebbed from his face and he fell back exhausted.

"I am sorry." On an impulse, Narcissa walked over to the bed. Thaddeus's left hand, bunched into a fist, rested on the coverlet. Narcissa laid her own hand on top of his. Thaddeus stared at her openmouthed, apparently astonished into speechlessness.

"I am sorry for your loss," was all she said. Thaddeus Harrald's hazel eyes, wide with surprise, looked over his pince-nez into Narcissa's dark brown ones.

"Good-bye," she murmured. "I am sorry what I said was distressing to you." Then she crossed to where Aurelia was standing. Aurelia, too, looked on the verge of tears, her lips pressed tight together as she stared at the old man. *She would like to comfort her father, and be comforted by him,* thought Narcissa. *But she is too afraid of his anger.*

Aurelia led Narcissa out into the dark hallway. Mirrie was standing near the stairs, making no secret of her readiness to leave. As they came up to Mirrie, Narcissa put her mouth close to her friend's ear and spoke in a low tone. "Leave us alone a few moments." Mirrie nodded and swept down the stairs. Narcissa, glancing around, saw no sign of the house's other occupants.

Aurelia blinked away tears, but her voice was bitter. "I know you must have wondered about us, what kind of family we are, that we did not have Josiah cared for here in our home. I tried to explain to Josiah, when I visited him, but he didn't understand. He said such things to me, called me such names, told me not to come back. . . . The truth is, Father is morbidly afraid of sickness, disease, disfigurement — so much so, he let his son die among strangers!

"I defied him," she continued, her chin lifting with pride. "I had Stansbury inoculated when I learned Josiah had contracted the disease."

"And you? Were you inoculated?"

Narcissa asked.

Aurelia hesitated, as if she would rather not answer the question. At last she said, "No. The idea of having that filth introduced into my body . . . I couldn't bear it."

So Aurelia was not immune to smallpox. Nor was she immune to the prejudices of her father. Narcissa felt a stab of anxiety. "If there are boys, your close neighbors perhaps, who have been exposed . . . I am glad that Stansbury is immune. But you must try to keep him at home. All the Cats are in danger, not just from rocks and bricks. A slave boy was found dead, shot. He was not one of the Cats, but he may have been involved with them."

"How terrible!" Aurelia recoiled, her eyes wide with alarm.

Narcissa decided to push no further for the present. The strain of her brother's death, her father's guilt, and her own vulnerability had come near to unseating Aurelia's reason. In a few days, if Aurelia seemed stronger, she would raise the subject again. But she had to find out about the rest of the household. "What does Aaron believe concerning inoculation?"

Aurelia thought for a moment. "It may not be my place to tell you, but since you are concerned from the medical point of view, I will say that he was inoculated while in college. Those few years when we were in school away from home gave us all a chance to slip the harness, at least temporarily. You see how willingly we have returned to it, after all: to the stall and the trough. And he was inoculated again after Josiah fell ill. He was feverish a few days after. I was afraid he would prove Father right."

"And your servants?" Narcissa pressed.

"Yes, someone from the hospital inoculated them."

"Did Josiah have a manservant with him in camp?"

"Yes; but he is no longer with us. He was sold to another officer in Josiah's regiment."

Hmm, Narcissa thought: perhaps this sale was the source of the money in Josiah's uniform jacket. "Sold by Josiah?"

Aurelia shook her head. "No, the sale has only just been concluded."

Narcissa came to the last item on her mental list. "Aurelia, forgive me for pressing this, but — do *you* think a woman could have visited Josiah? If so, she could be in danger."

Aurelia shook her head. "Josiah had no fiancée, and no women friends that I know of. Perhaps it was simply one of those kind women who visit sick and wounded soldiers."

"Yes, that's most likely, isn't it?" Narcissa frowned down at the figured carpet. It would be difficult to locate one among the many women who visited the hospitals. But then . . . what Private Simms had described sounded like a rather more intimate encounter. Was it possible that Aaron's mistress had visited Josiah? She could hardly ask Aurelia that question.

Aurelia turned away then, and Narcissa followed her down the stairs to the entrance hall. She looked around for Mirrie and saw her standing in the front parlor where the family had been gathered when they arrived. Now Mirrie was alone, standing near the fireplace and turning the pages of a thick, squarish book in an elaborately tooled and gilded binding. It looked like one of those albums in which friends and acquaintances inscribe a message, usually sentimental or religious, for the owner. Mirrie put the book down and crossed the room to where they were standing. The servant Aurelia had summoned handed Narcissa and Mirrie their bonnets, wraps, and the still-damp umbrella.

As they walked out onto the steps, a

stylish carriage pulled up. Narcissa, turning back to look at Aurelia, thought at first that the sight of the carriage had frightened her. Aurelia was standing straighter, her eyes wide. Then a smile transformed Aurelia's face, dimpling her cheeks so that she looked younger and far happier. The smile vanished, but the look of anticipation lingered. Narcissa knew before she looked who the newcomer would be — Roland Ragsdale.

Embarrassed at having suddenly become de trop, Narcissa hurried down the steps, conscious as before of Ragsdale's eyes on her. He stopped; then, as Narcissa and Mirrie came abreast of him, he bowed, doffed the hat, and murmured in a low, insinuating tone, "Mrs. Powers. Delightful to see you again so soon. And you, ma'am," he added to Mirrie. Narcissa nodded and stepped past him, then looked back to see if Mirrie was following. As she did so, she caught sight of Aurelia in the doorway — looking still at Ragsdale, not smiling now but betraying her emotion by two spots of color high on her cheeks. As Narcissa looked, Aurelia ushered him inside, and the door closed behind them.

"A splendid example of the kind of person this war is benefiting," Mirrie remarked acidly as they stepped onto the sidewalk. "I am surprised Aurelia would know such a person, much less entertain him as a suitor. But I think she does. The leveling influence of wartime, I suppose. Who is that man? And how does he know *you*, come to that?"

"Roland Ragsdale. He's the man I mentioned to you who came to the hospital the day Josiah died, seeking to make a donation."

Mirrie frowned. "He obviously has it to spare! Look at his clothes, when most Richmonders have had nothing new since last year! How strange the Harralds would welcome such a man into their house. Aurelia welcomes him, at least," she added dryly.

"I feel sorry for her," Narcissa said warmly.

"And I feel a profound urge to slap her!" Mirrie retorted. "She need not accept her father's and brother's bullying."

Narcissa protested. "Even Aaron couldn't break away from his father! You said he dared not marry a woman his father disapproved of."

Mirrie was adamant. "Aurelia could change her life if she wanted."

Narcissa sighed to herself. Mirrie

preached bold defiance in all things, but she had lived quietly with her father all her life, save the years she'd spent at boarding school. Mirrie would never understand what it felt to be trapped by circumstances. But Narcissa could recall a time a little more than a year ago when she herself had been in a situation resembling Aurelia's, living with her half-brother and his wife in her family's farm home in western Hanover. She had been without object for her energies and affections, and without much hope for alteration in the future. Mirrie had rescued her from that. For Aurelia, apparently, there was no Mirrie, and no rescue.

It *was* a puzzle, how Ragsdale had come to be acquainted with Aurelia Harrald. And it worried her, Aurelia's obvious partiality to a speculator, a man of the world in the worst sense. . . .

Tsk! Narcissa shook her head, exasperated. It was so easy to read people's thoughts, their intentions; and so easy to be wrong. If Ragsdale's money were tainted by its having come from the pockets of gamblers, well, human frailty was the basis of many a fortune. The Harralds, like many other Richmond families, had made their money on tobacco, the

175

use of which had been considered a weakness by some as far back as the English king for whom the James River was named. Still others built their fortunes on selling slaves, or maintained their wealth and status by slave labor. Though she was not an out-and-out abolitionist, as Mirrie was, Narcissa could no longer rest in her old, comfortable assumptions about caring masters and grateful servants. She had seen too much of the world.

Aurelia Harrald was an unmarried woman not in her first youth. As each year passed, Aurelia was seeing her hopes grow fainter: hopes for a home of her own, a little realm of which to be queen, to order things according to her own taste; for a companionate marriage; for children. . . .

Then, what about the woman who had hoped to be Aaron's wife? Was that the worst, to have the man you loved, but to have him in secret, in shame? What could drive a woman to accept *that?*

"Mirrie, I want you to find out about Aaron's mistress. It may be that she visited Josiah in the hospital. I ought to speak with her."

Mirrie nodded. "I can do that." Then she added, with a sidelong glance at Narcissa, "Did you know Cameron Archer used to be one of Aurelia's beaux?"

"I — no," Narcissa answered. What had Archer said when she had spoken to him about Josiah's death? He'd made no reply at all, or an offhand one — nothing to indicate he had known the Harralds well.

"Yes!" Mirrie laughed a little. "I found Aurelia's landscape album among the books decorating the parlor. Cameron Archer's entry was quite flowery. Of course, it was a dozen years ago now. But there hasn't been much written in it since then."

"Oh?" She wanted to know more, but she wouldn't ask. Mirrie was too quick to imagine she knew what Narcissa was feeling, especially when — as now — Narcissa didn't quite know herself.

They had passed halfway down the block when they heard swift footsteps coming behind them. Narcissa turned to see Stone running toward them. He skidded to a stop in front of her, looking a good deal more distressed than he had at the funeral.

"I heard they're holding one of the Butcher Cats in Castle Godwin."

"Who told you that?"

Stone shrugged. "Everybody knows." He was staring into her face as if trying to read her expression. "It's Coffin, isn't it?"

"Yes — it's Coffin," she answered. "But not because he is guilty. Only because he has no one to look out for him, no mother or father."

Stone looked at her, confusion in his face — wondering, perhaps, at the rebuke in her voice. Then he responded, with the undisguised egoism of a child: "*I* have no mother or father."

"You have security, a roof over your head, food, clothing. And you have your aunt Aurelia, who loves you very much. Coffin, it seems, has no one."

"Well, Coffin killed one of his own boys."

Narcissa hesitated, then answered cautiously. "We don't think so."

Stone was frowning now, not meeting her eyes. She tried another tack.

"Do you think Coffin stole the small-pox-infected clothes to hurt you and your friends?"

"Yes."

"*Why* do you believe that, when there is no proof, and Coffin says he knows nothing about it?"

"Of course, that's what he *says!*" Stone answered back. "Why would he be in jail, if he hadn't done anything wrong?"

Narcissa drew a deep breath and let it out slowly. She reminded herself that Stone wasn't to blame for repeating what he'd heard others say. "Because the newspapers criticize the Military Guard for not putting a stop to you boys' fighting. You two are mirror images, you know, the Butchertown gang and the Shockoe Hill gang, and each of you claims the other is to blame. But you, who have an influential family, who are friends with President Davis's son — *you* cannot be arrested. So you allow the Butcher Cats to be your whipping boys."

"We have to fight them." Stone seemed intent on getting her to agree with this premise. "If they come onto our territory, and we don't fight them, we're not men. Men defend their honor. Men defend their homes."

Over Stone's head, Narcissa could see the wry expression on Mirrie's face. What could she, Narcissa, say to contradict what was bred in the blood? She contented herself with asking one more question. "I wonder, if you were to put yourself in his place, whether you would be so quick to condemn him?"

At that, Stone gave her one startled look, turned, and fled.

Brit's first call of the day had been at the telegraph office on Main Street, where his operator friend Yancey often provided him with tasty bits of information. Now he was cutting across the Capitol grounds in the direction of the passport office on Ninth and Broad. Jefferson's noble Capitol was before his eyes, but a very different scene was in his mind: the Federal warship *Galena* as it steamed away from Richmond, a floating charnel house. Word had made its way back from the Union command concerning the debacle at Drewry's Bluff. Confederate shot and shell had rained from the bluff, blasting through the ship's inadequate iron plating, blowing to bits at least a dozen men. It had been like shooting fish in a barrel — shooting them, God help us, with a howitzer. . . . Meanwhile, most of the *Galena*'s shots had missed the target altogether, with some shells exploding in farm fields two miles distant from the river. Though some had hit the target, to devastating effect. He remembered with a shudder the men he had seen blown apart on the bluff. Still, to die in the open was preferable. . . .

With that thought, he filled his lungs

with fresh spring air and lengthened his stride.

Those seeking to go north into enemy territory, or to travel in regions of the Confederacy under martial law, had to seek permission at the passport office. Many had honorable motives, personal or relating to business, that required them to travel. But others traveled as smugglers, speculators, and spies. Rumor attached charges of bribery regarding passports to the names of high government officials, and every conceivable ill — from high prices to military defeat — was laid at the doorstep of the passport office.

The appearance of the office did nothing to counter its vile reputation. The building smelled like one of the city's hospitals, but the bodies lying about on the filthy floor were the indolent clerks employed at the behest of General Winder — employed, it appeared, to perfect their aim in spitting and in throwing cards into a hat. They were taking turns at this entertainment, laying and collecting bets on the outcome. At Brit's arrival, one of the clerks propped himself up on his shirtsleeved elbow and inquired offhandedly whether he'd come for a passport.

"No. I merely need some information."

The clerk grinned. Tobacco stained his teeth, and a wad of it distended his left cheek. "We don't have no information. We're the passport office. If it's information you want, go to the information office." He turned to enjoy the admiration of his fellow clerks. Brit heard him make some remarks under his breath in which the word *foreigner* appeared.

"I'm prepared to *pay* for the information." Brit pronounced the word quite clearly, and it got the clerks' attention. The one who had jested at his expense — Brit dubbed him Wad — got to his feet first, whereupon the rest subsided into listlessness.

"What kind of information is it you want, sir?" Wad's smile was even uglier at close quarters, and Brit could smell the liquor he exhaled.

"Can one buy a uniform here?"

Wad gave a sneaking glance toward the door. "One can, for a price."

Brit nodded genially. "A dead man's uniform?"

The smile disappeared from the right side of the clerk's mouth. The left side grinned on, stretched into a semblance of good humor by the lump of chewing tobacco. "Reckon they won't be needing them no more. We got hundreds of them down in the basement."

Yes, I can smell them, thought Brit.

"You'd be getting a bargain."

Brit leaned his elbows on the counter. "A dead *officer's* uniform?"

Wad stood up straighter, backing away. "You got a right to wear it?"

He's getting suspicious. Let him. Brit brought out a stack of Confederate money and put it on the counter. Wad eyed it coldly, turned, and spit in the general direction of the filthy cuspidor.

Brit took out a twenty-dollar gold piece and laid it on top of the stack. "I'm not asking to wear it. Just to buy it."

Wad's expression was that of a starving man at a rich man's feast. "I reckon I could sell it to you. I reckon we could work something out."

Brit put his hand on the money. "But could *I* sell such a uniform to *you?*" He stared into Wad's muddy brown eyes until the clerk looked down — reassuring himself, maybe, that the money was still there.

"Depends." Wad shrugged. "Where'd you get it?"

"I got it from an enterprising young boy, about six years old. Perhaps he's sold things to you, or to your colleagues here."

"I ain't seen nobody like that." Wad was getting impatient.

"Ask them," Brit insisted, gesturing with his head toward the other clerks.

"You boys bought any uniforms from a kid? You seen any kids in here?"

They all shook their heads. One spoke up. "Send him to Miller. He'd love to catch one of them Cats selling stolen property." He pronounced it *propitty*.

Brit recognized the name of one of the most notorious plug-uglies. "Where can I find Miller?"

"You can find him at the Golden Arrow," answered one of the lounging clerks. Then they all chuckled and exchanged knowing glances. Apparently they admired the drive and initiative of Miller in making himself a fixture in Richmond's highest-toned gaming-house-cum-bordello.

Brit swept the money back into his pocket. "Well, this boy — I told you he was enterprising." He was speaking to all of them now, and they were listening, though Wad was staring sorrowfully at the pocket into which the gold piece had disappeared. "This boy stole the uniform from the smallpox hospital."

Wad recoiled, backing away from the counter. "Smallpox? Jesus! I ain't fool enough to buy nothing like that." The others stared, shaking their heads in response to Brit's inquiring gaze.

"Well, if you see such a boy, let me know. I'm offering a considerable reward." Brit flipped an engraved card onto the counter. Wad picked it up, read it, and stuck it in his vest pocket. Brit, satisfied he had made his point, walked out into the bright light of day.

CHAPTER FIVE

SUNDAY, MAY 18

The desertion of Richmond by many of its most prominent families left a number of pews unoccupied at St. Paul's Church. But the person Narcissa and Mirrie had come to see — Dr. Stedman's redoubtable wife, who knew everyone and enjoyed sharing her knowledge — was much in evidence. As usual, Mrs. Stedman wore shades of pink that brightened her ruddy complexion to the sunburned hue of a farmwife. Her daughters clustered around her, and she held her month-old grandson on her lap. The family's prayers would be earnest, Narcissa knew: the baby's father was a captain in the Richmond Grays.

Narcissa tried to make her prayers earnest, too, but the events of the past few days entangled themselves with Dr. Minnegerode's words. The second lesson was the story of Lazarus. *Then said Mary unto Jesus, Lord, if thou hadst been here, my brother had not died.* Could they, she and Judah Daniel, have saved Benjy? Was there still a chance they could save Sam and Timmy? Maybe it was wrong to care so much, since Jesus had conquered death. But Jesus had wept for Lazarus.

After the service, Narcissa and Mirrie hung back to greet the Stedmans and walk out with them. Mrs. Stedman fixed Narcissa with a shrewd look. "My husband tells me you are trying to prevent an epidemic. Good for you. I would help you if I could, but —" Mrs. Stedman indicated her daughters. Slender and pretty, all of them, they clustered around their stout mother like peonies tied to a supporting stake. There was such a thing, Narcissa reflected, as being *too* good a mother.

Mirrie spoke in a low tone to Mrs. Stedman. "Narcissa needs to ask you something."

Mrs. Stedman held out her hand to Narcissa. "What is it, dear?"

"A woman visited Josiah Harrald. No one seems to know who she was. We need to find her, to make sure she did not carry away the smallpox infection. The soldier

187

who saw them together thought that she might be his fiancée."

Mrs. Stedman's eyes widened. "If Josiah had gotten engaged, I hadn't heard of it."

Narcissa went on in a lower tone. "Aaron and Aurelia Harrald say that Josiah had no women friends. But I've heard that Aaron has a mistress, and I wonder if it could have been she? Who is she?"

Mrs. Stedman nodded, her lips pressed together in a disapproving line. "Serena Warren. She deserves better than Aaron Harrald. He made promises to her, but he proved a coward in the end. She lives in a boardinghouse on Cary Street —"

A wail from the baby interrupted her. "Give him to me," Mrs. Stedman told her oldest daughter, who seemed relieved to hand over the screaming infant. Mrs. Stedman put him on her shoulder and began a rhythmic bouncing and patting that silenced the child at once. She gave Narcissa the address. "Not the worst block of Cary Street," she added, over the baby's back, "but not so very nice, either."

Narcissa asked, "Could I call on her there?"

Mrs. Stedman glanced shrewdly at Narcissa. "She may have enough honor left to be ashamed. Then again, I expect she is very lonely. Why not send her a note asking if she is able to receive you?" Then she added, "Serena lives a very retired life. . . . Aaron, surely, has been inoculated?"

Narcissa understood what Mrs. Stedman was getting at. If Serena Warren were herself immune to smallpox, but carried the effluvia on her person, whom could she have infected? "Aaron has," she answered, "but Aurelia has not."

"Well! You must persuade her," was Mrs. Stedman's brisk response.

Narcissa smiled. "I'll try. I'm very obliged to you."

Mrs. Stedman smiled in return. Then she set off up the street, her girls trailing her.

Judah Daniel had vowed to keep going back to the Evanses until they gave up and let her talk to Sam. Cassie Terry, too: if she wanted to lead her life free of Judah Daniel, she was going to have to yield up Timmy for her questioning. Both the Evanses and Cassie were hiding more than their sons, after all. Mal was selling illegal liquor; and Cassie was buying liquor, somehow, though the money she came by legally could scarcely stretch that far. Neither Mal nor Cassie would want visitors, or questions, and Judah Daniel suspected they'd give up their children before they'd give up the secrets they were hiding.

But there was something she had to do first, and so she had come back to the alley behind the free school. She had to break the cup that had belonged to Benjy. She would have broken it on his grave, but the Military Guard had Benjy's body. How would she know when or where they buried him? And it was time, past time, to release his soul. So she would break it on the spot where he had died.

She held Benjy's cup between her two hands as if making an offering. Her grief sighed in her, a hollow sound like the winter wind. *Gone, gone,* was its moan, *to a better place, and this one darker, lonelier, more desolate.* She raised the cup high in her arms. She would have to dash it hard onto the still-soft ground to break it.

Release Benjy's soul, for he is free now. . . . No!

She froze. Then, very slowly, she lowered the cup. She stood still, waiting for Benjy to tell her what he wanted her to do. No word came, but she found her mind growing clearer, her eyes growing sharper.

At last she saw it, straight in front of her across the alley: a thumb-sized hole in the door of the shed. The gray wood around the hole had splintered, showing pale wood that hadn't had time to weather. She crossed over to examine the hole. It was about waist-high to her, but Benjy was smaller than she. If he had been standing just here, the ball could have torn through his chest, then buried itself in the wood.

She probed the hole with her forefinger. She didn't think the ball had gone through. Had someone dug it out?

Judah Daniel tugged on the door, and it swung open. The smell warned her. Someone had been sick here. She stepped forward once, twice, taking in what she saw. The straw on the floor was clumped into two pallets, old feed sacks serving for sheets and blankets. Between these make-shift beds stood a tin cup holding — she looked to see — water. The cup was like those they used at the hospital. Benjy had come here, she thought, bringing water. For himself and another? She measured Benjy in her mind, then the straw beds. No . . . two smaller boys. At least one of them puking.

Now Benjy was dead. Where were the boys? She couldn't answer that question.

But who they were, that she thought she knew: Sam Evans and Timmy Terry. The pest-house thieves.

The dark, stinking space felt suddenly cold. She took two steps back to stand in the door. She brought Benjy's cup up. "You can go now," she whispered to it. "I'll find them. I promise."

She opened her hands. The pottery cup dropped onto the wooden doorjamb and broke into pieces, exposing the raw red clay from which it was made. *Clay is all we are,* the voice spoke in her. *Clay, and the breath of God.*

Judah Daniel went first to Cassie Terry's. The door and windows were shut up tight, and her knocking and calling raised no response. Maybe Cassie and her brood were at evening church service, but Judah Daniel didn't think so. Like as not, Cassie had seen her coming and was playing possum.

Judah Daniel kept calling for several minutes, using every threat she knew: disease, death, the police. The last, at least, was an empty threat: the police would not respond if she, Judah Daniel, went to them. And if she told her suspicions to someone to whom the police *would* respond, Dr. Archer for example, the upholders of the law would tear through the lives of Cassie and her children like a tornado.

Judah Daniel gave up finally and stood looking at the shanty in which daily misery flared up every so often into violence and death. It would almost be a relief if Cassie and her brood had skedaddled. But did they take the smallpox with them? She turned her cursing against Cassie into a prayer for Timmy, and for Cassie's other children.

By the time Judah Daniel walked into the Evanses' confectionery, she had worked up a full head of steam. She was ready to lay them out, Juney and Mal both, if they played dumb with her about Sam's whereabouts. But at the sight of the doc-toress, Juney hurried out from behind the counter.

"Judah Daniel." Tears trembled in Juney's voice. "I got my boy Isaiah upstairs for you to inoculate him."

"What about Sam?"

"I can't find Sam, he ain't been home in days." The words poured out of Juney in a wail. "I reckon he's afraid Mal going to beat him. Sam ain't done nothing, you got to believe me. My boys can't be getting no smallpox."

Judah Daniel put her hands on the woman's shoulders. "Why you so shook up about this?"

Juney's tears came faster than she could wipe them away. "If one of my boys got the smallpox, and had to go to the hospital, they'd sell him into slavery 'less we could pay the bill! It'd cost hundreds of dollars, the hospital, and we ain't got that kind of money! Judah Daniel, I couldn't stand it. If anything happened to my boys, it'd be the death of me."

"Ssh, ssh, Juney." Judah Daniel soothed her as if she were a child. "Who told you them tales? If one of your boys did get sick, wouldn't I take care of him myself? Anyway, ain't you ever heard *sufficient unto the day is the evil thereof?* I got to inoculate Ise and talk to him, alone."

Juney wiped her eyes and smiled a little. "All right, Judah Daniel. Mal ain't here," she added in a lower tone.

Well, I knowed that, honey, Judah Daniel thought to herself. If Mal had been here, Juney would have kept quiet as a stone, however much her heart was breaking.

"All right, let me see Ise."

"You wait here, I'll bring him down."

Judah Daniel sat out on the steps. In a few minutes, Juney came out with five-year-old Isaiah, known as Ise.

Judah Daniel waved Juney away, then pulled Ise down next to her on the step and looked him square in the face. "Ise, you know where Sam run off to?"

Ise shook his head, slowly and cautiously, as if he was afraid it would fall right off his neck.

"But you know why he run off, right?"

Ise continued to shake his head in gentle, careful denial.

Judah Daniel decided to be blunt. "I think Sam sneaked into the pest-house with Timmy Terry. He's afraid something terrible going to happen if anybody finds them. But listen to me, Ise: don't nobody care about what they stole. They won't get in trouble for that, I promise you. But they could catch the smallpox, and get real sick. And they could spread it to other folks — like, to you — just by touching the things they stole. Did you know you could catch it that easy?"

Ise stared back.

"Can you *talk?*"

"Yes, ma'am," he whispered.

Judah Daniel sighed. "You know I'm here to help Sam. Maybe you don't know where he gone. But if you do, if you can get a message to him, tell him to come to me. It'd be a whole lot better that way. Less trouble. Less danger, for everybody."

There wasn't much of anything left to say. She motioned to Juney to come on back. Then she rolled up Ise's sleeve to bare his arm, made the cut, and applied the liquid. Juney comforted her son. When he raised his tear-streaked face off his mother's shoulder, Judah Daniel said, "I'll be back, Ise. So think on it." Ise gave her one last look and ran into the house.

Judah Daniel sighed again. She could tell Mal Evans her suspicions, but Mal would likely beat a story out of Ise — a story that might not be true.

Something had scared Juney beyond the disease itself. Where did she get the idea that a free black treated for smallpox could be sold into slavery to pay the medical bill? Judah Daniel had never heard of that, not that she didn't believe it could happen. But Juney was not the kind of woman who dreamed things up. Someone had put the idea in her head — but why? Did that *someone* want to scare her into revealing Sam's hiding place? Or scare her into keeping him hidden?

Weeks in the rain-sluiced trenches around Yorktown, days on the march with little or no food, had sickened hundreds of soldiers. They languished, many of them, victims of those most stubborn and enervating illnesses: catarrh and bronchitis, rheumatism and neuralgia, diarrhea and dysentery. The soldiers gathered to defend the city were sleeping on the rain-soaked ground, wearing clothes that never had the chance to dry out completely, eating undercooked meat — if they had any meat at all. And they were falling sick, joining their fellows.

These days, as Narcissa moved among the sick men, she looked into their faces for the characteristic reddening of first-stage smallpox. So far, she had found nothing.

As she glanced into the first room, she saw Tunstall. He looked pale and feverish, but he was smiling. Sitting next to him was a woman, still dressed in a sooty traveling cloak and dirty boots, holding his hands in hers, laughing and crying at the same time.

Narcissa went over to them. "Sergeant Tunstall, is this your wife?"

Both nodded. Tunstall cleared his throat and whispered, "My wife — Annalise. My dear, this is Mrs. Powers. She's a good nurse."

The woman slipped her left hand out of her husband's and held it out to Narcissa. "Thank you," she whispered. Her eyes looked into Narcissa's for a moment. Narcissa could see the fear in them, warring with joy and hope. Then Mrs. Tunstall turned back to her husband.

Narcissa bathed wounds and replaced the bandages for several patients. Coming into one of the rooms, she found a half-dozen convalescent soldiers grouped around the window, looking out into the street. They were grinning and talking among themselves. One of them, Private Hodges, who at seventeen bore an empty sleeve as the badge of his patriotism, caught sight of her and called out, "Mrs. Powers! Simms's wife is here — he's just gone down to her, saw her when she was halfway down the block." He turned to look out of the window again. Narcissa reached the window just in time to see Simms catch his wife in a bear hug and spin her so that her skirts rounded out like a bell, showing white stockings and petticoats. The men in the window whistled and applauded, calling out "Hoorah for Mrs. Simms!" At last Simms loosened his grip enough to look up and wave. Mrs. Simms hid her face on her husband's shoulder as the men called and whistled all the louder.

"He's lucky," sighed Hodges. "The doctors give him two days before he has to rejoin his regiment."

Two days, thought Narcissa. Only two days to put the spirit back into the husband and the wife, so that they would be strong enough to carry on alone, for who knew how long? Two months, two years, maybe. How long could one live upon two days?

Simms and his wife were heading down the street now, arm in arm, his face bent to hers. As Narcissa watched, she spotted a slender, dark-skinned woman — Judah Daniel. Did she have any news? Narcissa excused herself and hurried out to meet her.

Judah Daniel told Narcissa what she had found behind the free school, at the place where Benjy was killed, and explained her fruitless quest for Timmy and Sam. Narcissa, in turn, told Judah Daniel about the Harralds, about Aaron's mistress, and about Coffin and Stone. When Judah Daniel suggested one of those two boys,

Coffin or Stone, might know something, Narcissa agreed, and promised to try and find out more. But she had to force herself not to defend them, to deny the possibility that the two boys who had won her sympathy could have any knowledge of either the thefts from the smallpox hospital or the shooting of Benjy. The two women parted company, Narcissa returning to the hospital and Judah Daniel to the Chapmans' house.

The sky darkened to indigo. Tyler Chapman, his deliveries for the family bake shop concluded, sat on the steps of the sprawling wooden structure that was home to four generations of free black Chapmans. He was paying little heed to the comings and goings on Second Street — whatever he was looking for, he wasn't going to find it there. Then a movement caught his eye: a small black boy, taking to his heels at the sight of Tyler.

"Sam!" Tyler called out.

The boy looked back over his shoulder, and froze — eyes wide, mouth a frightened *O*, body poised to run again.

In a half-dozen swift strides Tyler closed on Sam. "You was one of them Cats stealing from the smallpox hospital. Ain't that right?"

Sam sagged sideways as if his knees were buckling under him. Tyler caught him by the arm and held him up. Tyler's one hand, forefinger meeting thumb, encircled the boy's arm. *So little. Not much older than my boy.* Tyler felt his anger slip a little.

Tyler took a deep breath and let it out slowly, getting himself under control. "You can't just run off like that. In times like these, Sam, a boy got to act like a man. A good man got to stand with the other good men. He ain't going to turn his back. He ain't going to close his eyes and hope he ain't needed, hope they can do it without him. He ain't going to think about saving his life. What good's life to a man if he ain't a man no more?"

Tears were running down Sam's face. Tyler still held him, but gently; now that the anger had gone out of him, all he could feel was a terrible sorrow.

"I ain't . . ." Sam whispered the words.

Tyler, himself on the point of tears, shook his head. "God have mercy, Sam. You a little boy, you ain't no man. But you got to tell the truth."

Sam stared up, his face as blank and far away as the moon. He seemed to be gathering himself for some hard task. At last the words came out of him, one at a time, as if it was taking all his strength to speak them. "I . . . don't . . . know." Then he tore himself from Tyler's grasp and ran away down the street.

Judah Daniel walked up from the hospital to find Tyler sitting on the bottom step of his family's house. He had his elbows on his knees, face buried in his hands. Then he dropped his hands, fingers interlaced, between his legs. When she saw his face bared, the teasing words she had been about to say melted like snowflakes on her tongue.

Tyler broke the silence. "Judah Daniel, I ain't no kind of a father."

The misery on his face held her speechless. She knew what he was going to say, just as he knew everything she could say in argument. But you don't argue with a man whose heart is breaking.

"I got to go join the Union. Here I got the *name* of a free man. There I got the chance to *be* one."

"They ain't going to let you fight," Judah Daniel said quietly. "You won't be no more than a contraband of war, set to doing the hard labor, just like you done here."

"Maybe someday they let me fight. I can hope. But when I'm a old man I'm going to tell my children I done what was right." Tyler laughed, a dry cough of a sound. "To think I told Sam to stand up and be a man. Well, I'll show him I can be one. I'll show them all."

"*Sam* was here?"

Tyler nodded. "I had him. I — I don't know, something come over me, like it was me I was talking to, not Sam at all. The words poured out of me like Reverend Truesdale preaching a sermon. He got out of my hands, and he run away."

"Did he say anything about the thieving from the pest-house?"

Tyler smiled wearily. "Said he don't know nothing about it. But I reckon he know something. Why else would he be so scared?"

Judah Daniel watched as the dark settled like a velvet mantle onto the city's shoulders. She wanted to tell Juney that her son had been seen, but she dared not. Mal wasn't to be trusted. He had beaten the boys before, and his wife. Fear and anger could make a man do ugly things.

Had Sam found himself a safe place for

the night? If not . . . Her hands bunched into fists, fingernails digging into the flesh of her palms. Sam would not wind up like Benjy . . . not if she could help it.

CHAPTER SIX

MONDAY, MAY 19

The Powerses' hired coachman, Will Whatley, delivered Narcissa's note to Serena Warren and returned with her reply: that she would be pleased for Narcissa to call on her in the late morning. At eleven o'clock, the rouged and shrewd-eyed landlady of the Cary Street boardinghouse showed Narcissa to the rooms in which Aaron Harrald's mistress made her home.

Serena Warren proved to be a tall, rather gawky woman with graying dark hair worked into ringlets around her face. The fabric of her unfashionable dress blended green and yellow in an unappetizing plaid. With the awkwardness of one who does not often play hostess, she ushered Narcissa into a tiny sitting room crowded with heavy furniture and smelling of dust, mildew, and eau de cologne. Taking Serena

Warren as an example, the life of a kept woman had all the romance of a wet washday.

When Serena seated herself opposite Narcissa, her gaze was direct. "Miss — pardon me, *Mrs.* — Powers, you must forgive me." Serena fingered the tarnished gold trim of a hard cushion. "It's been quite a long time since I have had a caller. You think I may have been exposed to smallpox? I am well, as you see. As for the idea that I may be spreading contagion" — Serena gestured around the room, a wry smile twisting the corners of her mouth — "I very rarely leave these rooms."

Narcissa tried to keep the pity she was feeling from showing in her eyes. "I know it seems strange, Miss Warren, but the fact is, doctors don't know by what mechanism smallpox spreads. Dr. Archer told me Josiah Harrald could have contracted the disease by brushing past someone on the train. If you visited Josiah when he was in the hospital —"

The dead man's name evoked an immediate response. "Josiah!" Serena almost spat the name out. "I have not been in his company for years."

"So you did not visit him?"

"If I had, what reason would I have to

pretend otherwise?" Serena pushed the cushion away from her and sat up very straight. "Although I *would* like to have gone to his funeral, to see him lowered into the ground! He made no secret of despising me, and he kept at Aaron incessantly to give me up, to buy me off. As if Josiah, or any of the others of his family for that matter, had any right to look down on *me!*" Serena pressed her lips together and turned away for a moment before resuming. "Aaron saw him in the hospital. He came by here afterward, beside himself with rage. I thought he was going to get one of his headaches. Imagine, going to the bedside of your dying brother — we thought the amputation would finish him, even before he came down with smallpox — and having him lecture you about business!"

Narcissa frowned sympathetically. "Josiah did that?"

Serena nodded. "He did! And he away from home for a year, playing soldier, doing nothing but drawing on his family's finances. He would never admit they were in dire straits. And Thaddeus is the same." Serena's face darkened as she spoke the name of the man who was Josiah's father, and Aaron and Aurelia's. "If it were not for

Aaron, they would have had to face the truth, both of them."

"So Aaron found a way . . . ?" Narcissa prodded gently.

Serena nodded. "Aaron was a better businessman than Josiah, but Josiah was the eldest, and his father's favorite. And when he joined the army, all Josiah did was draw on the family funds."

"To pay gambling debts?" Narcissa inquired.

Serena stared at Narcissa for a moment, then shook her head. "No . . . Josiah never gambled. That was not one of his vices."

Were there other vices that could have put a large amount of money in Josiah's pocket? Narcissa couldn't think of any. But there was another question she had to ask.

"Do you know if any other woman visited Josiah — besides Aurelia?"

Serena shook her head as if the question didn't interest her and reverted to the earlier subject. "Now that Josiah is dead, Aaron will have a chance to straighten out the family finances. Whether Thaddeus will be grateful or not . . . But it should be better for us."

Serena spoke casually enough, but Narcissa found her choice of words interesting. *Better for us.* Serena was bound to

Aaron Harrald with ties as binding as those of marriage. More binding, perhaps, since to be with him she had given up every other tie.

Narcissa chose her words carefully. "Josiah had a great deal of money with him just before he died. Could Aaron have given it to him?"

Serena's wistful smile vanished. "He had money? How do you know? What happened to it?"

Narcissa told the story again. Serena listened, the expression on her face passing from anxious to angry to resigned. At last she said bitterly, "There never was any money. Josiah imagined it."

Narcissa recalled that Aaron Harrald had said much the same thing.

Serena gave a little nervous cough. "Is it true what my landlady tells me — that meats of all kinds are selling at fifty cents a pound, and tea for *ten dollars?* She claims she has to charge me forty dollars a month. I can scarcely believe . . ."

Narcissa tried not to stare. Did Serena really never leave these rooms? "It's true," she answered. "Coffee is cheaper — a dollar-fifty a pound. That is, if you can find it. . . . As for meat and produce, the farmers have to have passes in and out of the city. They're forced to wait for hours to get them. So many of them aren't bringing their goods in at all."

Silence fell between the two women, then both spoke at once.

"I am very much obliged —" Narcissa began.

"Well, I suppose —" Serena's mouth twisted in an embarrassed smile.

They stood up and faced each other. It was not likely they would meet again. What was there to say? Narcissa felt again the impulse to pity. "Will things change for you now, do you think?" she asked.

"Perhaps, but . . . Thaddeus still lives," Serena answered in a small voice. Then she led Narcissa the few paces across threadbare carpet to the door.

At home that evening, Narcissa received a note from Cameron Archer, which proved to be a copy of the necropsy report on Benjamin Givens — Benjy.

Examined the body c. 10 P.M. on the evening of the 16th inst. Determined death occurred between 24 and 36 hours prior to examination. Rigor mortis had passed over, and the body was cool. The wound of entrance was small, typical of the ordinary conical bullet used in revolving pistols, and situated two inches below and a little inward from the left nipple. On opening the chest more than two quarts of blood were found in this cavity and that of the pericardium, the lung being compressed against the anterior parietes. From its entrance between the fifth and sixth ribs, the ball had passed almost directly backward, inclining very slightly downward and toward the middle line, perforating the pericardium and the heart near its apex, and had emerged between the sixth and seventh ribs of the left side. The wound of exit was larger by one-half than the wound of entrance. Distension of the pericardium would have obstructed circulation and caused almost immediate death. — C. Archer, M.D.

The dispassionate wording of the report chilled her at first. But as she read it again, she realized she had to be grateful to Archer. He had obviously done the necropsy within a few hours of receiving her note — although it had taken him three days to inform her of the results. But at least he had wasted no time in examining the body. And he had confirmed Judah Daniel's observation that Benjy had been dead long before the Cats' fight. Not only that: he'd observed the wound to be characteristic of the conical ball used in revolvers. The pistol Brit had taken from Coffin, then yielded up to the plug-uglies, was an old single-shot horse pistol that would have fired a spherical ball. There could be no doubt now that Coffin was innocent. With the realization, her heart lifted a little. Coffin would go free — but go where, and to what?

In the shadow of the siege, Richmond's bawdy houses glowed with a subdued flame. Many of the more successful among the Cyprians had fled the town along with their neighbors. Their places had been taken by refugees from the Peninsula, but these were storm-tossed birds with ruffled feathers, thought Brit Wallace.

The Golden Arrow on Cary Street was a place for those who considered themselves men of the world — including many leading lights of the Confederate administration and the army — to gather in surroundings like those of a luxurious private home, only without the constraints. Here a man could relax and smoke a cigar amid the attentions of bright-gowned sylphs and white-jacketed slaves bearing wine. The pleasures of conversation cost nothing. Ragsdale counted on his employees' ability to turn the visitor into a customer, either at the faro bank or in the private rooms upstairs. On this evening, the Golden Arrow was officially closed. So it was with some surprise that Brit, admitted to the grand saloon by one of those white-jacketed servants, found it quite busy. A few men in civilian dress lolled upon the settees, but the spirit was supplied by a dozen young men in privates' uniforms who were clustered around the piano, singing "Dixie" and stamping their feet so that the candlesticks atop the piano jumped in time. A rather fat red-haired woman was playing, her elbows pumping up and down as she struck the keys, and a few females — young and pretty, at least from a distance — joined in the singing.

Brit was amused at first and imagined adding the detail to one of his dispatches — until he caught the eye of Private Archer Langdon, who winked and waved. Then it struck him that these young men would have the devil to pay if they were found here. He wondered if even Langdon, with his family connections and his personal bravery, could escape stern punishment.

Brit moved away, ignoring Langdon's beckoning gestures, and strolled over to an elegantly coifed Cyprian who was amusing herself with a game of solitaire at one of the green-baize-covered tables at the far end of the room. He stood behind her chair, leaned over close enough to brush her blond hair with his cheek, and advanced her desultory game by lifting the trey of spades and putting it down, with a snap, on the deuce. She turned to give him a practiced smile.

"Pardon me, Miss —"

"Dunbar, Sophie Dunbar," the Cyprian replied.

"Miss Dunbar." Brit bowed. "I wonder if you can tell me whether Mr. Miller is here tonight?"

Her eyes appraised him again, weighing his value to Miller — and perhaps to herself as well. It was, Brit thought, rather like examining a ripe peach and having it examine you back. Would she know his expensive clothes were a year out of the fashion, in England?

"He's here, through those doors there" — she nodded toward a set of double doors at the end of the room. "He's with

Mr. Ragsdale," she added, whether as a promise or a warning he could not tell.

"I'm very much obliged to you, Miss Dunbar." Brit bowed again, playing the courtly foreigner to the hilt, before walking away from her in the direction of the double doors.

One of the white-jacketed servants opened the right-hand door, and Brit strode into the room. Here the serious gamers had gathered, though they were still standing around, helping themselves from an array of refreshments as luxurious as any Brit had seen in months. Where did they get *champagne* . . . ? With difficulty, he turned his attention to the men, who upon his entrance had fallen silent. From descriptions, he recognized the lean, dark-jowled Miller. But in the instant he transferred his interest from Miller to the man whom Miller had instinctively glanced toward, deferred to. This man had wavy brown hair and a close-cropped beard, full, mobile lips, arched and satiric eyebrows over protuberant eyes; and, withal, the satisfied sleekness of an animal that has just licked from its lips the blood of its prey. His eyes locked on Ragsdale's, Brit stepped forward. "Mr. Ragsdale," he said. "Brit Wallace, at your service."

Ragsdale took Brit's offered hand and shook it, his massive gold ring cold against Brit's palm. "The British journalist. Are you celebrating another victory for *our* side?"

Brit felt his hackles rise. Was it because Ragsdale had assumed his sympathies lay with the Confederate cause? Or because Ragsdale himself had no reputation for patriotism? Perhaps he just did not like the look of the man. Whatever the reason, Brit's response was uncharacteristically prim. "A journalist gains his victory when the truth is told, Mr. Ragsdale."

Ragsdale's smile broadened as if in appreciation of a good jest. "And I have no doubt that you will find . . . some . . . truth to tell, Mr. Wallace." The hesitation was as good as an insult. "But I thought the Confederate cause had touched your heart more nearly than that?"

Narcissa Powers came into Brit's mind, and he almost said out loud, *How did you know?* He recovered himself and answered, "I have spent most of my time with Virginia regiments. The first man who called to me for help as he lay dying was a Confederate. The first man to point a pistol between my eyes and threaten to pull the trigger was a Confederate as well. So, for me, the war has a Confederate face."

Ragdale laughed heartily, looking around, inviting the others to show their appreciation of Brit's satire. Brit, who had been completely serious, put on a rather tight smile. Behind it, he was trying out and discarding subjects with which to engage Ragsdale and Miller in conversation. One stolen jacket might interest Miller on his own, but not in the company of Ragsdale. No, he had to propose a higher stake. . . . Ah, that was an idea. . . .

"Of course" — Brit smiled more easily now — "even though we live in the Confederacy, we are still citizens of the world." Brit stuck his hands in his pockets and waggled his eyebrows significantly.

"Ha, ha! Of course —" Ragsdale was watching him, waiting for the proposition to come. Miller looked on, a tolerant-verging-on-bored expression on his saturnine face.

"My cousin, for instance." Brit glanced around as if wanting to keep the subject secret from all but the dozen or so within easy sound of his voice. "Irish peer, more money than brains."

"I have no objection to those qualities in a business partner," Ragsdale commented smoothly.

"He wants to equip a blockade-runner, bring it over. He wants me to advise him what cargo to carry, and who should handle the transactions once he's arrived. And, of course, what cargo he should take back with him."

Ragsdale considered, or pretended to. "Well, as to delivery, of course the Confederacy prefers munitions, iron, and steel. But you should warn your — cousin? That kind of cargo slows a ship down, increases the risk of capture. Something light, now, brandy, wine, silks and laces . . . all profit, and far less risk. As to who should handle the transactions, I could advise you there. As to our exports, there are only two of any interest: cotton . . . and tobacco."

Ragsdale looked as if he would say more, but the dour Miller leaned over and whispered something in his ear.

"Oh, do you think so?" Ragsdale answered Miller, examining Brit again as if someone had mentioned the name *Wallace* in connection with *leprosy*. "Well, let me just say that, when your cousin's ship arrives in Jamaica, be sure to talk with me again." Ragsdale continued to smile, but it was clear the interview was over.

"Well, thank you, then," was about all that was left to Brit to say. He bowed and walked away, conscious of having been outplayed, but not yet willing to fold.

Back in the more public of the Golden Arrow's drawing rooms, Brit's gaze fell again on the golden head of Sophie Dunbar. She looked up at his approach and smiled flirtatiously. "So you're a newspaper reporter. Did you find out what you wanted from Miller?"

"Your loveliness makes me quite forget who I am," Brit answered lightly, wondering how she had learned who he was so quickly — had she listened at the door?

Sophie fluttered her eyelashes. "I don't spend time in the company of a nobody."

Brit pulled out the chair to her right and perched on its edge. "Then you force me to admit, I am the man. William Wallace, at your service."

"Are you going to write about the Golden Arrow?"

Brit shook his head. "I am here not to gather news but to deliver it."

"What news?"

"Actually, I need to deliver it in person. To Miss Pauline Avery."

Sophie grimaced, the corners of her

mouth turning down. "She's upstairs, in her apartments. She's Mr. Ragsdale's private stock."

Brit thought he detected envy in Sophie's pique. Perhaps she coveted Pauline's exalted status.

"Well, Mr. Ragsdale is otherwise engaged, and promises to be for some time. Could you go and ask if she will see me? I have news of her son."

There was no reaction to this last statement in Sophie's flat stare, but at last she gave a little yawn, stretched, and stood. "I won't be long," she said. "Why don't you play your own game?"

"I am very much obliged to you, Miss Dunbar."

As she walked away, Brit watched the lines of her silk dress sway.

He gathered the cards, riffled them in his hands, then laid them out in the seven rows of solitaire, hidden and revealed. He began to turn the remaining cards. The game went his way. In a few minutes he could see that he had won. Not bothering to finish, he scooped up the cards, shuffled, and laid them out again. This time, after a few promising trips through the stack, he found himself stymied.

"I wonder," he murmured aloud to himself, and lifted a black queen he had declined to move when he had the chance, choosing the other black queen instead.

"Thinking of cheating?"

The blond Cyprian had returned. She was leaning over the table, and he found himself taking in the view of her décolletage. He had been wrong about her hair being her finest asset.

"Would that all our decisions were so easy to revisit," Brit said, picking up the trey that had been covered by the queen. "We could go back and experience all that we have missed."

Sophie's reddened lips widened. She reached out, touched his hand, and winkled the trey from his fingers in a move as adroit as any riverboat gambler's. "Opportunity can be had, experience can be had. Anything can be had — at a price."

Brit rose to end the game. "Another time, perhaps."

Sophie took her dismissal with a shrug. "Come on with me."

Brit followed her through another saloon, this one deserted; down a hall not dressed for the public eye; and up a flight of dark and narrow stairs — the servants' stairs — to the second floor. At the first door, Miss Dunbar motioned him to wait;

she knocked softly, and the door was opened by a woman he guessed was Pauline Avery. One look at her told Brit that Ragsdale had had some success in bringing luxurious goods through the blockade. Yards of bright pink silk had gone into making her wrapper, with its enormous skirts, open from the waist in the front to display a froth of white petticoats, all of it — neck, front opening, hem, and wide pagoda sleeves — bordered with paisley silk a hand's-breadth wide. Her glossy brown hair hung in loose curls down her back.

"Thank you, Sophie," the woman murmured. The blond Cyprian, accepting the dismissal, turned back the way they had come.

When Sophie was out of earshot, the woman spoke. "Mr. . . . Wallace? I am Pauline Avery. What news do you have for me?"

She feared bad news: that he read in her wide eyes. But could this woman — young, possessed of a distinctive beauty — really be the mother of the rough youth who called himself Coffin? Brit hesitated, about to apologize for his mistake, when Pauline Avery spoke again. "Is it about my son?"

"A boy has been arrested. It's all right,

he's quite safe. He told me his name was —" Brit hesitated.

Pauline Avery smiled, her relief apparent. So she had expected something worse than arrest. "Coffin. His real name is Claude. An elegant name — French — but not one that suits him very well, I'm afraid. Where is he? What do they say he's done?"

"There is no specific charge against him. The boys had a fight, the Butcher Cats against the Hill Cats, and a boy was killed."

"What boy?"

"A slave, Benjy. Your son is innocent; he simply picked up a pistol in the street. It's only that the Military Guard have had no more effect against the Cats than the city police. So they are making an example of Claude as one of the leaders. One of the Butcher Cat leaders, of course," Brit added dryly. Pauline Avery took his meaning — her steady gaze and ironic smile assured him of that.

"Coffin." Pauline pronounced the name carefully, as if she wanted to hear the sound of it. "It's the name he chose, and it suits him better than the one I gave him. To name a poor, fatherless boy *Claude* . . . well, I was naive, and very young. Where have they put him?"

"In Castle Godwin. Please do not worry overmuch. I will use every means at my disposal to make sure he is not blamed for something he did not do."

Pauline nodded slowly, setting the frothy lace in gentle motion around her face, but Brit could not read her thoughts. "Would you like me to take you to see him?"

Pauline looked away for a long moment, then back at Brit. "No, thank you." Then her eyes narrowed, just as Brit became aware of a noise at the end of the hall. Two uniformed men were hurrying toward them

"Wallace!" It was Archer Langdon, he saw now, and Langdon's friend Henry Watkins. Brit chuckled with relief.

Langdon bowed to Pauline, "Pardon me, ma'am." Then he turned to Brit. "Miller's coming after you. Appears he took offense at your conversation with Miss Dunbar. I don't know what she told him, but —"

Watkins, who was practically dancing with nervous apprehension, spoke up. "The Baltimore detectives have taken over the place: the drink, the gaming tables, the girls, everything. We've got to get out of here — now!"

Brit turned to Pauline Avery. The smile

on his face vanished when he saw the frown on hers. "You'd better go," she said. "Don't take the stairs! Can you get through the window?"

She pointed to a narrow window at the end of the hall. As Brit remembered the situation of the house, this window over-looked the space between buildings.

"All right, then," Brit muttered. He wondered if this could all be an elaborate charade designed to pull his nose. But he bowed to Pauline Avery and led the way down the hall.

The window was wide enough for a slender man to wriggle through; fortunately, the three of them qualified. He slipped over to the window and tugged on the sash. It wouldn't budge. He cupped his hands around his eyes to shield them from the light and looked through the glass. There was a space of about four feet between the window and the wall of the next house. He could not see the ground. Still, it was no worse an escape route than some he'd used before, if only he could get the window open. "Come help me!" he called out in a whisper. Langdon darted over. Together they shoved with all their might, but the window would not budge, though there was no catch visible.

"Must be nailed shut," Brit panted.

Langdon pulled off his belt, wrapped it around his right hand, and drove his fist through the window. Langdon's desperate action made up Brit's mind for him — he pulled off his shoe and commenced knocking away the remaining shards of glass.

With most of the glass removed, Langdon pushed Watkins on ahead. The youth started to put his head out the window. "No, the other way," Brit cautioned. Watkins swung one leg over and out the window; brought up the other; then, muttering what might have been a prayer, he let himself drop.

A heavy thud met Brit's ears, then "I'm all right."

Archer Langdon took this as the signal to slip his own skinny frame over and through the window. Brit heard the thump, then a yelp of pain. A flurried exchange of anxious whispers and muffled moans rose to meet Brit's ears as he threw his legs over, hung suspended for a moment, then dropped, bending his knees to cushion the jolt. The impact took his breath away for a moment. It was pitch-dark, but enough light escaped the curtained windows for him to see Langdon clutching his left arm.

"He thinks it's broken," Watkins whispered.

"Move your fingers," Brit ordered. Langdon looked down at the fingers on his left hand as if they did not belong to him, but the fingers wiggled.

"Bend your elbow." Langdon winced, but the lower arm responded with a cautious flex up and down.

"You're all right," Brit pronounced. "Now, let's clear out of here."

Finally arriving back at his rooms at the Exchange Hotel, Brit was thinking over the events of the evening. How could he tell Narcissa and Mirrie about Sophie and her games, about Archer Langdon and Watkins and their undignified flight through the window? How could he tell them about Pauline Avery, who had told him to go away, even as her eyes, her whole manner, beckoned him to come closer? Sometimes he got so caught up in the game, he forgot there were players more experienced, and much more accomplished, than he.

He thrust that thought aside to focus on what he had learned, and what steps he would take next. He would find out about the warehouses Ragsdale had bought, find out how much tobacco was stored in them, and what other things — several thousand pairs of shoes? — might be stored in them as well. He would try to figure out a way to help Coffin: if Pauline Avery should happen to be very grateful to him, well, he could hardly help that. And he would avoid the plug-ugly Miller and his light-o'-love Sophie Dunbar.

CHAPTER SEVEN

TUESDAY, MAY 20

Narcissa arrived at the hospital early in the morning, intending to help with the doling-out of breakfast, but a note left for her there the previous evening made her change course. It was from Aurelia Harrald, asking to be inoculated.

Narcissa sent for Judah Daniel to come along. As they walked, Narcissa told what she had heard. She ended by asking Judah Daniel, "You don't think — do you? — that Stone or Coffin could have killed Benjy?"

Judah Daniel took a minute to reply. "Benjy was hiding them boys who stole from the pest-house. I'm just about sure it was Timmy Terry and Sam Evans. Their mothers is both scared — though they got different ways of showing it. Got different reasons, too, maybe. Sam, he been seen in

the street. Timmy . . . well, his mother
. . ." Judah Daniel shook her head slowly,
as if to indicate that Cassie Terry was
capable of anything.

Narcissa thought about this. "So Benjy
was killed because he was hiding them?"

Judah Daniel looked away, frowning.
"Them boys know who killed Benjy, I'll be
bound."

"We could look for their hiding place,"
Narcissa suggested.

Judah Daniel nodded. "Reckon they
ain't gone too far from their homes.
Reckon they hiding someplace in Butchertown."

"Well, it's about time to check on the
inoculations. In those that were successful,
the pocks will be forming at the inoculation site. This time, let's go together."

When Narcissa and Judah Daniel arrived
at the Harralds', they found Aurelia white-
faced but resolute. They followed her into
her private sitting room, where Aurelia
unfastened her bodice and bared her left
arm from shoulder to elbow. Narcissa,
smelling salts at the ready, sat at Aurelia's
right and tried to distract her with small
talk while Judah Daniel scraped a coin-
sized patch of skin off her arm, patted the

blood away, and affixed a preserved scab to the open wound.

By the time the procedure was finished, Aurelia's skin had a greenish tinge, and she said to them, "Now leave me, please; I will join you downstairs."

As Narcissa and Judah Daniel went out into the hall, the sound of retching could be heard behind them. Aurelia had not exaggerated her horror of inoculation. Narcissa wondered if she should go back and offer to help, but decided that a witness to her distress would be the last thing Aurelia wanted.

Judah Daniel left then to return to the hospital. Narcissa waited in the Harrald's front parlor, relieved to think that Aurelia should be safe now from smallpox. At last Aurelia returned, still pale-faced but composed. Narcissa rose, expecting a polite dismissal from Aurelia. Instead, Aurelia had the servant Jensie bring tea. Narcissa sat down again, and Aurelia seated herself next to her.

Aurelia sat very straight. She reached up to tuck a loose strand of hair behind her ear, then clasped her hands together on her lap. "I want to tell you the truth," she said, looking down at her hands. "There *was* a woman who may have visited Josiah. A

231

prostitute. I . . . and you . . . we are not supposed to know about such women. But my brother made her what she was, and linked her to him, and to my family, forever, by getting her with child."

Aurelia was now staring off across the room. Why did Aurelia feel the need to tell her this — that Josiah had fathered an illegitimate child — especially as the disclosure was so obviously painful? Narcissa tried to think of something to say that would relieve Aurelia's embarrassment, but before she could speak, Aurelia went on.

"You wanted to know about the money Josiah had in the hospital, about who might have known it was there. Well, she could have known — it could have been for her. Pauline Avery."

Narcissa was too shocked to respond. *Pauline Avery?* Coffin Avery was Josiah Harrald's son?

"It was years ago," Aurelia said, her voice flat. "I have not seen the woman in years, and the boy, never. He is a young man now, about the age of Stansbury. I only found out about him when Josiah fell ill. A dreadful woman came here, asking for the payments. Not — the mother. A slatternly woman Josiah was paying to keep the boy. I gave her some money, just to —

to make her go away. I didn't believe it at first. Then I thought back over things I had heard, arguments between Josiah and my father, and Josiah and Aaron. At last I decided it was true. But the woman hasn't come back. . . ."

Narcissa said nothing. It seemed impossible. But — why should she think so? Children like Coffin had mothers, and fathers, at least in the biological sense of the word, though the behavior of the parents may resemble that of alley cats. So Coffin Avery could certainly be Josiah's son . . . Thaddeus's grandson . . . Aurelia's nephew, and Aaron's, at least as close to them in blood as Stansbury Harrald, though not privileged to bear the family name.

Narcissa asked, "Do you remember the name of the woman who came to you?"

Aurelia nodded. "It was an Irish name. Terry, that was it. Carrie — no, Cassie — Cassie Terry." Aurelia shuddered. "She stank of cheap brandy."

Narcissa realized then that it was true. Coffin Avery had boarded with Cassie Terry, until his father Josiah fell ill and the payments to Cassie stopped. Maybe Cassie had thrown Coffin out of the house, but in any case, the boy preferred living on the street to being boarded with her. To think that he had been consigned to that filthy hovel when his blood kinsman and sworn enemy, Stone, lived in this fine house. That was something to fight about, indeed. But there was nothing to indicate Coffin knew who his father was.

Even if he knew, what could he do about it? What claim could he make on his father, when his mother was a prostitute? She, Narcissa, knew a good deal more about prostitutes than anyone would expect a lady to know. The diseases they carried were not mentioned among ladies, but nurses came to know about them. From overhearing the doctors, Narcissa knew that syphilis was treated with mercury; gonorrhea, with astringent injections — men screamed through this procedure more loudly than through amputations, and the doctors seemed reluctant to blunt their suffering with chloroform, probably believing the afflicted soldiers deserved to be punished. The consequences to the men's wives, and to their future children, could be terrible. Considering the horrors of the diseases and their treatments, she wondered that men continued to seek the companionship of women whose embrace was likely to poison them.

Would a woman who was not careful of herself with these diseases also take risks with exposure to smallpox? With this thought, it occurred to Narcissa that Aurelia's disclosure had not answered all her questions. If Josiah had had the money with him to give to Pauline, where did he get it? and why did Pauline not take it?

As Narcissa struggled to gather her thoughts, a floorboard creaked across the room. Aurelia whirled around to stare at the door leading to the next room. It stood a few inches open, but Narcissa, who was facing it, had seen no one passing. By the time Aurelia turned back, Narcissa had decided not to question her further. Aurelia had shown real courage today in accepting inoculation and in telling her of her family's shame. It was pointless and cruel to ask more of her. But there was one thing that Aurelia had to know.

"About the boy — do you know where he is now?"

Aurelia shook her head.

"In Castle Godwin. Not because he has done anything wrong — not more than the other boys who fight with the Cats — but because he has no place to go, no one to speak for him."

"Did he not kill that boy, then, that

slave?" Aurelia had gone very white again.

"No." Narcissa shook her head. "Benjy was killed long before that shot was fired."

Aurelia sagged wearily against the horsehair sofa. She looked relieved, but also exhausted. Narcissa summoned the servant to see to Aurelia, then took her leave.

Would Aurelia find it in her heart to do anything for Coffin? Narcissa wondered as she walked away from the Harralds' dark house, into the warm sunlight and caressing breeze. In the corner of the yard were three or four rosebushes, scraggly and untended, but bearing aloft a profusion of scarlet blooms. She stepped over to them, cradled a blossom in her hand, and bent down to inhale its fragrance. As she did so, she heard a little scuffle behind her, then *"Whsst!"*

Narcissa knew it was a mark of her own increasing secretiveness that she didn't turn right around in response to the low whistle. Instead she straightened slowly, looked around as if taking in the scene, and only then glanced over her shoulder in the direction of the noise. Stone was peering around the side of the house.

"Meet me at Pizzini's!" he called in a low voice, then disappeared.

★ ★ ★

A short walk brought Narcissa to the town's best confectioner's, where Stone was already waiting with his selection of candy sticks. "She'll pay," he said to the dark-haired Pizzini cousin behind the counter. Narcissa obligingly dug a half-dollar bill out of her reticule and set it on the counter, not waiting for change.

They walked out onto the sidewalk. Stone held out the bag for her to help herself, but the sight of his grubby fingers made her decline. He thrust the bag into his pocket without taking any himself and set off down the sidewalk, Narcissa close behind.

"Is it true, what you said to Aunt Aurelia?"

"I — I don't know what you mean." The fact that Josiah had had an illegitimate child was Aurelia's secret to keep or to tell. To have it found out this way . . .

"Benjy was shot before the fight?" Stone asked.

With a little sigh of relief, Narcissa answered, "Yes. Coffin was not guilty."

"So he will be released?" Stone was frowning; was he disappointed to see his rival escape further punishment?

"I assume so."

Stone stopped abruptly. He looked as if

he were going to be sick. "The day of the fight — I fired that shot."

Narcissa looked at him, wondering what she should say.

"When I heard you tell Aunt Aurelia that somebody was killed, a slave boy, I thought I did it."

He looked up at her then, his face a picture of misery. "I thought I should confess, but . . . when you told me I should put myself in Coffin's place . . . I couldn't go to Castle Godwin! I just" — he swallowed, looked away — "I just couldn't."

There was no point now in saying she hadn't meant it literally — no point explaining that, even if he had told the truth, Stone would never have had to take Coffin's place in jail.

"The pistol was one of Uncle Josiah's. I knew how to load it. I watched him do it lots of times. I got it out of the cabinet that morning. I pointed it up, I just wanted to scare them, but — the noise — it seemed to blast all around me, and I dropped the pistol, and — I ran. I just wanted you to know."

Stone stuck his hands in his pockets and, apparently reminded, muttered, "Thanks for the candy." Then he set off at a run up the hill.

Narcissa stood looking after him. It seemed that Stone had heard only the last part of her conversation with Aurelia. He didn't know that Coffin, the boy he despised, was his close relative. Still, she felt uneasy. If Aaron and Thaddeus got wind of the secret Aurelia was keeping, the storm would break over Aurelia's head.

At the Powerses' house, Narcissa found Brit Wallace waiting. He hurried up to her before she had even gotten her bonnet off, took her arm, and hurried her off to the back parlor, where Mirrie was sitting, an expectant look on her face.

Brit took his favorite spot on the hearth rug and began rocking back and forth, heel-to-toe. "I've found no one in the uniform-buying business who admits to purchasing a smallpox-infected uniform jacket from a young boy. And since I offered a substantial bribe, I think I *might* have heard if such a thing was done. But, listen to this: Roland Ragsdale's been buying up tobacco warehouses. He's been buying up goods — like shoes." He glanced down in the direction of his own ruined pair. "He has connections in the passport office, and he has connections among the blockade-runners. He's up to something, no doubt of that."

Narcissa's heart sank. She was thinking of Aurelia. It seemed more sorrow was coming her way.

"And listen to this," Brit went on. "I spent hours in the courthouse today looking up deeds. One of the warehouses belonged to the Harralds! The money that Josiah had in the hospital may have come from Ragsdale. He's owned the building for almost a year now, but Josiah's been away, so —"

That, at least, Narcissa could respond to. "Aaron Harrald has been managing the family finances for the year that Josiah has been away. It's more likely the money was paid to him. I heard that from Aaron's mistress," she added, turning a little pink.

"Well!" Brit's eyebrows went up. He leaned against the mantelpiece. "Whether it was a good decision on Aaron's part remains to be seen. If Ragsdale manages to hold the tobacco and sell it at the right time, well and good. If the worst comes to the worst, the tobacco will go up in smoke — or down into the drink — and Aaron Harrald will have won the toss. But I'd put my money on Ragsdale. He's a thriving example of that noxious species, the army worm."

Narcissa hesitated. It sounded as if Brit Wallace was about to get himself in trouble with the local authorities once again. Still, Ragsdale's manipulations angered her as well. Finally she asked, "What he's doing may be wrong, but what can *you* do, if the provost marshal's office ignores it?"

"Write about it, for my British readers," Brit answered loftily. "If there's one thing the Confederate government is united on, it's wanting the good opinion of England."

Mirrie got up then and left the room, returning in a moment with an envelope in her hand. "Speaking of Ragsdale, this came for you today." She handed the envelope to Narcissa. "It has both our names on it, but it's really for you, of course."

Narcissa lifted the seal with her thumbnail and drew out a folded piece of paper — of such quality, she couldn't but notice, as was rarely found in shops these days. A few handwritten lines stated that Ragsdale planned to make his gift of ten thousand dollars to the Confederate hospitals on Friday — three days from now; and he was requesting their presence at a buffet supper. At the bottom of the page, Ragsdale had signed his name with a flourish worthy of John Hancock.

She handed the paper to Mirrie, who scrutinized it through her pince-nez, then said, "Mr. Ragsdale fancies himself a man who gets what he wants. But that does not oblige *you* to be at his beck and call."

"May I?" Brit took the letter from Mirrie and read it, a grin spreading across his face.

Narcissa was considering what Mirrie had said. "And you?" If Mirrie would not accompany her, perhaps the Stedmans . . .

Mirrie laughed dryly. "It's not me he's interested in. Although certainly I will go, if you insist on doing so. Why not write him and say that it is not convenient for you to come on Friday? Perhaps he will relent and simply give the money to the hospitals, rather than insisting on a grand presentation."

"It is no trouble," Narcissa had replied mildly, "for me to spend an hour or so in Mr. Ragsdale's parlor, listening to speeches about his generosity. It will benefit the hospitals, and it certainly will not harm me. I'm sure Dr. and Mrs. Stedman will be there. . . ." She glanced at Brit, expecting him to offer to escort her and Mirrie, but he seemed not to be listening.

When Brit spoke again, it was on a different subject. "Coffin Avery is still in Castle Godwin, despite Archer's verdict on the timing of Benjy's death. They are claiming it's because he has nowhere to go, no one to claim custody."

"I have an idea about that," Narcissa said slowly. "I believe that, if it were handled carefully, the Harralds might be persuaded to take Coffin into their home. The truth is, Stone Harrald fired that shot. He told me so himself. I think he is ready to own up to it."

"Didn't I say so?" Brit gloated briefly, then put on a repentant face.

"Stone puts great store by his *honor*," Narcissa went on, exchanging a knowing glance with Mirrie. "It may be that he can persuade Aurelia to help him make up for his lapse. Whether the two of them can persuade Aaron and Thaddeus . . . But there is an even more important reason for them to help Coffin Avery. Aurelia told me: Josiah Harrald was Coffin's father. Josiah was paying Cassie Terry to keep the boy. Cassie Terry called on Aurelia to ask for money. Aurelia was too shocked by the news to respond. But Aurelia told me that Pauline may have been the woman who called on Josiah in the hospital."

Brit spoke then. "I talked to Pauline

243

Avery, two nights ago now. She never told me who Coffin's father was. She cares about the boy, very much" — Narcissa saw Mirrie roll her eyes — "but she cannot have him with her, of course."

"Where did you find her?" Narcissa asked eagerly. "I need to see her, to find out if she visited Josiah. She may have been exposed to smallpox. And she may know about the money."

Brit hesitated. "Do you really think —" he began, but the expression on Narcissa's face silenced him. "Well, she can be found at the Golden Arrow, but I hardly think — No, really, Mrs. Powers, stop frowning at me like that! It really is impossible for you to go there."

Narcissa spoke calmly, keeping her exasperation in check. "I am a nurse, Mr. Wallace. I am charged with preventing an epidemic of smallpox. Isn't that more important than protecting my delicate sensibilities?"

Brit paused, apparently weighing the question, but finally said, "Very well. You may run into Mr. Ragsdale there; apparently Pauline Avery is a particular *friend* of his. But I can tell you, she shows no sign of smallpox, and there's certainly no quarantine been imposed. Can't we put our efforts into getting Coffin out of jail?"

Narcissa thought it over. "I will call on Pauline Avery first thing in the morning. You and I can meet at Castle Godwin in the afternoon, after dinner. If I cannot persuade the Harralds to take him in, we will bring him here." She glanced at Mirrie as she said this. When Mirrie nodded, Narcissa smiled her thanks, grateful that Mirrie would agree so easily to taking a wild Cat into the house.

CHAPTER EIGHT

WEDNESDAY, MAY 21

On further reflection, Narcissa chose mid-morning as the best time to call on Pauline Avery. She figured it would be quietest then, the male visitors of the night before having slunk off to wherever it was they were supposed to be, and preparations for the coming night not yet begun. Despite her bold resolve, Narcissa could not deny that she felt uncomfortable, even guilty. She had an open and honorable motive for calling on Pauline: to offer the protection of smallpox inoculation. She also had a motive that, though concealed, was no less honorable — to find out whether this woman, wearing a red dress, had visited Josiah Harrald. But Pauline Avery had been Josiah's mistress, had borne his son. Pauline's story was as much of a tragedy as Serena Warren's . . . more so.

A sleepy-eyed young maidservant let Narcissa in. "Mrs. Powers, to see Miss Avery," Narcissa said. "It's a personal matter," she added, though the servant had not asked.

The servant returned after a few minutes. "You can come on up," she said carelessly, and led the way, not waiting for an answer.

The maid led her up a grand staircase, worthy of a hotel or private home aspiring to grandeur, and down a dark hall that smelled unpleasantly of stale liquor and perfume. She stopped at the last door and knocked. It was opened by a dark-haired woman dressed in a quite incredible wrapper of pink silk, trimmed with pink and orange. The ensemble would have made most any woman look like a sofa pillow, but this woman — tall, slim, ivory-skinned — could carry it off. The woman — Pauline, no doubt — met Narcissa's gaze with a wryly mocking expression that said, *Do you like what you see?* But her actual words were, "Was it quite necessary to call at this hour?"

Narcissa apologized, red-faced and awkward. This was going to be more difficult than she had imagined. "I am a nurse at the medical college hospital," she explained. Pauline's eyebrows climbed a fraction higher. "There was a smallpox case about three weeks ago, a man who — whom you may have met. Josiah Harrald."

A slight widening of Pauline's eyes, a trembling of the lips, showed Narcissa that her guess was correct. "You visited him in the hospital after his amputation, did you not?"

Pauline gave a thin-lipped smile. "Why would I do that?" She had her hand on the door now as if prepared to close it.

There might not be time to say much more; she had to make her words count. "I believe you have been exposed to smallpox, and that your son, Coffin, may have been exposed as well. I know he has had the disease, but —"

"Go back to your hand-holding and Bible reading. *I* have no need of a nurse." Pauline shut the door, not gently, in Narcissa's face.

Narcissa hurried back down the stairs, indignation burning her cheeks as hot as if Pauline Avery had slapped her. The maidservant's derisive glance had the effect of strengthening her resolve. Narcissa walked right up to the young black woman and said, "There have been instances of smallpox in town. Do you know of any such in this house, or among the . . . visitors?"

The servant shook her head. "We was all inoculated. Mr. Ragsdale ordered it."

This was interesting news. Why had Pauline not mentioned it? "How long ago was this?"

The servant considered. "About a year ago, I reckon. About the time we come here from Norfolk."

"But none of you was sick with smallpox?" Narcissa persisted, though the servant was looking away, clearly impatient with the questions.

"No'm, like I told you," was the terse response.

Narcissa gave up. "If you do hear of anyone sick with smallpox, please — what is your name?"

"Liza," said the girl.

"If you do, Liza, send word to the medical college hospital. We can help you."

The servant's eyes shifted, and she smiled, needing no words to express her disbelief.

Narcissa walked out of the house and into the street, oblivious now to her surroundings. Ragsdale had been concerned about smallpox a year ago. She had learned that much, at least, from her visit to Pauline Avery.

It was midafternoon when Narcissa arrived at the Harralds' to find that Stone had already broached the subject of their taking in Coffin Avery. Aaron seemed surprisingly uninterested; though Narcissa examined his face closely, looking for signs of guilty knowledge, she could not tell whether he knew Coffin was in fact his nephew. Aurelia's distress showed on her face — she had dark circles under her eyes and a weary droop to her shoulders — but she appeared resigned, at least, to having Coffin stay in their home. No one mentioned Thaddeus, and Narcissa wondered whether they had told the old man — though surely they could not keep Coffin's presence a secret from him.

They met Brit Wallace sheltering from the rain in the building's little entranceway. After introductions, he spoke in an aside to Narcissa. "They know about the necropsy report Dr. Archer did on Benjy. I don't think they" — he nodded toward the jailers — "can refuse to release Coffin, as long as the Harralds have agreed to take him in."

"Did you say *Archer?*" Aaron glared at

Brit. "Cameron Archer? Is he involved in this?"

Narcissa took a step toward Aaron. "He is involved only because I asked him to examine the body of Benjy — the boy who was shot. Dr. Archer did so, and that is how we know that Benjy died much earlier than the Cat fight."

"Oh, well, then . . . I suppose . . ." Aaron's anger subsided into disgruntlement.

They walked into Castle Godwin — Brit and Narcissa in the lead, followed by Stone, with Aurelia and Aaron bringing up the rear.

The red-faced farmer-turned-jailer looked surprised to see Brit accompanied by such an entourage. As Brit explained to him their errand, the jailer turned to stare at Stone.

"Why don't you keep *me* here," Stone said to him, as if he had suddenly come up with an idea that would please everyone, "in Coffin's place? Keep the leader of the Hill gang an equal length of time as the leader of the Butchertown gang."

Narcissa heard Aurelia gasp.

"Don't reckon there's any need of that," the jailer mumbled, sounding disappointed to turn down the offer. "So, let me see: you folks are willing to take custody of this boy, Coffin Avery" — as he said the name, he looked at Aaron and Aurelia as if to make sure they understood who it was they were taking on. "*You,*" he said to Stone, who stepped back from the jailer's scowling gaze, "say it was you fired that old horse-pistol."

"Yes, sir — can we have it back? It belonged to my uncle."

The jailer ignored Stone's question. "And *you*" — the jailer's eyes were on Narcissa this time — "got this here army surgeon to examine that dead nigger and say he died a day or more before the Cats had their fight."

Narcissa nodded.

The jailer sighed loudly. "All right, then." He turned to a younger man who carried a dozen keys on a chain around his waist. "Bring out Coffin."

As the Harralds signed papers, Stone stood, straight-backed, waiting for the first sight of his old enemy. When Coffin appeared, looking thin and sallow, Stone marched up to him like a soldier. "I fired that shot," he said, "and I dropped the pistol. I didn't mean to hurt anybody, but I did — I sent you to jail with my cowardice. I'm sorry. I want you to come home with me, to stay . . . for a while."

Coffin looked stunned. He looked around at the assembled group — at Brit and Narcissa, who were smiling encouragingly, and at Aaron and Aurelia, who were stony-faced — as if debating whether Castle Godwin might be preferable. At last he shrugged. "I reckon I will."

At last, after several days of trying, Judah Daniel found Cassie Terry at home. Whether Cassie had been away, or just too drunk to come to the door, she couldn't tell. The door swung open at Judah Daniel's knock, and she let herself in. The room reeked of alcohol. Cassie sat slumped in her chair. She turned toward Judah Daniel — turned her whole head, very slowly, as if a sudden movement might jar it loose.

"Get out of my house," Cassie growled.

Judah Daniel knew Cassie wanted to scare her off, but it was hard to be scared of a woman who could barely sit up and whose eyes were rolling in her head like peas on a plate. Judah Daniel stood her ground. "I need to check the places on your children's arms," she told Cassie, wondering if Cassie was sober enough to understand.

Cassie's frown deepened, and she rasped, "They's sick. You done something to them."

Judah Daniel felt a stab of fear. Inoculations did produce some fever. But what if the inoculations had been too late, what if Cassie's children had come down with smallpox? She hid her dismay and spoke firmly. "What I done was to keep them from getting the smallpox. Now I got to see them."

Cassie stared for a moment, her eyes little boot buttons in her bloated face. Her jaw worked as if she was getting ready to fight back, to press her accusation that Judah Daniel had harmed her children. Poor whites like Cassie — Judah Daniel didn't call them trash, but other people did — were quick to feel picked-on. They were quick to protest it, too, when they could afford to — and often when they couldn't afford to, when their anger and violence would get them locked up by the police.

At last Cassie muttered, "Do what you want," and pointed to a curtained-off part of the room.

Judah Daniel walked over and pulled back the curtain — a filthy sheet hung from the ceiling. There Cassie's children were lying huddled together, plainly sick, but not badly afflicted. It looked as if the inoculations had taken. The bad news was, Timmy was nowhere in sight.

Rose, the oldest, sat up and stared at Judah Daniel with an I-dare-you look that resembled her mother's. Judah Daniel went to her first and saw that the inoculation had produced a raised pustule on the arm, as well as a few scattered pocks on Rose's chest and back. "These spots itch like hellfire," Rose spat at Judah Daniel, who handed her a pot of salve and showed her how to use it. Judah Daniel then checked the rest of the children, five of them, down to the littlest, the girl that Cassie had said was almost three.

At last Judah Daniel went over to where Cassie was sitting. "You got to keep these children clean, give 'em water to drink, and good beef tea. If you don't, the scabs won't be worth nothing to the medical college," she added, hoping the threat would get Cassie's attention. "Now, I ain't seen Timmy."

"Can't get that boy to stay home," Cassie mumbled.

Judah Daniel folded her arms across her chest and stared down at Cassie. "How long's it been since you seen him?"

Cassie frowned. "I sent him out. . . ." Her eyes wandered over to the corner of the room, where Judah Daniel could see a whole collection of bottles, some empty, but a few filled with a cloudy-looking, amber-colored liquid. From the look of it, and the smell in the room, it was the rotgut brandy called applejack.

"Sent him for liquor?" Judah Daniel finished Cassie's thought. "When was that?" Had it been before or after the theft from the smallpox hospital? Was it possible Timmy had given his mother some of the money he and Sam had stolen?

Cassie twisted away from the question. "I got to have it," she whined. "When I can't get it, the pain's so bad, I feel like I'm going to die." She shrunk into her chair as if she could see the pain across the room, coming for her. "He tore me all up inside, when he kicked me. I didn't drink none before that."

Big dog gone, little dog get the bone, Judah Daniel thought. Now that Cassie's last man was dead, she was having her turn, seeking pleasure or at least numbness in alcohol. It looked like Cassie had done well for herself, boarding hired-out slaves like Benjy and whites with no place else to go, like Coffin Avery. But Benjy had been killed and Coffin taken to jail. Yet Cassie had money to buy liquor, even when it was illegal, and so more costly than usual.

"You done lost your two boarders. How'd you get money to buy liquor?

Cassie's slack mouth stretched in a smile. Then she turned away and settled her head onto the back of the chair.

Judah Daniel sighed. "I'll come see you, bring some medicine. If you see Timmy . . . Cassie?"

Cassie was sleeping, eyes closed and mouth open.

Judah Daniel snorted with exasperation. Then she went back to where the children were lying and crouched down beside Rose. "Rose, where's Timmy? I got to know. I reckon he got the smallpox."

Rose looked away from her. "I ain't seen him."

"You got to do what I say. If you don't, I'll tell the doctors and the police too" — Rose shrank from her at the word *police* — "that one of you got the smallpox. They'll put you in the jail where they put sick folks who won't do what they's told."

Seeing she had Rose's attention, she went on. "You got to stay here, in your house — not go out, and not have other children come here."

Rose shrugged, "We ain't been out since I can remember. And don't nobody come here, ever."

Judah Daniel went on. "If your ma can stay here too, and not go out, that'd be best." At least Cassie's got enough liquor to hold her for a while, she added to herself. "If she does go out, she's got to wash herself and put on clean clothes. If the police see her out in them clothes, she'll go to jail for sure, for breaking quarantine."

She knew she was taking a chance. But she had no proof of her suspicion that Timmy had stolen the tainted money from the smallpox hospital, and that he had given at least some of it to his mother. With nothing but a suspicion, she could not convince the police to impose quarantine on the Terry house. But this unofficial quarantine, if it worked, might keep the family from spreading the smallpox further. "I'm going to bring y'all something to eat, and some medicine. You got to promise me you'll hold out."

Rose seemed to have taken it all in. "Yes'm, we promise."

CHAPTER NINE

THURSDAY, MAY 22

"Halloo! Mr. Wallace!"

Brit looked up to see two boys running toward him — Coffin and Stone, with Popcracker bounding delightedly alongside. Brit stopped and waited. Boys and dog skidded to a halt in front of him. Popcracker, his earlier fright forgotten, pushed his head under Brit's hand. Brit obliged the mongrel by scratching his ears.

"Popcracker's happy you've made peace," he remarked to the boys.

Coffin nodded. "He weren't easy about it at first. He ain't never seen the good side of a Shockoe Hill Cat — uh, boy," he amended, *cat* being an insult reserved for the enemy.

"He likes me now," Stone declared happily, throwing an arm around Popcracker's neck and receiving a sloppy kiss in return.

"Where'd the name come from?" Brit asked Coffin.

"Oh, he come up with a soldier from the trenches at Yorktown. They used to tie things around his neck, Rebels and Yanks, tobacco and coffee, things like that; trade 'em back and forth across the lines. But when the shooting commenced, he'd run hide. So they called him Popcracker because he hated the sound so much." Coffin was grinning; then the smile faded. "When the soldier got shot, Popcracker wouldn't leave him. Come all the way up here to the hospital. Just before he died, the soldier gave Popcracker to Benjy. But Cassie Terry wouldn't let Benjy keep him, the witch." Coffin scratched Popcracker's ears. "So me and my boys looked after him. And he belongs to all of us, now. Reckon if he could go back and forth between the Rebels and the Yanks, he can go back and forth between the Butcher gang and the Hill gang."

"Ha! A brave dog. And how about your friends, are they pleased to have the truce in effect?"

"They don't know yet. We've got a big surprise planned," Stone announced. "We're going to get them all together, not knowing it's us, you know, and then jump out. Some fun!"

Brit smiled. Then a thought struck him. The boys were all over town, no one paid any attention to them — unless the bricks were flying: they would make excellent spies. "Well, when you've made peace between your factions, I have a job for you. There's a bad man around town, Roland Ragsdale. He's one of the ones responsible for the high prices people complain about, and he may be behind the thefts from the smallpox hospital. I want you to watch the places where he goes: his home, his warehouse down in Butchertown" — Brit left off the Golden Eagle; the Cats' mothers would never forgive him setting their sons to spy on a brothel. He described the locations, and Ragsdale's appearance. "If you see anything suspicious, I want you to report to me at the Exchange Hotel."

Coffin straightened up and gave a mock salute, but his face was serious. "You think this Ragsdale had something to do with Benjy being shot?"

Brit returned his solemn gaze. "I think he might have. And so you must be very careful. Don't let him see what you are up to, and don't follow him. Just play among yourselves as you ordinarily would, but keep your eyes open. All right?"

Coffin nodded, and Stone called out, "We'll do it," then motioned to his friend. "Come on!" They ran off, waving and calling their farewells, Popcracker at their heels.

In the alley behind the free school on Marshall Street, hidden from view in a little space between two buildings, the Butcher Cats were hunkered down around a pile of stones and broken bricks that reached waist-high on the shortest of them. The shortest was Ise, Sam Evans's younger brother, a skinny, wide-eyed, dark-skinned boy five years old. The largest — and therefore the leader, in Coffin's absence — was Michael O'Brien, called the Majer, aged ten, who even in these thin times managed to have some heft to him. The Majer wore a peaked cap pulled down low over his blunt-featured face, sandy hair sticking out all around. His gray-blue eyes were alight with anger. Reproductions on a smaller scale were his younger brothers, Patrick and Dennis, sandy-haired twins called the Soljers.

The Majer sat on his haunches; the others mimicked him. "Look what they done to us," he said in a low voice. "Coffin ain't done nothing, but they keep him in jail. Benjy's dead."

One of the Soljers licked his lips nervously and started to cross himself. His fellow Soljer gave him a cuff that tipped him onto his bottom. It looked for a moment as if a fight would break out between the two of them, but a glance from the Majer quelled it.

"And Timmy and Sam is missing," continued the Majer. Ise looked as if he might start crying again. The Majer went on hastily, "And them Hill Cats sits up there and laughs at us! They done sent us a challenge." He pulled out a grubby piece of brown paper, written on in pencil. *"Come out at four o'clock today,"* he read. "Maybe they expect us to turn tail and run. But we ain't going to do it!" With these words he rose to his feet and punched his fist into the air.

The younger boys jumped up and imitated him. The fist of one of the Soljers grazed the arm of the other, who wound up to deliver a punch in retaliation. The Majer pulled his cap off and whacked them both with it, then settled it back on his head.

"Still, might be there's more of them

than there is of us. Might be they got guns. So I got a plan. I seed that old broken-down cart blocking up the end of the alley, that's what got me to thinking of it. Me and the Soljers, we been constructing emplacements like this all along the alley. We get them chasing one of us into this alley, with the rest of us manning the emplacements, like. They's caught —"

"Like rats," one of the Soljers muttered appreciatively.

"— and we hammers 'em." The Majer was grinning. "We got emplacements there, there, and there." He pointed. "Ise, you get them to chase you in here. Run all the way to the end, *there*." He pointed again. "Duck in at the last minute." He looked around the little group. "Don't start shelling till I give the signal. Now, you all understand what you supposed to do?"

The littler boys nodded. Ise looked as if he might have reservations about his role as rabbit to hounds, but he kept them to himself.

At Pizzini's, the Hill Cats were eating candy and planning their attack.

"Looks like Stone's not going to show

up. That makes me leader," Nat McClennan asserted with easy self-importance, looking down his patrician nose at the others. He was half a head taller than the rest, as well as the oldest, having recently turned twelve.

Charles McMurray, Jr., protested, his black eyes sparking. "You don't even live here, really! Your family's from Norfolk. *I* should be leader. Anyway, I'm the one they sent the challenge to."

"*My* father's a colonel," Nat snapped back. "Don't forget that, Junior." He added, a little more kindly, "You can be leader next year when I join up with the Young Guard."

Junior McMurray sneered. "Your mama won't even let you wear long pants!"

Nat blushed with anger. "She will! It's just her dressmaker refugeed to North Carolina."

"Our father outranks yours," piped up Spider Jones. "Yeah," his brother — called the Sharpshooter — agreed.

Nat scowled. "If you want to be leader, you're going to have to fight me for it. Who wants to go first?"

After a few moments of looking up into Nat's fiercely frowning face, the others backed down.

"Now that we're *agreed*" — Nat drew out the last word, looking around into their faces — "here's my plan. This challenge, come out at four o'clock: we better take for granted it's a trick. They've tried tricks before — stealing from the smallpox hospital! They wanted to hurt us, but they weren't smart enough. Now one of them is dead and a couple others may be sick. Their leader Coffin — a thief and a liar — was caught with a gun last time we met, and put in jail."

Nat's hazel eyes were cold as he looked around the assembled boys who stood listening, treats forgotten. "They'll try some trickery, of course. But it won't do them any good, because this time *we'll* have the pistol." He reached into his jacket and drew out a boot pistol a little longer than a man's hand. "We'll make them afraid to come troubling us. We'll make them pay for what they've done!"

Junior looked incredulous. "How'd you get that?"

"Easy. My father brought it to my mama, told her to use it to protect herself if the Yankees come."

Junior frowned. "It's not right. Somebody could get killed."

Nat's mouth twisted. "Somebody

already has. We were fortunate it wasn't one of us."

The other boys looked at each other. One by one their expressions hardened from doubt to certainty.

Nat spoke again. "It rang three o'clock a while ago, and now it's looking like rain. I say we get up on the hill where we can see what's happening down below. When they come out, we'll pelt 'em some, but fall back, like they've got us whipped. When they're just about to cross into our territory, I'll bring out the gun, just wave it around, shoot into the air maybe, scare them. They run like Hades, and we're left in possession of the field."

The other boys looked at Junior, who seemed to be thinking it over. "Very well," he said at last. Nat clapped him on the shoulder.

"Let's go down there now," said the Sharpshooter, crunching the last of his candy stick and wiping his hands on his pants. Nat leading the way, the boys streamed out into the street, chanting war whoops with their palms closing and opening over their mouths Indian-style.

"Quiet down!" Nat warned them in a stage whisper. "Don't give the alarm. We'll separate, but keep within sight of each other. If you see any of the Butcher Cats, give the signal." He stared at each boy in turn. Spider saluted briskly. Nat returned the salute. The boys swarmed away.

A half-hour later, Spider and the Sharpshooter had their heads together, apparently plotting desertion. Junior was playing on the iron fence that ran around the Egyptian building. Nat himself was leaning against one of the big pillars, arms folded across his chest, looking down the hill. All at once Nat's gaze fixed on something, and he jumped up, arms pinwheeling in a come-here-quick gesture. First Junior, then in a moment Spider and the Sharpshooter, saw his signal, jumped up, and began running toward Nat. In a moment all four boys were running down the hill, closing on Ise, who stood frozen. Suddenly he broke and ran, bare feet slamming the dirt. He was headed straight for the alley where the Butcher Cats waited.

In the alley, Ise slowed, looking around him. Then he put his head down again and ran, arms pumping, straight toward the broken-down cart that blocked the way. At the last minute he pulled up, turned, and slipped through loose boards into a shed bordering the alley. As he did so, the first brick flew, launched from the Majer's hiding place. The brick sailed across the eight-foot breadth of the alley, smashed against the opposite wall, and exploded into pieces. The war whoops of the Butcher Cats rose, echoing off the walls, mingling with the screams of fear from the Hill Cats as they realized they were trapped.

"I've got a pistol!" Nat held the revolver out at arm's length, his intention to fire into the air apparently forgotten. Some of the boys scrambled for cover, while others froze. Judging by their reactions, Nat's friends were as frightened as his enemies by the sight of the wild-eyed Nat and his pistol.

"Butcher gang! Hold your fire! It's me, Coffin!"

"Pax, boys! Jesus, Nat — watch what you do with that pistol! You're pointing it at me!"

The Hill Cats and the Butcher Cats froze in their places, looking around for the source of the voices. At last they looked up, at the top of the abandoned cart, where an ill-assorted pair of boys was standing, one pockmarked, small, and skinny, the other handsome, tall, and well nourished. Pop-cracker was beside them, barking and dancing with excitement.

Junior McMurray was the first to speak. "Jupiter, Stone, where did you come from?"

Stone laughed and jumped down from the cart. Coffin clambered down after him, Popcracker following. The Butcher Cats had come out of hiding now, and all the boys clustered around Coffin and Stone.

"Listen," Stone told them all, "we were wrong about Coffin and the Butcher Cats. Two of their boys are missing, Timmy Terry and Sam Evans. If they stole from the smallpox hospital, they didn't do it to hurt us. Now they may be lying sick somewhere."

A sob burst from Ise. Coffin put his arm around the boy's shoulders.

Nat spoke to Stone, ignoring Coffin. "If that's so, why did they put Coffin in jail?"

Stone pushed his hair back off his forehead. "They put him in jail instead of me. I fired that shot. They did it because my family has money. And that ain't fair!"

The Hill Cats stared at Stone, then exchanged looks. Spider giggled. "You're starting to talk like him!"

Stone ignored the jibe. "I reckon they're afraid of Coffin, that's why they wanted him in jail. They'd be happy for us to kill each other."

Coffin stood straight. "Butchertown boys, listen to me: the boys from the Hill is our friends now, no difference between us, for the duration. If you ain't going to accept that, get on home."

Stone looked around at the faces of the Hill Cats. "What Coffin says goes for me too. Shake on it." One by one the Hill Cats and Butcher Cats shook hands with each other.

The Majer stepped up to Nat and asked, "Can I see it — the pistol?" In a moment the other boys were crowded around, jostling each other for a glimpse of Nat's mother's pistol.

Popcracker nosed up among them, probably imagining, in the way of dogs, that the object of so much interest must be good to eat. Nat humorously held the pistol down for the dog to examine. Popcracker's body stiffened, the hair along his spine standing up in a pronounced ridge. His lips curled up over his teeth, and a low growl came from deep within his chest.

Nat stuck the pistol inside his shirt. "He's scared of it," he said, looking around at the other boys.

Stone stared thoughtfully at Popcracker. "Reckon he knows it was a gun that killed his old master — the soldier?"

Coffin nodded. "And Benjy, too — reckon Popcracker was there?" Coffin held out his hand to Popcracker, who sidled over, tail between his legs, to the boy and accepted his embrace. Coffin looked up. "Reckon he saw who it was shot Benjy?" He and Stone stared at each other for a long moment. Then Coffin buried his face in Popcracker's matted fur.

Stone turned to Nat. "We'd all feel easier if you discharged that pistol."

Nat's face lightened. He aimed the little pistol into the ground under the wagon, pulled back the hammer, and fired. The boys jumped as the sound, amplified by the small space, went through their bodies. Popcracker gave an anguished yelp and took off down the alley toward the street.

By late afternoon, the clouds were heavy, though no rain had fallen. The warm, damp air clung to Narcissa like a blanket that grew heavier with every step. She felt she would prefer Judah Daniel's looser, thinner clothes to her own well-tailored calico dress, close-fitting over layers of undergarments.

But what hung on her worse than the weather, and on Judah Daniel too no doubt, was the frustration, almost desperation, of having made no progress in their search for Timmy and Sam. They had gone down to Butchertown together, checking inoculations but also hoping to find some sign of the boys. So they were not only calling where people were at home; they were circling warehouses, sheds, houses left empty by owners who had fled the siege. They had found no cases of smallpox but a good number of successful inoculations. In those few cases in which the inoculation had not produced a pustule, they had performed the procedure a second time. As far as Timmy and Sam were concerned, they had found nothing.

As they turned onto Clay Street, Narcissa noticed a house standing a little apart from its neighbors. Its windows were shut and its curtains drawn. Tall weeds choked its pretty flower bed. "Who lives here?"

"Dressmaker," answered Judah Daniel, who had paused beside Narcissa to examine the house. "Name of Sullivan. Neighbors across the street told me she refugeed some weeks back."

They followed the untended walkway to the front door. Stuck to the door with two pins was a piece of lined paper that looked like it had been torn from a ledger. On it someone had printed in neat capitals, GONE TO NORTH CAROLINA.

"You go around to the back," Narcissa said to Judah Daniel. If the boys were hiding inside, the sound of Narcissa at the front of the house might drive them out that way. She waited a few moments, then knocked on the door, good, hard knocks that made her knuckles hurt. She waited, slapped at a mosquito buzzing near her ear, knocked again, waited.

At last Judah Daniel came back around, striding through the tall grass. "You try the door?"

Narcissa grasped the carved, well-worn doorknob, and it turned in her hand. She glanced back at Judah Daniel, glad of her presence, then swung the door open.

The smell hit her, and she gasped, stepping back into Judah Daniel. It was worse than the hospital, worse even than the smallpox ward. She fought down nausea. At last she managed to say what Judah Daniel surely knew: "Someone's died here." *Is it Sam, Timmy?* "Wait in the yard. If it's smallpox, there's no use in us both being contaminated."

Fear for the boys' fate drove Narcissa over the threshold into the dark and silent house. It was like being shut in a tomb. She couldn't breathe. Death was around her, reaching for her, pulling her down. Her head was spinning, her hands and feet felt like ice. . . . She brought her handkerchief up to cover her nose and throat, drew in a breath through the lavender-scented cotton. Gradually her head began to clear. She went to each of the three windows in turn, tying back the curtains and throwing up the sashes. Light poured in, and blessed fresh air. Now she could make out the paraphernalia of the dressmaker — the scissors, tape measures, and pincushions, the sewing machine, the bolts of material, black and a rainbow of colors — green, yellow, salmon pink, rose-red. There was a bodice pieced together, black silk . . . there, what looked like an entire dress in emerald green plaid, cut out and pinned. Narcissa walked around, looking under the tables, peering into the corners. There was no one in this room, alive or dead. But at the far end of the room was another door. She pushed it open and looked in, dreading what she would find.

The thing on the bed was so advanced in

decay that only its hair showed it had been a woman. But . . . the boys weren't here. There was nowhere for anyone to hide in the little room — not that Narcissa could imagine any human being so desperate as to take refuge in this place. She closed the door and started back across the room, then paused at the sewing table. Something about those scraps of material . . . She fingered them, wondering. The rose-red silk glowed in her hand, sparking an image in her mind: a beautiful woman in a red dress, leaning close to Josiah Harrald.

Narcissa dropped the scrap as if it had burned her. A red dress . . . Miss Sullivan had not had time to sweep away the scraps; she must have finished it just before she fell sick. But the dress — where was it?

She ran to the door and called out to Judah Daniel. "The boys aren't here, it's a woman."

Judah Daniel came closer, within a few yards of Narcissa. Her eyes moved over Narcissa's face, and Narcissa knew her distress must be showing there.

"You think she died of smallpox?" Judah Daniel asked.

Narcissa nodded, still struggling to catch

her breath and calm her racing heart. "I think so."

Judah Daniel nodded as if taking in what Narcissa was saying. "You calm yourself, now. Maybe her spirit tell you something. I'll go up to the hospital and fetch Dr. Archer."

Narcissa watched as Judah Daniel started up the hill in the direction of the medical college. She filled her lungs with air, exhaled slowly, breathed in again. Then she turned and went back into the house. She would have at least twenty minutes, she estimated, before Archer would come. But it was possible that some curious neighbor had noticed the activity and sent for the police. She had to be quick. She knew Judah Daniel was right: the dead woman could tell her — or at least, the records she had kept could tell her — the name of the woman for whom the red dress had been made.

Narcissa searched the room again, more carefully this time, peering under bolts of cloth and cut-out pieces, looking through drawers, riffling the pages of *Godey's* and *Vanity Fair*. A few more minutes of searching failed to turn up several other things whose absence was puzzling: a ledger of bills and receipts, a list of customers, and money.

Narcissa glanced at the closed door and made a grim face. She dreaded going into that room again. She tried to recall . . . yes, there had been a low dresser, with perhaps a half-dozen drawers. She should look there at least. She went over to the door and opened it, careful not to glance in the direction of the bed.

A tatted runner adorned the top of the dark-wood dresser, and on it sat an ivory-backed hand mirror, a comb, and a brush that held strands of hair, chestnut mixed with gray, that matched what she had seen on the bed. In the first drawer were some inexpensive pieces of jet and garnet jewelry, hair pins and tucking combs, gloves, handkerchiefs, little pieces of tatting and crochet — no paper at all. The second drawer held letters, yellowed with age, the sealing wax crumbling. Narcissa turned them over, but nothing resembling a ledger was among them. In the three larger drawers she found only clothes. She drew a breath through her handkerchief and hurried out of the room, closing the door behind her.

There had to be something. . . . Then she noticed a bolt of cloth hanging over the side of the big table. She pushed the bolt aside and saw what the material had hidden: a cut-out space about a foot across where a drawer had been.

The drawer lay on the floor beneath the table. She had seen it before but missed its significance. There was nothing in it, nothing under it.

She was about to go around the room again when a voice calling from the yard made her jump nearly out of her skin. She smoothed her hair and went to the door. A worried-looking woman was standing in the yard.

The woman's eyes moved over Narcissa, then back to the door, which Narcissa closed behind her. "Is Miss Sullivan all right?"

Narcissa stepped out into the yard, closing the door behind her. "I'm afraid she's dead. You mustn't come too close — she may have had smallpox."

"Oh, no . . . no," the woman moaned, putting her hands up to her face. The reality of it hit Narcissa then, and she felt tears prickle in her own eyes. She had been so relieved not to find two little boys — but Miss Sullivan had been a living human being, who worked, and dreamed, and who loved beautiful things. Narcissa felt the tears spill over and run warm down her cheeks. But she wiped them away and willed herself to be strong. There was simply no time to cry, while death walked in the city.

At last Cameron Archer arrived, accompanied by his manservant Gideon and a medical student, with Judah Daniel following a little behind. The stern-faced men cut a path through the weeping women who had gathered there. Archer half-bowed in the direction of Narcissa, then stalked into the house.

A few minutes later, two policemen arrived — civilians, wearing the badge of the Public Guard. As the guardsmen passed her, Narcissa touched the sleeve of one. "Sir, Miss Sullivan may have been robbed."

"You need to get on away from here, ma'am," the guardsman replied without looking at her. He seemed so intent on the trial he was about to undergo that he had no mind for anything else. At that moment the door swung open. "Ah, officers," she heard Archer say, "you might be interested in this." Archer's leather apron and over-sleeves bore hideous stains, and the fetor that clung to him was well-nigh unbearable. The guardsman Narcissa had spoken to drew out a large red bandanna and tied it over his nose and mouth. His comrade followed suit with a plain white handkerchief. Then both men went after Archer. Narcissa remained near the door, afraid to join the other women lest she carry the smallpox contagion among them.

The little group of neighbor women stood at the edge of the yard. Judah Daniel walked up to them, mulling over what Narcissa had said about Miss Sullivan maybe being robbed. A short, plump black woman named Annie recognized the doctoress and came over, blowing her nose noisily. "Oh, Judah Daniel, it's a terrible thing, just terrible. Yes'm, I used to clean for her. I cleans for most of these ladies, helps out on washdays — things like that. Miss Sullivan, she was a good woman."

The prospect of getting to tell their stories again drew the half-dozen white women to join in. In short order, Judah Daniel learned that Susannah Sullivan had had a flourishing business; that she made dresses for ladies in the best circles of Richmond, including the wives of several high-ranking officers; and that she had not told anyone about her plans to refugee: in fact, several of Miss Sullivan's clients had come knocking on the neighbors' doors, angry that the dressmaker had left without finishing items she had promised. But this was back in early April — no one could remember having seen any activity at Miss Sullivan's for weeks. No, Miss Sullivan had no family. She had come from Ireland twenty years back, with a sister who had died. No family at all.

"Oh, Lord, it's been close on two months ago since *I* seen her!" Annie exclaimed. "Mrs. Patterson" — she nodded in the direction of one of the white women — "she told me about that note on her door. Made me mad, I admit it, her leaving without letting me know, or paying me the money that was due me. Course, now I know she was in there sick, dying —" Annie broke off with a shudder.

"Did she keep money in the house?"

"Oh, yes, she paid me out of the cash box in the drawer. I seen it open plenty times. You don't mean to tell me she was *robbed?* And her laying in there sick?"

The other women joined in; after a few minutes, Judah Daniel had an exact description of where Susannah Sullivan kept her money, her account book, and her list of customers.

★ ★ ★

"Halloo! Mrs. Powers!" It was Brit Wallace, riding up on a scrubby-looking nag that was, these days, all the livery stables seemed to offer.

Narcissa came down the path toward him. "Don't come too close! It's small-pox."

Brit grimaced with concern. "In there? Someone sick?"

"Dead," Narcissa corrected. "And, listen to this —" She told him what she had found, and not found, among Miss Sullivan's possessions. "There are scraps of red material, but no red dress. No financial records, no list of her customers, and no money."

"Did the Cats steal from her, too?"

"Perhaps," Narcissa said slowly. "But she disappeared weeks ago. The note on the door says she went to North Carolina — a nice, indefinite destination! But there was no sign she'd been packing up, getting ready for a long journey — no sign of anything but of her working, falling sick, and dying."

Brit looked for a few moments like he was trying to puzzle it out. If so, he gave up. "Well, let me tell you what *I've* been doing. Searching Ragsdale's warehouses!

283

They're well guarded, better than you'd think, these days. A couple of them he's protecting under foreign flags — you know, the tobacco owned by foreign nationals is not to be burned. But a couple he's emptied, and filled with goods he's hoarding — shoes, liquor, loads of things. And the tobacco that's *supposed* to be in them, is — where?"

"What about the warehouse he bought from the Harralds?" queried Narcissa.

"I was just going there; it's not far from here." Brit waggled his head in a more-or-less northerly direction. Narcissa recalled some of the warehouses she and Judah Daniel had prowled around for signs of the missing boys and wondered if it was one of them.

Brit went on. "I hear he's got one or another of the plug-uglies stationed there day and night. But I have a pass, signed by Roland Ragsdale himself!" Brit reached into his jacket pocket, took out a slip of expensive paper, and held it up for Narcissa to read. *Admit Mr. William Wallace to examine the contents of my warehouses,* it said, over the same important-looking signature she had seen the day before. Startled, she examined the paper more carefully. Yes . . . it was the *very same* signature. Brit must have pocketed the letter without her or Mirrie noticing. He had cut off the top part of the invitation, and, in the space above Ragsdale's signature, written the false pass.

Narcissa frowned up at him. "If Ragsdale finds out —"

Brit laughed and stuck the falsified pass back in his jacket. With a wave, he turned and rode away.

A few minutes after Brit Wallace came the Cats themselves, a half-dozen boys, with Stone and Coffin in the lead, a dog at their heels. They came running up, halting when Narcissa called out warning of possible smallpox contagion. Coffin grabbed the dog by the scruff of the neck and forced him to stay. In answer to the boys' questions, she told them that the woman who had lived there had died some time ago.

One of the older boys, a Hill Cat by his clothes and manner, called out, "That's my mother's dressmaker. I've been here lots of times. Are my long pants in there?" He scowled toward the house as if threatening to go in after them.

"Nat!" Narcissa called to him. "Remember me? I talked to you about the thefts from the smallpox hospital. You can't go in, it's really not safe. But — when did you last stop here with your mother?"

Nat screwed up his face, thinking. "Well, it was April first or second — right before my birthday."

Narcissa took out the scrap of red silk and held it up so that he could see it. "Did you see a dress made out of this material?"

"Yes, I saw that dress," Nat replied. "I had to stand there forever without moving while she stuck pins in me. I was staring at it most of the time. It had big bows on the skirt, and it was cut low here" — he indicated the bodice — "and filled in with some lacy stuff. My mother asked who it was for."

"What did Miss Sullivan say?"

Nat shrugged. "She didn't. She laughed and said something like, 'You'd be surprised.' She said it cost forty dollars. My mother said later the color was vulgar, but I thought it was pretty."

The boys were getting restless, shoving and punching each other. "Well, we've got to go," Stone called out to Narcissa. "Sorry about your friend." Then they were off, headed for the stream.

After another ten minutes or so, one guardsman emerged, pulling off his bandanna and wiping his face with it. Gideon and the medical student followed him. The other guardsman appeared from behind the house, walking like a drunken man, beads of sweat standing on his pale face. Archer came last, striding down the walk to where Narcissa stood with Judah Daniel.

Archer was speaking to the guardsmen. "We're through here. I'll ride over with you to talk with the coroner. In a minute," he added, and paused beside Narcissa. "You were right, Mrs. Powers: she died of smallpox."

Narcissa tried to organize her thoughts. "Could she have been the one who infected Josiah?"

"In theory, yes," Archer replied. "She's been dead for weeks. But whether they met each other —"

"She was a dressmaker," Narcissa ventured. "If she had made a dress, as she was falling ill, and someone got it from her, and stole her money —"

To her surprise, Archer looked interested rather than impatient. "So you think the Cats began here, with their stealing? It's possible. I'm beginning to despair of your finding those boys — finding them alive, that is."

"So am I," Narcissa whispered. Archer had spoken to her deepest fear. "But," she persisted, "isn't there another possibility? Suppose a woman came to the hospital, wearing a dress that had been tainted with smallpox? She could have infected Josiah. Maybe she gave him money as well, money that was stolen from Miss Sullivan."

Tainted money. Those had been Josiah's words. What if he meant that the money was already tainted, that it had made him sick?

Archer looked at her, his hazel eyes searching her face. "I don't suppose we'll ever know," was all he said. It was a dismissal, and meant to be kind, but it sounded to Narcissa like a challenge.

After Archer had taken his leave, Judah Daniel walked up, stopping several feet away from Narcissa, and recounted what the women had told her about where the dressmaker kept her money and papers.

Narcissa nodded vigorously. "That was the drawer I found — and it was empty! I have to get back to the hospital, to speak to Private Simms. I think the woman he saw, the one he thought was Josiah's fiancée,

288

may have been wearing a dress made by Miss Sullivan — the last dress she ever made," she added significantly.

Judah Daniel nodded. "Reckon I'll look around here some more."

Narcissa gave her a worried look. "I hope you find Sam and Timmy."

Dr. Stedman, who'd learned of Narcissa's grim discovery from the returning medical student, got his wife to come to Narcissa's aid by sending one of their daughter's old dresses to the pest-house. There Narcissa washed and put on the clean clothes. Then she went over to the hospital, where she almost collided with Dr. Stedman. He asked a number of questions about Miss Sullivan, some of which she could answer; others would have to await Archer's report. Then Stedman listened fairly patiently as Narcissa explained that the woman who had visited Josiah Harrald may have brought the infection from Susannah Sullivan. "I carried away a little scrap of the red material. I left it in the pest-house, with the clothes I was wearing."

"Show it to my wife," Stedman told her with an avuncular smile. "She has an eye for that sort of thing. You can make it safe by soaking it in vinegar — though to be perfectly safe I recommend burning tainted material if it can't be cleansed thoroughly with nitric acid."

Tainted . . . that word again. "What about money? Would you recommend burning money?"

Stedman nodded emphatically. "Yes, there are some who argue it can be fumigated, but I always say, why take the chance? Roland Ragsdale asked me that question, you know, about money, and I told him the same thing — burn it, by all means."

Narcissa stared at Stedman. Did he know what he was saying? "When was this?" she asked, trying to sound casually interested.

"Oh, ages ago . . . almost a year, I suppose. He had only just come here from Norfolk."

"Do you know why he asked?"

"Can't recollect that he told me," Stedman replied with another bland smile. "We often get questions like that. And now, my dear, I really must go."

Narcissa stumbled through apologies and thanks, not knowing or caring if she made any sense. Ragsdale had had some money that was contaminated with smallpox. Of course, he had not told Stedman that, but presented it as a *what-if,* and Stedman had given him an answer he surely hadn't wanted to hear. So, despite what Stedman had told him, Ragsdale had not destroyed the money.

Could this money have surfaced again, almost a year later? Could it have been used to pay Susannah Sullivan for making a red dress? Could the money have been used, too, to pay Josiah Harrald for a warehouse? And could Ragsdale have known, because of what had happened to Susannah Sullivan, that the payment would likely end Josiah's interfering forever?

How did Sam Evans and Timmy Terry — and through them, presumably, Benjy — get caught up in the dealings among these people, who seemed so far removed from their young lives? She couldn't see that now. But Cassie Terry was involved with the Harralds, and with Pauline Avery; Mal Evans sold liquor, which Ragsdale supplied, and Cassie drank. . . . Somehow, it all fit together. Sooner or later, she — or Judah Daniel, or Brit Wallace — would grab the right thread, and the whole intricate design would unravel.

CHAPTER TEN

FRIDAY, MAY 23

On the evening of Roland Ragsdale's reception, Mirrie said, with a note of resignation unusual for her, "It's no use. I can't leave Father alone. And besides, there's no one to drive the carriage."

Narcissa looked up from fastening the bodice of her dark-green silk dress. She had already done her hair, catching it up in a caul of pearl beads attached to a wreath of green velvet leaves. "Will's not turned up either?"

Mirrie shook her head. "No. Neither of them. This has never happened before. I almost wonder whether they've run away to the Federals. But why should they? They are free, we pay them for their work." She frowned, her shortsighted eyes focused on nothing. Then she gave a rueful laugh. "Of course, if they have run away, I should be congratulating them, not whining like a spoiled plantation mistress! It's just that Father's so frail, and with Beulah, I feel he's safe. . . . Oh!" An outburst of barking from Friday sounded from the downstairs hall. "Someone's here. It can't be Beulah or Will, Friday never barks at them. I'll go," Mirrie, already hurrying down the hall, called over her shoulder.

Narcissa stood listening. After a long moment, she began to undo the fastenings. It was not Beulah and Will who had come: Mirrie would have called up to let her know. In Beulah's absence, she hesitated to leave Mirrie alone with Professor Powers, although Mirrie claimed to be strong enough to manage her father, whom age and failing strength had reduced to the size almost of a child. And in any case, as Mirrie had pointed out, the absence of Will Whatley rendered the horses and carriage useless. But she was not resigned to it, as Mirrie appeared to be; she was burning with vexation. She had hoped to learn something tonight about Ragsdale. . . .

Mirrie's quick tread in the hall brought her out of her reverie. "Mr. Ragsdale has sent his carriage for us! I cannot go, of course, but you can — if you insist on it.

There is a lady waiting. I just caught sight of her. She declined my invitation to come inside."

Narcissa hesitated. "I don't want to leave you —"

Mirrie shushed her. "Don't worry, Father and I will get on fine. Use us for an excuse to leave early," she added with a shrewd glance. "And, Narcissa — be careful."

A liveried servant handed Narcissa into the carriage, where a young blond woman, wrapped up in a cloak, accepted Narcissa's self-introduction with a languid nod. "I am Sophie Dunbar, Mr. Ragsdale's . . . niece. He was most anxious you be able to join him this evening."

Narcissa smiled her thanks, then sat back, wondering. What cause had Ragsdale to be anxious?

Roland Ragsdale's house, located on Franklin Street, stood midway down Linden Row, a line of ten connected houses distinguished by Georgian simplicity. The row was raised high off the street and surrounded by a cast-iron fence twisted with thick ropes of wisteria. The curtains were pulled back from the ten-foot-tall windows so that the light from the chandelier flung diamonds onto the velvet darkness of the night.

Narcissa and Sophie Dunbar entered the ladies' withdrawing room together, but by the time the servant had taken Narcissa's mantle and smoothed her hair with a big silver-backed brush, Sophie was nowhere to be seen. As Narcissa went out into the hall she caught sight of their host, resplendent in a black tailcoat, his waistcoat of damask, blue on black. He greeted the others first, with offhand politeness, then turned the full force of his attention on Narcissa.

"Ah, my guest of honor! Come, I must take you in myself, and introduce you."

He drew Narcissa's left arm under his right. Narcissa smiled to think of what the sardonic Mirrie would have said concerning Ragsdale's gallantry.

The smile stiffened on her face as she entered the drawing room. There stood Aaron and Aurelia Harrald, a small crowd of people she did not recognize, and, at the other side of the room from the Harralds,

Cameron Archer. There were perhaps a dozen men — all save Archer dressed in civilian clothes — and a few matronly-looking women. Two younger women stood a bit behind from the rest, arms linked. The eyes of all these persons were fixed on Narcissa and Ragsdale. As for the ones she knew — Archer and the Harralds — they could not have looked more disapproving if they had been gathered for her execution. And here was Ragsdale, showing her off as if she were some bauble he had recently acquired.

Ragsdale stopped and turned to look at her, keeping her arm in his own. His flushed face and bright eyes made her wonder if he had been drinking. "Ladies and gentlemen, allow me to present Mrs. Narcissa Powers. Mrs. Powers is a graceful representative of the Richmond ladies who have come forward in response to their country's need as nurses in the Confederate hospitals."

One of the two young women was whispering to her companion, whom Narcissa now recognized as Sophie Dunbar. Here was the ostentatious luxury Narcissa had expected in Ragsdale's home: these two women, in their bright, low-cut silk gowns and jewels, seemed like animated accessories to the man who was now holding her arm. As she looked, the dark-haired woman brought up to her cheek a mother-of-pearl fan trimmed with white feathers. If she sought to hide her face, it was too late; Narcissa had seen the mocking smile. Pauline Avery. The sudden realization made her cheeks burn even hotter. To think she wouldn't have known, had she not visited her that very morning. . . .

Ragsdale's oration ended — Narcissa had heard none of it — and the guests applauded politely. Archer did not applaud, but bowed, as if in acknowledgment of something Ragsdale had said. Aurelia, looking embarrassed, played with the strings of her reticule — how odd Aurelia should be here, so soon after her brother's death. Aaron joined in the clapping as if realizing it was expected of him.

"Now, everyone, please enjoy the hospitality of the house!" Instead of leading the way, Ragsdale gestured with his left hand in the direction of the dining room, where Narcissa could see a long table laden with trays and decanters. Then he turned back to Narcissa. "I want to show you some of the treasures of my collection." Apparently he meant the paintings that hung on the walls, mounted in heavy gilt frames. "I paid a pretty penny for them; I'm told they're quite fine. I wouldn't know, I'm afraid." He lowered his voice to a confidential murmur. "I'm only the son of a mercantile clerk, after all! But you, I'm sure, can tell me whether their beauty of line and color indicates true worth." Ragsdale's eyes on her face made the comment uncomfortably personal.

"Mr. Ragsdale, you are mistaken in me. I was born on a farm in western Hanover County. I never learned to paint in oils, I have never been to Italy or France. What is it that you want of me?"

"My dear Mrs. Powers." Ragsdale waved his hand as if brushing away her words. His smile grew broader, more insinuating. "The question is, what do *you* want of *me?*"

Narcissa looked him full in the face, angry words on her lips. Then she hesitated. If she took offense, she might lose the money for the hospital — and also lose the chance to question him about smallpox.

"Mr. Ragsdale, you must know how deeply all of us appreciate the gift you're making. You cannot live in Richmond without feeling the effects of this war. You've seen the wounded soldiers in the streets, making their way along with a leg missing, an arm, an eye, or blind even. . . . You've been in the hospitals, you've seen the ravages of diseases . . . such as smallpox. . . . I believe you have some experience with that?"

Her little speech seemed to throw him completely. He was staring at her still, but the smile was gone. "Yes, well, of course, the hospitals . . . I've been moved, of course . . . as you say. . . . Well, let's join the others, shall we?" He bowed her ahead of him, not attempting to take her arm again.

In the dining room, Ragsdale moved away to speak to other guests. Narcissa saw Cameron Archer step up to him. Then a servant came up to her with a tray full of punch cups, offering her one. By the time she had accepted the cup and turned back to look, both Ragsdale and Archer had disappeared. She stood sipping the delicious punch and thinking about what had happened. She felt sure the mention of smallpox had alarmed Ragsdale; but he was not one to be surprised into a revelation.

After a few moments she became aware of the conversation going on next to her. A tall, dark, sour-looking man was talking about a meeting the Confederate secretary of state — he called him "that Jew" — had supposedly had with a certain count who represented the French government in Washington. "Dividing up the tobacco spoils, in case the city falls. Sixty million dollars worth of tobacco." His black eyes gleamed with an avaricious light that belied his stiffly solemn expression.

Another man, whose diamond ring sparkled in the light from the gasoliers, joined in. "The pettifogging bureaucrats want to blow it up! Save it from the Yankees!" The others laughed.

What was the war for these men? A game of chance, in which a clever player just might beat the careless dealer of the cards? And who was dealing, really? President Davis and his military adviser, General Lee? Or Secretary of State Benjamin, who was called "that Jew" and worse and accused of everything from self-interest to treason to mulatto blood?

She could not see the speaker who asked, "What about all that tobacco Ragsdale bought?" She froze, unwilling to breathe lest she miss the answer.

The tall, dark man answered. "He's banking on the city holding out. He means

300

to do nothing with it until the war is won — by the South, of course!" Laughter, ambiguous in its import, greeted his words. Then the little knot of men began to break apart, with a few heading toward the buffet table and others talking among themselves.

Archer followed Ragsdale out of the room. He knew he might be about to throw away ten thousand dollars that would have gone for the care of wounded soldiers, but it would be worth it for the pleasure of wiping the smug look off Ragsdale's face.

"How dare you bring ladies into a place like this?"

Ragsdale smiled as if nothing could please him better than to see Cameron Archer lose his temper. "This is my home," he answered smoothly.

"It's a whorehouse," Archer snapped back. "If you don't know any better than to bring a lady into the company of whores, it's time somebody taught you."

Ragsdale arched his eyebrows interrogatively. "Is that a challenge? Very well, I accept. For weapons, I choose knowledge:

yours against mine. You know that some of the women present have rather more worldly experience than is thought appropriate to ladies. I might ask you how you came by that knowledge — but I won't."

Archer frowned, wondering where this was leading.

Ragsdale went on. "And *I* know something about you, and how you behave toward ladies whose virtue should command your protection. Perhaps we should invite Mrs. Powers to join us and decide which of us has behaved more offensively: I, by having two charming ladies of questionable virtue to entertain my guests, or you, by —"

"That's enough!" Archer's hot anger had gone cold. "What are you getting at, Ragsdale?"

"You know very well what I'm getting at. I admit, I was naive. I was taken in by the *lady's* manner and pedigree. I am only glad I learned of my mistake before I pursued her too far." Ragsdale's voice was growing rougher. "Pursued her, until she caught me." He gave a short, angry laugh. "But perhaps I am wronging you," he said with a glance at Archer. "Perhaps you were her victim, just as I nearly was."

It had to be Aurelia that Ragsdale was

speaking of, though he was avoiding using her name. Perhaps he feared that, if he did name her, he would not escape an exchange of pistol shots with Archer. But Ragsdale's indirect way of speaking, together with his own shocked surprise, left Archer unsure of how to respond. He could not tell how much Ragsdale knew about what had happened between him and Aurelia, but the threat was clear enough: Ragsdale would tell Mrs. Powers. And Archer wanted very much to avoid that.

What could he say, what counterthreat could he make against Ragsdale? Archer could think of nothing. At last he turned on his heel and stalked out of the room.

Archer had vanished, the Harralds as well. There was no one with whom she could easily start a conversation. The men talked among themselves, as did their wives, their circles closed. Then she caught sight of Pauline Avery and Sophie Dunbar, hovering near the table like brightly colored butterflies, Pauline in cerulean blue with a headdress of ostrich feathers, Sophie in pink with damask roses in her hair. Each held a wineglass in her hand. It was a heaven-sent opportunity to question Pauline further — or perhaps it came from the other place; still, she could not let it go by.

Narcissa strolled over to the table and circled it slowly, as if searching for a tidbit, until she was standing next to Pauline.

"Good evening," she said. The pair stood looking at her, their rouged mouths forming polite smiles that did not show their teeth. "Miss Avery, you may remember me: Narcissa Powers."

"Oh, yes . . . I remember you," replied the one so addressed. She brought up her fan so that the tips of the downy white feathers traced her cheek and chin. Sophie Dunbar looked from her to Narcissa with a startled expression.

"Have you achieved your purpose?" Pauline asked Narcissa.

"Not entirely," replied Narcissa. "I have reason to believe that all of you may be in danger" — there was a flicker of uncertainty in Pauline's dark eyes then — "from exposure to smallpox."

With a graceful gesture the Cyprian brought her white fan to rest against the ivory skin of her left shoulder, then raised her left hand to sip from her wineglass. It's like sleight of hand, Narcissa thought, every movement planned to draw the eye, to reveal one thing and conceal another.

"As I said before — I cannot help you," Pauline said at last, and turned away.

Narcissa saw Sophie smile and flutter her eyelashes at someone behind her. It was the man who had called Secretary Benjamin "that Jew." He strode up to Sophie Dunbar and put his arm around her waist. "Good evening, Mr. Miller," Sophie cooed up at him. Narcissa turned away, wondering how soon she would be able to leave. As she did so, she caught sight of Ragsdale coming her way, shoulders forward and a scowl on his face. What was he going to do to her?

But he stalked past her without a glance in her direction. "Miller!" he snapped, then turned on his heel and walked back toward the entrance hall. Narcissa caught sight of a man waiting there, bearing a rifle, bayonet affixed, at parade stance — an army private or, more likely, one of the provost marshal's men. Miller went after Ragsdale, giving Sophie Dunbar's waist a final squeeze. Sophie's gaze, however, was fixed on Ragsdale.

Ragsdale returned and set himself to mingling with his guests again, though the fixed expression of his mobile features showed he was still angry. A few minutes later, Narcissa felt a tap on her shoulder. She turned to see Sophie.

"Pauline wishes to speak with you — in private." Sophie's eyes darted to where Ragsdale was standing, his back to them, as if reassuring herself he had not noticed their conversation. "Can you come with me?"

"Very well," said Narcissa. She trailed Sophie up a narrow stairway to the second floor of the house. Soon she found herself in a small, simply appointed room crowded with a large desk, a chair drawn up to it, two chairs facing it. Sophie motioned her to wait, then left her alone.

The minutes dragged by. Narcissa's excitement turned to anxiety. She turned this way and that in the confined space, looking for something in which she could pretend to be interested should anyone other than Pauline — God forbid it be Roland Ragsdale — come in and find her dallying there. Surely it would be better for her to return to the public rooms with an excuse prepared for her absence?

She had taken a step back toward the door when it swung open. Ragsdale stepped inside, pushed the door closed behind him, and stood leaning against it, looking at her. His presence made the small room feel crowded.

"Mrs. Powers, I understand you were asking after Pauline Avery. How does a lady such as yourself come to know the name of a whore?"

Ragsdale had used the vulgar word deliberately, watching her face, smiling as if anticipating her reaction. She determined in that moment that her reaction would not be what he expected.

"Josiah Harrald was right about you."

Certainly, Ragsdale had not expected that. He moved forward swiftly, his footfalls silent on the carpeted floor, and stood over her.

Narcissa kept talking. "He said your money was tainted."

Ragsdale was listening intently. "And yet my money is good enough for his brother — and his sister."

"I don't believe she sees you for what you are."

"I believe she does." Ragsdale's smile was back. "I have something she wants. And she has something *I* want. More to the point, Mrs. Powers . . . I see you for what *you* are. Would you like to know what that is?" His tone was smooth as silk, but there was steel behind the silk.

Narcissa did not answer.

"For me you put on a face of virtue, of devotion to duty — to get my money."

Narcissa's face burned. It was true she had held back, had not objected to his sly inferences, because of the money he had promised to the hospitals.

"What do you put on for Cameron Archer? For Brit Wallace? And what is it you expect to get from them? They are using you, believe me, as you use them. And what does that make you? Not so very different from Pauline Avery — are you? A cool handshake from you is not enough for me. I deserve more. This *invitation* is costing me more than I ever expected." With that, he reached into his vest pocket, pulled out a crumpled piece of paper, and held it out so that she could read it. It was the pass Brit had forged, allowing him to search Ragsdale's warehouses, on the invitation Ragsdale had sent to Narcissa. Ragsdale balled it up in his fist and threw it to the floor. Before Narcissa had time to react, he had grabbed her arm and was twisting it behind her back, forcing her up against him. She had never been afraid of a man in quite this way before. But she couldn't scream, bring in all those people, staring and whispering, Pauline giggling behind her fan. . . . It was too shameful, it was her own fault she'd allowed him to get her alone like this. . . .

"Will you call for help, Mrs. Powers?" he whispered. "Will you tell Brit Wallace, or Cameron Archer, that I insulted you? I think not."

She said nothing. She knew his words were true. To speak of this to any man would be like undressing in front of him. To a husband — to Rives — she could have told it, and he would have avenged her, somehow. Her thwarted anger collapsed upon itself, leaving her struggling against tears.

Ragsdale brought his hand up to stroke her face. She could only stare back in defiance, willing herself to cold disdain. His voice grew soft, caressing. "It would not do to have you upset on this festive evening, in front of my guests. Believe me, I mean you no dishonor when I say that all women in whom youth runs high and hot are secret Cyprians. How could I blame you?" He ran his forefinger down the line of her jaw to touch her lips. She stayed still as a statue, but her muscles knotted, ready to leap away. "You have had the merest taste of what I could give you. But don't be against me" — he put his mouth close to her ear, his breath hot against her face —

"or I will *bring you down.*"

Then, abruptly as he had grabbed her, he let her go. He stood aside and bowed. Narcissa swept past him to the door, opened it, stepped out into the hall. She could feel the muscles in her jaw bunched. Her left temple was throbbing. At the other end of the dark corridor she saw the silhouette of a woman vanish through the door that led to the public rooms. Had Sophie, who had drawn her into Roland Ragsdale's trap, stayed to witness her humiliation? Or was it Pauline Avery who had planned this humiliation for her?

She stood in the dark, half expecting some further insult, either from Ragsdale or from the unknown woman. As minutes went by and nothing happened, her heart gradually slowed and her breathing grew more regular. She unclenched her hands and smoothed her hair and her skirts.

After a few minutes Narcissa retraced her passage to the public rooms. She held her head high, her outward composure, at least, regained. Pauline was nowhere to be seen, but Sophie gave her a curious glance before turning away.

A servant came up to her. "Your carriage is waiting, Miss." She thanked him with a smile that she hoped concealed her inner turmoil. Then she reclaimed her wrap and stepped out into the warm, sweet-scented night.

Will Whatley was standing by the open door of the Powerses' carriage. Narcissa said a prayer of thanks at the sight of his familiar face and hurried to him. "Are you all right? And Beulah?"

"Yes, ma'am. A wheel come loose and had to be fixed. Beulah," he went on, "she got word her aunt was sick, that Miss Powers done told her to go there. Turned out she weren't sick at all. Strange doings." Will shook his head perplexedly.

More mysteries. Or perhaps no mystery at all. Ragsdale had wanted to get her alone. But how had he gotten hold of the counterfeit pass drawn up by Brit? Had that guardsman brought it? Ragsdale had returned from the interruption angry, and far more disdainful in his treatment of her. Miller hadn't returned at all. None of these developments augured well for Brit.

"And one more thing," said Will, "that Miss Powers asked me to tell you. Mr. Wallace been arrested, he's in Castle Godwin."

Ragsdale thought she had given the invitation to Brit to use as a passe-partout to examine Ragsdale's warehouses. Ragsdale

311

had been using her own modesty, her sense of shame, against her.

Back at the Powerses, Narcissa found Mirrie waiting for her, together with a young man Narcissa had never seen before. She would have remembered, because he had a twisted body, with one shoulder higher than the other. Mirrie introduced him as Mr. Yancey, a friend of Brit Wallace.

Narcissa remembered then that Brit had mentioned him. "From the telegraph office?"

Yancey smiled in acknowledgment. His dark eyes sparkled with intelligence. "When I heard they'd arrested him, I went right over to Castle Godwin. It appears the plug-uglies took him up as a favor to their friend Roland Ragsdale. Whether he will be prosecuted or not . . . well, it seems unlikely. Ragsdale might not want to invite too much scrutiny. I'm here because Brit asked me to bring this." Yancey handed a folded-up piece of paper to Narcissa. "And now, I must be going." Narcissa shook hands with him and, as Mirrie showed him to the door, unfolded the paper.

Don't come here, she read, underlined twice. *No need to have them after you. The H— warehouse —* Harrald, she supposed he meant — *is the closest-guarded of all — yet it's almost empty but for a large trunk, full of CSA bills. Thousands, or hundreds of thousands. Why not in a bank, or making more money for R?*

Money, under guard in an empty warehouse — two people dead of smallpox, a seamstress in Butchertown and a wealthy man, an officer, on Shockoe Hill — and money stolen from both — tainted money, death-bearing — a warehouse owned by Ragsdale, who a year ago had asked for advice concerning smallpox money — *Destroy it,* he had been told. *Thousands, or hundreds of thousands* — more, she felt sure, than could possibly have been stolen from Josiah Harrald and Susannah Sullivan. So, not stolen from them, but infected earlier . . .

Her head was hurting with the effort to make sense of the disparate bits of information. *It's like one of those little round puzzle boxes that you hold in your hand. The challenge is to get all the balls through the maze and into the capped circle in the center of the box. You move the balls by tilting the box. Sometimes the balls line up nicely and roll along, one after the other, into the center, and stay there; but more often, when one ball nears the opening, the others roll out.*

All at once she saw the incidents line up in a different order. The money had borne its taint to Susannah Sullivan and Josiah Harrald, sickening and killing them. The taint of smallpox from a year ago, carried on money that Ragsdale, against Dr. Stedman's advice, had decided not to destroy. So . . . this spring, after almost a year of waiting, Ragsdale had gotten greedy. Maybe he'd thought he'd waited long enough. He had paid Miss Sullivan for a dress for one of his paramours. Miss Sullivan had fallen sick; Ragsdale had covered up the truth. And then he had thought of another use for the money — to kill Josiah.

Then, why not take it a step further? Why not steal the money back, employing two little boys whose parents were in no position to resist a man with wealth and power, a man who treated the military authories as his hirelings? Why not kill a third boy who had found out, it may be, and threatened to tell? Whether or not Ragsdale had pulled the trigger, he had killed Benjy. But what could they do about it, she and her friends, when the authori-

314

ties were on Ragsdale's side?

Then a new thought struck her. In fact, Ragsdale was frightened of *her*, of what she might have found out or guessed. He'd been trying to drive her away, so that she would not come too close to whatever it was he was trying to hide. And he was doing the same thing with Brit by having him consigned to Castle Godwin. Judah Daniel would be in danger too, if Ragsdale learned she was asking questions.

Ragsdale was afraid of her! She laughed to herself as the realization swept away the shame and guilt she had been feeling. Nothing she had done as a woman, no glance or smile or word, had inflamed Ragsdale to press himself upon her. He had locked Brit in Castle Godwin, and he had tried to lock her in the chains of female modesty. And he had come near to succeeding. But now that she understood his game, she could play it on her own terms.

CHAPTER ELEVEN

SATURDAY, MAY 24

When Narcissa awoke the next morning, she found she had gained a little distance from the problem — enough, she thought, to begin to devise a solution. Three women had their hopes pinned on Roland Ragsdale. To Aurelia, he offered the promise of escape from her family. To Serena, he represented a business alliance that would enrich Aaron and secure her own future. To Pauline, he gave the freedom to refuse other men's money. It was possible that these women knew what kind of man Ragsdale was, but felt they had no other choice than to trust him. It was possible, too, that they did not know. It was even possible that one of them had put on the red dress for him and gone to visit Josiah Harrald, taking the money that would poison him. She would pay a call on each of them, with Judah Daniel along to question the servants, who often divulged what their masters and mistresses wanted to hide.

It was difficult to suspect Aurelia. As she was not immune to smallpox, she would have been incredibly fortunate not to fall ill herself from the exposure. Serena might have done it for Aaron, but would Josiah have engaged in intimate conversation with a woman he had apparently despised? Pauline was beautiful . . . if the ailing Josiah had had an ounce of susceptibility in him, he would have accepted a visit from Pauline.

At the Golden Arrow, Pauline Avery greeted Narcissa with bemused politeness. The Cyprian sat, cheek on hand, little finger just touching her bottom lip, long-lashed eyes playing over Narcissa's face. The pose was so contrived that Narcissa wanted to jump up and pull Pauline's hair.

"Why do you insist upon bothering me? I assure you, I don't have smallpox."

And you have no interest in protecting anyone else from the disease, Narcissa thought. "Josiah Harrald was the father of your child. He was badly injured, perhaps dying. . . . What more natural than that you would go to him?"

"Natural?" At last Pauline's composure was shaken. Her long-nailed fingers curled into fists. "Because Josiah Harrald was such a fine man, an officer, upright, a man of honor? Let me tell you what Josiah Harrald was. He was a rich and selfish boy, completely under his father's thumb. He was a coward, who loved a girl from a poor family — yet left her at a word from his father — left her with his child."

Pauline's sudden vehemence rocked Narcissa. "You must have been very young," she said at last. It was all she could think of to say.

"I was fourteen years old when Josiah became my seducer — he was nineteen — and fifteen when I bore his child. Fool that I was, I thought that he would marry me. A hasty marriage is not such a mark of shame in Butchertown. But up on the Hill, I was trash. A little whore in the making. Aurelia ran away at the sight of me, as if what I had was catching. They were sent off to school, then: Josiah and Aaron to college, Aurelia to some finishing school. Thaddeus came down from the Hill and gave my father some money."

Fifteen. Pauline had carried this burden almost half her life. And yet Coffin's lot had been worse — boarded with that slattern Cassie Terry. Narcissa steeled herself against an excess of sympathy. "Aurelia Harrald said Josiah paid your son's board up until the time of his amputation."

Pauline looked a little embarrassed at that. "Well, why shouldn't he?"

Narcissa had no answer for that. "It may be that the Harralds will make it right. They have taken Coffin in, did you know? Aurelia knows he is Josiah's son. I believe she would like to see him take his rightful place."

" 'His *rightful place*'?" Pauline repeated. "When a white man rapes a slave, the child that results is a slave. When a white man seduces a woman of his own race, and doesn't marry her, he makes her a whore, and their child a bastard."

Narcissa kept a stubborn spark of hope alive. "Aurelia —"

Pauline raised angry eyes to Narcissa's face. "Aurelia Harrald had better watch herself, or she may end up where I am. Roland Ragsdale wants her for her name, her family connections, and he is willing to pay. But if he were to suspect the truth about her — he does not pay for damaged goods — and if he suspects he has been cheated . . . I believe you know something of what I am talking about," she added with a cruel smile.

Narcissa resolved to try one last time to shake Pauline Avery. "You say Ragsdale doesn't like to be cheated. He must have been angry indeed, when some of his money became tainted with smallpox. Then, when someone else seemed about to get the better of him, he decided he would use that money. You visited Josiah, didn't you? Wearing a dress Roland Ragsdale gave you? Carrying money he gave you, to give to Josiah? Did you know it was smallpox money, that Ragsdale had been hiding? It killed Josiah! And the boys who stole the money back for Ragsdale — are they dying alone, somewhere in this city? Do you ever wonder?"

Pauline winced as if she'd been slapped. She pushed herself up from the table and hurried away from Narcissa without a backward glance.

Judah Daniel was back in the kitchen of the Golden Arrow with the cook, Winnie, and one of the maids, a girl named Liza. Judah Daniel had listened to Winnie complain about her aches and pains and offered some suggestions. Now she was turning the conversation to what she wanted to know.

"Y'all get some baked goods from Chapman's, ain't that right?"

Winnie agreed, beginning a commentary on the relative merits of the Chapmans' baking and her own. Liza broke in with a giggle. "That Tyler, he sure is handsome." The three women laughed over that for a minute. Then Judah Daniel circled closer to the subject. "Still, I reckon this place make a lot more money off liquor than pies. Where do y'all get that?"

The cook wrinkled her nose. "That sorry man Miller have it brought in. He always looking at me like he think I'm going to steal it. And let me tell you — I ain't tempted. One look at his ugly face, you think you drinking embalming fluid!" They laughed again.

"Ain't he one of them plug-uglies? Ain't he supposed to keep it from being sold?" Judah Daniel acted scandalized.

"Yeah, reckon he is," Winnie chuckled. "Him and Ragsdale, they's in each other's pockets."

"They sample the girls, as well as the liquor?"

"Pauline Avery and Sophie Dunbar, they like to pull each other's hair out over

Ragsdale. Pauline winning that fight, for the moment anyways. Sophie got to content herself with Miller. But she all time got her eyes on Ragsdale."

"Either of them girls wear a red dress? Seem to me I seen one of them, riding in a carriage one time —"

"Pauline had a red dress," Liza spoke up, "and she give it to me. Sophie seen it and bought it off me, told me she was going to have it cut down. But I ain't ever seen her wearing it. Pauline probably said something to her — Pauline's got a sharp tongue, and she know just what Sophie's up to. Wish she'd give it back to me," she concluded with a sigh.

"How long ago was this?" Judah Daniel could see that Liza was wondering what all these questions were about, but the girl answered anyway.

"I reckon it was about Christmastime."

Judah Daniel hid her disappointment. If Narcissa had read right the signs in Miss Sullivan's sewing room, the dress they were looking for could not be that old. "You ever hear of a dressmaker name of Susannah Sullivan?"

Both Winnie and Liza shook their heads. "She do good work?" Winnie asked.

"She died. Got the smallpox. Didn't no

one know she was sick, and she just lay there in her house for months, down in Butchertown." Judah Daniel shuddered, remembering.

Winnie and Liza tut-tutted. "That Butchertown, I hear that a rough neighborhood. I wouldn't want to live there," Winnie said, and Liza nodded.

Walking down Cary Street through the fine mist that had fallen all morning, Narcissa and Judah Daniel took turns telling what they had found out. Narcissa was most interested in the news that Sophie Dunbar aspired to take the place of Pauline Avery. Sophie, and every other woman at the Golden Arrow, perhaps, would see the position of Ragsdale's mistress as a step up from prostitution. What one of them would refuse to put on a dress and make a visit to a wounded soldier, if Ragsdale asked her to?

They went next to Serena Warren's. With the rain outside, the smell of mildew in the stairwell was stronger than ever. What topic would engage Serena so thoroughly that Judah Daniel could slip into her bedroom and look through her clothes? Narcissa thought she had one. After going through the formalities with Serena, who seemed surprised but rather pleased to see her again, Narcissa asked the question she had prepared. "How much did Roland Ragsdale pay the Harralds for their tobacco warehouse?"

Serena might well have wondered how Narcissa knew about the sale, but she didn't pause to ask. "Nothing!"

Narcissa looked a question, and Serena explained. "Aaron agreed to take a share of the proceeds when the tobacco is sold. What with tobacco falling into enemy hands in many of our Southern port cities, and so much less of it coming to market, for want of labor to grow and transport it — it will fetch a good price." Serena smiled, looking happier than Narcissa had ever seen her.

Narcissa was very much afraid her next words would shatter Serena's complacency. "Does Aaron know there is no tobacco in the warehouse?"

Serena rose, folding her arms at her waist as if hugging herself. Narcissa looked up, fearful that Serena would notice Judah Daniel's absence, but Serena was pacing, staring at the carpet. She had worn the pile almost off, in an S-shaped path leading from the door, around the chair, the sofa, the table . . . "What can it mean?" Serena said at last, lifting a worried face to Narcissa.

"Come and sit down," Narcissa said, half-rising herself. "It's nothing, I'm sure. Men, you know how they are sometimes. Aaron probably just forgot to tell you —"

Serena grabbed the hard, tasseled pillow from the sofa and clutched it to her like a shield. Narcissa realized, heart sinking, that for Aaron to receive payment from Ragsdale, and not tell Serena, was worse news for her than if the Harralds had been cheated. If Aaron started keeping secrets from her — especially news of some money coming in — Serena would take it as a step toward estrangement. As, indeed, maybe it was. Aaron had finally come out from under the shadow of Josiah. With a fresh infusion of money, he could find himself a woman who was younger, prettier, free of Serena's shame and the depression that seemed to result from it. Whether Aaron wished to do so or not, Serena feared he might; and that very fear might drive Aaron from her.

Judah Daniel slipped soundlessly into the room behind Serena.

Narcissa stood and put her hand on Serena's arm. "I must go now. Please don't worry. I'm sure everything will be all right."

As Narcissa and Judah Daniel made their way back out into the street, Narcissa felt Serena's burden on her own shoulders. By Judah Daniel's report, Serena had only three dresses: the unbecoming plaid she had been wearing both times Narcissa had called; a winter-weight black dress, years out of fashion; and a calico that had been inexpertly altered so that darker fabric showed along the seams of the faded brown material.

Despite her reassurance to Serena, Narcissa was far from sure that everything would be all right for her. If Aaron cut off his support, what could Serena do, where could she go? Perhaps it was desperation, not devotion, that kept Serena tied to Aaron Harrald.

Serena might have hated Josiah, even wished him dead. But to imagine that Ragsdale had approached her, given her a boldly colored dress and a handful of Confederate notes, and given her some pretext to visit Josiah Harrald in the hospital — it was impossible.

It was a long walk to the Harralds'. By the time Narcissa and Judah Daniel arrived, the fine mist had wet them through. Narcissa found Aurelia Harrald in the back parlor, lying on a chaise longue. Though it was quite warm, Aurelia was wrapped in shawls and blankets. "A touch of fever," she said to Narcissa, "to be expected after inoculation. No, no pustules yet." She shuddered, then smiled with self-deprecating humor.

In response to Narcissa's inquiries about Stone and Coffin, Aurelia smiled again. "They're getting on quite well. Stone seems happy to have a companion, and Coffin looks up to Stone, I can tell, copies his table manners and way of speaking. I am glad they are friends." Aurelia looked down then, fearful perhaps that Narcissa would ask whether the boys would be told they were in fact cousins.

Narcissa drew a deep breath and plunged in — there would never be a better time, she told herself, than now. "I believe you know Mr. Ragsdale."

Aurelia nodded. "The donation he made to the hospital was very generous, don't you think?"

"Generous, yes, but —" Narcissa searched for words to warn Aurelia. "He is a wealthy man, but where does his money come from?"

A line appeared between Aurelia's eyebrows. "From business . . . investments . . ."

"Some say," Narcissa ventured, "from profiteering. And from the vicious habits of men who can ill afford what they lose."

Aurelia smiled, apparently unconcerned. "I know he has gaming houses, faro banks. What of it? The most important men in our government, our army, go to the gaming houses. It's common enough to be almost the rule, among gentlemen."

It was the reaction Narcissa had expected, but it did not make her task any easier. She had to touch Aurelia's feelings, to make her see what Ragsdale was. "And consorting with prostitutes? Is that the behavior of a gentleman?"

Aurelia's smile vanished and she struggled to sit upright. "How would you know about such things? Mr. Ragsdale has always behaved in a gentlemanly way to me. It is you — you, who are no lady, coming to me with accusations that show your degraded imagination."

Narcissa, wanting nothing more than to walk away, forced herself to ignore Aurelia's abuse. She had taken on herself the responsibility for warning Aurelia, saving her, it may be, from the fate of

Serena Warren. It was a difficult task. Aurelia was not, could not be, happy so long as the very things that sheltered her — family, home, social standing — also confined her. But she could be so very much more miserable without those things.

Narcissa took a deep breath and tried again. "In my capacity as a nurse, I have had occasion to speak with a few of the prostitutes, concerning the danger of smallpox infection. I know that at least one of them is the paramour of Mr. Ragsdale." She did not want to say that it was Pauline Avery, the mother of Coffin — this news could not but harm Coffin's chances of being accepted into the Harrald household.

Aurelia's angry, contemptuous expression did not change. "You knew my brother Josiah. You looked after him in the hospital, you were with him when he died. Had things been different, perhaps you would have considered a proposal of marriage from him — though I doubt he would have offered marriage to you! Did it ever occur to you, as he lay there ill — grateful to you, admiring you — that he had consorted with loose women? But he did! All men do. If a man sought to make you his wife, would you ask him whether he paid women to lie with him — paid them with money, or with flattering attention? What would your suitor think of *you,* for asking such a question? What about Cameron Archer? Have you ever asked him what women he has had?"

Aurelia was sitting bolt upright, the covers fallen away. The heat of fever had reddened her cheeks and curled the loose hair about her face, but her expression was one of cold hatred. "Perhaps you know better than I what men do. Perhaps you know from your own experience how Mr. Ragsdale entertains himself. Are *you* his paramour? Are you envious of me, because he intends to marry me?"

Narcissa stood, letting the cruel darts strike. "Aurelia, I am sorry I have offended you, but *think:* is Roland Ragsdale the kind of man you want to marry? Think of the kind of life he has led. He could give you a disease that would maim you and doom your children to madness." She hesitated, still unwilling to say the words that would make Aurelia see the truth about Ragsdale, but that might harm Coffin Avery. At last she decided she had to take the risk. "Ragsdale's mistress is Pauline Avery."

"No! You're lying!" Aurelia was shrieking, clutching her cashmere shawl so tightly that her knuckles showed white. "Get out!"

Narcissa fled, forgetting Judah Daniel until she almost ran into her where she waited on the street.

"Weren't no red dress," Judah Daniel said. "Leastways, I didn't find one."

Narcissa told Judah Daniel what Aurelia had told her. As she talked, she grew calmer, her thoughts clearer. She ended by pulling a handful of Confederate notes out of her pocket and handing them to Judah Daniel, saying, "Give these to the Harralds' maid, Jensie. Tell her to let you know if Aurelia shows any signs of turning Coffin out to fend for himself. I would have you ask Jensie to contact me, but I'm sure she will feel better dealing with you."

Judah Daniel nodded and headed around to the back of the house. Narcissa walked away, heavyhearted. Had she really thought it would be so easy to unknot the web of evil Ragsdale had spun, in which so many people had been caught? All she had accomplished was to bring disturbing news to three women, and to jeopardize the future happiness of a young boy. She reminded herself that Ragsdale had caused the harm, that she had only tried to tell the truth, tried to make them see what he was. Surely the truth was preferable to comfortable ignorance?

What was it Aurelia knew about Cameron Archer? Was she, Narcissa, just as guilty of preferring ignorance?

Judah Daniel came back around the corner. To Narcissa's surprise, two boys followed her — Stone and Coffin. They came up to her and allowed her to hug each of them in turn, but they brushed off her inquiries and asked a question of her instead. "Is it true that Mr. Wallace has been arrested?" Stone asked with a frown.

Narcissa sighed. "Yes, it's true. He expects to be released soon —"

Coffin broke in. "Was he going after that Ragsdale?"

Narcissa drew back in surprise and looked from one boy to the other. "What did Mr. Wallace tell you?"

The two boys exchanged a look, then Stone spoke. "He told us to keep an eye on Ragsdale and report to him if we saw anything suspicious. So now, who do we report to?"

Oh, no, Narcissa thought. *Aurelia, close as she is to a nervous collapse, must never get wind of this.* But Stone and Coffin looked so eager. . . . They were awaiting orders, she realized, like the soldiers they imagined themselves to be. She found herself wanting to box the ears of the foolish Brit Wallace, who had made the game all the more exciting by getting himself arrested.

Narcissa looked a question at Judah Daniel, who answered it with a sidelong glance and an almost imperceptible nod of her head.

Narcissa had her answer. "You report to me. But now you know how careful you must be. Mr. Wallace was snooping around the warehouse Ragsdale bought from your family, Stone, when he was arrested. He believes the smallpox money is hidden there. You *must not* go near that warehouse — that's an order, understand?" She scowled furiously at the boys, making herself their superior officer. They nodded and ran off.

Narcissa turned to Judah Daniel. "I'm afraid I've just made that warehouse the most attractive place in the world. But if my words don't scare them off, maybe the guard Ragsdale has stationed there will."

Judah Daniel looked after the boys, a thoughtful expression on her face. "Least you ain't told 'em to stay home. They'd just make up their mind then and there to keep you in the dark, like they does the Harralds."

Narcissa knew Judah Daniel was right: an order to stay away from Ragsdale would have meant the end of the game, and they would not have obeyed her.

CHAPTER TWELVE

SUNDAY, MAY 25

To his surprise, Brit Wallace found himself released from Castle Godwin as abruptly as he had been thrown into it. Early on the morning after his arrest, he found himself a free man again. Miller, who had released him, seemed not to recall his former animosity in the matter of Sophie Dunbar. Brit was walking up the street, enjoying a heightened appreciation of his freedom as well as the pleasantly cool day, when he heard his name being called. *Damn — Miller's changed his mind.*

But it was Archer Langdon, heading back to camp in the gloom of early morning. When it came to military regulations, Langdon could wriggle off the hook as neatly as any trout in a Highland stream.

"Come back to camp with me, Wallace," Langdon offered genially. "You'll want to write about this. Today is the drumming-out of Peters and McCardle."

It wouldn't be a bad notion, thought Brit, to put as much distance as possible between himself and Miller — and of course Ragsdale. "What did they do — Peters and McCardle?" Brit asked.

"Deserters." Langdon spat out the word. "Peters is a man born to hang if ever there was one. He has a cold-blooded sort of courage, but no loyalty, and without that . . . He deserted rather than get a knife in the ribs for his thieving, I'll be bound. But McCardle . . . he broke down in the trenches at Yorktown. God knows, I can't really blame him." Langdon's mouth shut in a tight line.

Brit thought about what he had heard of the drumming-out ceremony. It was not the severest of penalties, in that the offending soldiers were allowed to leave the camp, never to return. To a man just released from jail, it seemed little enough punishment.

An hour's walk brought them into the labyrinthine mass of tents that was the encampment of the Alexandria Rifle

Grays. Brit greeted some of his old acquaintances. At last the bugler called the men to assemble in the big open field used for drill. Brit watched as the hundreds of men came together and found their places, drawn up in a line as if upon dress parade, the ranks in open order. There was some banter at first, but not much of it, and the men fell silent as the adjutant marched to the center of the line, took a paper from his sash, and read from it. Brit couldn't make out the words from where he stood, but he knew their import. Peters and McCardle had been charged, tried, and found guilty.

The drum started up at the left of the line, rumbling like thunder and rattling like hail, beating out the jaunty "Rogue's March." The fife joined in, screeching the tune. Brit, who'd stationed himself behind and to the right of the great line of men, moved forward to catch a glimpse of the prisoners. Their heads were shaven; stripped of their uniforms, they wore only their shirts and trousers. They were too far away to judge their expressions, to see if their faces wore a brand of shame. But the smaller of the two — McCardle, he guessed — had his head down, and stumbled along as if some numbness ran along his legs. The other — a fair-skinned man whose pale scalp contrasted with his sun-burned face — seemed bolder, and glanced around as if he himself were an onlooker at the spectacle.

What did he see, this deserter, when he looked at the men who had been his neighbors and his friends before they became his comrades-in-arms? Their faces were as solemn as if it were a funeral procession passing before them. And indeed, it was. In soul, in self-respect, in all that belonged to a man save the animated clay, Peters and McCardle were dead men. How could they walk away, feeling on their backs the damning gaze of their fellow men? How could they go home, if those at home cared for honor?

The little procession reached the end of the line. Brit could see clearly now the two men. Peters's composure was brazen, while McCardle's head drooped so low that only the bared top of his head showed his alternating blush and pallor. Guards marched on either side at fixed bayonets, while behind the condemned men were several more guards at charge bayonets, apparently ready to run them through if they should balk. Behind these came the fifer and drummer, still keeping up the

"Rogue's March."

Brit felt sick of it, but he could not turn away. What would be the effect of turning men loose upon the world when their epitaphs had already been written, carved in stone, never to be erased by any future act of courage or kindness? If men were marked down as lost souls, it only stood to reason they would behave that way.

CHAPTER THIRTEEN

MONDAY, MAY 26

Cameron Archer watched MacKenzie Stedman close the door, then go around to sit behind the big, paper-strewn desk. Stedman dropped into his chair like a man exhausted and laid his hands palms-down atop the stacks of paper, where they trembled so that Archer had to force himself not to stare.

"The fewer who know about this, the better," said Stedman, as Archer took the facing seat. Stedman went on in a low, uninflected voice. "It's fortunate the message was sent to me instead of to that jackanapes Randolph."

Archer was stunned to hear the name of the secretary of war.

Stedman went on. "I've taken a risk by deciding to let you handle it — least damage done, if we keep the politicians out

340

of it. And that seems to be what Goodell wants."

"Goodell?"

Stedman nodded. "It seems a slave skedaddled out of town to the closest Federal encampment. They're harboring him as a contraband of war, according to the bastard policy foisted on Lincoln by Frémont. Now the slave has come down with smallpox. Goodell is charging that the slave was sent into their camp on purpose, to spread infection among their soldiers." Stedman gave a dry chuckle. "Why should we send a slave to do what the Chickahominy fever is doing all on its own?"

Archer nodded. "You might also say it serves the Federals right. Since they first set foot on Virginia soil they've been buying information about our troop movements from runaway slaves. But what does Goodell want *me* to do?"

"He wants you to take the slave back to Richmond. Then he wants you to interrogate the slave — assuming he survives, question anyone else who might know anything, and report to him whether this was a deliberate act by someone on our side."

"Smallpox." Archer was thinking out loud. "We've had two cases to crop up here in Richmond, the Sullivan woman and

Josiah Harrald. The slave must have come into contact with one of them. And then, there's the matter of the stolen money, and the killing of Benjy. Perhaps this slave is the key to those mysteries."

Stedman shrugged. "Talk to Mrs. Powers. She's been going around asking questions ever since Josiah died. The idea that we would do it on purpose is ludicrous, of course." Stedman's frown deepened. "Goodell knows Virginia, he went to school here — he should know we are gentlemen. We could simply send back to say that his request is denied, or ignore it. There could be trouble, I don't have to tell you, if they decide to believe the worst and retaliate in kind. But —"

Archer cut him off. "I'll go. Will you arrange it so that I can travel to Casey's camp under a flag of truce to meet with Goodell?"

"When?"

Archer didn't hesitate. "As soon as it can be arranged. Tomorrow."

Judah Daniel pushed open the door to the Evans confectionery. Inside, the still air was heavy with the throat-clogging smell of sorghum, loud with the buzzing of flies. She walked up to the counter. It was covered with dust and dotted with dead flies.

Judah Daniel went around the counter and opened the door behind it. The door opened into a space just big enough for two people to pass one another — the landing for the stairs to the second floor. "Mal! Juney!" She went up the steps slowly, pausing to call out again. Soon she had climbed high enough to see into the second floor. The one open room was sweltering hot, dimly lit through the closed shutters. There were some pallets made up there. On one of them lay a small boy — Ise. Juney knelt over him, her face streaked with tears. Mal stood with his arm on Juney's shoulder, his face holding a mix of anger and fear that caught at Judah Daniel's heart.

Juney held her hand out. "Oh, Judah Daniel, my baby's done got the smallpox. Oh, God, don't take my baby!"

Judah Daniel sniffed the heavy air. There was a stink, all right, but it wasn't the smallpox. Still, might be he was in the early stages. She went to the boy and put her hand on his forehead, on his throat, on the crook of his elbow. Ise opened his eyes a fraction, then shut them tight. She looked closely at his skin. "What'd he bring up?"

"Brown stuff. It smelt something awful." Juney's voice was faint. "Then the last couple times, wasn't nothing but water, looked like."

"What he eat?"

Juney glanced at Mal. "Nothing since last night. Corn bread . . . crowder peas . . . with a little fatback in it."

"How long it been in the pot?"

"Oh, Judah Daniel, please don't let them sell him into slavery!"

Out of the corner of her eye Judah Daniel saw Mal's grip tighten on Juney's shoulder. She saw Juney twist away from her husband's hand. "No!" Juney's voice whipped out, low but fierce. "All this happen on account of *you* want to play the big man. You supposed to be free, but you done made yourself a slave to that Ragsdale. You ain't no kind of a man."

Judah Daniel braced herself to save Juney from Mal's punishing fist, but the blow didn't come. Mal stood, tears running down his face.

Judah Daniel spoke again. "It ain't the smallpox. Something Ise ate done give him a bad bellyache. I reckon it's about run its course. Give him some water with a little sugar in it, just a spoonful at a time till he keep that down. I'll bring by some tonic."

Juney sank to her knees. Her hand caressed her son's forehead.

"Mama . . . I ain't going to die?"

"No, baby," Juney cooed in response. "Ain't you heard what the doctoress say? It ain't the smallpox."

Judah Daniel straightened. "Mal?" She gestured with a motion of her head toward the stairs. Mal followed her, moving as if he had shrunk down inside his big body.

Judah Daniel went down the stairs and into the shop. She crossed her arms over her chest and looked up at Mal. "Where Sam at?"

"I swear to God, Judah Daniel, I don't know." Mal drew his arm across his face, wiping the tears onto the rough fabric of his shirt. "You think I'd let Juney suffer like this, if I knowed?"

For the past two days, Narcissa had been sticking close to the hospital, doing whatever she could to help with the patients. Feeling she was doing some good for the soldiers helped distract her from the uneasy awareness that she had done mischief to Pauline, Serena, and Aurelia — and through Aurelia, to Coffin. She had meant to warn the women about the danger they were facing, each of them in a different way, from Ragsdale. But what was the good of warning, when there was no safety to be had?

And she thought about what Aurelia had said, that all men are the same when it comes to women. She wondered about all the times she had seen a man cling to life in the hope of seeing a beloved face again, all the tender reunions she had witnessed, and the heart-breaking farewells. How many of those men had sinned against their marriage vows? If a man sinned by lying with a woman who was not his wife, did that mean he did not truly love his wife? And the wife who loved him — would she love him still, if she knew?

"Mrs. Powers."

Archer's voice startled her from her reverie. A convalescent soldier stepped up to take the bowl and cloth from her hand. "I'll do this for you, ma'am," he said politely. Archer moved away, striding through the line of beds to stand near the window. Narcissa followed, as she knew he expected her to do.

Without preamble, he told her, "A slave ill with smallpox has been found in the Federal camp. There's an accusation that we sent him deliberately to infect their soldiers. Where does this fit in with what you know — or suspect?"

Ragsdale, Narcissa thought, then stopped. Why did she think so? She spoke carefully, trying to make sense of it for herself as well as for Archer.

"Ragsdale has money hidden in a warehouse he bought from the Harralds. I believe the money was tainted with smallpox, and that Ragsdale has used it at least twice: some of it to pay the dressmaker, Miss Sullivan, and more to pay Josiah Harrald — maybe, to kill him. A woman may have helped Ragsdale kill Josiah, whether she knew it or not." She explained about the question Ragsdale had asked Stedman, the money in the warehouse, the scraps of red . . . Somehow, spoken out loud to the skeptical Archer, the threads no longer made a tapestry.

Archer frowned. "You have no proof of any of this, have you?"

Narcissa shook her head. "No, I haven't, though I believe Ragsdale is capable of having done it. He is unscrupulous, and he is greedy. But as to whether he would send an infected slave into the Union ranks . . . Why would he do it? What would he have to gain from it?"

Archer shrugged. "It's worth questioning the slave about, when we take custody of him tomorrow."

He took his leave then. Narcissa looked after him, thinking how noble and fine he looked in his uniform, and thinking how deceiving looks can be.

CHAPTER FOURTEEN

TUESDAY, MAY 27

A lieutenant bearing a limp white flag of truce and carrying a pass signed by General Johnston led the ragged little procession out of Richmond toward the spot six miles east of Richmond where Brigadier General Silas Casey's division had its camp. Cameron Archer kept his mount's pace to that of the wagon in which the diseased slave would be brought back to Richmond. Private Archer Langdon, wide-eyed and solemn-faced, drove the wagon, while Judah Daniel, who would tend to the patient's needs on the way, sat in the wagon bed, which was covered with an improvised tent to keep off the rain. A yellow hospital flag drooped despondently from the back.

They drove south and east along the Williamsburg road past the shipyards at Rocketts and on beyond the city's inner defenses. The crowded wooden buildings of the wharves yielded to an undistinguished landscape of churned red clay and skinny pines. A half-hour's ride brought them in hailing distance of the Federal pickets. The lieutenant beside Archer displayed the truce flag, then advanced cautiously to show their pass to the blue-uniformed men. After a few moments Archer saw one of the pickets give the signal for them to pass. As they did so, several of the bluecoats came alongside as escorts. Langdon cracked the whip, and the wagon lurched forward.

Out of one prison, into another. Archer found himself wanting to put the spurs to his horse and ride, on and on, past the Federal encampment, past every armed camp from here to Canada. For a moment he indulged his imagination in a wild flight north, to a wilderness in which he would live like an animal. He imagined a cold black sky filled with innumerable stars.

Another half-hour brought them to the Federal encampment. The blue-coated men were thicker along the road now. But the trees were thinner, lines of low stumps and gaping holes showing where they had been felled or pulled loose from the clay soil. Off to his left Archer could see one use to which they had been put: an abatis of whole trees, tangled together with thick vine-ropes of poison ivy and Virginia creeper, ran between the woods and the clearing, ready to block a Confederate attack. Archer continued on past earthworks and a cannon emplacement into the camp itself. Before him spread row upon row of tents forming a play city far more orderly than the real one he had left behind.

At the southeast edge of the camp, a red hospital flag marked a Sibley tent set well apart from the others. Archer saw that their escorts were leading them toward it. When they drew close, he dismounted, handed the reins to his young cousin Langdon, and went along with the escorts. He ducked to pass through the opening. Inside, at the center of the cone-shaped tent, he could stand upright. Despite the warmth of the day, a low fire burned. He saw Goodell first, greeted him briefly. "I want to examine the patient."

Goodell nodded, his face expressionless, and gestured toward a heap of rags that lay in the dimmest quadrant of the tent. Archer bent down and looked closer. He had been expecting a grown man, but the slave was only a child, small and thin. He looked feverish, but the scattered pustules were distinct, indicating a relatively mild case. Well-marked pustules, together with fever, indicated the disease was at its turning point: the boy should recover.

"Goodell, I'd like your permission to bring in the nurse I brought with me. I think she may know this boy."

Goodell's eyebrows rose, but he nodded. Archer strode out of the tent and beckoned to Judah Daniel.

Some nasty job none of the white folks want to do, Judah Daniel thought as she climbed out of the wagon in response to Archer's wave. But she was glad enough to be called, to put an end at last to the questions in her head.

It's just a little boy. She knelt beside the heap of rags. She saw his eyes widen, saw a look of relief in them before he skooched up close to her and rested his face on her skirt. *It's Sam. And he looks like he's going to make it. Praise God.* She touched him lightly on the head. "Hey, sugar," she said softly. "How you doing?"

"Thirsty," Sam whispered. There was a cup with water in it sitting on a box near the straw pallet on which Sam lay. She worked her arm under him, holding him up to take a drink. He took several swallows, coughed a little, then lay back down. "You come to take me back?"

Not knowing how Sam would like the answer to his question, she asked one of her own. "How'd you get here, honey? You walk all this way, sick as you been?"

"Yes'm, I walked. Some of the folks here been good to me and some of them been mean, but I can't go back."

Judah Daniel knew the white men, Archer and the Union surgeon, were listening behind her. It was best the truth come out, whatever it was. Maybe the Union doctor would force Archer to let the boy stay. It almost made her laugh out loud to think of Cameron Archer having to take orders. But here his army rank, his surgeon's status, his family connections, meant nothing; he was just a gray-coated minnow in a sea of blue.

"Why'd you steal them things from the smallpox hospital?"

Sam hesitated, his eyes dark wells of sadness. "My family gone be sold as slaves if I tell."

"Who was it told you that, baby?" Judah Daniel asked gently.

Sam shook his head. "I can't say. I want my mama." He sniffed. "Judah Daniel . . .

am I going to die?"

"No, you ain't. That why you ran away, 'cause somebody scared you?"

"Yes'm. And 'cause of what Tyler said."

Tyler. Now Judah Daniel wished she hadn't questioned him in front of the white men. Would Sam say something that would get Tyler into trouble?

Sam went on, his voice was growing weaker. "He told me to be a man and do what's right. I was scared. But I wanted to be brave. So I ran away to help the Yankees. Tyler, he —"

Judah Daniel put her finger up to her lips. "Ssh, Sam. Rest now." Maybe she had shushed him in time, before Archer became suspicious of Tyler.

She heard Archer's voice behind her. "Did you hear that, Goodell? The boy came wanting to *help* your side." She turned to get a look at Archer's face. He was smiling a little at the notion of a little black boy helping the Federals. But there was something else in his eyes — a gleam of anger. "That's the explanation, after all your charges against us. Some bully made his life miserable in Richmond, so he ran away." Archer was silent for a moment, then said, "Well, it's time we were off. Judah Daniel, you help the boy to relieve himself, clean him up, and get him into the wagon. Goodell, I'd like a word with you. Shall we walk?"

Judah Daniel got Sam's filthy clothes off him and began to sponge him off with a rag wrung out in tepid water. She asked Private Langdon to fetch the clean shirt from the wagon, and he jumped to do it, no doubt eager to escape from the fetid air of the tent. The man's homespun shirt she had brought would hang almost to Sam's ankles. She had expected to find a full-grown man, fled for his freedom — a man like Tyler. Instead she had found a boy, and with him the truth, at least some of it. What Sam had said, and what he had been afraid to say, made it as clear as spring-water to her. Someone had used the smallest of the Cats, Sam and Timmy, to slip through the window of the Egyptian building and bring out money and cloth-ing. Sam, scared — whether by Benjy's fate, or some spoken threat, or both — had run away. She tried to remember what Tyler had told her about his encounter with Sam. Tyler had been upset, she recalled, torn between his desire to join the Yankees and his fears for his wife and son and unborn child. He'd said to Sam the words that he heard in his own head day after day.

"Sam, you told me Tyler had something to do with your running to the Yankees. It ain't safe to talk about that in front of the white folks, might get Tyler in trouble. But you can tell me now, if you feel like it."

Sam nodded. "Tyler asked me things. I didn't tell him nothing. I was afraid."

"Not of Tyler, surely?" Judah Daniel asked.

"No." Sam clamped his mouth shut on the word.

"Don't be scared, Sam," Judah Daniel soothed him. "Whoever done this to you ain't no brave man nor no smart man. He ain't nothing but a coward."

Sam nodded again. The disfiguring pustules made his expression hard to read, but Judah Daniel thought he looked a little cheered.

"But you been brave, Sam, and you done as much as a man can do."

Sam's cracked and swollen lips curved up in a smile at that. "I reckon that's so."

It was too bad Sam had got caught up in Tyler's private war, but maybe running away had been the best thing he could have done. Maybe it had saved his life. Now it was up to her and any friends she could find to make sure his life stayed saved.

When Archer decided he and Goodell were safely out of earshot, he began. "When last we met, you talked about honor. You brought up a certain matter as evidence of your own honor. Only a few days later, I had that same matter thrown in my face as a taunt by as contemptible a blackguard as I've ever met. So I ask myself: how did he learn of it? Not from me. So it had to be from you, or from someone you told."

Stephen Goodell looked into Archer's eyes. "I told no one. I can only believe you were mistaken to think no one else knew. Some servant, probably —"

"No!" Archer's hands balled into fists at his side. "No one saw."

Goodell shook his head impatiently. "We were young then. The young think only of themselves. It may well be that no one *saw* the two of you that night. But a disarrangement of the hair or the dress . . . Even less than that: a smile, a word, a look exchanged . . . Don't you know, now that you are a man, the many ways we betray ourselves?"

I think you betrayed me. The words burned in Archer's head, but he did not say them. He had to admit that Goodell might be right. Anyone who had seen him in conversation with her must have known his interest. And if the signs of her encouragement were there for him to read, others could have read them too.

Goodell turned away, saying, "You had better go. We've had word there's fighting up at Hanover Courthouse."

The wagon that carried the boy Sam back to Richmond was the one allotted for transporting smallpox victims wherever it was necessary for them to go: the smallpox hospital, or the cemetery. It was someone's old farm wagon, drawn by a broken-down nag. Archer told his young cousin to go slow along the muddy, rutted road, out of consideration for the sick boy; but had he ordered him to make all speed, it likely would have made little difference. So Archer held his horse to an amble and allowed himself to remember.

It was spring, how many years ago now? A dozen or more. He had been twenty-one or thereabouts, Aurelia just seventeen. When he thought about it afterward, in cool reflection, he knew what he had done was dishonorable. But she had thrown herself at him, let him know a thousand ways that he could come closer. . . . At last it had seemed almost ungentlemanly of him to refuse. Foolish, he knew now. Far better he had insulted her with a rejection.

For a while during medical school, he, along with Stephen Goodell, had lived at the home of his late sister's husband on Shockoe Hill. It was the home he had since inherited, in which he now lived alone. Aurelia Harrald had appeared at parties to which they were invited. She was a lovely girl, but there was something about her . . . now he would see it as loneliness, a desperate longing to be accepted, the result perhaps of her father's pushing her into company that looked down on her lack of brilliance. There were rumors about her — that she would allow liberties other girls would not. Now it seemed pathetic. Then, it had been exciting. He had had experience, a little, paid for in the accustomed way. He had never intended . . . but somehow she had wound up in his room, when there was no one to know what they did. At last Goodell had knocked on the door to warn them.

For a few days, weeks perhaps, he had wondered: would her parents hear of it? Would her father demand a marriage? Then he had heard she had gone away. It had felt like a release, though there had been moments in which he had burned with shame for his cowardice in not offering to marry her. When at last they did meet again, they had treated each other with the calm cordiality of mere acquaintances.

Aurelia Harrald had escaped disgrace. All this time he had thanked Goodell for that. But now . . .

Darkness was gathering as Judah Daniel walked back from the pest-house, where she had left Sam in the care of Narcissa Powers and Jim Furbish, to the Chapmans' home, where she had been staying with her ward, Darcy, ever since her own house burned. She and Darcy had come to think of the rambling wooden structure that housed the extended Chapman family as their own home, or almost. John Chapman ruled his family with a strong but loving hand, so that the lack of a strong, grandmotherly woman — the woman John Chapman's wife would have been, if she'd lived — wasn't felt too sharply. Judah Daniel sometimes felt that John would like her to step into that role, but she resisted even acknowledging his interest. She worked, and lived — for her work was her life, the thing that fed her spirit — best alone, training Darcy to be doctoress after her.

Tonight, though, she found herself longing for the welcoming embrace of the Chapmans, the warm, noisy rooms, the smiles and teasing among the generations that began with old Honus Chapman, grew, and blossomed in children, grand-children, great-grandchildren. Since Benjy's death, a hard, bitter feeling had settled on her — behind her eyes, in her throat, at the pit of her stomach. If the feeling could be put in words, it would say something like, *None of it matters. Human life, human love. We're alone in the grave.*

When she opened the door to the Chapmans', all these thoughts fell away. Elda jumped up — she must have been sit-ting staring at the door — but when she saw Judah Daniel there, she stood still, hesitating. Clearly she'd expected someone else. The room was crowded with eight or ten women, aunts, sisters, nieces of John Chapman.

"Judah Daniel, you got to talk some sense into her," said Phyllis, one of John Chapman's sisters, the closest to him in age.

At this, Elda stepped forward and put out her hand. "Judah Daniel, you got to let me go!" She took hold of Judah Daniel's arm and shook it, like a child begging her mother for some favor.

Judah Daniel patted Elda's arm and looked over her head to Phyllis. "Elda, you can't go nowhere, think of your condition. Go let Phyllis get you into bed. You let me take care of whatever it is."

Phyllis came up and put her arm around Elda, who fixed Judah Daniel with a pleading look but allowed herself to be led away. Some of the other women went with them, murmuring encouragement.

Another one of the sisters, Betty, came up to Judah Daniel. "Them plug-uglies was snooping around the bake shop today. John got it in his head they going to break into the shop tonight. Him and Tyler went down there." Betty spoke in a low tone, her face tight with anxiety. "They say they ain't going to fight, but they ain't got to do no more than show their faces, and they'll get taken in by the guard."

Judah Daniel felt herself respond to this new threat, felt her head go up and her lungs fill with air. She knew what it was to want to fight, to hold anger in until it couldn't be held any longer. She knew John and Tyler were both holding in anger — at the unfair laws, at the men who enforced them, and not least at each other. She hoped she could get there in time to talk some sense into them. Good thing she had her pass from Dr. Archer: she might need it if she were caught out after dark.

Well, at least she couldn't get all down in the mouth about the worth of a human life while she was being asked to save two of them. "I'll go see what's going on. Most likely nothing." She said this to reassure the women.

Judah Daniel took a careful path along the half-mile from the Chapmans' house on Navy Hill to the bake shop on Main Street, feeling her way down dark alleys and pressing in between buildings where only the thinness of her frame allowed her to pass. Remembering what John Tyler had said about the trapdoor, she eased her way into the stable. There was the big horse Raven, tied to the side of the stall. And there were John and Tyler, hunkered down in the straw. They were crouched low, ready to jump on the intruder, but relaxed at the sight of her. She lowered herself to sit beside them, and they accepted her presence, more intent on keeping quiet than on shooing her away.

About a half-hour passed that way. Judah Daniel's pounding heart had slowed, her legs were cramping, and she was wishing she had chosen to reassure Elda with words, when they heard hurrying footfalls in the rain-softened dirt of the yard between the stable and the bake shop's kitchen. There was silence for a moment, then a thumping noise, then what sounded like a muffled curse. Then she heard pounding, heavy and measured, a man's fist against wood. Someone was trying to break into the bake shop.

She felt Tyler shift beside her. In a moment he was up and running into the yard, John Chapman right behind him. Judah Daniel stood more cautiously. If she didn't rush out into the arms of the plug-uglies, maybe there would be something she could do to save Tyler and John.

She saw two, no, three figures wrestling in the dirt. Oh, they were fighting all right. This couldn't be good, no matter how it turned out. At last two of them seemed to subdue the other. She heard her name called softly, urgently. If they'd jumped one of the plug-uglies in their anger, it made no matter if they'd won or lost the fight. How could she get them out of this? She crossed the little yard slowly, trying to think. Then she saw that the man was black. A moment later she recognized Mal Evans.

"Bring him into the shop," she heard John tell Tyler. "Mal, don't you try and run away."

Judah Daniel was making for the door of the shop, feeling her way in the near-dark. Her foot struck something lying on the ground — a bag of flour, it felt like. She reached down to push it away, and her hand touched skin, hot with fever . . . skin whose smooth surface had erupted in rough, raised bumps.

She moved to the door, and it swung open — Mal Evans must have pulled on it with such force that the lock had broken. The banked fire in the oven gave a little light to the scene.

Tear tracks darkened the dirt on Mal's face. "Before God, Chapman, you got to believe me. She told me my sons be sold as slaves —" Mal Evans was sobbing, pleading. John and Tyler had Mal up on his feet now, one on each side of him. Mal was a head taller and a good deal broader than either of the Chapman men; if he'd tried to, he could have shaken them off. They didn't seem to be holding him back, though, as much as holding him up.

Judah Daniel knelt by the ragged bundle and turned his face to the light. It was Timmy Terry. "Cassie Terry told you that?" she asked Mal.

Tyler glanced at the ragged bundle on the ground. His eyes widened. "Jesus, Mal, what you bring that white boy here for? Look like he — oh, God, he got the smallpox."

Tears and sweat ran down Mal's face. "Cassie told me to dump him here. I had to do it. But it ain't going to make no difference. Why would she care about *my* sons, when she don't care nothing about her own?"

Judah Daniel crouched next to the boy, got his arms around her neck, then lifted him. He wrapped his legs around her waist — he was a child, after all, not so many years past being carried — and tightened his grip around her neck. His hot face rested on her shoulder. *Jesus, help me keep this one safe*. Then she looked up at the three men. "You got to hide. The plug-uglies going to be here any minute. They think they done found a way to close down Chapman's bake shop." As she started to leave, she turned back to Mal. "Tell Juney: Sam's alive."

As Judah Daniel hurried out of the yard the way she had come, she saw the three men disappearing into the stable. Not a moment too soon. From the street beyond the bake shop she could hear the sounds of horses and men.

Holding Timmy's fever-hot body in her arms, Judah Daniel passed through the alley, the yard behind the next house, and on to Franklin Street. She walked fast, and she thought. Mal's command from Cassie was to leave Timmy in the bake shop, but that was only half of the plan. The plug-uglies had followed Mal and ridden up in force to *find* the sick boy who, with his obvious signs of smallpox infection, would give them an excuse to shut down the Chapmans' bake shop, at least for a while. Most of the things stored there would have to be burned, and when word got out, people might refuse to buy from them even after it was safe. That would be their way of punishing John Chapman for refusing to sell liquor for them.

Mal hadn't known the plug-uglies were following him. He'd taken his orders from Cassie Terry. Hard as it was to credit, Cassie must have offered her own son to the plug-uglies. What was Cassie getting in return, other than enough liquor to dull any grief or shame she may feel? And what would the plug-uglies do now that their plan had failed? Would they go through the town looking for Timmy? Did they have reason to fear what he might remember, and tell, if he recovered from the disease?

She had to take him someplace safe — where nobody could hurt him, and where his smallpox could not hurt anybody. She thought of the Chapmans'. Tyler, John, Elda, Young John, Darcy — all, she knew, had been inoculated against smallpox. But she could not be so sure about the other family members and friends who wandered in and out of the Chapmans' house. And soon there would be a baby.

What about the medical college, the makeshift pest-house where Josiah Harrald had died? Jim Furbish would look after the boy, and she herself could keep an eye on him. Maybe that was best. She thought for a moment, getting her bearings. She could follow the alleyways up to Marshall Street.

If any of the night watch stopped her, she would only have to yell *Smallpox!* as hard as she could to raise a panic the Military Guard and civilian police together couldn't put down. Strange: the weapon this boy carried in his body could take a city without a shot being fired.

Mal went first into the tunnel. Tyler motioned his father in next. John frowned as if to argue the point but gave it up. Tyler stepped around to the head of Raven and untied him, then lowered himself into the opening and shut the trapdoor. With any luck, Raven would step over the trapdoor and obscure it from notice. There was no time left to make a better plan.

In a few moments heavy boot heels were tramping on the wooden floor just over their heads. There was a high whinny and stamping of hooves, then a muffled curse. "Damn horse used to niggers, I guess," came the voice of a man.

"Let's get out of here," said a second voice. "Anybody sees us, next thing you know the newspapers will be saying we missed them Cats again."

The first speaker seemed to agree. "Miller done took off already. He's been sour as curdled milk ever since that yellow-headed whore of his took up with Ragsdale."

The Chapmans and Mal Evans, lying on their sides in the tunnel, heard the men leave. But was it safe to come out? Suppose the men had only pretended to leave? Once Tyler prodded his father with the toe of his shoe by way of asking, *Can we come out now?* His father grabbed his ankle and held it: *Keep still.* They stayed there for what must have been two hours. At last John said, "All right, Tyler, reckon it's safe." Tyler raised the trapdoor and peered out into the dusky predawn light.

Judah Daniel was stopped only once, by two men of the night watch. One of the men held his pine-knot torch close to examine her burden, then stepped back and waved her on. When his companion protested, the man warned, "Smallpox — eat up with it."

In the basement room of the Egyptian building, all was quiet. Narcissa rose from her seat near Sam's pallet. She spoke gently to Timmy and smoothed his hair. While Judah Daniel settled Timmy on a pallet close to Sam's, Narcissa busied herself gathering a tallow candle, a bowl of water, and some clean rags. She knelt near Timmy and held the light so that it shone down on his face.

The boy didn't wake. Maybe he'd been doped with something. He was filthy, his hair matted. The pustules were clumped more thickly around his mouth and along his cheeks, forming a sort of band across his face. Narcissa lifted one of his hands, then the other. There, too, the bumps were clustered braceletlike around the wrists. She examined his trunk and legs. The same band of angry bumps circled each ankle.

Judah Daniel, who had been watching, said at last, "Look like he been tied up. Wrists and ankles and across the mouth, too."

Narcissa nodded, anger rising in her. She had seen it on smallpox patients before, that anything binding or rubbing the skin — shirt cuffs or collars, for example — stimulated the pocks. In this case, the pustules left a record in the flesh of the cruel treatment Timmy had received. Who had done this, and why?

Judah Daniel plucked a small object from the straw, placed it in her palm, and held it out so that Narcissa could see it. "What you think about this?"

Narcissa looked at it, rubbed it between her thumb and forefingers. It was a feather, an inch long or a little more, once white, now gray and gummed together with filth. "Where do you suppose it came from?" she asked. "A mattress?"

Judah Daniel shook her head, puzzling over it.

Narcissa let the feather fall from her hand. "It looks like these two boys were our thieves. I think their exposure came at the same time. Benjy must have hidden them, but when they fell sick . . . maybe he was afraid to keep their secret any longer. Then someone killed Benjy. After that . . . Maybe they will be well enough soon to speak for themselves. Sam is faring a little better — thanks to our enemies."

Jim Furbish came into the room. "It's him, ain't it?" Jim asked in a sad-sounding voice. "The little boy I seen come in through the window."

Judah Daniel nodded. "They dumped him in the street." She trusted Jim, but the fewer people who knew the Chapmans were involved, the better. "I reckon it was the plug-uglies that dumped him."

Jim's eyes widened. "You think the plug-uglies got him to steal the smallpox money? Think maybe they killed Benjy, too?"

"I ain't sure."

Jim Furbish looked back at the boy and shook his head. "Beats me how people can be so hardhearted."

Ragsdale, Narcissa thought. *He chooses his victims carefully . . . frightened little boys, desperate women . . . and me.*

She spoke aloud. "These boys are still in danger."

Judah Daniel nodded. "Might be they know who killed Benjy. Might be they even seen it done. But they's too scared to say."

Narcissa made a decision. "We'll watch them — you and me, Judah Daniel, taking turns, and Jim and Nahum — two of us, all the time. That way, we can keep them safe, and also be ready to hear when they are ready to speak. I'll take the first watch."

"Judah Daniel!"

How long had Betty been standing at the door of the Chapmans'? And the other women had waited with her: Judah Daniel could hear their voices, one by one, exhaled like bubbles bursting, releasing the pent-up air.

"It's all right," Judah Daniel called out. She heard her words repeated, relayed from one woman to another within the house. She could only hope the words were true.

Once she was inside, the women fell silent, waiting. "Tyler and John are all right." She saw the women darting nervous glances at each other, and at her. What was worrying them, if not John and Tyler?

The answer came from somewhere back in the house: a moan, low and pent-up, but growing, rising, pushing its way through the throat of the sufferer, forcing apart the clenched teeth, bursting forth as a wail.

"It's Elda." Betty's gentle face was sharp with worry. "Seem like the fright brought on her pains."

So the baby was coming: early, but not by much. Judah Daniel had expected Elda to begin labor with the next full moon, two weeks away. Not enough to worry about, in normal times. But with the strain Elda had been under . . . The women were clucking like chickens watching over their biddies, but Judah Daniel felt the power coming into her, muffling their voices and all other concerns. God was getting ready to bring new life into the world, using her mind and her hands.

"I'll see to her, don't you worry about that." Betty's face lost its pinched look.

Judah Daniel felt a touch on her elbow. "I's here, Judah Daniel." It was Darcy, her apprentice, called by the power before Judah Daniel could speak her name. "I got the tallow fat warming on the stove."

CHAPTER FIFTEEN

WEDNESDAY, MAY 28

Judah Daniel hurried down the hill to the Terrys' ramshackle dwelling. When she saw the shutters closed against the sun-drenched morning, her feeling of dread grew stronger.

She knocked at the door, then pushed it open. What she saw, and smelled, made her stop. In a moment she had herself composed again. She went into the room.

The reek that assaulted her nostrils carried the sick-sweet smell of applejack and the bitter tang of vomit. Maybe Cassie was only passed out, slipped from her chair into that awkward position on the floor. But as Judah Daniel moved closer, she knew she was in the presence of death. Cassie Terry lay curled up, her legs drawn up and her backbone curving so that her head almost touched her knees. Given her bulk, it was likely that some sort of spasm had contorted her body into the pose just as it had killed her.

Judah Daniel went around Cassie toward the back of the house, where she had found the children before. Rose, her young face thin and grayish, moved out of the shadows to meet her. Behind her, a keening wail told her the children were grieving for their mother. Or maybe they were just hungry.

She walked out through the back of the house into the little yard she had seen before. Something about it, something she couldn't quite call to mind, tugged at her. All at once she knew what it was. She picked her way through the mud and filth to a wooden structure, little more than a thrown-together collection of boards that at its highest point reached about to her breastbone.

Judah Daniel bent down and peered inside the jumbled boards. There was evidence of chickens — the smell of dried droppings was unmistakable. There were bits of feathers all around, too — maybe a dog or a fox had ended the Terrys' attempts to raise chickens. In the corner was a little heap of soiled rags.

Judah Daniel thought of the times she

had come to this house, asking after Timmy. He had been here all the while, ever since he had run or been driven from the hiding place Benjy had made for him and Sam. Here his mother had kept him, gagged so his cries would not be heard. But someone had paid her, maybe given her liquor too. And maybe put something extra in the last batch, to make sure she didn't tell. If it turned out there was poison in it — if the police ever bothered to check — things didn't look good for Mal Evans.

She heard a little noise behind her and turned to see Rose. She had been crying, crying so hard the youth and life were about washed out of her. "Mama had somebody come and take him away. She said he was going to die anyways."

Judah Daniel stood and gathered Rose to her. "Timmy's alive, honey. Don't you cry no more. Don't cry. He going to live."

Judah Daniel stood in Mal Evans's shop and told him again the news she had called out over her shoulder at the Chapmans' bake shop. "Sam's got the smallpox, but he done got over the worst of it."

"Praise God. Where he at?"

"Someplace safe. Tell Juney she can see him soon." She wouldn't make Mal suffer more than she could help. But what she had to know, in order to see justice done, was inside his head — so close she could almost touch it, but she had to get him to say it.

Mal stood there, shoulders slumped and arms loose at his sides, given in to what he knew was coming.

"You been helping Ragsdale."

Mal nodded, his attention on something that wasn't in front of his eyes. "His man Miller got me to selling liquor for him. It broke the law, but I didn't care nothing about that. Don't know what kind of law they can call it anyway, where a handful of men makes the rules to help themselves. But then the plug-uglies gone after John Chapman, to get him to sell liquor. John so damn proud, he just played like he didn't know what they was getting at till they give up, I reckon. So they come to me, told me I had to get the Chapmans to go along. When I said I couldn't, Miller told me — it was the second time I seen him — he told he'd have me thrown in prison for selling applejack, have my boys sold as slaves. Arrest *me* for selling liquor, when *he's* the one got me to do it!"

By the look on Mal's face, he would have killed Miller. But there was nothing he could do, nothing that wouldn't wind up destroying him and his family. Judah Daniel felt for him, but she had to press on.

Mal passed a big hand over his face. "I heard Miller and Ragsdale had a falling-out over some woman Miller thought was his property. She's took up with Ragsdale, Miller's high and dry, so all of a sudden he ain't so happy working for Ragsdale no more. Anyway, it weren't neither of them got me to dump that poor boy at the Chapmans'. It was the boy's own mother did that. Cassie told me he was dead. I was halfway to the Chapmans' before I seen he was alive. I reckoned I couldn't take him back —"

Judah Daniel broke in. " 'Cause the plug-uglies was going to be looking for a sick boy at the Chapmans', and you was afraid to disappoint them?"

"No! It weren't me told them. When I heard them standing right over where we was hiding in the tunnel, I thought I was going to die."

"Well, Mal, I reckon that's how it was. These folks is mighty good at getting other folks scared of them. That's how come Sam run away."

Mal put his hand to his forehead. He looked like he didn't want to believe what she was saying. "My boy run away?"

Judah Daniel felt bitter anger flame up in her. A man's pride depended on being able to protect his children. What black man, slave or free, could do that?

She believed what Mal had said. But the plug-uglies had been on the spot. Someone must have set it up with Cassie Terry, then followed Mal as he left her place for the bake shop. If things had turned out different, if Mal had been caught with the body, chances are the Military Guard would have grabbed him and charged him with the murder of Cassie Terry, maybe other crimes as well. Even though he had escaped capture, there was nothing Mal could do, since the law took no notice of a black man's accusation against a white man. When Ragsdale hurt somebody, he picked somebody who couldn't hurt back.

"I been a fool, Judah Daniel." Mal's deep voice was soft, ragged with emotion. "I done throwed away everything."

Judah Daniel thought for a minute. "If Miller and Ragsdale's turned on each other, they won't be worrying about Cassie

Terry. Let's you and me go see her and see if we can get the truth out of her."

Mal straightened his shoulders. "All right."

Judah Daniel waved her hand. It seemed Mal really didn't know. "Cassie Terry's dead. Poisoned, unless I miss my guess. If you smart, you'll take all them bottles and drop 'em into the river."

Cameron Archer had dreams in which Roland Ragsdale and Stephen Goodell were whispering against him, pointing and laughing, while he burned with shame. He woke convinced that the two men were somehow conspiring against him and against the Confederacy. Even as reason returned, the notion haunted him. Nothing was what it seemed. No one could be trusted. Sam Evans's claim that he had acted on his own by fleeing to the Federal camp was not enough to dispel Archer's suspicions. Someone had scared Sam so thoroughly that even now the boy clung to the story he'd been ordered to tell.

Neither was Archer inclined to credit Goodell just because the man had been a friend, and Archer had always believed him to have the highest regard for honor. If honor had once been an absolute, it was no longer.

The question he kept returning to was, what did Ragsdale have to gain from loosing smallpox among the Federals? At last he concluded that the only thing to do was ask Ragsdale himself.

Ragsdale, still at home in the late morning, displayed his usual sang-froid. He settled back in his chair, smoothed the fine silk fabric of his smoking jacket, and smiled. "So good to see you again, Doctor. Please forgive me if I don't shake hands — a little, er, soreness in my shoulder. I suppose you've come to ask for the money I promised for the hospital."

Archer got to the point. "I am wondering if your patriotism extends further than that . . . if perhaps you have been working behind the scenes as well."

Ragsdale looked at him over steepled fingers. "I'm afraid I don't know what you mean."

Let's get to it. Archer drew a deep breath. "The recent outbreak of smallpox here in Richmond began with some tainted money. I believe it was yours."

Ragsdale smiled coldly. "No. Those who

work for me are immunized at the least hint of an outbreak. In a business such as mine, a rumor of infection would be" — he smiled a little — "fatal."

"Rumors are grist to your mill, are they not, Ragsdale? Perhaps you've heard that a slave ill with smallpox has turned up in the Federals' camp. Some think he may have been sent on purpose to spread the disease. An advantage to us, if the Federals should be decimated by it." Archer's tone was light. Boasts always came easier than confession: let Ragsdale think him capable of admiring such an act.

Ragsdale looked up, seeming surprised. "Is that so? It sounds like the merest accident to me. I doubt we have anyone clever enough, or bold enough, on our side to manage a deliberate attack on the health of the enemy. Still, it's as you say, a benefit for us. Do they know how many Federals have fallen ill as a result?"

Archer temporized. "So you know nothing of this?"

"Not I," Ragsdale responded lightly.

Why had he thought this would be easy? Ragsdale was too much a man of the world to be rattled by an accusation that — short of the slave's own evidence — would be the devil to prove. And the slave could not testify against Ragsdale in a court of law. Still, if he trod carefully . . . "But you condone it?"

"Wars are won by weapons, Doctor," Ragsdale replied coolly. "Our side lacks manufacturing capabilities, raw materials, trained workmen. While we — or perhaps I should say *you,* since I do not come from wealth and privilege — were living a dream from a sentimental novel, the North was building factories. If we expect to win this war, we must use the weapons to hand."

Archer frowned. The man's complacency was pulling at the edges of his temper. "Some weapons blow up in the faces of those who would use them. Smallpox would be such a one."

Ragsdale's smile was condescending. "While Richmond is under siege, we are all soldiers, like it or not. And there are always accidents."

"Those who lower themselves so are rogues, not soldiers, and do not deserve to prevail."

Ragsdale's retort came quickly. "If we are not willing to scratch and claw for any weapon that will give us an advantage — *any* weapon — we may as well surrender here and now."

Archer, uncomfortably aware of his own

defense of torpedoes, said nothing.

Ragsdale's smile grew triumphant. "We used smallpox to kill the Indians, with infected blankets. Your friend Stedman told me that. What is a slave with smallpox, after all, but a human torpedo?"

Archer stared at him for a moment, then said, not trying to hide his disbelief, "And yet you say you had no hand in it?"

Ragsdale stood up. "I have said not. But you do not believe me. You think you are a gentleman, and I am not. Yet you yourself have been a habitué of the gambling hells. Or perhaps it is my other business that you pretend to disapprove of. And yet you yourself have known the delight of plucking forbidden fruit, despite the fact it is not yours to enjoy. In at least one case, the lady in question was an amateur. That makes it worse."

Ragsdale went to walk past him, but Archer caught him by the arm and turned him around. "I will assure my Federal counterpart that no more infected slaves will be appearing in their camp. And if I hear about one more outbreak of smallpox in this town, I will come after you. Do you understand me, Ragsdale?"

Ragsdale shook off his hand. "Much better, I think, than you understand me."

Mirrie, waving a folded newspaper, met Narcissa at the door. "Read this!" she exclaimed, and thrust the day's *Dispatch* into Narcissa's hands. There was a small item circled in pencil. Narcissa held it up and read,

The Cyprian Polly Avery, who affects the name of Pauline, was apprehended late last night at the home of a certain prosperous gentleman. The Cyprian must have been preparing to sell what is left of her soul to the D—, for she had buried the blade of her penknife in the gentleman's chest. The gentleman was not much hurt, giving credence to the belief current in some quarters that he is the D— himself. Miss Avery has taken up temporary residence in Castle Godwin.

"Ragsdale! Well — now Aurelia can have no doubts."

Mirrie nodded vigorously. "Mr. Wallace came by to tell you. The news is all over town. And now, read *this*." She refolded the paper and pointed to another item circled in pencil.

Mr. Roland Ragsdale, who gave

$10,000 for the care of our sick and wounded, is offering further proof of his patriotic fervor. He has announced plans to destroy the tobacco in his warehouses. Though the destruction of tobacco in danger of Federal seizure has been ordered by the Confederate government, no holder of tobacco in this city has yet to carry out the order. It remains to be seen whether Mr. Ragsdale's patriotism will be emulated.

Narcissa looked up. "What does it mean? There *is* no tobacco in his warehouses, most of them. Does he mean to destroy the smallpox money? Or does he want us to think so?" Narcissa handed the paper back to Mirrie. "I must try one more time to speak with Pauline Avery. The night of the reception, she seemed to be doing Mr. Ragsdale's bidding. But now . . ." Now, she thought to herself, Pauline had faced the truth about Ragsdale. The truth that she, Narcissa, had forced her to confront. So this would be an end of it at last. Pauline would confess to having done Ragsdale's bidding, admit to having visited Josiah with money from Ragsdale, money that had carried the smallpox contagion. If Ragsdale had used her in that way, without any warning as to the dangers of what he was asking her to do, of course Pauline would be furious. Surely, now, Pauline would be ready to tell the truth.

Narcissa watched the scene play out in her mind's eye — Pauline on the stand, pointing an accusing finger at Ragsdale; Ragsdale breaking down, being led away in chains . . . Then, like a cloud-castle, this pleasant vision changed shape. She saw the judge, the jury, the officers of the law, all pointing at Pauline, all laughing, all whispering, *Whore* — Ragsdale laughing most of all. No, it wouldn't end that way, it couldn't. . . . Narcissa felt Mirrie's gaze and looked up. The cloud-picture blew away.

Concern, and curiosity as well, furrowed Mirrie's brow over her pince-nez. "You know, you've never said much about what went on at Ragsdale's."

Narcissa grimaced. "If you're asking whether I've wanted to take a knife to the man myself, the answer is yes."

At Castle Godwin, Narcissa was relieved to meet up with a jailer who did not recognize her. Pauline Avery was sharing a bare, rough, and foul-smelling room with two other women whose gaudy clothes and rouged cheeks revealed their profession. Narcissa handed Pauline a bundle containing bread, fruit, and some clean linen. Pauline's cheeks flushed red, and she clutched the bundle in her lap.

Narcissa spoke first. "I read in the newspaper that you were accused of attacking Roland Ragsdale. I would have liked to do it myself, if I had the nerve," Narcissa hastened to add, lest Pauline take offense.

Pauline gave a slow, mocking smile. "If you were not such a lady. You were raised to smother your impulses, not give rein to them. As was I, come to that; but I find I come nearer to getting what I want by going after it."

"What *do* you want?" Narcissa surprised herself by asking.

Pauline seemed to consider the question. At last she answered, "Something that is my own."

"You have that in common with Aurelia Harrald," Narcissa responded.

Pauline smiled again. "But with a difference. Aurelia is still waiting for someone to give it to her. I learned long ago that that will never happen."

"Are not both of you looking toward the

same source?" Narcissa probed carefully, avoiding the name of Ragsdale. But Pauline only shrugged and looked away. Narcissa decided to be more direct. "I think Mr. Ragsdale was displeased that I had sought you out. Maybe he threatened you."

Narcissa saw a change come over Pauline's face. "Ragsdale made a promise to me. If I kept a secret for him, he would reward me." Pauline broke off, looked away. "But Ragsdale grew greedy, and careless." Then she shrugged. "I thought that I would kill him — ha! What do I know about a knife? I drew blood, I had that satisfaction, but I did not even slow him down."

"Are you afraid of him?"

Pauline did not have to answer the question. Narcissa could see the fear in her drawn face, her clutching hands.

Narcissa moved closer to Pauline, turning away from the curious stares of the other two women. "Tell me if I am right. About a year ago, Ragsdale came into possession of money that had been tainted by smallpox."

Pauline hesitated, then nodded. Then she spoke, her voice eager, as if she had been longing to tell someone. "It was just as he was preparing to leave Norfolk for Richmond. One of the girls at Ragsdale's gaming house stole a great deal of money, the entire takings of a Saturday night. He tracked her down, but when he found her, she had a full-fledged case of smallpox. The money was with her. It should have been destroyed, but he couldn't bring himself to burn so much money."

Pauline lapsed into silence. Narcissa prodded her. "You knew about it."

"He told me he would not spend the money until enough time had passed to render it harmless. He told me if I kept his secret, I would never lack for anything." Pauline stared down at her interlaced hands. Then she looked up at Narcissa and smiled faintly. "I found I was wrong about you, Mrs. Powers. I did not think you would have the courage to carry on with what you started. He blames me, you know, Ragsdale does. He thinks I am the cause of the questions being asked by Cameron Archer, and that reporter — and you. He was furious with me, and with Miller as well, though I'm not sure what he thinks Miller has done. So he's gone and installed poor little Sophie Dunbar as his favorite, punishing both Miller and me with one stroke."

The newspaper account had pointed to Pauline's jealousy as her motive in stabbing Ragsdale. However much she denied it, Pauline looked and sounded like a jealous woman. Sophie, always her inferior, now held the position of power, while she sat in a filthy jail. But there was no point in antagonizing Pauline by questioning her version of what had happened. There was another question Narcissa had to ask. "The money you gave to Josiah, when you visited him in the hospital — Ragsdale didn't tell you, did he, that it was tainted with smallpox? You must have been very angry when you found out."

Pauline's mouth twisted with irritation. "I told you before, I didn't see Josiah in the hospital! Not that I wouldn't have gladly seen him dead, or killed him myself."

Pauline's cellmates laughed aloud at this.

Narcissa sat in silence for a moment. At last she thought, no matter. Pauline has told me enough to know that we were right. The smallpox money is hidden in the warehouse Ragsdale bought from the Harralds. Ragsdale may have tried to wait until it was safe, but at last he broke down and began to spend it. He paid for a dress: the dressmaker fell sick and died. He paid

Josiah Harrald for his share of the tobacco warehouse: Josiah sickened and died as well. It mattered little who among Ragsdale's women had worn the red dress to visit Josiah. The truth was out, and Ragsdale knew it; at last he would destroy the money.

But Ragsdale's cruel and callous evil was still claiming victims. Narcissa had one more thing to ask of Pauline. "What you have told me might save another woman from making a terrible mistake. Would you be willing to speak to Aurelia Harrald, to tell her what you have told me?"

"You want me to convince her that Mr. Ragsdale is not an acceptable suitor for her?" Pauline framed the question with a lift of her eyebrows. "Do you think that she will believe me? Or even admit me into her presence?" Suddenly Pauline began to laugh. "Aurelia Harrald is another reason Ragsdale is angry at me. When we came here from Norfolk, he took advice from me. This is my hometown, after all. I recommended he go after the Harralds, make them his business partners, marry into the family. . . . He would have done it, too, but someone told him the truth about Aurelia, and he told me. Aurelia Harrald is no more a virtuous woman than I am." Pauline laughed a short, bitter laugh. "He was furious, he blamed me. . . . Oh, I'm sorry, you don't know? That boy Aurelia pretends is her nephew, or cousin, or some such, is really her son! It revolts you, doesn't it? I can see it in your eyes. Such a hypocrite she is! She thought no one would ever know, that she would trade her family name for a life of wealth and ease. Well, that won't happen now. Someone has seen to it that that won't happen."

As Narcissa walked away from Castle Godwin, Pauline's words hung on her like the invisible taint of disease. Fire could burn the smallpox money, but it could not burn away the evil that was poisoning so many lives.

And what about Timmy and Sam? They had been infected, in every sense, by the evil that Ragsdale had loosed in the city. But something was missing, some link that bound Ragsdale and his money to the boys. The haughty Ragsdale had not gone down to Butchertown, recruiting boys to steal for him. And what about Benjy? Unlikely that Ragsdale had pulled the trigger, though he may have given the order. Judah Daniel, she knew, suspected both Cassie Terry and Mal Evans. But . . .

Narcissa could not imagine Ragsdale lowering himself to deal with those two, either. The plug-ugly Miller was the likeliest, and he hated Ragsdale now; but, even so, it was impossible to approach Miller directly.

Sam and Timmy, they had to hold the key. Someone had told them where to go and what to do, had taken from them the money they had stolen, had frightened them into running away. It seemed they would recover. If they could feel safe enough, they would tell what they knew. The thought made her quicken her pace. No one, save Jim Furbish and Nahum McCall, Judah Daniel, and herself — and Archer and Stedman, of course — was supposed to know where the boys were, or even that they were alive. But, eager as she was for the boys to tell what they knew, someone must be even more eager for them not to tell.

CHAPTER SIXTEEN

THURSDAY, MAY 29

Narcissa's last encounter with Aurelia, almost a week ago now, had ended with Aurelia accusing her of lying, screaming at her to go away. Narcissa had not expected to see her again. But with the shocking story Pauline had told, Narcissa found she could not stop thinking of Aurelia. What would Aurelia do, now that Ragsdale believed she was a lost woman, the unmarried mother of a child? Was the story even true, or had Pauline invented it as some sort of revenge for slights she had suffered? Pauline seemed bitter against everyone — Aurelia, Sophie Dunbar, and Ragsdale himself most of all. Had Pauline made up the story because she was envious of Aurelia?

On the other hand, Aurelia's exaggerated anxiety over Stone, witnessed by Narcissa particularly on the day of the Cats' fight, might argue for the rumor's truth. The worst of it was that, once the rumor became known, whether it was true or not would hardly matter.

So the note from Aurelia, delivered to the pest-house where Narcissa was now staying twelve hours a day to care for Timmy and Sam, struck her with surprise and something close to fear. Aurelia had been overwrought, hysterical, the last time Narcissa had seen her. Was Aurelia summoning her back to blame her for something else? Had Aurelia heard the ugly story — ugly in intention and in effect, whether or not it was true — that Pauline was circulating about her?

While Judah Daniel took over the care of the young patients, Narcissa readied herself to obey Aurelia's summons.

At the Harralds' house, Jensie took Narcissa up the stairs to Aurelia's bedchamber. The room was dark and close — the curtains pulled tight against the morning sun. Aurelia was lying in bed, propped up on pillows. Jensie showed Narcissa to a chair near the foot of the bed and then left the room. The sickroom atmosphere filled Narcissa with nervous foreboding. Aurelia could be suffering the effects of the inoculation, but suppose she was actually ill with smallpox? Narcissa started to rise and go to her.

"Don't come any closer." Aurelia almost whispered the words, but the coldness in her voice froze Narcissa. "I don't like you, and I don't want you here. I brought you here to warn you, as you were *considerate* enough to warn me. You know what they are saying about me, don't you? Stone is my son."

Narcissa couldn't answer.

"I see by your silence that you do know. It surprises you that I didn't die, after having been seduced and abandoned. That is what always happens in stories. My mother was the only one who knew. She told everyone I was going north to school, then sent me to her sister, who hid me away. My aunt kept the baby, and I returned home. My mother died, and then her sister died, and Stansbury came to us. That has been my unlooked-for blessing, but also my torture, because I could not tell him what he was to me."

"Aurelia —" Narcissa began, but again she failed to find the words. She thought of all the men she had seen, terribly wounded or wasted with disease, for whom a woman — wife or sister sometimes, but almost always *mother* — gave solace on earth and hope of heaven. Aurelia's loss was great, but Stone's was greater still. Why should shame be stronger than love? "Aurelia, you must tell him. Tell Stansbury you are his mother."

"Tell him?" Aurelia chuckled dryly. "You have no idea what you are saying, how many lives would be disrupted. Including yours. Stansbury would want to know who his father was, wouldn't he? Suppose I were to tell him that? *You* can guess who his father is, can't you? Cameron Archer."

Narcissa found herself wanting to say that it wasn't true. But how could she? The cold knot in the pit of her stomach told her that it was true, that she had suspected it all along, from the moment Pauline had revealed Aurelia's shame.

Aurelia gave a cold little laugh. "It's amusing, isn't it, that you warned me against the debauched Mr. Ragsdale. All I have to hope for, now, is to share in that debauchery. He will not marry me — very well; I will become his mistress. When I am lost to society, lost to heaven as well, then perhaps I will be able to tell Stansbury that I am his mother. I don't believe he will thank me for it."

"Aurelia —" Narcissa wanted to plead

with her, to tell her there must be a better way, that all could not be lost. But what could she, Narcissa, advise Aurelia to do? There was one thing. . . . "Talk to Cameron Archer. He ought to —"

"No!" The energy of her anger brought Aurelia upright. "He humiliated me. How could I live with that, day after day, if I forced him to marry me?"

Narcissa felt sick. How could she have admired Cameron Archer? How could he have deceived her? But he had never tried to deceive her; she had deceived herself. She had seen his strength and courage as a surgeon, and attributed those qualities to him as a man. It was possible to be a very good surgeon and a very bad man. . . . She saw that now, but even as she struggled to accept it, grief and anger roiled in her. She told herself it was for Aurelia.

Aurelia sagged back into the pillows. "Leave me now," she whispered.

Narcissa stood, but she hesitated. "Aurelia, don't throw your life away. God forgives —"

"*God* may." Aurelia's voice was small and dry. "But my father does not. Society does not. Go now."

Narcissa left then, wiping the tears from her face with the heels of her hands. She thought of the children who needed her, Timmy and Sam. It would not do for them to see her cry.

It was near midnight when Cameron Archer came to the Egyptian building. He peered through the little window in the door, trying to get a glimpse of — of Mrs. Powers, he admitted to himself. He could not go in. He had no clothing to change into.

Strange . . . The barrier between himself and Narcissa Powers had shifted. He hadn't understood before that the barrier was in himself. Now he knew it had been, and he cursed himself. He should have had the courage to break through, to speak to her, at least to see if she could care for him. Now the barrier was outside him, and it was Aurelia Harrald. He had been young when he met Aurelia, unready for the test; and he had failed it. Never before or since had he taken advantage of a virtuous young woman. The question of what he was to do about it now perplexed him. He had seen no sign from Aurelia that she expected or desired a proposal of marriage from him; indeed, she seemed hardly to know who he was. He certainly had no wish to make such an offer. Maddening though it was to admit it, the expectation that he would do the honorable thing seemed to be coming from Narcissa Powers. Why should he offer marriage to one woman, because another woman would think it the right thing to do?

He was leaning far to the right to look through the door, but could catch no glimpse of her. The window, though . . . Well, it was dark; no one would see him acting the fool. He looked around, saw he could not be seen from the street, then stepped into the ditch dug along the sides of the Egyptian building. He found a spot where the black fabric that covered the windows had come loose and looked in at the scene lit by a glowing tallow candle. There she was, sitting in a chair near to the two boys; near enough to bend down and soothe a forehead or take hold of a hand. The boys were asleep, and she seemed to be as well, turned sideways in the chair, her head resting on her arms. A white cloth covered her hair; in the dim light, it resembled a nun's headdress.

Men make angels of women they scarcely know, based on a gentle manner, a shy smile, a certain curve of the cheek. . . .

Further acquaintance proved these angels only human. He was likely quite wrong about what Narcissa Powers wanted. Perhaps, if she knew everything, she would view his seduction of Aurelia as a terrible lapse, but not one for which he should be punished ever after. But it stood between them now, and would do so, until he told her about it, and had her absolution. And he could not tell her. He could not put his pride on the line, knowing that she might not absolve him.

CHAPTER SEVENTEEN

FRIDAY, MAY 30

Narcissa figured the throbbing in the left side of her head must have finally succeeded in pounding her awake. The pain in her head traveled down through her neck into her shoulders and back, which ached as if she'd been at hard physical labor. Her stays were poking into her soft flesh, and her legs felt numb.

She opened her eyes, blinked, and took in her surroundings. Streaks and smears of morning sunlight made their way into the room around the edges of the curtained windows. She was in the pest-house, and she had fallen asleep in the chair. The awkward angle had caused her head to hurt.

Her concern for her patients pushed aside her own discomfort. She stretched and stood up, then knelt between the little pallets. Timmy and Sam were asleep, their breathing deep and regular. They were doing well. Chances were good for their recovery — unless Roland Ragsdale learned where they were, and decided their knowledge put him in danger.

Narcissa looked up to see Jim Furbish standing at the door, talking to someone outside. Jim turned and came to stand near her. "Beg your pardon, Mrs. Powers. They's some boys out here wanting to speak with you. They say Judah Daniel told 'em you was here."

Narcissa went to the door that led out into the hall and looked toward the outside door. There stood Stone and Coffin, and between them Nat McClennan. "Good morning, Mrs. Powers," Stone said. "We're reporting, as you ordered."

"We couldn't find Mr. Wallace," Coffin added.

Narcissa smiled an abashed welcome. She had worried about the boys — how long ago was it now, a week maybe? — when she'd found out Brit Wallace had told them to spy on Ragsdale. But days had passed, she'd heard nothing worrisome . . . at last, she had forgotten. Now, here they were, looking for some response from her.

Narcissa arranged her face in an officer's

scowl. "What do you have to report?"

"You know that red dress you were asking Nat about? Well, he thinks he's seen it." He nodded to Nat, who took a step forward.

"I was walking down past Linden Row with my mother this morning, in front of Ragsdale's, and there was this woman going into the door of his house. And she was wearing a red dress with a big skirt and a low neck. And I said to my mother, isn't that the dress you liked at Miss Sullivan's? And she looked and her face got all red and she said no and she practically just about dragged me away."

Ragsdale's house. "What did she look like, the woman who was wearing the dress?"

"She had yellow hair down on her shoulders. She looked pretty. I couldn't tell much. . . ."

"Thank you, Nat."

Then Stone stepped forward. "Coffin and I were there earlier, when Ragsdale went out. He goes out every morning, but we don't see him come back. It must be after dinner. Wish we knew where he went," Stone added regretfully.

Well, thought Narcissa, at least Brit Wallace had refrained from having them watch the Golden Arrow! "Thank you, Stone, and Coffin. I appreciate your telling me." They left then, but Narcissa stood in the doorway, deep in thought. There could be a hundred different explanations, but the one that came to mind was that Sophie Dunbar had been at Roland Ragsdale's house, wearing the red dress made by Miss Sullivan — the dress poisoned with smallpox.

Had it been Sophie, all along — Sophie who had worn the dress to visit Josiah? Of all the women for whom Ragsdale held the key to happiness — or the purse strings to happiness, it might be — Sophie had come out the winner. As soon as Judah Daniel came to relieve her, she would go in search of Sophie Dunbar.

It was after noon when Narcissa knocked on the door of Ragsdale's house. The silver-haired servant she had noticed before opened the door. "Mr. Ragsdale ain't in," the old man said. "Yes, I reckon you can wait. He ain't expected anytime soon, though —" The servant finally led Narcissa to a low sofa in the front parlor. She refused his offer of tea. At last he disappeared down the hall that led to the back of the house.

How did one pay a call on a kept woman at the house of the man who was keeping her? Narcissa had received no instruction from her mother in this particular branch of etiquette. When she'd learned Ragsdale would be out for some time, she'd decided that, rather than having the servant announce her to Sophie, she would try to find her herself. Perhaps, by catching Sophie off guard, she could surprise her into some revelation. With this thought, Narcissa got up from the sofa and strolled, very slowly and casually, into the hall. It was deserted. She gathered her skirts and ran up the stairs.

On the second floor, Narcissa peered into one beautifully appointed bedroom, then another, her mouth dry with fear that she would be discovered. At the third door, she hesitated, then went in. Here was a private sitting room fit for a lord, with dark, satiny-finished furniture and jewel-colored carpets that yielded to her step like the cool, prickly-soft grass of a newly mown lawn. Through a half-open door at the far end of this room she could see into the bedroom. The bedclothes were in a tangle on the massive four-poster. Could it be that Sophie Dunbar was lying there still? Yes . . . her blond hair lay spread out on the pillow, and her bare arm and shoulder were visible. Whatever Sophie was wearing now, it wasn't the red dress.

Narcissa stood frozen, certain that she had done a very stupid thing by coming here. She turned away from the bedroom and saw, coming toward her through a door she hadn't noticed, a woman, plainly dressed and bonneted, face very pale, dark eyes wide with fright — Oh! It was her own reflection in a huge cheval-glass. She walked toward it and entered a third room, smaller than the other two, dominated by the mirror, a huge wardrobe, and a dresser covered with silver-backed brushes and little bottles. She was looking for something red, and at last she saw it, under the wardrobe. She teased it out with her foot. The red dress — or at least, the fabric — she was sure of it; she had stared at the little patch of it she had found at Miss Sullivan's, memorizing the shade. . . . She probed with her foot, caught a fold, and tugged it loose — a little pouf of a sleeve, cherry-red, with a second pouf of sheer ivory tulle. It was delicate, sumptuous, thoroughly decadent. Surely this had to be the dress.

Narcissa straightened up and took a deep breath, trying to slow her racing heart. She had to confront Sophie now, before Ragsdale returned. Now she had seen the dress, she had the evidence to press Sophie. They could leave together, she and Sophie, if Sophie were innocent. If not . . . She pushed that thought aside and strode into the bedroom.

The sight that met her so unstrung her that she grabbed one of the bedposts for support. Sophie lay there, tangled in the bedsheets and in her light hair — light, save where Sophie's blood had darkened it to near-black. Sophie's blue eyes stared at nothing.

At that moment, she heard footsteps coming up the stairs — quick, heavy, clearly belonging to the master of the house. To Ragsdale.

Narcissa ran out of the bedroom and closed the door behind her. She was standing in the little sitting room, her breath coming in painful gasps, when Roland Ragsdale came into the room.

"Mr. . . . Ragsdale," she panted out, "I . . ." — and then she fainted.

When she came to, she was lying on the chaise longue. Ragsdale was bending low over her, holding a glass of brandy to her lips. She pushed his arm away and sat up. In the few moments of her swoon he had taken off her bonnet, undone the hook-and-eye fastenings at the top of her bodice, and taken the tucking combs out of her hair so that it lay loose on her shoulders. He was bending very close to her, so close that she could smell the brandy on his breath. He offered her the glass again: when she shook her head, he said, "No? Pity." He drained it in a draft, then set the glass on a little table near her elbow, next to a nearly full decanter of the deep golden liquid. Ragsdale leaned closer to her. "I know this is hard for you," he murmured, his hand in her hair, "but I'm glad you've come. I want to show you" — he brought her hand to his lips and kissed it — "how very glad" — then turned it over and kissed her palm — "I am."

Narcissa sat frozen, afraid to move even her eyes, lest a frightened glance at the bedroom door communicate her knowledge to Ragsdale. He must not suspect she had seen the dead woman in his bed . . . not even if she had to make him think she wished to join him there.

In the courtyard behind the elegant row houses on Linden Row, Coffin stood with

412

his bare feet planted on Stone's shoulders, fumbling with the bottom sash of a narrow window.

"Hurry up!" came a whispered warning from farther down the alley.

Coffin jerked his forearm sharply upward. The window flew open. Coffin dropped the broken-bladed knife he'd been using to pry open the sash and disappeared headfirst through the opening. His eyes widened in horror as he saw the door swinging open. A thin, white-haired black man came through the door, an abstracted expression on his face, as if his thoughts were far away. To Coffin, it seemed an age for the man to look up, focus on him, recognize him as someone who had no business being where he was.

Narcissa moistened her lips and tried to smile. Ragsdale hung over her, his left hand still entangled in her hair, his right hand now clasping her waist.

Narcissa cleared her throat. "Do you know . . . I believe I will have some of that brandy?"

Ragsdale knelt closer, his other hand at her waist. "Darling, I —"

"Please. . . . It might help me . . . relax." She twisted away from him and reached for the decanter, a clumsy move that knocked the little table off its spindly legs. The decanter fell, spilling its precious contents onto Ragsdale's trousers.

With a muttered oath, Ragsdale pushed himself up from the chaise longue and stalked out of the room. "Tom! I need you! Tom!" No answer from the servant, apparently — she heard Ragsdale clattering down the stairs, still calling. In another minute she could no longer hear him.

Coffin whipped around and went back the way he had come, boosting himself into the window. At that moment he heard another man, somewhere in the house, shouting. It had to be Ragsdale. "Run like the devil!" Coffin called to the boys below. They instantly obeyed, except for the dog, who took all the excitement for a game. Coffin turned to lower himself through, feet-first it had to be this time. He was hanging there, hands gripping the sill, when the servant reached the window. They looked into each other's eyes for a second. Coffin looked down, gauging the

414

fall, let go with his left hand, and swung, ready to drop.

Crash! The window slammed onto his right hand and bounced up again. Coffin dropped six feet or so to the ground, bending his knees to cushion the fall. He stifled a wail of pain and thrust the three wounded fingers into his mouth. He and Popcracker took off down the alley as if the hounds of hell were after them.

At long last the pounding of Narcissa's heart communicated itself to her legs. She rose from the chaise, gathered up her bonnet and shawl, and ran out into the hall. A glance down the stairs showed no one below, and she passed down them full tilt, her hand brushing the satiny wood of the banister. In the entrance hall she paused just long enough to fasten her bodice and plop her bonnet on her head. There was a great deal of noise coming from the back of the house, shouts and cursing. Thankful for the distraction, whatever the cause of it might be, she threw open the door and ran out into the street, pulling her shawl around her. She hurried away from Ragsdale's in the direction of the medical college. A few people looked at her curiously, or pityingly, but in these times, the sight of a distraught woman half-running in the street drew no particular notice.

She would tell one of the doctors what she had seen. There was nothing to be gained from telling the police, who were in Ragsdale's pocket. Then, when she had done her duty by poor Sophie Dunbar, she would go to the pest-house to take her turn caring for Sam and Timmy. There she would be safe. Jim Furbish would be standing watch, and the smallpox itself would protect her — not even the plug-uglies would venture into the pest-house. . . .

"Mrs. Powers!"

It was Cameron Archer. She was opposite his house, she hadn't realized — she could tell him, and then it would be over.

"Major Archer . . . Ragsdale killed . . . a woman . . . in his bed . . . *Go!*" She was near to sobbing, panting out the words. Archer was shaking his head, reaching out to her as if she were the one who needed the help.

"*Go!*" she screamed again. She was trembling from head to foot. She folded her arms at her waist to keep from reaching for him. "She's lying there . . . all bloody . . . *Go!*" she screamed one last time, and started to run, away from Archer and Ragsdale and the dead Cyprian, toward the safety of the pest-house.

The rain that had fallen since noon showed no signs of letting up. Rather, the descending darkness seemed to unleash the full force of the storm. Narcissa lit a candle and positioned it where its faint glow would not irritate the eyes of the sick boys. She had arrived at the pest-house shaking head to foot, almost unable to speak. Judah Daniel had put her to bed on clean straw and for several hours had waited on her as well as on the boys. At last Narcissa had felt the strange weakness lift. Now an unexpected serenity buoyed her. All would be well — the boys would survive, not much hurt or scarred.

Where did this faith come from? It wasn't always with her. Sometimes, when she nursed men whose life was slipping away, the wish that it would not be so had torn her apart. She knew what it was to pray without ceasing, even when she could not craft a prayer God would answer, save

Thy will be done. But now, she knew in her heart that the boys would survive.

She heard footsteps in the hall — not Jim or Nahum, but an unfamiliar step, faster and lighter than theirs or the doctors'. Judah Daniel got up and crossed to the door, where she spoke with someone, then turned and motioned to Narcissa.

Aurelia Harrald stood at the end of the little hallway. Her right arm cradled something, wrapped in rough sacking — a *baby?* No, a parcel of some kind. Her left arm held a bull's-eye lantern stiffly away from her body. Aurelia's face was as wet and white as a drowned woman's. Wet ropes of hair lay along her cheeks and shoulders. Her dress hung on her, heavy with water as a marble statue's sculpted robes. She opened her mouth to speak, and Narcissa heard her little gasp for air. *She's been running* — just as on the day of the Cat fight, when she had run into the street after Stone.

Aurelia's words came in a rush. "Sophie Dunbar's dead. Ragsdale's saying Stansbury was there, and Coffin. He's saying they killed her!" Aurelia swayed and clutched the doorjamb for support. She took a breath and spoke again. "Stone and Coffin have run away. I know where they've gone — they took the key — to the warehouse Aaron sold to Ragsdale."

Narcissa put her hand out as if to stop Aurelia, but Aurelia was too far away, and in any case, Narcissa knew she could not stop her. Still she had to warn her. "Aurelia, you can't go, there's smallpox there. I will go."

Aurelia shook her head. "I know the place. Come with me!"

"But you —"

Aurelia shook her head impatiently. "Stansbury is in danger!"

Narcissa jumped to her feet, her skirt striking the tin cup next to Sam's bed and sending it clattering on the stone floor. At the sound, Sam shifted on his pallet and moaned, a sad, lost sound. Narcissa knelt next to him. Sam's eyes opened, gummy and unfocused. His cracked lips parted. Narcissa knelt closer to catch the whisper. "Don't hurt me . . . please. . . ." The boy's whole body seemed to shrink away from some threat.

Narcissa put her hand on his shoulder with a firm, gentle pressure. "No one will hurt you," she whispered. She could hear Aurelia calling for her to hurry, but she did not move until Sam relaxed, his eyelids closing again over his unseeing eyes. Then

Narcissa went over to Judah Daniel. "This is my fault. I was afraid they might go there. I have to go with Aurelia. Please, Judah Daniel, can you stay?"

For an instant, Judah Daniel's tall, straight form lit up, blanched by the cold glare of lightning. Then came darkness, then a rumble of thunder. As it died away, she heard Judah Daniel say, "I'll stay."

Narcissa's hands shook as she went through the ritual of washing and changing clothes. Her earlier serenity had vanished. The news about Stone and Coffin depressed her spirits until every thought, every memory, seemed an omen of horrors to come. Catastrophe was gathering, closing in on them all, falling from heaven to burn among them like a refiner's fire.

A few minutes later, Narcissa stood with Aurelia at the edge of Marshall Street, looking down toward Butchertown. In the dark and the driving rain, she could barely see a foot in front of her. Aurelia's lantern served only to illuminate the slanting silver curtains of rain. Then Aurelia set off, aiming the dim lantern light down onto a dirt footpath, now the course of a rivulet down the steep, rain-slicked hill. Narcissa followed, her heart in her mouth. It would be all right, she told herself. Aurelia had been inoculated, after all. And couldn't she understand that Aurelia thought the risk worth taking, to get to Stone? Would she not do the same, if Stone were *her* son?

Aurelia was going fast, too fast for the treacherous path. Narcissa was falling behind. She could barely make out the faint glow of the lantern. Suddenly Aurelia went down. Narcissa made her way to her — fortunately Aurelia had not dropped the lantern, but the bundle she carried lay near her on the ground. Aurelia snatched it up and pulled away from Narcissa's extended hand, then got to her feet and ran on, leaving Narcissa to follow as best she could.

At last Narcissa felt the ground level off. They made their way among the warehouses, up to their ankles in standing water and mud. At last Aurelia halted in front of a big brick building. Its windows were boarded and its door padlocked. For a moment the lantern light played over the facade. Then Aurelia said, "Let's go around back."

They walked along the side of the building. The lantern shone on Virginia creeper coming up through the scraggly grass, clinging to the rough mortar between the bricks. *Indomitable spring.* If, a year from now, these bricks lay scattered on the ground, tumbled by cannon blasts . . . or stood blackened by fire . . . the creeper would come still, and grow unchecked until it covered all.

They turned the corner. Here at the back were big wooden doors through which the tobacco hogsheads would be rolled. A massive chain with a padlock spanned the doors, but Narcissa could see that one door stood an inch or so out of flush. A hiding place for — what? Frightened boys? Or runaway slaves, or derelicts from the wharves, hiding out from impressment?

Aurelia seemed to feel no such uncertainty. She rushed up to the little space between the doors. From inside the warehouse Narcissa could hear a scuffling noise that made her heart thump painfully. The darkness within lightened a little. Then a hand appeared, illuminated by Aurelia's lantern. In another moment the big door swung inward, the chain sliding loose.

As Aurelia was about to step inside, Narcissa rushed up and caught her by the arm. "Don't go in there! Tell them to come away!" Narcissa was pleading now, but Aurelia did not even seem to hear her. She stepped into the warehouse, and Narcissa followed her into a big, barnlike room with rough wooden walls, floor, and ceiling, empty save a few tobacco kegs up against the wall to the left. Half-hidden among them was a wooden trunk with leather straps, standing open. She couldn't see inside it, but she knew it must hold the smallpox money.

It was Stone who held the candle. He was looking at Narcissa, frowning. "We're safer here than anywhere else. The plug-uglies are after us, didn't you know?"

"Stone!" Anger warmed Narcissa like a drink of brandy. "We've been through hell for you this night, and you *will* listen!"

Stone blinked and his eyebrows rose as petulance gave way to shock. He looked at Aurelia, whose earlier certainty seemed to have deserted her. Narcissa spoke to Stone and Coffin. "You must come with us, now, both of you. The contents of that trunk are tainted with smallpox; you mustn't get close to it."

"We know about the smallpox," Stone answered with a little smile. "You told us. That's why we knew this would be a good place to hide. Ragsdale and the plug-uglies would figure you'd warned us not to come here. But Coffin's had smallpox, and I've been inoculated —"

Narcissa shook her head, exasperated almost beyond words. "We've got to get out of here, *now*."

With the storm sluicing the roads and lashing the trees outside, Brit found himself among others taking shelter at the Monumental Hotel across from the Capitol. Archer Langdon was there, apparently with bona fide authorization this time, since he was making no effort to hide from the crowd of officers gathered around the big table in the center of the room.

Langdon smiled wryly in response to Brit's query. "But I'm under strict orders to return tonight, and — well, you've seen it out there! I'll have to swim back. Still, tomorrow should be a day of rest. Look, there's Carlton — let's see what he has to say on the matter. He should know all about wet weather: they say he got his corporal's stripes about the time of Noah."

The jest was not far off the mark, judging by the officer's flowing white beard and general air of omniscience. Brit and Langdon sidled closer.

"The Chickahominy," said the old man,

leaning back in his chair, "where it parallels Richmond, is nothing much more than a ditch through a swamp. McClellan's already found this out, to his sorrow. A moderate shower fills the ditch, which is about a dozen yards wide and some four feet deep. A continuous rain floods the swamp and the lowlands around it. As wet as it's been this spring, the swamp and bottoms are all flooded. Infantry might pick their way through the swamp, up to their armpits in mud, but horses and artillery trains would be hopelessly mired."

"Could not bridges be put up?" someone asked.

"Yes," the officer replied with a sly smile, "if the pilings were laid on Church Hill."

"So, no fighting tomorrow, sir?" Langdon asked eagerly.

"That's right, son. You boys will get another day to work on keeping your powder dry."

At last, around ten o'clock, Langdon rose. "Well, it looks as though there's no help for it. Come back to camp with me, Wallace. The officers will be at their ease tomorrow; you should be able to obtain an audience with any one you choose."

"Very well, then."

Brit claimed his battered felt hat and followed Langdon out onto the hotel's portico. Rain was slashing down. In one moment the street was lit to blinding radiance. In the next, it was plunged into darkness.

Brit wished he had refused Langdon's invitation while they were still holed up in the Monumental's comfortable saloon. If he were to back out now, Langdon would think him a coward. So he would go. Even as the decision was made, Brit realized something more was driving him than the fear of losing Langdon's esteem. It was portentous, this weather. Something was coming, something grand and terrible. He could hide from it, or he could go out and meet it. Grateful he had no decent boots to be ruined, Brit stepped out into the storm.

Judah Daniel stood at the window. The material that covered the glass, shielding the patients' eyes from the painful light of day, had torn away from the nail and hung loose along the wall. In the window she could see her reflection, distorted by the thick old glass in the diamond-shaped panes. When lightning rived the darkness for an instant, she could glimpse the low-clustering clouds, the sheets of silvery rain.

It was a storm like this, sixty years ago and more now, that drove down the slaves that was rising, following Prosser's Gabriel. It was a storm like this that rent the veil in the temple and shook the graves open, when God's Son died forgiving his killers. In a storm like this, God bellows, saying to men, you don't know My will. You don't know My ways.

Judah Daniel stood, looking at the alternating images of the storm and her own face. At last she raised her hand to refix the cloth. She hesitated, then let her hand fall at her side. The boys were sleeping now. She would replace the curtain when the dawn came. Until then, she would leave it as it was. She couldn't shake the feeling that a message, a sign of judgment, was going to come to her through that window, from that sky.

Brit slogged alongside Langdon for what seemed like hours through mud that at times came up to their knees. The rain continued to pour, and the darkness was absolute. If they had had more to do than follow the broad turnpike, their fate would have been by no means sure. But Langdon — led by habit or some animal instinct revived by soldiering — found not only the camp, but within it the tent he shared with Watkins and a half-dozen others. Still following close behind Langdon, Brit crept inside and felt his way past the warm, softly breathing lumps to a space where he himself could lie down. Stopping only to make a pillow of his wet sack coat, Brit lay down on the muddy ground.

Archer Langdon settled in next to him. Within moments, Langdon's breathing relaxed and fell into the abandonment of sleep. Brit was the only one awake now, and he stared into the darkness as if eager to catch the first light. If the sun came out and stayed strong all day, it would go far to drying his clothes — and the roads. Would it bring a battle on the day after?

Why was he here? Why was he not in his bed in the Exchange Hotel, or even back in England? It was rank self-indulgence to denote himself a correspondent. For months he had not known whether the *Argus* was receiving his dispatches, or printing them if received. Was he simply following the path he had worn for himself? If some blockade-runner did not come through with money from his family, he would have to move out of his hotel and strive for a room in a private house, against the clerks, the wives, the hangers-on — all of whom, he had to admit, had more right to be housed in the capital than he himself did. But whenever he thought of leaving, he could conjure up no future, away from this place and these people, to draw him on. It seemed to him he was destined to be the observer, and sometime chronicler, of their drama. And so he relaxed into the mire, warmed now with the heat of his body, and slept.

Narcissa thought she saw a flicker of doubt in Stone's eyes. But then Aurelia spoke in a low, insistent voice. "We have to take the money. We have to make sure it is destroyed."

Narcissa turned to Aurelia. Had she, too, lost her mind? "Ragsdale is planning to destroy the money, Aurelia, didn't you know that? It was in the paper. Leave it, it doesn't matter. . . ."

"It does matter!" Aurelia's eyes were fierce in her pale face. "Don't you know you can't trust what Ragsdale says?"

Narcissa put her hand to her temple. It

seemed that everything she had said to anyone had had the opposite effect from what she had intended. She had told Stone and Coffin not to come into this warehouse, that it was dangerous — and they had sought refuge here, trusting its dangers to protect them. She had told Aurelia about Ragsdale, to warn her to stay away from him — and Aurelia had taken it on herself to stop him using the smallpox money. But wait: she hadn't told Aurelia about the smallpox money being hidden in this warehouse. She had intended to, all those days ago when she went to warn Aurelia about Ragsdale; but Aurelia's anger had driven her away. Stone and Coffin must have told Aurelia. Narcissa sobbed with frustration and fear. Why could they not see —

But they had delayed too long. The sound of splintering wood from the front of the building gave notice that the boards of the door, or a window, were yielding.

Stone darted behind the tobacco hogshead at the far end of the warehouse, motioning to the others to follow. Coffin went after him, then Aurelia and Narcissa. Aurelia shut the lantern to a faint glow and set it down on the floor. What was Aurelia doing, with that mysterious bundle she carried? As Narcissa watched, Aurelia pulled the sacking away and dropped it on the floor. In her hand was a revolver, an officer's side arm, heavy and menacing.

"Aurelia . . ." Narcissa whispered, "put the gun away, *please*. It will only make matters worse."

"*No*," was the only response.

Silence descended again. Narcissa heard the pounding of her own heart, then another, louder beat, quick footsteps coming down toward them, hard-heeled boots that struck like blows, coming toward their hiding place.

Narcissa gestured to Stone, Coffin, and Aurelia to keep quiet, then stepped forward, her own boot heels striking a lighter note on the floor. The intruder's footsteps halted at once, at some distance — fifty feet, maybe — from where she stood.

"Go back!" Narcissa called out. "Go away! There is smallpox here."

A beam of light, blinding in the near-darkness, slid across her, then settled on her face.

"Mrs. Powers!"

Ragsdale. His low-pitched voice, intimate and offensive as an unwanted caress, had always repelled her. Now it shocked and terrified her. Had he planned this, tricked them all into coming here?

Ragsdale stepped closer. "You are surprised to see me. And not, I think, pleased. Was it all an act, then, your coming to my bedchamber? Well, be that as it may . . . I have planned this trap for someone other than you. You must come with me. Don't think of running away this time."

Narcissa's voice came out in a frightened squeak. "Stansbury Harrald has smallpox." *But I must make him believe I'm the only one here.* "He's been taken away to the pest-house. I am here to — to destroy the things he touched."

She moved sideways so that the lantern no longer shone into her eyes. Now she could see Ragsdale shifting his weight, moving toward her smoothly, silently, with a feline grace surprising in so big a man.

He mustn't come closer. Narcissa took a step forward. "Don't you understand? You will be exposed. Your fine clothes will have to be burnt."

"I don't mind my clothes, Mrs. Powers. But you and I should talk. Come into the office, where we can see each other. Who is with you?" His voice was purring, seductive.

He wants to lure me away from here as much as I want to lure him. Narcissa won-

432

dered for a moment, then realized: the money, of course. He was hoping she hadn't seen it. The money had killed, would go on killing until it was destroyed, and no one had been found brave or honest enough to destroy it, simply because there was so very much of it, and greed rose up to protect it, unreasoning and instinctive, like a mother's love.

Now, ironically, Ragsdale's cupidity was protecting Stone and Coffin, and Aurelia. She could only pray they would get away quickly.

"No one," answered Narcissa, calmer now in the hope of their escape. "I am alone."

The little office, dingy at the best of times, was now covered with months' worth of dust and cobwebs. Ragsdale closed the door behind them. Narcissa looked around. There was a door to the outside; another door, six or eight feet away to her right, probably led to a similar sectioned-off room. If she had to run, which way would she go? Outside, she thought; the storm seemed to even the odds between them. Ragsdale's size and bulk, his heavy boots, might tell against him in the rain. . . . In fact he was not very wet; he must have come in a carriage, and if so the driver might be waiting for him. Would there be two men chasing her, then?

Ragsdale might pretend to threaten her, to force himself upon her; but, Narcissa told herself, his mind was on the fortune out there in the warehouse. He would try to insult her to the point that she would run away. She resolved to tolerate it for a few minutes — long enough for Aurelia to get the boys out safely.

Ragsdale's glittering eyes returned her scrutiny. He stood leaning against the door that led to the open warehouse, arms folded across his chest, the lantern dangling from his right hand. The gold of his ring sparked in the lantern light. "It's time we got to the bottom of this. Why did you come here?"

"I told you!" Narcissa replied, wishing she did not sound so desperate.

"Ah, yes, you told me — a pack of lies." His leer had vanished, replaced by impatience bordering on anger. "Have you come after that damned money?"

"Yes," Narcissa retorted, "to destroy it!"

"And just how did you plan to do that?"

She stared back at him. "I . . . to burn it."

Ragsdale gave a short laugh that bared his large white teeth. "Oh, it would be much easier than that. All you have to do is walk up to the trunk. There's a torpedo set in the floor to go off with the pressure of a foot. Even a small foot like yours."

Narcissa felt the blood drain from her face. She put her hand on the desk to steady herself. Aurelia, Stone, Coffin . . . pray God they were getting away, forgetting the money. . . .

Ragsdale was still talking. "The money will be destroyed. And the thief along with it. You don't know? Miller, Mrs. Powers. He stole some of the smallpox money — with Sophie's help, I imagine. I don't think he killed her out of jealousy. I think he was afraid she would tell me what they had done. I have a lot of money, I could have waited for the smallpox taint to pass off, but Miller could not wait. And he will come tonight, thinking to steal the rest of it before I burn it all to ashes. Which I will do, of course, and Miller with it. And there will be an end of it. Of course, I hope the Confederate government will see fit to recompense me for my loss."

Narcissa forced her numbed lips to form words. "Miller? I thought you were accusing the boys — Stone and Coffin — of killing Sophie."

Ragsdale laughed again. "Little boys? Do you think I'm stupid? Miller's known about the money from the first. The temptation was too —"

A single sharp report, loud and with a cleansing snap, rent the air. *Aurelia's pistol.* Ragsdale leaped away from the door and stood staring at it, transfixed, one second, two, three, as if expecting something — the blast from a load of black powder?

At last Ragsdale got himself under control, though when he spoke, his voice shook. "I thought we were about to join the angels, Mrs. Powers — or, in my case, the powers from the other place."

Narcissa's thoughts seemed to be moving with a dreamlike slowness. Ragsdale had accused Stone and Coffin of Sophie's murder . . . or so Aurelia had said. Aurelia had been looking for the key to the warehouse and discovered it had been taken by the boys . . . or so she said. Aurelia would not leave the warehouse, would not take Stone and Coffin out of this poisoned place, because she wanted to take the money away to destroy it . . . or so she said.

But here was Ragsdale, laughing at the

notion that he would suspect Stone and Coffin. Ragsdale had set a trap for the one who wanted the money enough to ignore its dangers, to kill for it even. And someone had risen to his bait. Not Miller. *Aurelia.*

"Aurelia's out there," she said at last, "with Stone and Coffin."

Narcissa reached the door before Ragsdale could move to stop her, swung it open, and ran a few steps into the warehouse. Ragsdale followed more slowly, holding up the lantern. If she were wrong, she would be taking Ragsdale to those he wanted to destroy. But . . . what if Aurelia had paid a dressmaker to make a dress like Pauline's, then paid her with tainted money? What if Aurelia had then visited Josiah, given him more of the tainted money, to stop him from interfering with the business arrangement Aaron had made with Ragsdale? And Aurelia could not, even now, let the money be destroyed, because it had given her power, promised her freedom, and these things were dearer to her than her own son.

Narcissa grabbed the knob and swung the door open. She saw no one, heard nothing, so she kept walking. Ragsdale followed.

"Mrs. Powers!" It was Coffin. His voice came from the far end of the warehouse, high and weak as if he were frightened. Behind her, Ragsdale raised the lantern, aiming it in the direction of the voice. Coffin was crouching low to the ground, supporting Stone, who was clutching his chest. Had Stone been shot?

Narcissa started toward them. Then she heard another voice that stopped her in her tracks. *"Ragsdale."* It was Aurelia. Narcissa turned. Aurelia had stepped out of hiding and was standing behind Ragsdale, holding the lantern in one hand and the revolver in the other. The revolver was aimed at Ragsdale.

"Stone's hurt!" Narcissa called to Aurelia.

"No!" "I'm not!" The voices came from the boys themselves, Coffin and Stone. Narcissa turned to look at them. They were standing now.

Aurelia was speaking to Ragsdale. "I thought you wanted a good woman, from a good family. I thought you wanted *me*. Then . . . I found you care nothing for good women. You spend your money on whores. I tried to make myself into a whore. I told you I had been shamed, borne a son — it was not even true! I gave

438

myself to you." Aurelia's voice broke off in a sob. "And then, to find that cheap little whore, Sophie, in your bed — the bed I had just left —"

Ragsdale broke in. "*You* killed Sophie?"

Aurelia spoke again, her voice stronger now. "I stabbed her. That slave boy, I shot."

Benjy. Had Aurelia ever even known his name?

"And Cassie Terry, I poisoned." Aurelia giggled, a chilling sound in the dead, empty silence of the warehouse. "And I will kill you too, unless I get my money. It *is* my money. God knows, I have earned it. Give it to me. That will be an end of it."

"Go get it then," Ragsdale answered.

As Narcissa watched, Aurelia stepped forward. She walked around Ragsdale, keeping the gun aimed at him. Narcissa watched the two of them. Ragsdale's eyes followed Aurelia's every move, but he looked relaxed, a slight smile on his face, his arms folded over his chest again. There was nothing in Ragsdale's manner to warn Aurelia that she was walking into a trap.

Narcissa watched as Aurelia drew level with her. The gun still pointed at Ragsdale. Narcissa tensed her muscles, judged the distance between herself and Aurelia. It was too far. If she made a move in Aurelia's direction, the Colt would blow a hole through one of them — Ragsdale or her, Narcissa — as it had through Benjy.

She should warn Aurelia, stop her before she stepped on the hidden fuse and blew them all up. But surely Ragsdale would not punish Aurelia at the cost of his own life. Ragsdale must know how strong the charge was, how much damage it would do. Narcissa weighed her choices: Aurelia setting off the torpedo — killing herself in the process, it may be — against Aurelia frustrated in her monomania, burdened with three witnesses, and armed with a six-shooter that had five rounds still loaded.

Narcissa saw Aurelia glance in her direction. Their eyes met for a long moment. Was Aurelia reading something in her face, some warning? If she was going to say something, to stop Aurelia from springing the trap, it had to be now —

No. She had made her decision. Aurelia was moving slowly backward toward the chest full of money, closer . . .

She heard Ragsdale move behind her, saw Aurelia's eyes widen, saw her aim the gun as she took one more step back —

"Stone, Coffin! Run!" Narcissa screamed

as she threw herself across the floor, away from the money and the trap it concealed. The boys' frozen figures sprung into motion, and she heard running, shouting. *Oh God, let Coffin and Stone get to safety.*

She felt the building struck, not by lightning but by thunder, blasting not from the heavens but from the earth, pushing the air away, pushing down on her.

CHAPTER EIGHTEEN

SATURDAY, MAY 31

Brit woke with a jolt and squinted against the sudden brightness. A lantern had been thrust through the tent flap — a lantern that swung from a man's hand, and behind it a voice: "Get up! Get up! Pack up your knapsacks and fall in!" His ears caught the beating of the long roll. Then the lantern was withdrawn. Having some idea of what was going to happen next, Brit scrambled out of the way and huddled against the tent wall while the soldiers, once again in total darkness, groped about for their accoutrements. In moments they were packed up and out of the tent. Brit grabbed up his knapsack and followed after them. The rain had subsided to a drizzle. By the light of their lanterns the sergeants were handing out the cartridge rounds and rations to men whose faces, each lit for a moment in its turn along the row, looked serious in the extreme. Brit felt a thrill of anticipation. Beyond the muttering and calling, the beating of the drum, the night was silent. If his guess was correct, this army was about to do something it had never done before: make the first attack upon its enemy.

The explosion had knocked her senseless for a moment or two, Narcissa realized. She was lying facedown on the floor, sprawled as if she had dropped exhausted onto her bed. She felt bruised all over. Her head ached abominably. But she had to get up, to find Coffin and Stone. The building might even now be burning. She licked her lips and tried to speak, but could manage only a cough. Her left shoulder and right hand were sharply painful, and her whole body ached like a bruise.

There was light coming from somewhere, not bright and hot like flames but dim and watery, just a little grayer than black. It was coming from behind her. Slowly, painfully, she turned herself on her side to look. There was a hole blasted in the wall where the smallpox money had been. She was looking through that hole out into the night. No fire, then. No immediate danger. She could rest a moment, gather her strength.

Was Aurelia dead?

Narcissa swallowed, licked her lips, and tried again to speak. "Stone!" Her voice was a rasping whisper. "Coffin! Can you hear me?"

"Mrs. Powers! It's me — Stone!"

Thank God. The tight band around Narcissa's heart eased a little. She heard a scrabbling noise and looked across the floor. There above the debris on the floor — broken barrel staves, clumps of smoldering bills — she could see a hand waving. She pushed herself up a little more. There was Stone's face, smudged but smiling. She managed a smile in return.

"Is Coffin with you?" she called to him.

"He went to get the boys. He's fine. I hurt my leg. I can't stand on it. Are you hurt?"

"Not badly. What about . . . the others?"

Stone was quiet for a moment. Then he said, "Aunt Aurelia . . . Coffin didn't find her. She may have gotten away. She told us to hide in here, even gave us the key to the padlock. But you'd told us not to touch the money, so we didn't. It wasn't such a big explosion, really. I reckon he wanted to scare Miller, not blow him to bits."

Stone spoke again. "Ragsdale's over there, near the door. Coffin said he's passed out, but not dead, thank goodness. Ha! I never thought I'd say *that*."

Stone fell silent. Narcissa tried again to rise, but the effort was too much, and she sank again to the floor. She would have to gather her strength to go after Aurelia.

A crack of thunder stirred Judah Daniel from sleep. She opened her eyes. Gray dawn showed through the window she had left uncurtained. She got up and stepped toward it. Nothing had come through that window, after all. Now it was light, and time to —

There it was. A face pale like death, come from the grave, looking, trying to come in. In the white blur of the face, she could not make out any features, just the hollowed spots of the eyes and the lank hair. Was it Cassie Terry, come from the grave to claim her son?

As Judah Daniel stared, the vision glanced away, then looked back. Something in that nervous movement told her it was a living woman. But the woman bore death on her as plain as any corpse.

Judah Daniel watched as the woman turned away. Judah Daniel's skin was prickling like a dog's scenting a bobcat. Swiftly she crossed to the door. She drew her breath to call for Jim Furbish, but there he was, lying in the doorway, his gnawed-looking face turned up to the gray light, dark blood on his shirt.

Judah Daniel raised her eyes to see the woman step over Jim. The woman too was hurt. Her skin was scraped raw, and though the rain had washed the blood away, it was welling again, turning the left side of her face red. Her tattered skirts, soaked and heavy, dragged through the blood on Jim's chest. The woman lifted her damaged face to look at Judah Daniel, and with the same motion brought up a pistol, which she pointed at Judah Daniel's chest. *It was a shot woke me. She must have held the gun pressed right up to his body, that muffled the noise; and then she come to look through the window.* At last, when the woman was close enough to touch, she recognized Aurelia Harrald.

"I have to kill those boys," Aurelia said. "If you help me, you may save your life. If you do not, you will die first." And she slid a few inches closer, as if to make her point.

Judah Daniel inclined her head to show agreement. If Aurelia killed her now, there would be no hope for the boys.

Aurelia motioned with the pistol for Judah Daniel to go back into the smallpox room. Walking slowly, carefully, Judah Daniel stepped between the pallets and stood to look down on Sam. He was the farthest from the door. She was trying to get Aurelia as far from the door as possible.

Aurelia followed her lead, walking around the pallet to face Judah Daniel. The heavy pistol drooped and jerked in her hand. Aurelia looked down at Samuel's thin form. "Kill him," she ordered. "Smother him. He is too weak to fight you."

Judah Daniel knelt next to Sam. She pulled the sheet off him and bunched it in her hands. She tensed the muscles in her thighs. More than enough strength in them to smother Sam. Enough to spring over him, to throw herself onto Aurelia and bring her down. Judah Daniel put a beseeching look on her face and looked up at Aurelia, gauging where to hit her.

From behind Aurelia, there came a scraping noise, and the sound of voices, young voices. Aurelia turned. *What was that?* Something came in through the window, hit the floor. For an instant, Judah

Daniel was too surprised to move. *A dog.* A sand-colored, mat-coated, not very big dog. In a moment it was on its feet and growling at Aurelia. A ridge of hair stood up along its spine. Aurelia was staring at it, trying to hold the gun steady enough to shoot. In the next instant, Judah Daniel was on her. Aurelia went down unresisting as an anatomist's skeleton. Her head hit the floor with a crack. The next instant the pistol discharged, with a report that Judah Daniel felt like a punch in the stomach. The ball buried itself harmlessly in the thick stucco wall.

As the ringing in Judah Daniel's ears died away, she heard Aurelia moan once. The dog backed away, whining. Judah Daniel took the gun from Aurelia's limp fingers. Stunned with the fall, Judah Daniel figured. She put her fingers on Aurelia's neck. No pulse. No, there it was, faint and erratic. Judah Daniel saw the blood, looked for the wound, found it, down under the ribs — and knew that death was taking Aurelia Harrald.

Cameron Archer held the little bottle of sal volatile close to the pale face of

448

Narcissa Powers. Stansbury Harrald said she had spoken, but — At last he saw her blink, recoiling from the penetrating odor. "Mrs. Powers."

She opened her eyes. He saw her take in the lights from the lamps, and the people's voices.

"Are you hurt anywhere?"

"Everywhere," Narcissa answered. Something between a smile and a wince crossed her face. "But not badly, I think."

Archer exhaled a sigh of relief and sat back on his haunches. "Aurelia is dead. She was injured in the explosion." He saw no need to tell her now that Aurelia had come after the boys, had shot Jim Furbish — though the ball had passed through the flesh of his shoulder, and he should recover. Nor that Judah Daniel had risked her own life to save the boys, Timmy and Sam. Nor that Aurelia had bled to death, pierced by sharp pieces of wood and metal hurled like missiles by the explosion. There was time enough for Narcissa to hear all that, when she was stronger.

"I have to go. They're expecting an engagement, the biggest yet. But I wanted to tell you —" He was speaking fast, trying not to think of how ridiculous he must appear to her. "I went to Ragsdale's, as you

449

ordered me to do. I thought you were raving, of course, but something . . . Anyway, he called me up and showed me the body. He thought Miller had killed Sophie. I examined her and told him to fetch the police. I must say I believed him when he said he didn't kill her. He seemed truly shocked."

Narcissa's eyes were on him. She looked apprehensive. Well, he had to go on.

"We exchanged some words" — no need to tell her exactly what the words were — "and then he said Aurelia had . . . had been with him, the night before. He brought it up to me that Stansbury Harrald was my son, mine and Aurelia's! And said she had told him so."

He was watching Narcissa's face, trying to read her reaction. Her mouth twisted down in the corners, her eyes looked away. She had known about the accusation, then. She had believed it; she believed it now. He had to make it clear to her somehow, but it was hard, after all those years of falsehood. He'd excused himself, told himself he need not offer marriage to Aurelia, on the grounds that he had not deflowered her, though that was due neither to her virtue nor to his, but to Stephen Goodell's interruption. Afterward, he had condemned

Aurelia for her looseness; he could not deny it, though he recognized the irony.

He fumbled for the words that might redeem him in Narcissa's eyes, even as he feared he did not deserve redemption. "I knew that Aurelia was lying. We were . . . indiscreet, and she would have been compromised, had anyone known. But there was no possibility of a child."

Were the lines of her face relaxing just a little?

Archer went on, trying to tell her as much as he could before he had to go. "When Ragsdale told me how Aurelia had lied, acted the part of a fallen woman . . . how she had given herself to him, I finally understood how desperate she had been. He told me, too, that she had lied about not having had a smallpox inoculation. You inoculated her on the left arm, didn't you?"

Narcissa nodded.

"But Aurelia is — was — left-handed. She had an old inoculation scar on her right arm. Ragsdale saw it, when they — he saw it," Archer concluded awkwardly. "Then I thought about how desperate she had been to get away from that terrible family, ever since I first knew her. I think that's why she let me take liberties. I thought about who had been infected with smallpox, and how each death or illness could be seen as benefiting Aurelia, or as protecting her from discovery."

Narcissa opened her mouth to speak. Archer put his head down to hear.

"The Harralds are rich — or they were — but Aurelia lived the life of a prisoner. I think Aurelia had already stolen the smallpox money to pay for a beautiful dress, not knowing it would kill Miss Sullivan, but willing to take the risk. Then Josiah came home and threatened to stop Aaron's dealings with Ragsdale. Aurelia couldn't stand that, because Ragsdale, and his money, seemed to be her only hope of escape. So she stole some more money, put on the poisoned dress, and went to see Josiah in the hospital. With Josiah injured, he stopped sending money to Cassie Terry for Coffin's board. Cassie went to the Harralds' house to ask for money, and she talked to Aurelia. I suppose Aurelia guessed Cassie would do almost anything to get liquor. Even force her own son Timmy and his friend Sam to steal the money back from the pest-house for Aurelia."

"Major Archer." The call, discreet but insistent, brought him back to reality. Soon the guns would begin to fire, and soon after that the wounded would be coming back through the lines.

"Good-bye, Mrs. Powers." He took her hand in his and pressed it for a moment, then got to his feet.

"God be with you," she called after him.

He gave the automatic response, but it carried his whole heart. "And also with you."

As the brigade set out, Brit fell in step. There was not time to get a horse or to prepare in any other way. If he wished to be along when they met the enemy, he had no choice but to join in the march. And so he plodded through the mud, forded the chest-high creeks. The light of dawn confirmed that they were marching eastward along the Williamsburg Road. Brit remembered that Langdon, who had been down this road a week before with Cameron Archer, would know what they could expect to encounter. So he put on a burst of speed and passed up along the line until he spotted Langdon, then fell in step next to him. He had no breath left over with which to question Langdon. But in a while

453

the brigade halted along the road between two stands of pine forest, perhaps five miles outside of Richmond. The drizzle at last began to abate, though the sky hung heavy and dull overhead. With much patience, the soldiers started small fires to boil their coffee, fry their bacon, and light their pipes. And there they sat, having dragged over stones, fence rails, and logs on which to perch above the mud.

"Are you going to attack?" Brit asked Langdon and the others who were hovering around the little fire, fanning and blowing and feeding in the driest sticks that could be found.

"Oh, I shouldn't think so," Langdon replied. "Perhaps it's just a show of force after all."

Watkins rebutted him. "Why would they give us three days' rations? The brass must have expected a Federal attack. Maybe they got slowed down coming through the swamp."

Brit and Langdon exchanged a glance. Would it be just as the white-bearded general had said?

"How far off do you think they are now?"

"Not far. Couple miles maybe," responded Langdon, his tone casual. He moved close to Brit and stuck a twig into the fire, preparing to light his pipe. "When we come to where you see the trees are cut, we're there. There's an abatis, some earthworks — then the camp. It's a good position. I hope it won't be our job to drive them out of it."

Boom! A cannon sounded on their left, followed by an answering cannonade. As the hearers recovered from their shock, they could hear the rifles joining in, rattling like dry peas in a gourd. Then more cannon joined in, more rifles, a deafening and discordant music toward which they stared as a gray smoke formed over the earth and spread upward to meet the lowering sky.

"Over the Nine Mile Road," Langdon guessed. Brit looked over to see him gazing with an expression of utmost concentration in the direction of the firing. But when the order came to move, it bore them to the right, away from the sounds of battle.

Until four o'clock, the firing kept up. The men of the First had begun to relax when the order came. "Fall in! Forward by the left flank! March! Double-quick!" And the men jumped up and ran, on and on for a mile, straight into the roaring mouth of hell. As they squelched through the mud they passed, coming the other way, the wounded, whom they themselves were going to replace. In a steady stream they came — on stretchers, swung in blood-soaked blankets, leaning on their comrades, or hobbling along, using their muskets for crutches. Brit, hurrying along to keep pace, heard a strange, strangled noise come from Archer Langdon. He looked; Langdon was laughing, pointing, and soon the whole regiment was laughing at a man, apparently slightly wounded in the left hand, helped along by two comrades, one on each side — and two more, following behind, one bearing the wounded man's musket and one, his hat. The hilarity of it seemed to raise the men's spirits even higher. "See that, Langdon!" one called out. "Go get yourself a hangnail! I'll make sure you get to safety."

The brigade, following some order passed down the line, bore to the right, into a field ringed by woods. Farther to their right, too far to provide cover, were a barn — this was somebody's farm, after all, whose harvest this day was men's bodies — and rows of tents. Was this, Brit wondered, the clearing Langdon had spoken of, in which Casey's men had camped? It was deserted, except for the dead; the rifle pits were empty; no enemy was in sight to offer resistance; why were they rushing to occupy it?

With the thought, he slowed to watch the Confederates race pell-mell into the clearing. Just as they broke into the open, shots rang out along the edge of the clearing, firing into it, into the charging men. *There* was the enemy, hidden in the trees opposite, so close he could smell the smoke from their artillery pieces. Brit saw men fall from the line, shot down like game flushed by a keeper. Charging as they were, one after another, the Confederates could not return fire for fear of hitting their own comrades.

Brit's heart was pounding so hard he could not catch his breath. He could not believe what he was seeing. Men were dropping now with every step, but the survivors ran on. Did the officer who gave the command know he was sending his men to slaughter?

But still the lieutenants waved their swords and shouted, "Forward! Forward! Don't stop! Charge right into the camp!" The men ran on, in their thin and desperate line, between the woodpile and the redoubts, past the barn and in among the tents. There they were penned, the air shrieking with a terrible rain that burst into fire and tore them down. With no orders given except to charge, with no opportunity to fire a shot, the brigade broke and ran. The flag went down as its bearer sank to the earth. Brit watched as first one man, then another, then another grasped the staff, raised it, and sank to the ground. But the colors flew, held by men who would die for the honor. Now at last it seemed the soldiers were running with a purpose: to save their lives. They scrambled into the rifle pits, some falling dead in the effort.

Brit's every nerve twitched with the instinct to run with them. At last he focused his eyes, his whole being, on the nearest of the rifle pits, and started out across the field. As soon as he began to run, the sounds of battle blurred into meaningless noise, and his vision narrowed. His fear pushed him, but it was outside of him now; he did not feel afraid.

He reached the pit, clawed his way over the slick clay surface, and dropped into waist-deep mud below. A crowd of men was sheltering there, from different regiments and brigades. He stood panting, catching his breath. His fear had caught up with him now, but it didn't seem to shake him as it had before.

Brit watched the soldiers around him. Now and then one or another got up his courage to look over the top. There was Archer Langdon talking urgently with some of the others. Langdon waded around to find firm footing in the mud — never mind that he was standing on enemy dead who had been killed there earlier — levered the barrel of his musket over the parapet, and fired off a shot.

Without looking to see whether his shot found a mark, Langdon handed down the musket to a man on his left, then turned and took a loaded musket from a man on his right. Langdon's friend Watkins gazed at him thoughtfully for a second, then took a stand several yards to his right.

For an hour at least the two youngsters returned the fire of the enemy — two against how many? — while the men gathered there rallied to help. Working quickly, methodically, a man would take out a cartridge, clamp the paper end between his teeth, and rip it open, then pour the powder down the barrel and press in the bullet. He would draw the ramrod from beneath the musket's barrel and ram the bullet home, then thrust the ramrod back into place. Then the soldier would reach into his little cap box for a percussion cap;

with the musket set on half cock, he would press the cap into place, then wait, watching his turn to hand the loaded musket up to Langdon. Brit marveled at the smoothness of their motions. It was automatic to them now.

Gradually, imperceptibly, late afternoon dimmed to evening. The enemy fire slowed, then stopped. Langdon looked around, shrugged. The men stopped reloading the muskets. Gradually they all grew bolder, peeking out over the edge. Had the enemy withdrawn? Had their own officers forgotten them in this hellhole?

At last a colonel jumped out into the open space and called for the regiment to form. From holes and thickets and corners the men came running, those of them who were left alive. Brit followed the soldiers out of the rifle pit, moving on the double-quick through the camp to the shelter of the abatis. Not a shot greeted them. They kept on into the woods, Brit with them. It was easy to see where the Federal line had formed to mow down the Confederates. Torn cartridges and ruined muskets lay scattered on the ground. The artillery pieces had been pulled out, to fight another day. Not a victory, then, for the

Confederates — not here, at least.

And someone had sent them into this, all those brave men, had let them be killed and sink down into the mud with their enemies. So were nations made, and unmade — on the bodies of the fallen.

EPILOGUE

SUNDAY, JUNE 1

The sounds of distant skirmishing around Seven Pines had died away. The afternoon heat bore down, gathering for thunder. Ambulances, litters, carts, every vehicle that the city could produce, carried their ghastly burdens up Church Hill to the hospital at Chimborazo, or to one or another of the hospitals improvised around them, in public buildings, stores, warehouses, and private homes. As pale and heart-sore as the wounded were the women and old men who moved through the city like ghosts, seeking their loved ones.

Judah Daniel carried another load of bandages in to the surgeons, stepping carefully so as not to slip on the blood that covered the floor. She wished she had an arm free to brush the flies away.

462

In her mind was Tyler. He'd fought his battle alone long enough. Now he had left Richmond to join up with the Yankees. She prayed he'd find another soul like him to stand next to, because that was what he craved. It was not that he didn't love his wife and children, but — in his mind anyway — they didn't make him a man. Fighting alongside other men, that's what would make him a man. Even the little boys understood it, Timmy and Sam. One black, one white. Now that they no longer had a common enemy, how long would they fight side by side?

Brit Wallace was driving the Powerses' carriage, filled with a load of wounded men.

What makes men risk their lives, follow orders that are suicide, ride into the valley of death though they know in their souls that someone had blundered, and that their lives would be the price?

Each other. That's not what the generals fight for, maybe, but the common soldier doesn't go out to stand against an enemy. He goes out to stand with a friend.

Brit saw again the gray-coated men,

brothers and cousins, boys from farms, villages, and cities. *They have come to fight together; to die together, it might be, in one charge, leaving a whole community bereft. Yet the ones who live through it, on both sides, will have something none of the rest of us can claim. After this war, Private Archer Langdon will have more in common with Billy Yank than he will have with me.* For some reason Brit could not explain, the thought made him sad.

AFTERWORD

Smallpox in Richmond, Virginia

1862-63

In this story, I try to give an accurate picture of smallpox in the 1860s. At the time, smallpox had a mortality rate of approximately forty percent. Its highly contagious properties were known, if not understood, and people were justifiably terrified of it.

People carried out inoculations themselves. *The Medical and Surgical History of the Civil War* (vol. 6, p. 625ff.) describes a soldier who "refused to be vaccinated by the surgeon of the regiment," saying that "when an infant his mother vaccinated him with a needle coated with lymph from the arm of another child." Soldiers inoculated each other, using dirty knives, on occasion spreading diseases that eventually resulted in ulcers, scarring, and even gangrene.

Most of the "lymph" was obtained from children, often slave children, who were inoculated up to a dozen times on each arm in order to produce an abundance of scabs. Healthy children were thought less likely to harbor illness that could be transmitted via inoculation. Those individuals who received effective inoculations did, in fact, come down with smallpox, but the disease was usually mild, and the mortality rate for inoculated individuals was much smaller — even today, we don't know why.

Money of smallpox victims created a problem. "The fear of this money becoming a smallpox vector disturbed Surgeon [G. W.] Semple to the extent that he ignored regular channels and wrote directly to Confederate Secretary of the Treasury Memminger requesting that these notes in his possession be destroyed because 'as to recirculate them would be attended with a dissemination of this great scourge' " (Dr. Charles F. Ballou III, address to the Richmond Academy of Medicine, October 1991; typescript in the Archives, Tompkins-McCaw Library, Medical College of Virginia).

I invented the outbreak of smallpox in Richmond in spring 1862. In fact, Richmond's wartime epidemic began in August 1862.

The first building to be used as a quarantine hospital, or pest-house, for smallpox-infected soldiers was the City Hospital across from Shockoe Cemetery. (This building had served as the hospital for the city's poor since the Battle of First Manassas, when the much larger Alms House nearby became General Hospital #1.) When the City Hospital became filled, Surgeon General Moore converted a tobacco factory at Cary and Twenty-fifth streets into a smallpox hospital.

In November 1862, the *Richmond Examiner* reported that the mayor "heard with great surprise that [this building] was filled with small pox patients" and "[urged] the Council to adopt some stringent measures to effect the removal of small pox patients and hospitals from our midst." At the time there were "fifty cases at one end of the town and seventy-five at the other . . . and twenty-one had already died at the city hospital of the disease. . . ."

The city council spent the following weeks discussing what should be done, and by whom. One such session was described by the *Examiner*'s reporter: "The Council evidently being possessed with the idea that they had got hold of a good thing showed a disposition to argue it all night. Every member, with two exceptions, made at least two speeches. When physical exhaustion intervened, [one member's] resolution was put and adopted" (Manarin, *Richmond at War*, pp. 241–44).

During this lengthy meeting, one council member stated, "the Council ought to urge upon the Confederate Government . . . not to establish their contagious hospitals on the highways leading to this city, as at Howard's grove for instance." Howard's Grove was exactly where the Confederate government did establish its smallpox hospital.

The city council finally made vaccinations compulsory in December 1862. In January 1863, five months after the disease entered Richmond, the city council was still arguing over what to do. The committee set by the Council to study the question recommended that householders indicate the presence of smallpox "by hanging out a white flag not less than twelve inches square in front of the principal entrance to the house . . ." The committee declined to recommend taking infected persons out of their homes and placing them in quarantine, saying that "this . . . would do violence to the feelings of those whose relations or friends or servants are the victims of this terrible disease" (Manarin, *Richmond at War*, p. 259).

The question of what to do about free blacks' being treated in the hospitals but unable to pay their bills led to a recommendation "that the Council petition the legislature to so amend the code as to allow free Negroes who are indebted to the City for hospital fees to be sold for the payment of them" (Manarin, *Richmond at War*, pp. 259–60).

ADDITIONAL SMALLPOX SOURCES

Blanton, Wyndham B. *Medicine in Virginia in the Nineteenth Century.* Richmond: Garrett & Massie, 1933.

Domestic Medicine, Surgery, and Materia Medica, "by a Practising Physician." Philadelphia: Lindsay and Blakiston, 1851.

Freemon, Frank R. *Gangrene and Glory: Medical Care During the American Civil War.* Madison, N.J.: Fairleigh Dickinson University Press, 1998.

Hopkins, Donald R. *Princes and Peasants: Smallpox in History.* Chicago: University of Chicago Press, 1983.

Houck, Peter. "Dr. Terrell's Pesthouse." *Virginia Medical Quarterly* 19, no. 4 (fall 1992): 232–36.

Kiple, Kenneth F., ed. *Cambridge World History of Human Disease.* Cambridge: Cambridge University Press, 1993.

Manarin, Louis H., ed. *Richmond at War: The Minutes of the City Council, 1861–65.*

Chapel Hill: University of North Carolina Press, 1966.

Roueché, Berton. *The Medical Detectives, Volume II*, 16–32. New York: Dutton, 1984.

U.S. Department of Health, Education, and Welfare. *Diagnosis of Smallpox.* 1966.

Wood, George B. *A Treatise on the Practice of Medicine*, vol. 1. Philadelphia, 1858.